MY OWN DEAR PEOPLE

BY
DWIGHT THOMPSON

BROOKLYN, NEW YORK

This is a work of fiction. All names, characters, places, and incidents are the product of the author's imagination. Any resemblance to real events or persons, living or dead, is entirely coincidental.

Published by Akashic Books

ISBN: 978-1-63614-191-6
Library of Congress Control Number: 2024940686

First printing

Akashic Books
Brooklyn, New York
Instagram, X, Facebook: AkashicBooks
info@akashicbooks.com
www.akashicbooks.com

To my mother
and my former lecturer, Lucinda Peart,
for unimagined possibility . . .

PART I

JACK TAR VILLAGE

CHAPTER 1

It was the whole ridiculous plight of wanting to write that set the flame alight even before I got home. I was on the bus dreaming I was the second coming of George Lamming, just as dashing, just as handsome in his BBC *Caribbean Voices* days, and just as talented, filling the airwaves with his mellifluous Bajan baritone. Well, maybe not *as* talented, but close, because Lamming was damn talented, the closest thing to what I'd ever consider Caribbean genius, and to be even half that good would have been its own reward. I smirked and looked out the window at vendors with plastic bags of roasted and sugar-boiled peanuts strung to wires stacked high on their heads. *That's the true size of Lamming's creative intelligence*, I mused, still smiling. *That's the measure of the man's nous—a brain so big it continues to grow outside his head and as tall as a peanut vendor's stack.*

I was so amused with my thoughts, I laughed out loud. "Nutsy!" I yelled from the window, then whistled and fished my wallet from my shorts. "Bring me a bag!"

The vendor approached with an unhurried walk. The girl sitting beside me regarded me with her eyes slanted. A thin little thing. I sized her up. Waistline twenty-nine, bust a C cup. A face about 8.5. She wore a pink blouse and jeans skirt and white slippers. Her heels were cracked. A slum girl on her way back to Montego Bay after partying in Kingston all weekend, I surmised, or if she has bags in the luggage compartment, probably a seller from the clothes arcade, returning home with cheap wares bought at Cross Roads and garment factories. She was a *dougla*. I could see she prided herself on her long lustrous ponytail that flowed to her back, and I had this weird fleeting attachment to it like I could feel its silkiness wrapped in my hands. I liked these types: young, coarse, abrasive, and cute.

"Hey," I said, my eyes lingering on her just long enough.

"Hi," she answered, smiling. Her breath might have been shot out of a cannon, it was that strong with the reek of Green Apple wine. I saw she had a hand on the bottle in her Perry Ellis handbag, slipping it out every now and then for a sip. A drunk? I was intrigued.

"Why don't we get to know each other, since we'll probably both be sitting here for the next hour."

She sneered and scratched the back of her hair. "I know all I need fe know 'bout yuh."

"Don't be too quick to judge."

She turned and gave me her full attention. "You're a college bwoy. I hear it in yuh voice. I fuck enough of dem at Negril ATI to know when I meet one."

She had bleached her whole face to a smooth starchy consistency, like a young mango, except for the backs of her ears that still showed her dark-brown complexion. A clothes vendor. Yes. A young entrepreneur who goes to Kingston to haggle and for debauch, trades of the very same nature. I'd been away from MoBay for three years but I could still tell what I was up against. Her perfume was faint, like a baby's sweet colicky breath. St. James girls could be so easy at times, so uncomplicated, that they could feel like a nuisance, and if you started treating them as such, cheating on them or occasionally hitting them or embarrassing them in public, they became desperate—desperate, that is, to prove their worth. Montegonian men knew exactly how to handle them. And they liked to be handled. If a Montegonian girl ever called you "quiet" or "kind" or, worse, a "gentleman," you were as good as dead; at the very least you were a laughingstock. It was like an obituary you couldn't recover from without acting a proper fool. That is, to raise yourself from the dead with a personality transplant.

She was sizing me up with furtive glances and coy little giggles, like a child licking a jelly spoon. She saw that I had noticed her black ears and designer bag and cracked heels. But her attitude was still like, *Yes, now that you know who I am and I know who you are, what yuh goin' do, bwoy?* It was the sort of challenge I relished, that was won or lost more by what was not said than what was. It was about mood, action, a quiet turbulence that had to exist between both parties where the air between you vibrates and your heart palpitates and flies to your throat and the heady fear of dying, the fear of falling, is the sweet relief of surrendering to someone who reads you perfectly without fulsome talk, because sweet words often spoil everything for us Montegonians.

I took her hand and studied her nails. They were jeweled, and the pink and purple nail polish was chipped at the base. She laughed and snatched her hand away. "But wha'ppen to dis bwoy though?" When I stared at her, her smile melted. She got nervous. She wet her lips and looked ahead and said in an off-kilter yelp that startled everyone, "Driver, turn up de music nuh, mek people enjoy demself in de damn bus. None ah we goin' funeral, enuh."

People cackled in soft murmurs and pointed at her with pushed-up lips because they knew it was the behavior of a girl made skittish by someone's hungry attention. The driver obliged and turned up the volume. "*One heartbeat at a time . . .*" Smokey Robinson crooned. She snapped her fingers and sang along.

"Me love oldies bad," she said without looking at me.

"Then yuh my type of gyal," I replied. "Nutten I love more than an oldies session at Pier One on Fridays."

She widened her eyes. "How long now yuh live a Kingston? Oldies Nite move to Wednesdays donkey years back. Friday Nite is Passa Passa now."

"Well, you'll just have to bring me up to speed then. What's yuh name?"

She still sang with Smokey to give the impression that we weren't talking earnestly to each other. She didn't want people witnessing how easily she was crumbling. "Andrene, but dem call me Dreenie. What's yours?"

"Nyjah . . . Nyjah Messado."

She said quietly, with an inflection to suggest deference, "What yuh want me call yuh?"

"Nyjah."

She put her hand in my lap as if it didn't belong to her, with her face turned away, almost as if she were handing over her purse to a customs officer. I massaged her fingers and studied her callused palm; she worked hard. She looked away the whole time. She was showing me who she truly was. I reached forward and rubbed her earlobe. She winced a little and looked around to see if we were being watched, then satisfied we weren't, she dropped her head and toggled through her phone while I felt against her neck and moved my hand down her shoulder, stopping at the swell of her small breast. She didn't flinch, but her breathing pattern changed. I wondered if she was getting wet. I passed my hand over her breast and down her slender side to her thigh. *Ask her her age. No, not yet. St. James gyals don't like that.* Her jeans skirt was hiked up and exposed her finely haired skin which was a shade darker than her face.

People understood what I was doing and consciously kept their heads trained forward because they didn't care to see anything improper, as much as they wanted to, kind of like looking away while two dogs mated in public, or two drunken revelers fucked in a corner street during J'ouvert or Mas—you glance but never stare because that'd make you queer and ill-mannered. It was a game of conditional manners West Indians have mastered. She was keeping her eyes peeled too, in case anyone had the temerity to look. A fat dark woman across from us became cross, looking at our looseness, but Dreenie stared her down and snarled at the woman to mind her own business, so the woman sucked her teeth and fanned herself and fidgeted her big frame in her seat. I caressed Dreenie's knees. She clamped her thighs together when my hand moved between them.

"Can I ask you sum'n?" she breathed.

"I'm waitin'."

"What yuh want from me, you . . . whatever yuh name, Nigel . . . Nyjah." Her tone meant she wasn't willing to give in totally just yet.

The bus stopped at Duncans Square to let off some Trelawny people and we had to get up so the heavy-chested woman could reach across us and wrench her crocus bag free from the overhead. When Dreenie stood, I took my time studying her slight figure; she glanced at me and waited out the inspection. She sat, but I said to her, "Let's go outside and catch some fresh air."

People wandered off to bathrooms and food stalls lined outside the small blue plaza. The woody smell of jerk pork filled the air. Dreenie excused herself to get us something to eat. I sat on a circular concrete ledge, took out my phone, and looked over the poem I was working on.

Mother, I Remember the Cyst on Your Neck

It's pleasant it is
to sleep and dream,
more pleasant it is
than all the years of
old men,
because in sleep
youth is recaptured
and bound
to the body
like blindness filling
eye wells of old men
like wet mud,
drying . . .
like dreams, dying.

I saw you,
you were young and beautiful again.
White skirts white panties white linen
white eyeballs white teeth.
How beauty fades fast.
A dream's memory fades even faster.

I wanted it to be more confrontational in tone, to say all I couldn't say to my mother's face when I saw her. Dreenie came back with the food, standing in front of me with her slim straight body planted between my knees, pulling strands of her long, slightly wavy hair from her high round forehead. My mind still on the poem, I asked, "Where's your mother, Andrene?"

"She hustlin' in Hen-gland."

"Used she to love you?"

"What?"

I chuckled. "I'm only kidding."

"You're makin' fun of me already."

"No, I'm not." I looked up at her as I bit into the wet peppery conch she handed over and thought of biting into her flesh. She smiled. She had an even row of strong white upper teeth but small crowded baby teeth at the bottom. She seemed conscious of this unevenness. She let out a nervous whinny. That was fine. I was searching for a flaw, a vulnerability I could use against her when the time came. She clamped her mouth shut, but I tapped her lightly on the leg.

"Smile for me, man," I said quietly.

Blushing, she pushed her fringes back again as the coastal wind was strong. "Why?"

"Because yuh beautiful, yuh my muse."

She squinted. "Yuh what?"

"A word I'll teach yuh through action more than language."

She shrugged and obliged me. But the smile this time was forced and silly. I reached up and pulled her neck forward and kissed her deeply. Her breath still stank of the stale Green Apple wine and she gave in to me completely. She kissed me as if she were thirsting for something—perhaps the truth of my intentions—and it was all bundled up in the tip of my tongue.

She pulled away when she heard the smoking men whistling. They flashed their lighters at us. "'Ow yuh mean? Go inna it, Starry!" they cheered.

I pulled her to sit beside me and she hung her head over, dazed, shy, perhaps even happy.

Again she asked, "What yuh want from me?" Her tone this time was serious.

I didn't look at her. I was looking at the poem again. "Eat yuh food," I said, sipping the bitter frothy stout. "I told yuh to get me a *hot* stout. I hate it refrigerated. The flavor goes out."

"No yuh didn't," she snapped. "Me ears nuh under me foot bottom. All yuh said was, 'Get me a Dragon.'" She watched me studying the phone and became annoyed. "Yuh girlfriend call yuh? She send yuh text?"

Dreenie didn't play the jealous type well but was willing to baptize our alliance with an argument. I showed her the phone screen. She read the poem and chewed her coconut *gizzada*, the sugary crumbs sticking to her pale mauve lipstick. "You're a writer." She sounded affronted, aggrieved, like Sancho having the courage to accuse Don Quixote of being a self-deluded liar.

"A poet," I clarified.

"Yuh goin' teach?" She wasn't interested in the silly side of my indulgence, she wanted to know what I had in mind for a stable self-sustaining life. I could almost laugh. I hadn't expected this side of her, and to be blindsided by it was poetic in itself. She wasn't looking at me now. All the play had fallen out of her and she was eating her *gizzadas* and drinking her bottled water at a rapid pace and watching the bus fill up again. She got up and dusted the seat of her skirt. "Come, Claude McKay, de bus ready."

I felt at pains to explain myself. I even felt a little ridiculous.

When we sat back and I finished my conch and tried to speak to her, she squinched her face at my breath and handed me a stick of Winter Fresh gum. Her attitude was like an adult accommodating a child. "Yes," I said, "I'm going to teach. But not for long."

"Hah, that's what I said 'bout sellin' clothes to trickify neagah . . . *not for long*. Lawd, gimme strength." She crossed her arms, sighed. Then she put her fingers to her forehead and shook her head and looked out the window, with an expression that said, *Dreenie, why de hell yuh pick up dis dreamer?* I felt annoyed: she thought she knew everything about life because she haggled clothes and had a "shop." But in truth, my confidence was shaken. I put my hand on her leg and she pushed it off.

"Listen . . ." I said, and at the same time wondered why I was so desperate to explain myself to a girl I'd just met. Something about her rebuff was making me confront my ambition, my fears. Something I hadn't always done. "I've got three teaching posts lined up. Did the Skype interviews."

"What schools?" she asked sharply.

"Glendale, Willocks, and Undergrad."

"Dem is all poppy-show schools!" she burst out. "I do a nursing course at Undergrad las' year an' when exam time come, de school tek we money an' when we go exam center we cyaan find we name to sit exam. Not one damn chair in there said *Andrene Singh*. Dem t'ief. And now I don't get a nursin' certificate!"

I swallowed my spit. I hadn't researched the schools thoroughly before accepting the preliminary offers, was only eager to land on my feet. But I couldn't let that worry me. I had student loans to pay.

She continued, "Mos' o' these new schools run by Nigerians who lookin' fass money. Yuh cyaan even pronounce dem damn name, much less hol' dem guilty."

"Did you get to sit the exam at all?" I said stupidly.

She didn't answer. Then she cracked a laugh. I couldn't tell if it was sad or mocking, if she was laughing at *her* dupery or mine. Her manner was different now, a change had come over her gradually from the beginning. No matter how slick or smart I thought I was, she hadn't been intimidated: she would force me to reveal who I was or to confront myself.

"Yuh can always come back to yuh course now that I'm teachin'." I didn't know why I said this.

She twisted to look at me again. I knew what she would say. "What yuh want from me?"

I said nothing, turned away from her, and peered out the window at Falmouth's redbrick buildings and primary school children buying salted green plums. The little girls dipped all the way to the bottoms of their Oxford-blue skirts to fish the copper coins out to make their purchases. Even at that age you could see in them an almost cynical maturity in the way they handled money, and the corresponding pride glowing in the rough sweaty faces of the stall women. They called the girls *darling* and *dou dou* and treated them with a special concern they never wasted on boys.

Dreenie leaned her shoulder into mine and said in a steady voice, "Me can cook an' me can clean. What more yuh want?" She waited to see how I would respond to this. She had answered her own question to rescue me. I eased back in the chair so she could lean into me. "Me have ambition too. Me nuh wa'an sell clothes de rest of me life like Norma. Me have some subjects an' me plan to sit for two or t'ree more. Me nuh go college but me can tek care ah yuh money. An' me wild ways done. Me nah look fe compete wid yuh. Me respect yuh as a man. Only *you* know what's right for yuh."

I breathed a little easier. But all my uncertainties were still crowding my head. I reached up and rubbed my fingers over her slightly pimpled features. The stout was sinking into me and I had an erection. My head felt woozy, and here an attractive girl was leaning against me. Outside the window was the sharp salty smell of the Flankers stretch of sea, green and rank in areas where beach was dumped up for new golf courses, villas, and hotels. *Sandcastles in the sea, built on perilous foundations*. I was almost home. My heart was dropping inside me. I was turning over the poem in my head and trying to keep my mother's image out of my musings. I wasn't ready to face her just yet. She would weaken my defenses, plunge my resolution into placidness with her calculated demeanor.

I reached over and squeezed Dreenie's hip. She nuzzled her little jewel-studded nose against my T-shirt. This was a girl I could never bring home. Who called her mother *Norma*. So typical of ghetto girls. Was she a part of my rebellion, my revenge? To break away from their dense deceit and give my new identity just enough teeth to bite them where it hurt? My heart hammered. I felt a little weak with all the possibilities. Home, after so long. This wild ambition to be a poet, and a successful one.

"I don't know what I'd do if yuh weren't from MoBay," I said. "If yuh had come off at Duncans or Falmouth I'd probably get off and follow yuh."

She wasn't flattered. "I ain't yuh modda. I not lookin' fe no young pup or maama man widout backbone. I don't want nobody followin' me."

"Yuh stayin' alone?"

"Uh-unh," she answered. "Me likkle chatterbox sister deh home wid we granny, up in Concrete. Me tribe waitin' on me."

"But I want to stay with yuh tonight."

"Yuh cyaan have me tonight . . ." Her voice trailed off in a way that I understood.

"Really?" I said, trying to hide my disappointment and alarm. I was so horny from feeling on her, I was seeing spots.

"It suppose to start today," she confirmed.

"I still want to stay with yuh."

"Then rent a place. No girlfriend from college?" she teased. "No Kingston brownin' wid Brazilian weave and Norbrook accent an' summer house in Negril?"

"Shut up and get some sleep. We soon reach."

We got off at the bus park and came upon a comical sight. A young gigolo was waiting to get on a Hiace bus to Ocho Rios with a skinny middle-aged tourist. The bus was already packed and the gigolo frowned when the conductor offered them both small padded seats behind the driver where engine heat was most intense, seats that were sold at a reduced rate, usually to children. "Come inna de bus, man," blustered the conductor, stretching his big gold-teethed grin. "See de nice lady gettin' sunburn an' ready to faint."

"I'm quite all right," smiled the woman, looking with dread at the "patty pan" seats, like a wall they shot people against. Perhaps it was the idea of sitting there with all those tense Black faces staring at her for two hours to St. Ann that made her visibly cringe.

The young man steadily refused. He knew he was being made fun of. The woman became embarrassed at passengers struggling to hide their amusement. "Trevor, let's go," she said softly, turning away, "let's get something else, babe."

"Ah chu him see white woman him a gwaan like him cyaan siddung pon de patty pan," a passenger observed.

"Trevor turn *risto*," said a woman emptying coconut drops into her child's cupped palm.

This released laughs they'd all been holding back. It was an assault that frightened and jolted the woman, like a slap. In a huff, Trevor, dressed for the beach in neon-green shorts, a tank top, and new slippers still bearing the tag, dragged his companion off to the other side of the park.

"Gwaan!" someone shouted. "Gwaan go spend Yankee dollar an' nyam Joe leftovers!"

We boarded, took their seats, and the bus drove away.

They let us off outside the pink cut-stone walls of Jack Tar Village at the bottom of Gloucester Avenue. I could see Dreenie was impressed that I could arrange a room on the Hip Strip on such short notice, in an exclusive hotel like Jack Tar. My friend Chadwell had a condominium there, a family getaway spot, that we had frequented as boys at Chester College, and I'd called him and asked a favor. The security guard checked my name and gave us two pink rubber bracelets. He asked a man in a buggy to carry our bags, and smirked at Dreenie's stiffness.

"Gwaan, me love," he said to her, "de white people won't bite." He looked her over and winked at me behind her back.

We checked in, got the keys, and walked across the property to the condo section on the beachfront.

"Me hungry," Dreenie said, sitting on the edge of the floral-patterned bedspread and browsing through menus.

I opened the white curtain and glass doors that led out onto the balcony overlooking the pink sand of the private beach. Guests were packing up beach chairs and umbrellas and getting ready to join dinner lines along a pool terrace. Beach attendants, in crisp black half-pants and short white jackets, were cleaning up after them, solemnly searching among the tourists' trash for anything useful, or helping women with little sandy-haired brats wearing bright-colored arm floaties, all so the mothers would reward them with soft thank-yous and profuse apologies and perhaps a tip, or a phone number and room invite from one of the cougars. The beach attendants were ravenous hunters. The word "tribe" that Dreenie had used earlier came back to me. I smiled, sipped the Schweppes from the mini fridge, and watched as from a gallery. When we'd brought girls here during our sixth-form days, this was one of our pastimes, watching attendants picking up tips and chicks, hustling lecherous, flabby women half-drunk on colorful holiday drinks.

"Nyjah, yuh ready to eat?" Dreenie said.

"Not yet," I answered over my shoulder, "lemme just chill." I sat there imbibing sea breeze. We were on the tenth floor, which commanded a view of the sun-glinted coast all the way down to Fletcher's Beach at the other end of the road. A boy was playing a curious game with his mother on the shore—he dug a trench beside her supine body as the radio on the beach table droned in the gathering twilight, "*God bless the day I found you . . .*" She was drinking what looked like a Dirty Banana, but probably because of her position she choked violently and the liquid frothed over her mouth as if she were having an epileptic episode. Then the towheaded child did something curious: he eased his mother into the shallow ditch that he'd dug, and it was amazing that it was just her size. As she lay in the hole, he put his perfectly sized hand into her mouth and fished out what must have been a citrus seed blocking her airway. He rolled it between his fingers as if he found all the meaning in the world in the thing that she'd choked on, that he'd pulled from her mouth covered in slime. His father rushed forward with a half-dressed hotel man, both looking frazzled and helpless and wobbly on their feet. The woman raised herself slightly on her elbows and waved off their fussy attention with a *t'chit* of her tongue. She had eyes only for her son—she looked at him with a profound and new appreciation. From where she sank into the earth, she raised her hand to him and he pulled her toward him. A mirage blurred the line of her knifelike body cutting windblown sand. "Lady Lazarus," I said with a quickening of breath. I remembered the body we had buried at school and left for dead. A Lady Lazarus without a savior. The whole reason why I had run away for three years.

I drained the Schweppes bottle. My loins woke suddenly, watching bare freckled flesh parading below, plodding on the sand, shrieking with laughter under palm-tree canopies stringed with bubbling pepper lights welcoming dusk, young women sticking thumbs under bikini bottoms to fix their swimwear and look presentable for buffet lines. And it was a welcome distraction from my guilt. The sun was going down with a burning hue of orange that turned the pink sand to a sea of jewels. I started in on a second bottle and went back inside.

Dreenie cast the remote control aside, as if ready to offer me payment for this immense surprise of luxury. She smiled and winked at my crotch. I was pulling off my pants and tumbled forward getting out of them. She laughed and fell back in the bed. I climbed on top of her.

"De AC too cold, Nyjah." She turned away from my kiss. "Did yuh hear me, bwoy? Me sey de blasted room too cold." She had the power.

I sucked my teeth and got up and cursed the little white remote when I couldn't work it. I almost chucked it.

She enjoyed my frustration. "Maybe we should eat now, I hungry too bad, enuh."

I finally clicked it down to a tolerable temperature. I turned around and she was sitting up, looking for her slipper. I wrestled her back down.

"Look here," she laughed. "Yuh bring me to Jack Tar to jump me like a ramgoat an' tear off me clothes?"

I couldn't work the damn bra latch. We started kissing but all she gave me was her teeth. I felt a little flushed with irritation.

"Remember what I said," she warned.

I panicked. I'd forgot.

"Don't look so cross," she said, "it's natural, a woman cyaan help it."

I got up and flopped down in the wicker chair and hung my head back.

Her voice drifted across the spacious white-tiled room: "What yuh want me to do?"

The words touched my thoughts where I sat with my eyes closed and my fire was lit again. I got up and walked over and kneeled by the bed and started sucking her small firm breasts.

"Nyjah . . . Nyjah, bwoy, yuh some kinda crazy." She moaned when I had her panties around her legs. The thin sanitary pad was dry and unspotted, only clotted with bits of pubic hair. I could've almost shouted, *Hallelujah!* A strong overpowering scent came from her when she was fully aroused, as repellent as it was magnetic, a smell I knew I could never do without.

She twisted her body. "Lemme go shower first."

"No," I almost shouted.

I buried my face in her crotch.

CHAPTER 2

The next morning, I put Dreenie in a taxi and walked up St. James Street. I stopped in front of Sangster's Bookstore to catch a ride to Bogue. A car came but I waved it on. I dragged my bags into the bookstore instead and browsed their shelves. I took up *The Naked Lunch*, Coetzee's *Disgrace*, and a volume of poetry by Louise Bennett. I wanted to buy a copy of a local X-rated magazine but the cashier was looking at me funny, as if sizing up my taste. I paid for the books, smiled at her, and left. I caught a minibus that had just loaded, mostly with morning-shift workers headed to Hampden Estate.

My mother had written me a strange letter. She'd never written me a letter before and it troubled me more than anything that she should do it now, when I was out of her clutches and aware of my own agency as an adult, not beholden to her emotional blackmail like when I was a child, when my mood would be poisoned by her disapproval and frowns. I was supposed to be *her* son and no one else's, not even my father's. I'd been a slave to her ambitions for me until I'd made the decision to go away for school and not stay in Montego Bay. But how wrong I was about my supposed freedom, because all it took was a simple letter from her and I was in turmoil again. I attempted to read what was *not* there, trying to understand what she was actually saying to me.

The crows have eaten all the tomatoes. You should see the yard.

All that's left is the sweet potatoes but I can't bear to eat them without you home. I worry, Nyjah, when birds eat the first crop a mother has planted it means her firstborn is primed for trouble. Come home.

It was the last part that got me: *primed for trouble*—it was open-ended enough to mean I may well be the author of my own destruction through dissipation, a ruin that wouldn't be my fault necessarily, but nevertheless very much my own in another sense, and her letter was an intervention, a forestallment to save me from myself. All because the crows ate her crop. I was equipped enough mentally to dismiss this as a ploy based on handy superstition, but then I had a wretched gut feeling which I knew she was counting on.

When I was much younger, I hated my mother's bread pudding; it had a texture as if it had been boiled and not baked. It was funny because she excelled at most puddings—potato pudding, cornmeal pudding, you name it—but was desperately bad at this and would watch us eating with an evil eye and grudging instinct as if daring us to condemn her for it. But we couldn't. Till one day I found the strength to blast her fragile confidence. "This puddin' taste like the last bullas at the bottom of milk boxes off the school truck."

She took awhile computing the condemnation, then exploded, "That's it, I'll never bake again in this house as long as I live!"

"Apologize," said my father, looking up from his odious mouthful of pudding which he'd been chewing since Adam was in short pants.

"But Daddy—"

He slapped the taste out of my mouth before I could finish. "Yuh goin' learn to never insult a woman's confidence, especially your mother's. Not if yuh want to live in peace."

This was the first time he'd ever hit me. And there was a lesson in that slap. But I was too young to appreciate it.

"Now nyam de taste-bad puddin'," he whispered savagely when she stepped out to weep at the fence, calling:

"Myrtle, dat bwoy I bring nine months an' who nearly kill me up ah Regional Hospital wid him big head jus' have de heart . . ."

I tuned her out.

My father rushed out to console her, dumping the rest of his pudding on my plate as punishment. That's how fathers make men of their sons in Montego Bay. And how boys learn to blindly hallow the industry and sacrifice of women with readymade blandishments and tact. Bread pudding made a man of me. I still eat it today and laugh.

I got off at the bus stop and walked down the potholed back road. The mango tree was in flower and the driveway was filled with white, yellow-hearted blossoms and the acrid smell from waxy mango sprouts. Ground lizards welcomed me as I pushed the gate, skittering up the gravelly carport. They were cooking in the open kitchen at the side of the house. I shook Mr. Senior's big hairy hand and greeted the women.

"Laney, him come," called Pearl to my mother inside. I heard her frying something and talking to Mrs. Senior. She came out carrying a silver tray of curried prawns and placed them on the long galvanized slab so the women could apportion them to Styrofoam boxes. She gave me a tight smile and scant attention. I was used to this anytime I visited her at work. She wanted to give the impression that she was slightly bothered by my lack of proactivity and right away started to complain to Mr. Senior, who sat shirtless on a lawn chair under the ackee tree, smoking a pipe like a grand overseer.

"Mr. Senior, yuh see how him lazy?" she lamented softly, leering at me. "Jus' come stand up lookin' at everybody like census taker."

"Yuh spoil him, Laney," puffed Mr. Senior on his pipe, turning me by my wrist and feeling my backside as if I were still a little boy. "Nyjah have as much gumption as butter ackee."

The ladies laughed. I was slightly annoyed by this behavior of hers, complaining to Mr. Senior as if he were some kind of god even though they were partners in the catering business, always flattering him and his wife with obsequious manners, gibes at my expense, not wanting to appear too proud of me, as if she viewed this as immodest.

"Leave de bwoy alone," said Pearl, "let him enjoy some life," smiling at me with her toothless gums, and chucking rice, macaroni salad, and beef cuts into small white boxes laden with gravy, her long skinny arms moving with graceful efficiency.

"Laney, look how long yuh nuh see Nyjah," said Mrs. Senior. "Give him a hug nuh, gyal."

My mother paid no more attention to this advice than if it had come from a parrot. "Nyjah," she almost shrieked, "help Char serve de soup!"

"Yes, Mummy," I said, and dropped my bags on the verandah.

Charmaine handed me vinyl gloves and a hairnet. She was habitually hot-and-cold around me, sometimes coy, sometimes bossy, ever since we were children. I had briefly thought of dating her but then she'd gotten pregnant and dropped out of school and thereafter came to work with Pearl, her mother, at the Seniors'. I didn't find her particularly attractive, yet I did. It was one of those faces that made you think, a compliment to her probably, but I found her basic nature the most appealing of all the girls I'd known; I could never sham anything in her presence. She used to go fishing with my father and me. Daddy would tease, "But Nyjah, Char is a better fisherman than yuh." She had a talent that made me envious and it hurt my pride to even vie for my father's favor with her. Now we were shoulder to shoulder and I felt I wasn't good enough for her. She was showing me how to wipe the edges of the Styrofoam soup cups.

Mr. Senior hobbled over to us with a friendly look. "What's going on between yuh two?" he ribbed. "What sweet yuh, Char? I never see dis gyal skin her teeth like dis before Nyjah come." Charmaine excused herself and went to the dooryard. "How the job huntin'? Things comin' along?"

"Things comin' along fine, Mr. Senior," Mummy preempted me. "He secured two teaching posts already, an' teachin' general paper at him alma mater."

"I'm not contracted to teach sixth form," I corrected her, "it's only a substitute gig till the teacher returns from maternity leave. I'm doin' her a favor."

"But still," interjected Mr. Senior, rubbing the white hairs on his big protruding stomach, "it's good to get a shoe in the door. A Chester job would stand yuh well in the long run. More secure than all these patty shops poppin' up all over town. Everybody have teacher's license nowadays."

"All dawg and puss," chimed his wife, wrapping a tray of saltfish fritters, leftovers from breakfast orders that the workers would have for lunch. "But things need time, eh, son? I'm sure yuh don't want to teach all yuh life."

"No ma'am," I offered. "But I'm prepared to do it as long as I have to."

"Then what?" Mr. Senior challenged, fingering the lint in his navel. "Poetry ain't go pay those student loans."

"No," I said under my breath, "of course not."

This was a point he had been looking to underscore ever since the discussion started, because he was my guarantor and never missed a chance to remind me about it, always obliquely complaining to Mummy about all the time and energy he'd expended in taking time off from his headmaster post at Bolton, a low-rent comprehensive school that a monkey could govern, so he could accompany me to the student loan bureau. I had hated this man ever since my father and I returned a day early from Blue Mountain camping and caught him in our house. Mummy had sworn it was an innocent visit, but her marriage never recovered.

Char came back and I immediately said, "How's Denzel?"

She looked embarrassed, especially since she saw that Mr. Senior was irritated at my changing the subject. "Him well," she mumbled, "startin' de las' year of primary school dis term."

"My, time flies, eh?" said Bev, the fat half-Indian dietitian who supervised the menus, using a knife to slice Bustamante backbone into soft brown caramelized cubes smelling richly of burnt ginger.

Char's son was a taboo subject since she'd given him her surname, not knowing who the father was. She handed me a warm white bag for deliveries. "*Mirror*. Tek de bicycle."

"Lawd, Char," I complained, "mek me cool off likkle bit nuh."

She took up a cube of Bustamante backbone and stuffed it in my mouth, rough-playing like a boy, then wiped the sticky caramel from my face and pushed her finger into my mouth so I could suck it. "There," she chided, "now yuh have de strength of a prime minister. Go forth."

The adults laughed and shook their heads. "But dis gyal nuh easy," Pearl said, not knowing whether to be amused or affronted on account of her daughter.

Char ignored them and packed the bags in a basket.

I was off, clucking at scampering ground lizards with their silvery green bodies and bloodred tails.

I pulled up at the *Western Mirror*, and the guard waved me on to the front-desk woman who was friendly enough, but insisted I deliver the orders personally since she didn't want the extra task. "Make sure yuh have lots of patience when yuh make change," she whispered, "newspaper people are bad at math."

I walked along the thickly carpeted floor, dropping off lunch orders at various desks.

An editor was saying to a colleague leaning over his desk, "Yvette, what yuh think about this phrase 'dereliction of character'?" The girl brushed aside her newly cropped hair to reveal a comely face on the verge of womanhood—an intern. The question was obviously a test. The bearded man continued looking at his computer screen and in the meanwhile shook a mint into his mouth and took it with a swig of water. She still hesitated, trying to appear thoughtful. But the copy editor wasn't fooled. He saw that she was afraid to state her opinion and court his disappointment. So he dismissed her.

I had a thought then to apply for a job, so I approached the secretary. "Who do I talk to about a job here?"

Her eyes snapped; she leaned back. I wondered if my tone had been too forward. "Aren't you the lunch bwoy?"

I grinned. "I suppose I am."

She waited to see if I'd take a hint. "Listen," she said, visibly struggling to keep her tone professional, "that's not how it works. You have to put in a formal application, in writing. I take it you mean a job in *this* office?"

"You take it right, miss."

She looked insulted yet concerned. "Have you even finished school?"

A young woman who'd been watching us from inside her office stepped out. "Marsha, what's going on here?"

"The delivery bwoy has ambition, apparently," said the secretary, spinning her chair away from us to answer her telephone.

I couldn't believe it—it was Briana. I'd been friends with her brother Perry in school and we'd had a harrowing intersection once—the three of us.

"I've been watching you," Briana started, "peeping over the writers' shoulders as you deliver food. You're interested in writing?" She winked. I understood the play immediately—she wanted me to pretend we were strangers to avoid any claim of nepotism.

So I shrugged. "It's a habit with me, I want to make it a profession."

"Really," she almost laughed, clearly taken with my acting. "Wow, I'm sorry, currently we don't have any office positions." Her tone was arch yet attentive; she might've been trying to figure out just how much I'd grown since we met last, the man I'd become. "So you write."

"I'm a poet."

"Hah," said the secretary, drumming her fingers on her desk and watching my face. "Now I've heard it all."

"Published?" said Briana, our ruse becoming real now.

"Yes," I said, almost too confidently, "in *Bim*, and my first collection came out last January."

Briana looked disappointed; we'd been young literary rivals in St. James. "What's your name?" The sham lilt was back in her voice.

"Nyjah . . . Messado. What's yours?"

"Briana Fischer." We shook hands. "Please sit down."

We sat before the secretary's desk. She did her best to ignore us, busying herself with work, but had her multipierced ears cocked, her little earrings dangling like chandeliers. I was slightly disappointed; for some reason I'd been hoping to be invited back into Bree's office.

"Is this the interview?" I asked, hoping she wouldn't take herself too seriously.

"It could be . . . Nyjah. Did I pronounce that right?"

I nodded.

"We're very progressive here. I'm sure you've noted how young I am. And we're not big on formalities, no need to set a date and come in a tie and jacket. You're here now, aren't you? So what do you want to do for us in a freelance position?"

"I want to contribute poems."

"We don't pay for those," she said quickly, and it seemed like she was about to get up.

"Wait. How about a movie review? I always read the *Mirror* hoping to find one and never do."

"A critic." She looked stirred at the idea. "Tell you what, send me a sample. Then we'll talk."

All in all, I felt it was going well. "I won't let you down."

"Don't let *yourself* down. I'm very hard to please."

"Really?" I smiled genuinely at her for the first time. The secretary had all this time been doing everything with a little affected flourish, even ripping papers up to throw in the garbage, as if she felt neglected. "Well, what has happened here?" I said. "Nyjah, you might just have talked your way into trouble, or at the very least a rejection email. And they're not even paying for the movie ticket."

Bree laughed, batting a loose strand from her face, her eyes twinkling. "You're funny, Nyjah. What are you reading now?"

I could see that she liked rediscovering my name, it gave her a secret pleasure.

"*The Tale of Genji.*"

"Poor Minamoto," she said with a shake of her head, using Genji's other name that's mentioned probably only once in the book, showing off her depth. "Has that witch from Kokiden died yet?"

"Not yet," I replied.

She recited: "*Tears dim the moon, even here above the clouds. / Dim must it be in that lodging among the reeds.*"

I recited back: "*In the sky, as birds that share a wing. / On earth, as trees that share a branch.*"

The secretary got up as if she'd heard enough, going over to the water fountain with short angry steps.

I think Bree was impressed, but she kept her expression neutral. "*The Song of Everlasting Sorrow.*"

"It's the best novel ever."

"No," she said, "*Don Quixote* is better, if only because Shikibu's book was unfinished."

"Tidy endings are overrated."

"And where's this headed?"

"Have lunch with me."

"We'll see."

"We can trade more *Genji* verses."

"Is that your idea of a good time? A challenge?" She was hiding her grin. "I'm still grateful for what you did for Perry, Nyjah. Don't think I've forgot." Her cheeks quivered with sober reflection.

"Much good it did him."

She looked at me desperately now, her face working wildly with the same fumbling determination it had when I'd gripped her waist on the school's steps back in ninth grade. "He's in trouble again, I know. But he's a big bwoy now." Her big brownish-red hair bun was streaked with silver. Her head hung for a moment, showing only her full lips—lips that I'd betrayed. When she raised her eyes, there was the same pleading question in them that had been there all those years ago when she'd sacrificed herself for Perry. "Please, Nyjah. Talk sense into him. Yuh have to get him away from that car-wash lot. I'm only a woman—he don't listen to me no more."

"No, Bree, no. Perry make him bed. Him haffe lie in it."

The secretary headed back over. Briana stood, shook my hand, and said shakily, "We'll be in touch."

The secretary could see something had passed between us. "Briana, yuh need a tissue?"

"No, Marsha, I'm fine," said Bree, irritably wiping a tear.

I left with a spring in my step. Dreenie texted me but I was so giddy about Bree I was almost disappointed to see her name. I ignored her message.

Chadwell called me right after: "What yuh doin'?"

"Makin' deliveries. Tell yuh what. Order food from Mummy's place so I can have an excuse to come see yuh."

CHAPTER 3

The disembodied voice in the supermarket followed us, chanting vegetable prices over the speaker. I pushed Mummy's trolley and said, "I wonder what that man looks like—the one who barks prices. His voice is like God's on Sinai touting commandments."

"I tell yuh what I goin' do. New commandment. I ain't givin' you no advance on yuh allowance to go gallivantin' at Yacht Club with Chadwell."

"But Mummy, yuh promised! And if yuh don't gimme the money, they goin'—"

"Dem go what?" She stopped dead in the aisle, shouting because she was a mother and didn't care. "Dem go know yuh poor? Learn to live within yuh means, Nyjah. Yuh not rich like de Crichtons. Remember yuh place!"

"I don't have a place. And yuh not putting me in none. This is a new day. Yuh time done!"

She slapped me. My words had stung so much, her eyes brimmed. She feared this wickedness of mine. "I regret the day I birth yuh. Raise yuh voice like dat to me—yuh mad?" Her voice was weepy, fragile.

I felt terrible but pressed on: "Why me? Why me?!"

"Sorry I ain't enough for yuh. Yuh high-minded friends goin' ruin yuh. Turn yuh inna scapegoat one day 'cause yuh lack yuh own spine."

"Hah, how Levitical. I don't care!"

"Push dis trolley 'fore I break yuh jaw."

The Delfonics sang angelically over the meat section's PA: "Are you gonna break your promise, baby? You said that you love me. Are you gonna break your promise to me?"

I sulked all the way outside but wondered at her prophecy. She was annoyingly skilled this way.

"Yuh clench yuh ass, yuh cyaan piss either," she remarked over her shoulder.

I wondered which I was doing: clenching or blocking my urine. How exactly was I sabotaging myself and when would it end?

I stared at my mother's calm back as she toted bags. This witch!

We passed a crowd in the parking lot idling, watching a woman changing her frisky infant who people made baby noises at. The kid's shit was a golden color and people marveled at it—and it was the strangest thing. I walked behind Mummy in silence because we couldn't speak another word, our hearts were so full. I felt then such an intense love for her I couldn't breathe. I felt like I wanted to jump back into her womb or fall and kiss her feet and bawl, Mother! Mother, release me! Say somet'ing! Spit on me even! *I nearly said it and she knew I was suffering but held back her pity. Her hair was thin at the top with grayish wisps and fuller at the bottom with thick scarlet curls. It was bewitching to look at, like an aging fox of duplicitous beauty. That was my mother: wise, venomous, and alluring.*

"De pussy sick?" deejayed a toothless man outside Canterbury, watching young girls traipsing to the family-planning clinic. "Bring it come mek me give it a new gear stick!"

Mummy made a face and spat. "Dutty neagah." Then she finally regarded me. "That's why I break me back to send yuh to Chester. So yuh can be a gentleman . . . respect women. Education is a fine t'ing."

I delivered lunches to Chadwell's after leaving the *Mirror*. I went behind the grill partition and sat down. "I tired too bad, Chad, ridin' over MoBay deliverin' food on my second day back."

His older brother, Ska, came into the shop with the electricians. "Yuh ever think yuh'd live to see the day, Nyjah?" Ska smiled broadly. "Yuh ever think yuh'd live to see me takin' orders from me baby brother and salivatin' to bite the hand that feed me?"

I chuckled.

The men sat in a corner to eat. I was waiting for Ska to pay me but he made no such movement. Finally, he said through a mouthful of curried mutton and rice, "Let the big boss pay yuh. I ain't givin' yuh a cent. My whole life has been a quiet protest 'gainst injustice. Look how white me hands be with stone dust, installing electrical pipes in walls all mornin', and Chadwell don't lift a feather from cock crow till now. Lemme eat me damn lunch."

The electricians grumbled their assent but were careful not to appear too worked up. They didn't like Chadwell—he was bossier than his old man, more exacting though less hands-on since he wasn't an electrician—so they could never fully respect him, and he was more money-grubbing; they called him Prince with sarcastic courtesy, especially when he paid them. Ska was the joker of the family, the mouthpiece, while Chadwell was quiet and serious. But under Ska's bluff charm, like his provocative words just now, was genuine rancor because their father had groomed Chadwell to take over operations, due to his obvious talent, and left Ska to do odd jobs connected with the business. Ska couldn't help being a little resentful, yet there was an interesting dichotomy: both sons had their father's gifts in great measure. Ska was an excellent electrician like Mr. Crichton, and Chadwell was a fine moneymaker, just a little more grasping—the endowments were exclusive, two sides of a precious penny. The two sisters usually steered clear of this feud; they wanted nothing to do with the business, and a younger brother (born when Mrs. Crichton was well into her forties) was still in high school.

Chadwell saw to some customers and sat down. "I've been on my feet all day too, tryin' to figure out why that damn store at Overton Plaza losin' money. I didn't even eat any proper food."

"Boo-bloodclaat-hoo," said Ska, draining his Ting bottle.

Chadwell started on the lunch but ate absentmindedly—you could almost see his brain working, going through accounts in his head. Money was all he cared about, that and watching people break sweat when pressured. He winked. "Had a good time at Jack Tar?"

I smiled down at my drink. "The cuts on my back weep angrily. They sing, *Freedom*."

"Liar," he scoffed, "no woman scratchin' your back unless she fit to be tied . . ."

I stared hard at him.

"In a straitjacket," he finished.

I laughed.

"Fuck it," he said, putting down the half-finished boxfood on a slot below the open counter. "Let's go for a drink."

"This time of day?"

He was already up. "Ska, watch the shop till I get back."

"Yes, boss. Anything else?"

We went to the Georgian, an upscale restaurant overlooking craft shops on Gloucester Avenue. We had three Sea Breeze cocktails, enjoying the chilly wind, hardly saying anything to each other. But I watched him. There was a distinction between Chadwell and me. We'd taken a liking to each other immediately in prep school, first as sporting and academic rivals, then peers. He'd pay me to get his lunch. I still don't know to this day why I did it. I didn't really need the money. He had a way of handling people, but it was subtle and almost unwitting on his part. If we went into a convenience store just to grab a bite and talk, he would murmur his order to the cashier, "Coffee . . ." and she would have to lean forward as if to pull the words out of his mouth. He'd never mention the size and she would have to ask, "Small, medium, large?" By then she'd know the type of person she was dealing with and adjust accordingly—that is, react differently to him than she did to my much pleasanter mien. Mine was the type of manners people dispensed with, his was the type that intrigued them. The cashier wouldn't just ring up his order but leave her post to get him the beverage at the coffee machine, offering unwarranted service, hoping that while she was taking her sweet time he'd say something to her, even simply thanks. All she'd want was an opening. She'd come at our table later with napkins and ask if there was anything we'd like, eyeing him in that way which showed she smelled money and wasn't shamefaced about her forwardness. I always laughed at these instances but wondered deep down if I envied him. He had the good looks to match his manner, which never came off as imperious, was always perfectly calibrated. And he was very intelligent, could size up a situation in an instant. It showed in the intensity of his face that people often looked away from. He was born to get ahead, or more to the point, get away with anything.

"Yuh won't believe who runnin' *Western Mirror* now. Briana Fischer."

"Perry's sister? Yuh ol' fire stick? Another gyal on yuh choppin' board. What did the other one tell you? 'Me can cook, me can wash, me can clean—what more yuh want?'"

I snickered at his gift for recall.

"The silly cow."

"But you should see Bree, Chad."

"No, Nyjah. Yuh don't know how to handle them, they do somethin' to yuh."

"Anyway, she's a boss-lady now. Still have her foot on me neck—"

"Like St. Elizabeth and the dragon," he interrupted.

"Like St. Elizabeth and the dragon," I echoed with a smile, and forgot what I was about to say.

We heard peals of laughter, like shrieks of Old Joes descending on the beach. Their giddy voices warmed you like afternoon sunshine: you could feel their power before you saw them. It was just after two thirty and they were making their way down the school hill and across the pedestrian crosswalk to hang out at seaside parks or help their mothers at the craft markets—the white-dressed, blue-tied girls from St. Helena's. We watched women presenting their daughters to customers outside their gaily painted shops.

"Those vendors should be ashamed of themselves, the way they advertise their daughters."

"But they're the biggest draw," Chadwell said.

We watched one of the craft vendors brightly introducing her kid to a tourist. The girl seemed shy, but her mother played it off with brawling laughs and pushed her toward the man. I wished I could hear just what they were talking about, the process involved in this matchmaking, this barter. The mother, tubby, deep-chested, and pleasant-faced, was watching to see how much the man would spend, but more important, how well the girl would do on her own when she stepped away, hovering close enough to jump in and give her pointers, like a coach. The stoop-shouldered white man, in plaid shorts, a long white shirt, and a straw hat cocked back on his head, never stopped showing his teeth, sidestepping browsers so he could have the girl to himself. People gave him funny looks but he never minded, there was no harm in talking to a local teenager.

"It's a retirement package, isn't it?" I said.

"Who tell yuh?" Chadwell responded. "Soon as that school gyal get the ring and fly up, she filin' for her mother to come live with them, turn the white man house into a proper gynecocracy, then watch how quick stress kill him. Don't feel sorry for them."

"Why's a local woman's life so complicated?"

Chadwell's face lit up. "That's what you should write about, Nyjah! I bet if you wrote about the ugly choices of women, the writing would never stop."

I leveled a wary look at him. He knew exactly what I'd been turning over in my head; he was perceptive this way, as if I could never fool him, as if he could see right through me whenever he wanted. "You're a fine one to talk," I said, surprised that I felt so exasperated.

He stirred his drink and looked bemused, then exhausted. "Yuh lost me there."

"You know what I mean—*her*."

"Who?"

But I broke it off.

He smiled his satisfaction, happy I'd backed down, had given him the advantage. "She's dead to you and me—it never happened. She's dead to Rory too, and the other bwoys."

"Is she?" I'd lost my appetite. "Why did yuh do it?"

"It all happened so fast, Nyjah, I can't even remember."

"Like hell yuh don't!"

"Snow made me do it."

"Shut up!"

"Okay . . ." A smile played around his thin mouth.

I couldn't bear to look at him now. I peered out at the white tumbling sea crashing against rocks below Margaritaville.

"What's best for yuh is to live in the present. Leave her where she is, in the past. Why punish yuhself?"

"But she still haunts me, Chad."

"That's 'cause yuh sensitive, it's yuh gift and curse. Yuh overthink things."

"And you don't."

"No, I'm the shopkeeper, remember? I put things in their rightful place and leave them there. Then I close shop. I don't take work home with me."

"And yuh worked her over well, didn't yuh?" I said.

"You're no better."

Listening to the girls laughing at the beach park across the road brought a sudden stab of recollection. I remembered the ripped blouse, the bleeding fingernails. I got up and rushed to the bathroom. All the conch salad came up, a long, slimy pink trail hanging from my mouth, with a sour bile-smelling haze floating around my face like a filthy halo. When I looked at my reflection I was horrified. My chest hurt. I washed up, popped a mint into my mouth, and went back out.

Chad was sharing some joke with the waiter, offering him a business card, totally at ease with himself again. I didn't want to be with him anymore. It usually happened this way when *she* came up. Something would sour between us and I would bridle against his tone to smooth things over, to "close shop" as he'd put it. I went back to the table but kept staring at my phone.

"Somethin' wrong?" he asked.

"It's Andrene, she keeps texting me. She thinks I'm with someone."

"But you are, your BFF, your inseparable twin." He was having another planter's punch. I could see that in the time I was away he'd also ordered a Dragon Stout. How long had I been in the bathroom lost in thoughts, facing my monstrous self?

"Bwoy, yuh really putting them away now."

"We came here to drink, didn't we?" Chadwell responded.

"We did?"

"Don't do that."

"Do what?"

"That—being prickly, like a bitch."

"How yuh want me to be?"

"Jesus, Nyjah, sit down." He called for the bill.

"I know why yuh had that pint so quickly and ordered another punch."

"Yuh seem to know everything today."

"It's because Maude came up—yuh not as in control as yuh'd like to think."

"Enough." His square jaw tightened. I could see frustration building in his face, in the way his nostrils flared. He took a deep breath. "And if yuh really want to know, I was headed to Shangri-La, just knocking on the door with one drink more before yuh fucked it up. Let's go, let's see this gyal of yours. I hope she's in a better mood than you are."

The parking lot attendant shambled toward us, shouting, "Hey, bredda, yuh cyaan read? Yuh cyaan park deh so! Yuh nuh see de big white sign *RESERVED*?" When he recognized Chadwell he gaped, backpedaled to his booth, slowly closing his mouth and raising his fat arm to wave. "Sorry, Missa Crichton . . ." The Crichtons owned the building and the man had a worried look, wondering if he'd just gotten into trouble.

Chadwell did nothing to relieve the man's nerves. He only acknowledged him with a frosty look as we crossed to the other side of the lot.

"Yuh not going to fire him, are yuh?"

"Stay out of it, Messado. This don't concern yuh."

He could be that way, suddenly cold. When we were boys, he could be vindictive over small things, as if something had snapped inside of him, a little piece of madness, like a dead man's switch going off somewhere in his head, cruel spontaneous behavior, just for kicks or to flaunt his ego. Once, in sixth form, we'd walked down to the study room where the upper-schoolers had classes. Sometimes we hung out with them. They were on a free period and had pushed desks together to play money football with coins and fudge sticks. Chadwell had walked ahead of me and greeted them, then smiled at a boy named Omar Binns. "Binnsy, who winnin' de game, man?" Binns might not have heard him in all the din or was just busy with his game. But Chadwell took umbrage and raised his voice: "Me sey Binns, yow tallist!"

Binns straightened up—he was tall, athletic, and always jovial, popular with the Helena girls. He walked over to Chadwell, all bluff charm, showing his braces. "Chad, wah gwaan?"

Chadwell looked at the hand Binns had raised for a dap like it had a scorpion in it. Binns, confused, dropped his hand and jocosity; the room went quiet. "How much money yuh win just now?" asked Chadwell quietly.

Binns, sensing something was off, tried to sound casual. "Three hundred and twenty dollars. Fulla luck yuh fuck dis mawnin', Chad." He tried injecting his voice with alacrity again, but was clearly nervous at Chadwell's deadly calm.

Chadwell snarled, "Me forget me lunch money today."

"So de man want a loan, no problem," said Binns stupidly.

Some of the boys snickered but others got mad. They knew it was the beginning of something ugly, a humiliation, a sixth-former taking the piss out of them, and they became territorial. Binns still tried to play it off with a cool demeanor but stepped back to deescalate the tension. There was something in his backpedaling, his scared face, that was similar to the parking lot attendant just now. As Binns stepped back, Chadwell had reached up and cracked him across the jaw and he had fallen on the money football tables, scattering coins and sticks. Binns got up and held his jaw and tears rolled down his handsome face.

Chadwell had smiled. "Yes, a loan, Omar. Between friends." While Binns shakily gathered his winnings to hand over, I just stood still and fumed like everyone else. That was Chadwell's power, his psychotic episodes worked either as a tranquilizer or stimulant for everyone else. But he wasn't through. He walked within an inch of Binns's face, singing, "*Sly mongoose, yuh name gone abroad*," meaning Binns's name would be broadcast now as a coward. "Dat gyal yuh have by St. Helena's . . . wha' she name, Dainty?"

Binns had nodded sheepishly. This girl Cari Mullings, whom everybody called Dainty, was Binns's steady and a bona fide beauty. She made our mouths water.

"I think I go fuck her for yuh, yuh know why? Don't eyeball me, pussy'ole!"

Binns looked away.

"Yuh know why, Binns? 'Cause yuh ah nuh man . . . yuh a man *frame*." He grabbed the taller boy's head roughly to his bosom and whispered, "Say it!"

"Me ah nuh man," murmured Binns, and it turned my stomach.

"Louder, pussy'ole! Like yuh mean it!"

"Me ah nuh man! Ma ah man frame!" Binns screamed, as if he'd sucked in and released all the tension in the room like a chemical process, turning oxygen into genuine pain.

"Now ask me politely."

"Chadwell, can yuh please fuck Cari for me?"

Some of the weaker boys had chuckled.

"Why, Binns?"

"'Cause me ah nuh man, me a man frame."

"Now down on your knees. Show me how yuh nyam Dainty pussy."

Binns straightened, sniffled, then adjusted his khakis and kneeled and cupped his hands like someone praying or drinking at a tap; he ran his tongue over his palms.

"Chadwell, that's enough!"

"No, Nyjah, wait. Look pon Binnsy." Chadwell had laughed, leaning against me and tugging my elbow.

"Omar, get up," I hissed.

But Binns didn't dare move.

Chad turned to the other boys and laughed. "Binns eat pussy like how pickney eat fudge."

But the boys had started filing out, they'd seen enough; it had to do with the sight of Binns's tears falling freely into his hands.

Yet a part of me said I should lay off Chadwell and take responsibility for my own failures of character for once. He was only human. Chadwell . . . human. I laughed and the echo in my head disturbed me. It was true. He suffered in silence in a way that no one else knew but me.

I had caught him slumbering on the beach once; the sunlight had spread under his armpit like golden wings, as if it had no space to shine and had penetrated his resting form, forcing him alive. He was sitting with his head thrown on his forearms and the waves couldn't have disturbed him he was so peaceful, and a laughing sickness overtook me because water was his nemesis, he hated anything he couldn't control, he couldn't swim, so I borrowed a bucket from one of the tourists' kids and scooped seawater and splashed him and he woke up screaming, "I didn't do it, Mommy, I swear!" He started weeping, "Obah-di-Obadiah . . ." crying the name of his baby brother who had died in his care. It was so odd this outpouring of his, so odd in fact that when I'd held him to my chest I was at a loss about what to do next. I didn't know how to comfort him. He was like a dead man in my arms.

"Is not your fault, Chad . . . is not your fault . . ."

He looked at me and I saw the dead boy in his eyes, I swear it, I saw the likeness of the infant aching to forgive his big brother and offer him comfort and reassurance.

"I was watching him de whole time, Nyjah," he had babbled, snot running to his chin. "I swear, I only look away once! I was . . ."

"Of course you were . . ."

"I was watching him. Yuh believe me?" His breath kept catching in his throat and he was so overcome with what he'd seen in his brief sleep that he'd lost his ability to speak. I led him back to the room at Jack Tar Village and emptied half a flask into a cup of warm milk and gave it to him and watched him curled up on the bed, hoping I would never see that side of him again; it was gratifying yet terrifying in a way. I felt ashamed of this double feeling, this sandbagging for victory, as if I'd deliberately underperformed in my sympathy because I liked to see him suffer.

CHAPTER 4

Six years earlier

Master Bremmer said, "Okay, since it's raining today, let's do a ball rotation. How many lines do we have here?" He counted them. "Seven. Gentlemen, I have three balls."

"Lucky you."

"Hahaha," the boys laughed.

Bremmer glared at the joker. "And I want three lines, and don't let me have to beg like my wife makes me do every Friday night." We laughed again, but less heartily; we were used to this joke, and the response that always followed. He grinned at us. "What you all laughing 'bout? At least I get it once a week, you sorry virgins." Then he made a monkey face and stuck out his tongue.

"Line up in order of height, from shortest to tallest!" commanded Maude Dallmeyer. A sharp burst of her whistle followed.

I was sitting close to the front and dragged myself up and pulled my shorts out of my crotch and said to Chadwell, "I had some fiber cookies this morning. I thought they wouldn't move me like the fiber cereal does, but they're moving me all right. I'm goin' to the back so I can be near the restroom."

Chadwell stamped his foot. "But I wanted yuh to be my ball partner! Now I'm going to have to toss and catch with Cress."

"Tough shit," I said, walking off.

"I hope yuh die on that toilet seat," he said to my back.

There was a thunderstorm outside. Lightning lit up the gymnasium brighter than the bulbs, then the power went out. Groans sounded.

"Three lines, ladies! Make it snappy. Don't tell me you're scared of a little lightning and darkness . . . and it's not even that dark." Another burst of the whistle. Another crack of lightning and boom of thunder.

Some of the boys made mock screams and flapped their hands and ran around bumping into each other. The power returned and at the back of the line I noticed Chadwell had followed me. I saw him crouched down with a medicine ball in his lap.

"What are yuh doing here?" I asked sharply. He stood up and grinned, talking louder than usual to catch the attention of Ms. Dallmeyer, a trainee from the sports college, G.C. Foster, who was doing her practicum at Chester that month. She was assisting Master Bremmer with rotations. She was pretty but seemed to have intentionally dulled her looks, wearing no makeup, with unprocessed hair in big schoolgirl plaits and boys' sweatpants, but still had a confident gait. Though I was convinced that she had a gentler, caring, sensitive side—after all, she wrote as a hobby and assisted Master Throckmorton with the sixth-form book club.

Now she marched toward us with a stern face, her chest bouncy under her fitted green G.C. Foster shirt. "Why are you down here? I said tallest to the front."

"Nyjah made me do it," Chadwell gulped.

"I did not." I flashed him a look.

She stared at me. "I forgot you two are joined at the hip. Say the word."

"Sorry," I muttered.

"Louder!"

"I'm sorry I skipped the line."

"The thing to remember is actions have consequences, a domino effect."

"I said I was sorry. Why isn't Chadwell apologizin'?"

She stepped to my face. "You speaking back to me, Messado?"

I lowered my head. "No ma'am."

"That's right—*I* say who does what here."

"I never could catch one of these properly," Chadwell said, glancing at her.

She snatched the ball from him with playful aggression. "Okay, Crichton, let's pick up where we left off last class."

I furrowed my brows at Chadwell. Ever since she came to Chester, the boys had been salivating over her, calling her Ms. Daydream, placing bets on who would be the first to ask her out or ask for her phone number or look up her skirt (if she ever wore one). We never took ourselves seriously, of course, it was all in good fun. But Chadwell had the daring to promise he would get to her first, and we laughed at him. It was entertaining to watch his asinine strategies to catch her attention.

She rolled the ball from arm to arm in an endless loop, showing off her dexterity. Then she got serious and said, "Now look sharp."

Chadwell made a catch pose but it was too late, she had already launched the ball, her motion barely noticeable, the force of the throw knocking him over.

"Get up!" she barked, and I was seeing another side of her. She was out to make it hard for him, as if to knock the clowning out of him for good. He got up and threw the ball back as hard as he could and she caught it in the crook of her arm. The boys *ooh*ed and *aah*ed. Chadwell made a catch pose again and she instructed in her authoritative way, "The next throw is coming at chest height. Make a strong catch-ready position. Bounce on your toes a little, Crichton, loosen up . . . and keep your legs at shoulder width. Your knees should be slightly bent and your hands should be floating above your hip. Here it comes."

Zoom! The throw knocked him on his ass again. More boys had gathered and were watching almost reverently. Some of them liked to see the stuffing knocked out of Chadwell because he was so full of himself. He simmered with impatience, but took a deep breath.

"Get over here," someone said. "Chadwell get knock on his ass by de gyal."

"Twice," said another boy, and it was becoming a full-fledged spectacle.

I could see the veins standing in Chadwell's neck. He hadn't expected this and now he felt out of control, and for him that was the worst feeling. He knew he was outmatched, had bitten off more than he could chew.

"All right, let's try again, throw it back," said Ms. Dallmeyer.

Chadwell threw even harder than the first time and she caught it easily.

"Now that's better. Watch me—your weight and balance must always be going forward toward the ball. See how I did that? Don't put your weight on your heels. Don't have your balance going back toward the ball. Ready?"

Zoom! This time he caught it and held on and staggered just a few steps. "I did it!" he exulted, and the response was so unlike him that he wasn't the only one immediately embarrassed. He sounded stupid and kiddish, like a lower-schooler.

The boys applauded sarcastically. "Attabwoy, Chad," one kid said. "Bravo, make Mommy proud. Catch it with no hands this time."

"Shut up!" he hissed, but they'd turned the tables on him; even Bremmer was enjoying it.

"Don't mind them, Chadwell," said Ms. Dallmeyer, "and you can do it even better. Now lean forward into your catch and attack the ball. Don't be afraid. Expect it, but don't be tense."

Chadwell stretched his shoulders. "Right . . . *expect it, but don't be tense.*"

"Make a diamond-shaped hand gesture, like this," she explained, "with your thumbs connecting at the center back of the ball. That's good, focus on getting your hands on the top two squares. Here it comes. Remember, attack the ball with your arms and put a slight bend at the elbows."

Zoom! This time the ball knocked Chadwell down again, and he rolled on the floor and yelped, "My finger!"

We ran over to him.

Ms. Dallmeyer shoved us back. "Let me see it, Crichton."

Chadwell offered the hand like a wounded paw and whimpered, "I think it's broken."

"No it's not," Dallmeyer said as she studied the finger. "But maybe we should stop."

"Chadwell's scared." This started us laughing again. "He broke a nail!"

"The sissy."

"Chadwell's a pussy after all."

"Cut it out!" Master Bremmer bellowed, his echo booming in the big maroon gymnasium, bouncing off the sober portraits of all the stuffily dressed past headmasters.

Maybe it was all those faces, alive and dead, looking down on him for once with unabashed scrutiny, that made Chadwell lose it. He jumped up and started shrieking at her, "I'm not scared! You bitch, I'm not!" His eyes misted. It was the first time anybody had ever seen him cry. Everyone looked at each other in shocked amusement.

"Crichton, that's enough, apologize this minute," Master Bremmer said.

Chadwell sulked. Bremmer grabbed his arm, but Ms. Dallmeyer put a hand on the man's big shoulder. "Coach, it's my fault," she said, softening her tone. "I pushed him too hard. I'll take him to the sick bay, if that's all right."

"You want to buy him a sweetie too?" Bremmer said. "Don't baby him, Dallmeyer. It's not like you. It's quite not like you. I approved your placement here for a reason. Show some sense."

Ms. Dallmeyer stayed quiet but resolute. Master Bremmer was upset, you could see his copper mustache moving with his whistling breath, and he had that wild look in his light-brown eyes. He was a Chester old boy himself—Big Red was his nickname back then—and had been on full athletic scholarship and perhaps still carried some of that old grudge against the privileged types like Chadwell. He saw that Dallmeyer would not back down from her decision, and though he probably felt her sympathy was misplaced, he seemed to appreciate her resolve and nodded. "You know where it is?"

"How hard can it be to find?" she answered.

"Okay . . . Rory, Marco, Castleigh, help them out." Master Bremmer blew the whistle and instructed us to work on our own for the rest of the session, since he had to go to Winners Sports downtown on business. I headed to the locker room for my raincoat and then through the side door out into the drizzle, and jogged up the slope by the cafeteria, pacing myself and counting steps.

At the top of the hill I turned right by the old chemistry lab and ran past Bailey House. The disused road forked all the way to the old cracked steps leading down to the back of Fuller Canterbury, the slum community whose thieves terrorized us. Fog spread behind the row of teachers' cottages. Sometimes fog rolling off the Albion hills was so cold it blistered your nose, leaving it with little red scars like pinpricks of blood. Pockets of cardboard hoppers—cardboard-colored grasshoppers—were jumping around, wet and nervous; they were considered a bad omen. I jogged down into the slope above J block and heard voices below.

The car-wash boys.

They called themselves that because they always hung out at J block, the fire-gutted building behind the industrial arts block, where they washed and serviced teachers' cars for a fee. They hardly attended classes. Most were automotive technology students, but it was exclusive company: all these boys were gay. At Chester, gay boys banded together. Loners were often persecuted. Choosing a course of study could sometimes be a matter of security rather than academics.

Philip Moodie playfully swung a three-star ratchet knife at Colin, who laughed wildly. Moodie, now pointing at Master Laird's white BMW, which was smeared with dirt, said, "Collie, that car needs to be cleaned."

Colin, slim, dark-skinned, tall, and fine-featured, with his bottom lip and eyebrows painted mauve, paid it scant regard. "No, enuh . . . me like a dutty bumper."

It took awhile for the joke to land among them. When it did, they all shook with laughter. "You were always a dutty bugger," said Fenton, drinking straight from the fat brown bottle of Clairin, Haitian liquor he'd taken from Smokey the groundskeeper's den.

Smokey was friendly with us and allowed us to relax there, to take a break from the rigor of school. We smoked, watched movies, read comics, and gambled in exchange for giving him school lessons and whatever schoolbooks he requested.

Colin held up his hands in comical guilt. "Persecute me, Fenton, me ready for it."

"What yuh willing fe do for it?" replied Fenton, leering. He had flared nostrils like a bull's with two ostentatious gold nose rings and tumbleweed hair like Don King—among the gay boys, he was the most outrageous, sometimes spraying his hair pink like cotton candy. And he was extremely vain, always titivating with a pocket mirror.

"I'll wash it," said Perry Fischer, a chum of mine, tall and gangly with a shaved head, a babyish face, and doe-like eyes. We liked Fish, he had a rare gift for improvisation that was never grandiloquent; we liked him in the way you might like a pet that's in the house but not yours personally, treating it with occasional friendliness or casual abuse that kept it confused and scared enough to always try to please you with tricks, licking your hand when you extended it, satisfied with a smack or an ear rub. That was Fish's life at school. We felt if anyone had the right to abuse Fish, it was us. He was a homosexual, a deviant, but still a Chester man who won school trophies in cricket and drama. Lately he had been slowly pulling away from us, probably realizing he'd reached a point in his life where he had to make a choice. So, though he was a prefect, he'd been hanging around the J block, kowtowing to the car-wash crew, running errands.

Just then, a dark-red van with a barnlike body attached to the vehicle, and the brown and white head of a smiling cow painted on the side, rounded the corner. Above the cow's pointy white ears ran the legend, *BARN APPETIT!* The cursive white legend above its barn door said, *ENJOY DELICIOUS GELATO MADE WITH FRESH MILK YOU'LL BE HAPPY YOU DID.*

Colin confronted the driver as he stepped out: "Where's the punctuation after 'milk'? Wha'ppen, yuh not a believer in full stops or commas?"

But Snow was barely listening; he was a sixth-former and entrepreneur like them, who drove the school's dessert van around campus during recess and lunch and other occasions like Sports Day. He was also a semi-hoodlum from Fuller who had a reputation for terrorizing vulnerable teachers, so the car-wash boys usually left him alone. "Wash de fuckin' van an' stop ask fool-fool question," he muttered. He had a small, smooth head and premature gray whiskers on his dark face.

"No, seriously, Snow," chuckled Marvin Mighty, a tall, well-built boy in a fade haircut who ran the gambling den by Smokey's, and operated at times as a loan shark and bully. He was the crew leader, sitting on the bonnet of a Lada puffing weed.

"I ain't de boss," Snow growled, eyeing the car-wash crew milling about, flicking towels at each other. "I don't make de rules, I only drive de truck." He said this as if his words had double meaning, shyly meeting Colin's eyes. It was the most I'd ever heard him speak. He was always quiet, dangerous-looking, tightly wound. Sometimes if you didn't have the exact amount, he'd just take all your money and drive off.

Colin smirked at the crew. "Him doh even talk in full stops either. Him perfectly suited for de job."

His cronies laughed.

"Snow, how much yuh make a week?" asked Fenton.

Snow stiffened; his eyes went flat.

"Answer de man before me mek yuh wash it yuh bloodclaat self," said Bolo, the fat one.

"Ten t'ousand."

"And tips?"

"Round out to 'bout twelve t'ousand a week," said Snow. "Same fe Lenky, de server." He was being strangely conversational; he looked tired.

Colin whistled mournfully. "Then Snow, yuh can mine yuh gyal on dat? It nuh better yuh come work for we?"

Snow wiped nervous sweat from his forehead. "Who tell yuh me have a gyal, Collie?"

"Not even a *sketel* from St. Helena's?"

"Yes," said Snow, changing his tack. "Me have a gyal . . . at Helena's."

"Describe her to me," said Mighty, drawing on his spliff and winking at the others.

"A f-fat gyal," Snow stammered. "She manny-manny though . . . but me cyaan cut her loose 'cause me love fat woman."

The car-wash boys cackled at this. He was obviously lying, making it up as he went along.

"Manny-manny like meself," clucked Moodie, throwing his leg over Fenton's hip.

Mighty walked over and placed his hand on the shorter boy's shoulder and slowly, erotically, put his spit-sodden spliff into Snow's mouth. He patted Snow's chest. "Nuh worry, Snow, we all have a fat unfaithful gyal . . . probably share de same one. Dat disgustin' pig."

Colin said, "Perry, pray fe Snow so him doh lose him fat woman. Give Gawd thanks fe all mampy-size gyal."

Perry, quick on the draw, kneeled before Snow as Mighty gently eased him against the wall abutting the corridor. Snow started heaving as Perry unzipped him—he was breathing so wildly, his mouth open, his chest moving up and down, it looked as if he would run if Mighty wasn't holding him firm. Perry was smiling, taking his time, praying nonsensically, "Fawda Gawd, t'ank yuh fe food, t'ank yuh fe de car-wash gang. Fawda Gawd, t'ank yuh fe fat gyal, anyt'ing over two hundred an' fifty pound, Fawda Gawd. Me know it tek whole heap ah time an' material fe mek dem sum'n deh, so me appreciate it. One rib mek mawga gyal, but fe fat gyal is either ah hand or ah foot."

When he slipped Snow's cock into his mouth, Snow closed his eyes and melted against the wall, whispering feverishly, "Mercy . . . 'Zaas Christ."

"Yes!" exhorted the car-wash gang. "Pray, Perry!"

When they saw Snow enjoying the blow job, when they saw him relaxing, accepting himself, they nudged each other. Moodie was on the wet ground rolling with laughter at Snow's face. Perry sucked his dick like he was starving, sealing his protection—he too knew there was no coming back from this, he was one of them now if they would have him. Snow gripped Perry's shoulder, approaching his climax.

Chadwell rounded the corner with Ms. Dallmeyer, Marco, Rory, and Castleigh.

"No! No!" Snow shouted, pushing Perry off and scrambling to tuck his hard cock into his khakis. "Hey, gyal, wha' de bloodclaat yuh ah look pon!"

Ms. Dallmeyer jumped at the harsh sound of his voice and backed up. So did the younger boys.

Snow kept making half turns to face the wall, twisting around then turning back as if he wanted to smash his way through it, his fists half-clenched, his cock still throbbing hard and hanging out his pants, as if begging to be sucked.

Castleigh Twentyman, Snow's younger brother, looked utterly embarrassed but was too stupefied to move. Mighty approached them with a wry nod. "Wait . . . wha'ppen, baby, yuh lost? What yuh doin' at de car wash on foot?"

"We took a shortcut back from the sick bay," Rory said.

"Grub, was I talkin' to yuh?" Mighty said.

Rory lowered his head, opened his mouth, but then thought better of the apology.

Mighty flicked away his spliff and his expression changed, his mouth downturned in a sneer. "Well, grub, did yuh tell de pretty miss dis is a cock roost? No hens allowed?"

"She might be a dyke, Marvin," Fenton offered, swigging his Clairin Sajous. "Look at dem awful pants."

Ms. Dallmeyer opened her mouth but released a weak push of air. The car-wash crew giggled.

"Wha'ppen, cat got yuh tongue?" said Fenton.

"Like she ketch a death of fright," said Big Eye. "She never see cock get suck before. Yuh have a boyfriend, darling—yuh know how to . . . ?" He moved his fist back and forth, working his tongue in his jaw, simulating fellatio.

Ms. Dallmeyer gulped, "I didn't see nutten."

"*I didn't see nutten*," Moodie mimicked. I could see his skin crawling to hurt her. He was the smallest, with princely features the Helena girls drooled over. He was also a certified psycho. But it was strange with Philip Moodie. He had a love of beauty. He could recite Keats and Shelley and embarrass teachers and he used words like *in toto*. But then he'd do things like carry a dead rat on his key chain for days, till it stank, things that made the masters shake their heads and sigh about what could have been. Sometimes he walked by St. Helena's with an empty leash and girls playing afternoon tennis would scramble to the fence and pant with their tongues out. *Take me, Philip! Take me!* Now he asked Bolo, "Who the fuck is this bitch?"

"De gym gyal—Bremmer's mistress."

"I didn't see nutten," Ms. Dallmeyer repeated like a morbid witness.

"Bremmer like dem young, eh?" said Big Eye, feeling her side.

"Take your hands off me!" she rasped, slapping his hand down. She trembled. She should have run then, before Mighty and Big Eye slowly circled her. She gripped Chadwell's hand tight.

Snow paced the corridor, his head in his hands. "Me ah nuh faggot . . . me nuh love man!"

"Tek it easy," Bolo said. "Yuh cocky never reach inna him mout' by accident."

Perry looked lost, slumped against the wall. Snow pushed him hard to the ground and kicked at him. Perry got up and hurried away.

"Me ah nuh bloodclaat battyman!" Snow had the look of a mongoose that had fallen into a bamboo box when the trapdoor fell *clat!*

"Whatever you are is your own business," Ms. Dallmeyer said quietly.

Snow stopped pacing. "Wha' de fuck yuh say, gyal? Talk again!"

Mighty and Big Eye laughed and slapped palms.

"Snow, go easy, badman," Fenton counseled. "Dis is a place of peace."

"Pandora, yuh haffe work out yuh own salvation," said Bolo.

"Yuh t'ink me a bloodclaat battyman?"

"Perry, come away!" Ms. Dallmeyer yelled, then to Snow, "It's all right. You don't have to hurt anyone. I won't tell a soul."

"Who de fuck yuh be to tell me what's all right? Yuh t'ink a class dis?" Snow closed the space between them. "Me go show yuh sey me a bloodclaat *man*. Nuh gyal nuh gimme order!"

She turned to run and Chadwell tripped her. She looked up at him as if she couldn't believe he'd done it. He glanced up the slope and our eyes met. I could've sworn he smiled.

"N-noo!" she wailed as Snow dragged her up. He twisted her arm behind her back and the pain was so sudden she gasped.

"Open yuh mout' again an' see wha' yuh get." Snow twisted her arm harder and she bit her lip; you could see the pain was such that she'd lost her voice, it was one of those stickup grips he used on women back when he snatched purses, running wild with the rest of the Canterbury boys. He dragged her toward Smokey's den. "Me go show yuh wha' bloodclaat clock a strike."

Ms. Dallmeyer whimpered, "No, don't do this . . . please!"

She looked to Mighty; he mock-grimaced, lit another spliff. "Me gyal, yuh jus' bad lucky. Yuh shoulda stay inna yuh bed today."

"Marco! Castleigh!" I called out. Marco and Rory looked up then quickly turned away, their faces registering fear of what might happen to them too.

"Cass, open de door," Snow ordered his brother. Castleigh

obeyed. "Come, grubs," Snow beckoned to my friends, "come fe oonuh share."

Ms. Dallmeyer started praying. It was strange, she prayed with the same earnestness Perry had, though his had been in jest. "When I wake up on the mountain, God, kill me, throw me to the bottom. Cast me upon the rocks and break open my flesh. Let the message be the sword and let the sword be the message. Fashion a stone out of the holy mountain with your hands and break me open. Break me open!"

Her words chased me across the hill. I slipped in the wet grass and fell on something—a John Crow had died on the knoll and the corpse had lain stinking days before, but today it was a macabre tangle of white bones, empty black feathers, and ants, because Smokey had thrown lime on it. Now white lime smeared my cheeks and hands and there were nasty feathers in my mouth.

When I barged into his office, Master Harding was bent over a rash of papers. He was wearing a cream-colored suit with high-waisted pants, I distinctly remember, to show off his diamond socks, and puffing on his pipe. Fright took the wind out of my lungs, I couldn't get the words out; I was stuck, in a horrible paralysis. Harding saw my distress and jumped around his desk and pulled me free and slapped my face. I heaved and opened my mouth and blacked out.

I woke up on his couch and he had a wet compress on my forehead. My yellow raincoat hung in the corner. He helped me to the chair and said, "I know something stupendous happened, something disastrous. It's written all over your face. Don't speak because words can sometimes betray one. Your gift lies with the pen. Here, boy, write it."

He had an annoying habit, Master Harding—he would correct your work, as if correcting your thoughts, as if he had the gift of putting on paper what you so desperately wanted to say. He articulated your vision but he made you earn it. What he'd do was make his revision with such poor script in red ink that you'd have to spend days deciphering it, and the effort was worth it because his advice and subtlety of thought were always so valuable. So I wrote down everything in a shaky hand and the words were as inscrutable as his when he gave good advice. But I'm sure he deciphered the SOS in that frantic ink.

He said something strange to me after glancing at what I wrote: "You lost the game, didn't you, Messado?"

"Yes," I panted, "yes, I lost badly!"

"But you enjoyed it, no?" He peered so deep into my eyes that I thought he would hurt me. The smoke from his pipe half obscured his strong-jawed face and it could have been a different man sitting across from me. I backed out of his office with my skin crawling at the steady screeching from his copier, as I watched him crush the paper into a ball and throw it in the wastepaper basket.

CHAPTER 5

Ms. Dallmeyer never returned to school after that day. Master Bremmer never disclosed anything beyond that she had discontinued her practicum for "personal reasons," but he was obviously troubled, and had an air as if he wanted to quiz us but didn't know how. I wondered at the refuge she'd found in her faith at that moment when she was about to be overwhelmed. The boys had taken to calling her the Epileptic St. Maude.

The incident was a fork in the road for me and my friends, especially Chadwell. I felt sometimes I had cobweb on my face when I thought of how Chadwell suffered for his dead brother, and it frustrated my rage toward him.

And I felt in my gut that Perry's persecution wasn't far away either.

Months before Ms. Dallmeyer arrived, we'd had School Barbecue. We had invited the St. Helena's girls as their school was just across the street. They reciprocated whenever they had Bazaar. I was running up the steps outside the library block to get the banner I'd forgotten to spread by the cafeteria where the funhouse was set up. I slipped and fell so hard on the landing that my body went into shock. I felt a boot on my back before I could get up. I turned angrily to shout at the prankster but heard, "Uh-uh, not so fast."

I knew the voice: Briana! My heart hammered. I reached around and touched the foot holding me in place, then the calf, then twisted my body to look her full in the face. A white shaft of light slithered along the floor like a snake. She gazed at me where I lay, her boot now on my chest, a closed-off look on her face. She was the female version of her brother, but so beautiful not even her glasses could blunt her looks. Her ruddy cheeks were a little puffy with deep dimples. I'd been trying to get with her since first form. I shuffled to my knees, ran my hands up her legs, thighs, while she stood there like a tailor's dummy, but her full lips quivered. My hands gripped the half-moon of her fleshy backside under her St. Helena's skirt and rose to her waistline to peel her stockings. I nearly exploded with excitement.

"Bree . . ." I breathed. "Why? Yuh told everyone I was ugly." I kissed her mouth, then saw him a few steps below us. It turned my gut. I pushed her back and moved aside. "What's this?"

Briana glanced back at Perry standing sheepishly behind her and said flatly, "Yuh have to promise to leave off me brother, Nyjah."

"Perry has a mouth for himself, let him speak."

But as soon as he opened his mouth and said, "Nyjah, what happened was—" I shut him down: "Quiet, yuh little *chi-chi* man. Bring yuh twin here to seduce me. You *bitch.* Yuh think I'll let it go so easy?"

"How much you want?" Perry said.

"Don't insult me."

"Perry, shut up," said Briana, whipping around. "I'll handle this."

"Yuh think yuh can throw money at me like yuh yard bwoy—is that what yuh think? You uptown types are very adept at *handling* things and people, aren't yuh, Briana?"

"He didn't mean it that way," she said.

"Yuh can read his mind too? Read mine." I grinned.

"You will!" Briana screamed, poking my chest repeatedly. "You don't get to hold this over his head." Tears wet her eyes. Perry ran up and held her elbow, but she pulled away. "Why are you bwoys so cruel to each other? I don't get it. You're no different than those Canterbury hooligans yuh set up high walls to keep out!"

I snickered. "I will, eh . . . okay . . . I'll let it go. I'll take the retainer." I leered; she held my stare. She was stronger than me then, and I had to look away. Perry stared over the railing to the pavilion and empty sports field. "I'll have her, Perry, and keep my mouth shut." I pulled Briana in for a kiss, feeling on her ass. I had an absurd sickening feeling that I was kissing her twin, that Perry's emotions ran poisonously—intravenously—in the kiss she gave back to me. We were in the Poetry and Languages Club our schools shared, but she always ignored me. I taunted as I cupped her breast, "*Poeta nascitur, non fit.*"

"A poet isn't made, but a coward certainly is," she snarled.

"Come to Jack Tar Village this Saturday by noon," I demanded.

Perry bammed the rail with his fist. "That whore's nest where yuh and Chad fuck *sketels*? No! No, Bree, it too much. Call it off."

I dropped my hands from Briana's waist and walked past them. "It's her choice, Perry, take it or leave it."

His sister held his handsome face, catching his tears with her palm. "It'll be all right, Perry." Her own eyes were dry.

He grabbed her fiercely to him and crushed her with his love.

I'd totally forgotten about the banner.

We had come back from the field and ran boisterously into the gym and Perry sat right at the door holding hockey sticks. "Two consecutive wins against the Tigers!"

Rory swayed, standing, pulling at his red shorts bunched up in his crotch.

"Speech, Captain!"

Rory held his hand up. Silence. "High on its summa cavea came shouts of Helena maidens screaming praises of the true gladiators!"

"Horatian Odes!"

"The Eagles who trounced the Tigers!"

We dropped our hands behind us and beat the wall to a deafening roar.

I was always messing with Perry, so I flopped down in his lap and ground my bottom against him. He looked scared.

They started hooting and taunting Perry, who knew better than to respond.

"Tek it out, rude bwoy," I teased him, wining in his lap. "Tek it out and wave it at me."

Our play was very homoerotic sometimes, with a sort of tongue-in-cheek devilry. But we thought nothing of it. Like feinting at each other's cocks when we lined up to piss at the urinal gutters.

But Perry looked trapped all of a sudden, his mouth kept opening and closing like a washed-up fish. We knew he was afraid to push me off and act outraged because then we'd accuse him of being a hypocrite, and if I stayed in his lap we'd tease that he liked it. It was a cruel game with no outlet. Perfect. The only games worth playing. You had to be a sportsman!

"Tek it out and wave it," Marco demanded.

And the boys started beating the windows and walls with laughter.

When I got up from his lap, Perry had a boner.

"Jesus Christ!" said Cresswell, as if he'd seen a dead body.

We all looked at Perry's erection and fell silent. He was crying like a little boy and biting his lip with his head hung over. We couldn't laugh anymore. We felt sorry for him. "It's okay, Perry," offered Castleigh. "We don't mind that yuh a faggot. Yuh still a Chester man."

But he was deeply ashamed and sad at the way his body had betrayed him. When he went to the showers we didn't follow, and Chadwell whispered, "Somebody keep watch, he's fragile now. He might try to harm himself." So we stood outside like gloomy sentinels—real Romans now—while he had the showers to himself. We were showing solidarity without even meaning to.

But something turned in me, became bitter. Maybe it was because I was the one who'd felt that rise of his nature poking at me. Such a strange thing. Or because they were all wealthy, and the real reason they were bonding was because he was elite—his last name German. A name established in St. James. Perhaps I had a proletarian eruption, because I shouted, "No! Him is a fuckin' battyman an' I go out him!"

We heard him wail inside the shower.

* * *

When Briana came to Jack Tar Village that Saturday afternoon, her throat was trembling like a bird's. The guard had buzzed her through to the beach cottages and she traipsed down the hallway toward me lost in protective revery; she looked into vacancy, pursing her lips. She stopped before me with sea light swimming in her eyes and said in hushed terror, "I'm a virgin!"

I pulled her, closed the door. My fingers trembled with regret. Afraid to touch her.

"Is like me head carrying me legs, Nyjah. I can't believe how tired I feel these days . . ."

She was begging to be spared with her roundabout talk—soliciting sympathy—as if I cared how exhausted she was.

"Look how me sweatin' . . ." She held her arm up and sniffed her armpit, her clothes dark with perspiration, as if trying to put me off, kill her own attractiveness. Her hair was cropped. She wore light-khaki capris and a cream button-up.

She looked like a schoolboy—like her brother, Perry.

I took the sunglasses off her nose. "Why yuh wear this? Why yuh look so different?"

She pulled away as I held her chin. "I don't want nobody to recognize me as one of Chadwell's whores."

"*Chad?*" I said, piqued. I could've slapped her. "But you came to see *me!*"

She smirked (or so I thought). "Yeah, Nyjah, but let's face it, this is Chadwell's castle."

"And what am I, his shadow?"

"You're *something* . . ." She shrugged, turned her eyes up at me. Her words riled me. Living, weaponized poetry!

Feeling emasculated, not worthy of my ill-gotten prize, ambushed, I tugged at her waistband, peeked at her kelly-green underwear—a thong.

Yet. Yet.

Her skillful poison!

I sat on the flower-patterned duvet.

She gazed out the glass doors, eyes roaming to the shoreline. "Can I have room service?"

"No," I answered sharply. "Quit stalling. This ain't Disneyland."

"Lawks, man, don't be so hasty." She jerked the pants over her soft bulging hips. Her beauty was unfathomable. Now *my* throat hammered like a bird's. She removed her soft canvas shoes. She swallowed. Walked into the dark squares of white marble as the cream-colored clothes peeled off her. She stopped before me.

I dropped my head. "I can't, Bree. Your brother did nutten wrong. Let him work out him own salvation. It's tough enough bein' a battyman without blackmail."

She was silent till I heard sobs and her naked stomach quivered with intakes of breath. Her tears plopped to the floor. Her saliva swung to her deep, smooth navel. She held my head. "Thank you. Thank you, Nyjah."

"Put your clothes on."

"Thanks, Nyjah, that's such a relief." She sat beside me, yawned. The white chiffon drapes fluttered behind the door leading to the balcony, which was ajar. The air was a mélange of her whipped-lavender and coconut-milk body cream and sea breeze.

"Tired?"

"Yeah." She stared at the seafoam-green walls.

"Yuh can nap here if yuh want."

"Promise yuh won't do nutten funny."

"Briana . . . what yuh take me for?"

"Nyjah, I ain't playin', enuh."

"Bree! Come on, what I go do? Trust me."

From an adjacent beach, we heard the klaxon of a head fisherman's conch shell—alerting others to his catch. I watched her in the net of the canopy.

"Awrite. And I still want that room service."

I went out to the balcony, my Parnassian hunger unquenched. I felt she'd cheated me somehow. Bested me as she did in poetry and French.

A white man walked the beach with careful alcoholic gravity, abusing his skinny young wife tramping ahead: "Git back hyar!"

"Fuck you and your draw-ma!" she yelled, gripping her wind-blown hat. "Don't call me like I'm your dog!"

"Gwaan back ah de villa, badman, dis ain't de place for it," said a beach boy, grabbing the man's hand.

The husband wagged his finger at the attendant. "Lemme give you some free advice: never try to buy a girl's affection, it always ends up bad for you."

"A woman's always right," the attendant smiled, patting the man's shoulder.

They were trained to deal with these types. I could see in his lecherous laugh—his gaze fixed on the wife's bony backside—that he was planning to seduce her.

The white guy said, "Aw phooey," and allowed himself to be led.

The buff attendant glanced back and winked at the wife. She responded to his effrontery with a shy grin. She looked like Susan Sarandon. She tossed her hat to the sand, signaling to him—a gauntlet. Then she called devilishly to her husband, "Go on, Ernie, go lie down, honey."

I went back inside.

Briana slept soundly on turned sheets, looking like a princess below the canopy. She breathed warmly and sweetly through moist parted lips. I stole a kiss. *Clackety-clack, clackety-clack*, went my heart like a broken machine.

Chadwell came back from the tennis courts and buzzed to see if I was still in.

I walked out to the honey-colored foyer. "She's sleeping."

"Market women always say if a tangerine is hard to peel, then it sour," Chad muttered with a scowl.

"The hell yuh know 'bout market? You have a butler."

"Her drawers peel easy? Sweet or sour pussy?"

"My lips are sealed." I looked beyond him and saw the beach boy wearing Susan Sarandon's hat. She giggled and clapped her veinous hands. He sliced a papaya, turned it oblong—so it resembled a uterus—and devoured its pink flesh piecemeal with snake swallows, the juice glistening in his beard. Her body appeared to tremble with all the possibilities of adultery.

His performance triggered a premonition: I saw it was Briana's brother who would end up saving *me*. Not the other way around.

PART II

SNOW'S RETURN

CHAPTER 6

An alert came on my phone as I left the job interview. I opened my email.

Nyjah,
I love your writing style . . . I am a big fan of reading movie reviews and I like how you come across :).

Now I have a few observations and suggestions: I do not like that logo for the movie review. I'm not sure you can always stick to that (undue pressure) and I actually don't mind you expounding on the plot. Which brings me to my next point: You do not have to be so vague, especially with the Mission Impossible *review. I read it without knowing any more than I watched in the trailers. I'm sure you can say more without giving away the plot :). And I see u have a stars system, I'm assuming it's out of 5?*

Final analysis: I want to use the reviews in the Mirror, *prolly twice weekly, if you can manage it. Just connect more to your readers by letting them in a bit more.*

I'm awaiting your response.

Regards,
Briana

I met Chadwell, then we went to see Cress at SG Investments where he worked. We walked down Church Street toward the LOJ Shopping Mall because the day was windy and it would be good to have lunch near the pier. I had a feeling that I'd always want my days as free as this, the city at my behest and my friends at my side. For a long time I had seriously considered staying away—getting a Kingston job and starting a new life there.

"How was the interview?" said Cress.

I was telling them when Chadwell cut me off: "Fuck that. Who text yuh?"

"Bree."

He narrowed his eyes, ready to give a reading.

"What?"

"She's a toothpick. Sometimes yuh don't need one, but if it's sticking out the pack, yuh take it anyway."

"*What?*"

He grabbed my neck.

I shrugged him off. "Fuck you."

He laughed. "Don't yuh know I want yuh for myself?"

We heard him before we saw him, a familiar voice that reeled our attention in. When we moved toward the commotion and confirmed our suspicions, it took my breath away. "Remember Snow?" said Cress. "He's gone mad, preaching like a drunkard and still drinking Clairin Sajous."

"Rum Preacher!" hooted a shirtless boy jumping beside a sweetie stall. We walked closer to get a better look. Snow rolled down the wide street on a wooden platform that took up all the space in the open body of a pickup truck—it looked like a carnival float and people, especially children, shouted, "Mista Big! Mista Big!"

The pickup rolled past and stopped outside the white Dyoll Insurance building, right in the sink of the road where minibuses picked up evening passengers on their way home from garment factories. Snow waved to the masses to quiet them down. He didn't look that much different from school days, except a little fatter in his black face. He still wore his hair cropped and still had his widow's peak and bright smile; he'd always had nice teeth, but his eyes were full of a deep stubborn pain that turned them red, like he'd been drinking from that Clairin bottle his whole life and couldn't finish it, like some mythological punishment. Now he worked his charm. He played peekaboo with one of the street boys near the van, playfully covering his face as his white teeth disappeared into the darkness of his coal-black hands. We called him Snow because he was the blackest boy we'd ever seen. Now the teeth, when they emerged from his playful gesture, spoke to me without the mouth—they exhorted, full of violence and casual cruelty. *I'm going to fix everything just the way it was before*, he said, nodding determinedly as he dragged her body and she prayed fervidly. *If my mind tries to run away, catch it, Father. My legs are falling off and I have no arms, no tongue, 'cause it is cut off by the wind . . .* The anger in his eyes, the white heat of it rolling off his body, threatened to burn everything around me. Setting things alight before my eyes. His face seemed to be pushing me backward into a porous invisible wall. I couldn't feel my soul in myself; he was carrying me on the invisible wave of his words, preaching a sermon only I could hear.

"I know who you are," I was mumbling between my teeth, barely aware of my reaction. "I know who you are!" But I might have been referring to myself. I crushed something underfoot, and when I looked down it was a dead bird's skull on the sidewalk. It had probably collided with the glass of the nearby flower shop—maybe seeing through the glass to the potted plants on the other side.

"Chief! Chief!" they shouted. "Mista Big!"

Snow soaked up the adulation. As ridiculous as it may sound, he was wearing a three-piece suit and spoke with a gentleman's whisper to those at the front, warming up his routine. There was a strange magnetism between him and us, as if we were boys still bumbling in the weak afternoon light, still slowly emerging from the Albion fog. We couldn't have moved if we'd tried. We hung anxiously like everyone else on his every word; it was as if he spoke for *us* when he raised his voice. A cock was crowing busily as he talked on about the past. A city cock, startled by the unexpected noises and sounding the alarm for his hens.

Snow looked across the street and saw us on the opposite curb. We three stood with our hands in our pockets, apart from the crowd that gathered in the sink of the road or sat along the wall fronting the building's underground parking. His red eyes lost some of their animation. I could see him working through the fog inside his head, the fog that was also inside of us, the common affliction. I never figured him for a public speaker, he was always an elite athlete—then again, I hadn't figured him to be a rapist either.

He cleared his throat, took a swig of the Clairin, and began again: "Bredrin, listen to de Rum Preacher. Yuh doh know what type of person yuh are until yuh faced with certain things. An' I folded, I folded to pressure dat day."

Chadwell glanced over at me. I knew what he was thinking, but was Snow really going to confess everything? Right here and now?

"Madness," Chadwell hissed.

Cress looked at him and then at me, but didn't say anything.

I stood there, hotly baffled, my feelings racing back and forth between despair and curiosity.

Snow's face went dead all of a sudden—he had a look as if lightning had struck his breast. The crowd hushed on their own. I realized this was what they liked about him, though not so much his words—they could get a glib sermon from any patty-shop preacher on any day of the week. What they liked was his emotional rawness and unpredictability; he was a performer in the way of our best street dancers, scrapping till their knees and hands were bloody, dancing till they were past exhaustion and the performance was ugly and you wanted them to stop. His gravel voice was hearty but ghostlike to my ears, as if coming from a coffin.

"Rich rumors of war an' strife, dat's de type of bile dat fill de heart of many people nowadays, friends. But de Rum Preacher have a different burden. Built up in me heart, like cancer, are some of de words me cyaan use, words dat never grant me freedom."

People seemed bemused; some rubbed their chins and drew closer.

Snow took another swig of Clairin, wiped his mouth. "There was a bwoy dere who had ah irrepressible spirit an' we kill him dat day. Him name was Perry Fischer. Him was de captain ah de cricket team an' a fine bowler, played basketball besides, an athlete to rival de best of us older boys, a successor, but even in him brilliant moments we withdrew from him an' he withstood de ostracism an' stayed strong an' genial an' his performances never wavered, as if quietly provin' himself against de odds, as if dere was a Cold War goin' on between him an' de virulent homophobes . . . but him reckonin' had come."

He took a break from monologuing to act something out, like a one-man play. "Bring Fish over here!" he commanded, big and black and looking a little crazy talking to himself in the back of an empty truck, pretending to hold someone down like a rugby tackler.

The crowd was enthralled, they kept whispering to each other.

"Bring him come!" Snow gestured to his invisible cast.

We stood transfixed, Chadwell and I, because a part of us was back at the industrial arts block, and at the same time in the back of the truck with Snow—he wasn't looking at us but we were responding to his gestures, as if we had a fishhook in our guts. Chadwell's hand shook and he had to put it in his pocket.

Snow broke off the impromptu play and said conversationally, "Back den, if a bwoy said something to yuh like, 'Why yuh wear your watch like a gyal, with de face pointing downwards?' yuh had to wear it facing up. Several t'ings have served to injure me t'roughout me life, and me not tryin' to sound innocent or blameless here, but dis alarmin' aggression, dis virulent homophobia dat seemed contagious an' a feature of peer pressure, was one-a dem, it shaped what yuh could an' couldn't say in public, an' to be silent sometimes was just as dangerous as to be apathetic or in opposition. So me became a soldier. Or a war horse, runnin' in blinders. Yuh had to sing 'Boom Bye Bye' like yuh meant it, like a war cry. An' if some suspected faggot was being tried *in absentia*, yuh had to agree along de lines dat yuh'd always seen de symptoms." He waved his hand in a vague gesture. "But me gettin' mixed up. Me just wa'an say today, people . . . Me won't miss dis life when me time come."

"He's doing penance," I said. "He's tormented, he probably can't sleep."

Grabbing my arm, Cress asked, "This has somethin' to do with that afternoon at gym, don't it?"

"Enough outta you," I said, pulling my sleeve away from him.

Snow walked slowly over to us, his arms outspread: "Me friends." He greeted Chadwell with a hug and whispered, "Bwoys of de Albion fog."

"Preacher," answered Chadwell tensely, going stiff in Snow's embrace and eyeing the inquisitive faces around us, "you look well."

Snow had a thin-lipped smile fixed on his clean-shaven face as he tried to hug me. "It was really foggy dat day, wasn't it? All dose cardboard hoppers like a plague. So thick yuh couldn't see yuh hands in front-a yuh face!"

I pulled away from him. "Yuh saw well enough, Snow. Yuh saw well enough to—"

He held up his palm. "Me doh go by dat name no more."

"Isn't that ironic?" I said. "A rejection of the name of purity because of its filthy association. What should we call yuh now?"

"A chile ah Gawd."

I laughed—it started slowly and built till it was tearing painfully through me.

Panic spread in Snow's face and he pulled us aside toward the underground parking lot.

"You're a fraud," I said. "We've been to war, Snow, yuh right. But we're not veterans, neither were we innocent bwoys. You're a murderer, yuh initiated the massacre."

"Hey, take it easy," said Chadwell.

"Yuh special," I mocked Snow, "real special, aren't yuh? I'd like to see the bum that baptized yuh. What yuh dream of at night—God on his knees sucking yuh big dick?"

"Gawd never take a day off," Snow challenged, jabbing his finger at us, some of his old aggression coming back, "an' I'm on His clock!"

"Whatever. All yuh've done is traded in the ice cream van for a propaganda van."

We were so caught up we didn't see Mad Lena's approach. "Self-hatred. You wear it like a poison mustache. You're hurt," she said, grabbing at my arm. She wore pancake makeup, big pearls, and a frowsy white frock, and always traipsed the Bay like a ghost looking for a home, toting a witching bag of junk. She was never usually this forward.

I snatched my arm away and noticed hers was covered with bruises and looked like a half-rotted chicken's foot with all the green veins below the wrinkly paper-thin skin.

"Preacher, they raped me again last night," she moaned, lifting her frock to show her bird legs, then all the way up to her filthy drawers, gray pubic hairs sticking out at the top. "The Dollar Boys . . . they did it under Fowler Bridge. One of them put his zinger in my mouth." As always, her manner and accent oozed bewildering refinement.

"Get away from here, you witch!" shouted Chad. "Filth!"

She drifted across the road staring crossly at us. "Little people," she fumed, sputtering saliva that ruined her silver lipstick; tears dripped down her mascara. "Maggots!"

"What yuh want from me?" Snow asked hotly, fiddling with his pocket watch.

"Nutten," I said. "Keep doin' yuh thing, *Preacher*. We'll see yuh round."

"Yuh cyaan walk away from dis, Crichton," he called after Chadwell. "Not twice in de same lifetime."

"Watch me," replied Chad over his shoulder.

The day was ruined and we could barely eat. Cress was moody because he'd confirmed that we had secrets between us. He barely answered when we parted company.

Driving home, I could still see Snow. My eyes were closing on his ghost—it truly felt like I had seen an apparition—but were opening widely on the memory of that foggy afternoon.

The orange tabby that frequented our yard was curled up on the mat. I sat on the top step and took her in my lap, stroking her ears. She stretched out her paws and meowed. "Yuh know why yuh always happy?" I said. "Because yuh have very low expectations of yuhself. Yuh don't even have a conscience."

She looked at me quizzically and jumped up, her tail held high. The sky was brilliantly sunlit, with a single cloud floating across it.

See, when we'd been boys at Chester College, there was a piece of rascality we'd engage in without thinking about it. We'd short-change the bus conductor, confuse him with a lot of coins, and by the time he'd counted them all and realized what we'd done, he would have to hop off the bus and chase us, but we'd stand together, five, six of us, and dispute every word. I now realized we'd done this cruel thing only after we ourselves had been hurt, from some type of public humiliation we couldn't live down, a caning or a reprimand from a superior that left us vindictive, feeling small, so we would leave school with the collective intent of taking out our frustration on someone else, actively seeking targets.

I took out my phone. Charmaine answered after the second ring. "What yuh doin'? Still at the Seniors'?"

"No, I'm home. Today I work from six to two. Heard yuh had an interview . . ." Her voice trailed off. I could hear her breathing expectantly on the line.

"Come over. I'll tell yuh how it went."

"Gimme five," she said, and hung up.

When she arrived, she still smelled like fried food, as if she'd never left off toiling over big pots. "Nyjah," she said softly, not wanting to protest too much as I fingered her buttons, "what's goin' on? Talk to me nuh . . ."

I took off my clothes as if they were on fire. "You can have me, Char," I said. "Isn't this what yuh want?"

She didn't answer. She turned her head away and looked out the window. I lay on top of her but nothing happened. I rubbed my soft penis on her pubes. She took me in her mouth, then looked embarrassed. Nothing I did worked. I was desperate. I grabbed her arm and tried sniffing her armpit.

"Nyjah!" she protested. "Wha' wrong wid yuh!"

I gave up. "Char, yuh remember that time yuh said I think I too good for everybody? I was ill, Char . . . still am. Yuh have it backwards. I'm the one not good enough for yuh, not good enough to lick even yuh toe corns."

She looked genuinely worried at my words, sitting up and covering her breasts. "Bwoy, what's goin' on? I know sum'n happen. What yuh talkin' 'bout?"

"I did something, Char. I did something awful and I can't function properly since. I'm like a man runnin' from himself."

"Doh worry 'bout that." She indicated my flaccid penis. "We can do other t'ings. I feel yuh come back home for a purpose."

"*For a purpose*," I snorted.

"Talk to me. Lemme help." She had her hand on my chest, peering into my eyes with her perpetually sad face.

"Char . . ."

We heard the key turn in the lock. My mother put down her bag with a soft noise as she entered, and proceeded down the passage, her footsteps a soft plunge in the rugs. "Nyjah . . . ?" I could tell by her tone that she'd seen Char's slippers.

Char muttered in dumbfounded panic, "Me rassclaat . . . Me naked, not even have on a bangle!" But it was too late.

My mother came into the room and spun in the doorway as if teetering on a precipice, then threw up her hands. "Jesus Gawd, me still in me own house? Charmaine, what yuh doin' here?"

Char sat on the bed's edge and wrapped the sheet around herself. I stared directly at Mummy; she knew I had intentionally laid a trap.

She was in a dangerous humor, had forgotten Charmaine temporarily. "Why yuh do dis—disrespect me in me own house?"

"Yuh wanted me home, didn't yuh?" I countered. "That's what yuh letter said. Well, here I am."

Her face sagged, and something inside her crumbled, maybe her sense of balance. "Get out," she said, holding on to the doorframe. "Pack your t'ings!" She looked at Char. "You too, yuh batta-eayz bitch. Out!"

Char didn't know where to run. So she jumped through the window.

"Dat's de type o' nastiness yuh bring in me house, a gyal who leave t'rough a window wid all her *kratches* outta door like a dawg!"

"And how did Mr. Senior leave?" I said. "Did his wife know that yuh fuck her husband?"

She choked on stunned outrage—or it might've been guilt. "Yuh not my son, yuh's a demon. Out!"

CHAPTER 7

Something caught my eye: an outdoor café festooned with blue and white streamers, on the savanna where we used to fly kites. "How long that there now?"

"'Bout two years," the cabbie replied. "Nice likkle eatery. Serve de best Blue Mountain coffee an' potato puddin' you can find."

"Gimme a stop, a me dis."

He pulled up along the curb and came out to help with the bags and cat carrier. Outside of the taxi he was small and slight in build, and bald-headed under the silk cloth cap.

"It's fine," I told him, but he insisted, taking the opportunity to slip his card in my pocket.

As I walked up the driveway, sun-drunk lizards slithered slowly under the crotons. I liked Rory. He could be a little high-strung at times but was usually mellow, and his laugh had a warm folksy sound to it, like a country boy's. He was on the balcony looking down and smiling.

"I'm clearing out the last paint cans—take yuh time."

"I'll be up in a minute."

I rang the door chime. His grandmother came out to the door-way. She was smiling with her mouth open and had a comb wedged in her hair. "Nyjah," she said pleasantly.

I opened the burglar bar gate and hugged her. "Mrs. Lombard."

She eased me back. "Always so tall. How long yuh been back now? Why yuh don't come round as before? Yuh used to be here all the time stonin' me young mangoes." I laughed shyly. "Before they were ripe!" she said, shaking my shoulders. She'd always had a funny bone.

I followed her in and took a seat as she went into the bedroom. There were family photos all over the living room. Rory's parents had divorced early, like mine; his father was a businessman in Switzerland, and his grandmother had practically raised him and his younger sister Jacqueline. We'd never asked him what it was his father did, but it was obviously very prosperous—they were always adding rooms to the original government-issued house, as if they had nothing else to do with their money. Rory lived alone upstairs since Jackie had gone away to a polytechnic in Switzerland.

His grandmother soon came back with the receipt book and plum juice. She sat beside me and pushed her fingers through her silky salt-and-pepper hair, taking me in with a rueful look. She looked like Marla Gibbs from *The Jeffersons* and *227*, that same working-class beauty that could be upgraded quickly to elegance with pearls and the right dress and makeup. "Yuh lookin' at me with yuh poet's face."

"I'm sorry." I dropped my head.

"I don't mind, it's good to be looked at once in a while." She handed me the glass. "I'm so proud-a yuh."

"There's nutten to be proud of."

"So yuh got the job—congratulations. Yuh grandmother told me."

"Yes ma'am, teaching. Slaving to pay back the government's money."

"And my rent!" She wagged her finger and we both laughed.

I got up and handed her the glass and money.

She wrote me a receipt and gave me the keys. "The electricity works fine."

"The water?"

"Sometimes we have problems with NWC in this scheme. But we storage tank full. Maintenance of the yard will be you bwoys' duty."

"Yes ma'am."

"Gwaan," she said almost sadly, "I know Rory dyin' to know what keepin' yuh."

I took a step into the side yard and the dog rustled its chain. I'd forgotten about him. He was big and black and blind in one eye. We called him Snow, because we'd hated Snow so much as a school bully that we gave the dog the name as a running joke. He was old but didn't look it. When I got upstairs, Rory was in his room.

"There he is," I greeted him gallantly, "my landlord!"

"I'm buyin' a boomerang on eBay," he said colorlessly.

"What? Why?"

He didn't answer. I went to my room across the hallway and started unpacking my things. It had been his sister's. The room stank of fresh paint, and the maroon louvre blades in the window frame were still shiny with a new coat. It was all white—white walls and white tiles and white curtains and bedsheets—and slightly bigger than my rooms at both my mother's and grandparents'. *I'll have to buy a TV*, I thought. *First paycheck.* I had that old worry about money again. Rory never had this worry his whole life. (None of my friends did.) He was an architect working for a new firm in Freeport, building condos, piers, a kind of mini city out west, a project he'd be on for at least eight years. I suddenly envied his financial security. I fed PJ, my cat, some canned tuna and corn, then went over to Rory's room.

"Listen, watch the cat for me. I soon come."

"Watch how? Yuh stupid or what, Nyjah? A cat ain't a baby, yuh know."

"Don't let Snow mess with her."

"What will be will be," he responded.

"Fine, I'll take her with me."

As I slipped on my shoes, a piece of one of the heels came off. I took it as a sign that things wouldn't go well at my grandparents' house.

When I came out, Mrs. Lombard was scooping dead roaches

into a mulch bag. She straightened up. "Eh-eh, is where yuh off to?"

I kissed her cheek and skipped down the steps. "I have to make a courtesy call."

"I guess yuh won't be needin' supper." She turned away without waiting for an answer.

The signs were all over the place as I headed to Tucker, just across the river. A scrawny hen was walking on the curb and when it heard an engine cough to life, it fluttered its wings and tried to run in two directions at the same time. I saw a man whom I'd known since I was a child coming down the broad boulevard. He was dragging an oxygen tank on wheels, rubbing his bloated stomach and complaining to anyone who would stop to listen. And lusting after women who walked past him, swiveling his head to watch their bottoms. He started murmuring something to a girl standing at the bus stop, a student waiting for the Teachers' College bus. "Trish. Trish Biscuit," I heard him say genially, licking his dry pebbly lips then whispering to her.

She feigned a slap at his round gray head. "Tom, which part ah yuh sick?" she laughed. "Yuh fat so till yuh look like yuh nyam yuh own neck."

He simpered and left her alone, making his way toward the riverside café. He was a retired police colonel, notorious for his venality during his heyday. He lived alone in Porto Bello, in a mansion no less—which people liked to joke he had built on his government pension—a broken, infirm, lonely widower. Going to the café might have been one of his regular jaunts.

An oldish aristocratic woman who was walking her poodle stopped. The dog started showering the sidewalk with so much piss that it ran toward me and I had to skip over into the dry gutter. The woman bowed apologetically, but there was something vinegary about her face that made me wonder if she meant it. She looked as if she had the world on her shoulders. She was getting ready to wash away the urine with a squeeze bottle when Tom verbally attacked her: "Yuh fuckin' rich bastards act like yuh own Porto Bello an' yuh animals can do as dem please."

The woman reddened and clutched the collar of her red coat. "Apologize this minute! The ruffians that have moved into this neighborhood—it's unreal!" She doused the pavement and moved briskly across the road.

Tom walked her down, wheezing and bumping the oxygen tank over the rutted road. "Lemme tell yuh sum'n, lady! Reality is reality, an' love come before apology. Yuh t'ink I fraida yuh mout'? Yuh people too damn coldhearted an' selfish. Dat's why yuh pedigree doh worth shit no more. Everybody mix up—everybody a mongrel now. All oonuh *stoosh* types go get wipe out!"

She had so many trinkets strapped to her that when she hurried along, she jangled like a rolling calf. Tom had a lazy eye that we'd always stared at as children, just to annoy him, whenever we rode our bicycles through the neighborhood. The lazy eye was now trained on me. "I know you," he said with a demented stare. "Yuh from around here . . ."

"Who was that woman?"

"Zetta Rosegreen," he said. "Dem used to own everyt'ing west of de train line, now dey doh have dry shit in dem ass. She passin' her days as a psychic up in dat ol' mansion. Talkin' 'bout she communin' wid spirits. Yuh wait till dem bwoy ready, dem soon kawn her."

I nodded, walked ahead. It jolted me how casually he had spoken of her vulnerability, alone in her big house, and her inevitable rape, as if it were some kind of retribution. I tried to put the thought away. I didn't feel she had any need for my concern.

I took a shortcut through Gunns Drive and entered a side gate. Through frilly curtains I saw the blue light of their TV set and the jagged silhouette of Hammer Mouth's rooster dreads. He kept his washing machine in the backyard, which I thought was odd since the bathroom, though small, could still hold his washer and leave space enough to maneuver. Then it occurred to me that it probably wasn't his doing but his girlfriend's, probably one of her coarse leftover habits from the slum they'd moved from. I'd met them only briefly on my last vacation from school. When they found out the house they lived in was mine, Hammer, a worker at my grandfather's cement factory, had gone slack with a look of vague surprise then embarrassment, but the woman, a hairdresser who worked in Marsh Head, the squatter settlement, had rescued the situation by thanking me for the courtesy of visiting them in person, saying something about my busy schedule. I'd been charmed by this. She wasn't bad-looking either.

I was trying to remember her name when I passed their verandah and saw her. She was resting her back on a silver stability ball, the back of her head held in knitted fingers, doing crunches. As soon as she saw me, she stopped and stood up. "What yuh doin' creepin' up on me like dat?" she demanded.

I dropped my amiable manner, annoyed by her tone. "Don't flatter yuhself. There's a side gate, if yuh care to know."

"Try usin' de front one next time."

I bit my lip. "Perhaps I should introduce myself properly—"

"You're a creep," she said, toweling sweat from her cheek, "a horny likkle toad."

Hammer Mouth came out, big and broad and black, like a square of bitter chocolate, muttering to himself, "When dese players act like savages, dem like to say dem have passion. Ever hear a t'ing like dat, Mel?"

Seeing his blunt nose, the tip like a porous strawberry, the sides of his mouth foaming spit, I wondered how a man like him kept such a fine woman. Even just a fleeting thought about their sex act was excruciating, so I tried to put my mind in a vise grip.

"Wait, what's happenin', landlord?" he said. "Inspectin' yuh house or me property?" He turned his girlfriend's back to me and ran his hand over her ass, gloating, watching my reaction. Leaning over the rail toward me, he whispered jovially, "She deceptious, nuh mek de angel face fool yuh, false modesty, but I would walk over broken glass for she. Climb *macca* tree naked too!" He exploded with a brawling laugh. She gave me a dignified glare and went inside.

Lightning had severed a coconut tree in the yard, the top of the scorched stump looking like a burnt match. I almost laughed. It might have been a monument to my relationship with my family. When I walked around to the front yard, a skinny shirtless boy of about ten ran up the steps past me as if I wasn't there, reaching for Cam's hand, but not before she gave him a hard rap on the side of his head. He rubbed it vigorously and moaned. "Camille, is what me do now?" he inquired through angry tears filling his eyes.

She didn't answer, just held out her hand for him to help her up. "Go get the gentleman's bag," she ordered.

He took the cat carrier without acknowledging me, sniffling and wiping his nose.

"What's yuh name?" I asked.

"Tony," he answered, "but everybody call me DJ."

"Why do they call yuh DJ?"

"'Cause me can deejay like Baby Wayne. Yuh wa'an hear?"

"Perhaps later, Tony, I'm tired." I walked up the steps and kissed my aunt. She was my grandparents' youngest child, just four years my senior, and taught at the nearby kindergarten, though she couldn't manage it on a regular basis because of her health.

"Look who's home," she said, "the poet."

I gave her my best smile. "Yuh look well."

She sat back down and folded her skirt between her slender thighs, peering up at me from under the hoods of her eyes. "Yuh sound disappointed."

"Who's the bwoy?"

"You have Lois and Papa to thank. They went shopping at Blossom Gardens orphanage. Now he's the little man of the house but still wild as anything, hell-bent on his vices. I had to whip him this morning."

"No," I laughed. "In your condition?"

She gave me a pressing look, as if anything would unloosen her tongue. She wanted me to ask what the child had done, but I wasn't in the mood. I wanted to lie down.

"Nyjah," called Mama.

I went into the kitchen and kissed her.

"You eat already?"

"I feel so tired, Mama, all this back and forth."

Lois walked past and flicked her finger against my ear, mumbling that she could smell her food burning. I went to the refrigerator and glanced sideways at some papers spread out on the table. They appeared to be utility bills.

An ugly noise filled the house, then Cam hobbled in on a crutch jammed under her left arm. "Nyjah, Papa wants to talk to yuh. And stop drinkin' straight from the milk carton. You're a pig."

"Lawd, Cam, is what Papa want so quick? How him even know I'm here?" I took out a plate of cold chicken.

"Yuh never see him workin' outside?"

"No. I took the back gate." I pushed past her to the table and she wheeled around to pursue me. "Listen, I know yuh miss me, but please control yuhself."

"Miss which part of yuh? And how yuh mean yuh don't see him, yuh blind? Him out there quarreling how yuh don't have no manners. Walk in him yard an' don't even tell him howdy."

"He didn't see me. It's that child, what's his name—Baby Wayne—who told him. Why is this place such a fiefdom?"

"Suit yuhself," she said.

"Yes," I exploded, "I intend to! I'm goin' lie down and get some sleep, if that's all right with yuh."

"Why yuh leave Elaine house so quick—is what yuh do?" She jutted her dimply chin and gave me her squint-eyed look. She had always felt like a lesser version of Lois; where all Lois's features were sharp and attention-grabbing like Cicely Tyson's, hers were softened by baby fat. She was the cute baby sister—not beautiful, but she had always competed with Lois for attention and invariably come out second best (Lois had poise she could never match, a certain unerring grace), rebelling during her time at Teachers' College and gaining a reputation with students and professors that made even me ashamed. Her dissolution was only checked by sudden illness. Whenever the lupus flared, her face got a slightly puffed-up look and it gave her the appearance of a round-cheeked doll. There was an infinite youthful quality about her, like a child who had never outgrown her petulance.

"Mind yuh own goddamn business, Cam. Since when yuh get so sanctimonious?"

She laughed out loud, enjoying my annoyance. I went to my room and lay on my back, looking at my old dancehall and new jack swing posters. Super Cat hadn't aged a day, neither had Tony! Toni! Toné! Whenever Cam cleaned my room or borrowed my novels and glanced at them, she would shake her head and snort: "Yuh so gay, yuh know that? This shrine to beautiful men—yuh jerk off in here too?" I always chased her out, but whenever I masturbated and glimpsed the gallery, her remarks would alarm me and sometimes affect my erection.

I knew my grandfather was waiting and I had to prepare myself. The chicken sat on my chest like stone. I was too keyed up. I cursed and got up and stormed through the door.

Papa came in gruff and silent, wiping his hands on his coveralls. Lois busied herself in the kitchen. Cam got the dishes out.

Tony brought the cat to me. "She scratch me," he said, pointing to his bleeding neck.

"I'm sorry, she's prone to anxiety and aggression when she travels."

"Lemme see that," said Lois, twisting the boy's face. "Go get the rubbing alcohol and some cotton."

"Yuh washed yuh hands?" asked Mama.

I lied that I had. We sat and she set the steaming dishes on the table.

Papa muttered, "Yuh know how much o' my money I spending pon dat crosses house?"

"No sir."

"Damn right! Jus' las' week I have to spen' thirty thousand to buy wastewater pipe to put roun' de side since raw sewage running over in Clivey yard. Week before dat I buy eight bag o' cement an' sand an' stone to make walkway for de tenant 'cause him complaining dat—"

"How come yuh buying cement when yuh own a cement factory?"

The innocence of the question staggered him, like an uppercut in a fistfight he thought he had under control; he never liked getting caught in his lies when being sententious. Sometimes it made him violent. So I looked away, tight-lipped, as if it had been a slip of the tongue.

After my parents split, my father had migrated to Florida and sent money to have a house built and rented to help finance my education: a six-compartment dwelling—two bedrooms, bathroom, living room, kitchen, and verandah—that stood in our backyard. But it had always been a point of contention between him and my grandfather. And I, as the beneficiary, was trapped in the middle of their financial feud. I didn't care for Papa's budget presentation now.

"Wha'ppen between you and yuh mother?" said Mama.

"I brought a gyal in the house."

"But what's de problem? You're of age now."

Cam smirked and watched my face. "Would you want him to bring a gyal *here*? I hardly bring anyone home. And Derek wouldn't dare kiss Lois, even on the verandah, when he comes here."

"Hush yuh mout'!" Mama shot back. "Why yuh feel yuh always have to speak for everyone? Give people dem natural space. A'ways playin' barrister in dis damn house!"

Lois was silent, composed. She was thirty but none of her boyfriends had ever slept over; Papa made them uncomfortable. Cam was different. She insisted that they sleep here and we even heard them having sex. Lois was now engaged to a divorcé, a man older than herself. The whole thing unsettled my grandparents slightly. He was trying too hard to please them. Cam, on the other hand, always acted as if she was out to prove something.

"And when we goin' meet dis gyal?" said Mama. "Nyjah, why yuh so secretive?"

"He'll never bring her here," prophesied Cam, "you watch."

"And why's that?" I snapped. "Yuh seem to know everything today."

"Well . . . are you?" asked Lois, joining the conversation while passing the bowl of stewed peas to Papa.

"I tell yuh what him goin' do," interjected Papa. "Him goin' apologize to Hammer Mouth for de state of dat peelin' paint."

This thing about paint was my trial. My father had wired me some money—a portion of which was Papa's—but I'd spent it all. Money for "upkeep." Failing to pay Papa back, I'd signed a Faustian contract stating I'd work it off at the cement factory. I never stayed at my grandparents' too long because Papa was a slave driver—and I hated working at the cement factory.

"Papa, now?" I said in half despair, scooping candied dasheen on my plate. "Can't I eat first?" My mouth was watering.

"Yuh see, that's how selfish Nyjah is," said Cam. "He feels the world should wait on him while he dines or thinks up pretty words. He wants to apologize to the tenants on his own terms."

The food smelled too good to wait. My stomach groaned.

"And what makes you such an expert?" Lois cut in. "Stop acting as if the world owes you something 'cause you have lupus. Always shooting off your mouth with an opinion on everything. The great unsolicited critic. Your words are as welcome as junk mail."

"Don't take out yuh frustration on me, Lois," said Cam. "Yuh belong in that museum. Yuh life is so inert. So mousy yuh can't even find a man for yuhself, have to settle for people ol' bruk. Too timid to even fuck him in yuh own house," she added under her breath.

Papa reached across the table and slapped her so hard her shoulder jammed into me. "Get up," he said quietly, already rising from his chair. We knew what was coming. He was reaching for his heavy workman belt that hung on the doornail. "Come." He stretched out his big hairy forearm. She was going to get the whipping he was dying to give *me*. Her exuberance had backfired.

"Anthony, please!" Mama bawled, plucking nervously at her dewlap. But she could do nothing else.

I stood and pushed Cam back into her seat with the same motion. "Papa, this has to stop."

"Oh?" He glared, raking a thumb over his graying mustache. "Who go stop me?"

"Sit down, Nyjah," said Cam, getting up, "this don't involve yuh."

"Papa, don't," cried Lois, "she didn't mean it."

"Maybe I was too soft on yuh," said Papa, pushing his dentures over his lip in a cold, unnerving gesture. "Yes, me take responsibility, but no more of yuh sauciness. Yuh mout' get yuh into trouble but your bam-bam go tek yuh outta it. Is my responsibility to make yuh decent enough for someone to marry. Me won't shirk me duty. Yuh growin' like wile bush." He reached out and gripped the fleshy portion of Cam's upper arm and she pulled away, but the set of his face melted her resistance. He led her by the hand into the kitchen and left the door open. Cam had a calm dead look; she didn't resist even when he put her over his knees in the old straight-back chair. It was the only thing that took her strength—being reminded of her physical frailty by someone else's tyrannical violence.

St. Maude! my brain flashed like a red siren, and I nearly blacked out. When the belt thwacked the back of Cam's pale thighs, she gave a muffled yelp. This was the only time we prayed with conviction as a family—for her relief. Little Tony was shedding tears for everyone else. He didn't understand this side of our family yet, this sudden calamity. I slammed the table and got up.

Outside, I scooped the cat up. I felt powerless and foolish walking away, knowing what was happening inside. Finally I heard Lois scream, "It's enough, Papa, look at the welts!" I felt I could kill him. I headed to the backyard and knocked on the door; I still had the cat in my arms.

"Yes," said the woman's voice inside.

"It's me, Nyjah."

"Oh," she said in a sarcastic tone, "de landlawd." She came out wearing a red belly-skin and pum-pum shorts, her stomach professionally flat, her navel jeweled, trailing a fine line of hair that disappeared into her waistband. She had fair skin, like Cam's; I could see that she took care of it. Her thick braids were caught in an untidy bun and some of them swept across her long, puffy-cheeked face. She was about thirty. It was my first time looking at her properly; she stared right back. "What yuh want?"

"To apologize for the—" I stopped short for words. "I'm sorry that I didn't . . . It must be awful to . . . Anyway, I was wrong. I'm sorry . . . I'm sorry for everything."

She gave me a strange look, pouting her full lips. "Yuh not apologizin' to me, yuh lookin' right chu me. Yuh apologizin' to someone else. I don't know who, but not me." I didn't say anything. "Wha' de cat name?" she asked, propping one foot on the other, meshing her red-painted toenails together.

"PJ. Yuh can talk to her, she's really smart."

"Yuh grandpoopa drag him foot after promisin' to repaint dis place how long, an' de whole time I have to live in dis bloodclaat house dat look like duppy vomit pon it, an' yuh come here wid yuh bright self askin' if me wa'an *labrish* wid puss? What I look like? I workin' for yuh?"

"Melissa, who dat?" growled Hammer Mouth.

When I returned to the house, Cam was in her room, her food covered. I made to go to her but Lois said, "Leave her be, come sit down."

"It's done," I said, taking my seat.

Papa ignored me and wiped fish oil from his bushy lip with his tongue. The candied dasheen had gone cold and crisp. I took up the knife and fork and started eating the fish.

"Lois cooked it," Mama croaked—her voice still tearful—noting the appreciation on my face.

Lois avoided eye contact, she didn't want a compliment.

Papa started chewing savagely, trying to make a show of enjoying his meal.

"Tony work real hard today," he said, smiling at the boy. "Him have de land in him blood."

I wonder now why I missed this remark. "The day yuh try to hit me, I'll kill you."

"Nyjah!" warned my grandmother.

"I know it," Papa smiled, returning my stare. "But is not me yuh want to kill, is somet'ing inside *you*. I been watchin' yuh."

"And I hope yuh didn't adopt this bwoy so yuh can bully him. I hate you!" I went at the snapper greedily, my hunger surprising me, my knife making violent little jerks. I swallowed the soft slimy okras and carrot slices nearly whole, then tore the back of the fish open and devoured the white meat. I dug out the eyes with my fork and sucked the jelly from the sockets with a crude noise, licking my lips. But the fish had a surprise for me. My knife sliced into something turgid, and I slit the stomach all the way up to the gill flaps. Lodged inside its mouth cavity was a white tongue-eating lice as fat as a toddler's thumb. I clamped my hand over my mouth and ran from the table.

CHAPTER 8

I saw Zetta Rosegreen and her dog on what was probably their usual run. She quickened her pace toward me, jerking the dog's leash so hard it protested with a cracking little bark that echoed through the empty street. I was a little confused and stood rooted to the spot momentarily. Maybe she thought I was with Tom, the man who had verbally assaulted her, and was out for revenge. But her expression told me it was something more personal; she was looking at me with a sad, heavy face, her stringy neck thrust out. I remembered what Tom had said about her being a psychic. She grabbed my arm before I could move away. Her painted lips curled into a snarl as she dug her fingernails into my flesh, forcing my palm open. I didn't dare move now—I was hers. She wore a dirty white silk headscarf covered with red carps. She shook her neck and scrawny shoulders as if somebody had dropped a snake down her bosom. The dog jumped and yapped at her feet. She continued doing her jerky movements that vibrated my hand and moved slowly through my body, as if we were physically connected, and kept flicking her tongue, then moaned as if she had a fever chill. "Be careful this morning! Love is hurt! A roaring lion wounded and scared!"

"What yuh mean?"

She was warming my hand with her grip and warming my heart with her strange intimations, her voice dark and foreboding. She raked her fingernails over my palm and it goose-pimpled my flesh.

"Tell me," I pressed.

She snatched her hand away as if bitten. "You've come back in a nest of vipers—beware!" She took a step back.

My eyes teared up—it might have been the cold morning air.

She reached out tentatively to touch my face. "Young man, what is this sadness you carry around? You don't look well. What did you see last night?"

"I dreamt I finally found the key for Smokey's den and got out, but it was a dream in a dream. I woke up and realized I was still on the bus heading back home."

"That man you saw attack me was a hooligan, don't you ever be like him," she said, though she might've been looking through me; her face had a penetrating stare as if she could see right under my skin. I felt exposed and anguished.

I grabbed her wrist. "But what does it all mean?"

She held one side of my face tenderly. "You couldn't live with your failure. Where did that bring you? *Back to me*. Now you're a devil tangled in the bushes."

Her mind was all over the place, as if she couldn't get a clear reading, but I was determined. I knew she could see something and could help me.

"Yes, Mother," I said, not knowing where the words had come from. I tried to kiss her hand against my own judgment. "I'm goin' to change! *She's alive* . . . and waitin' for me to do right. That's why I came back—somethin' pulled me—I couldn't stay away." My voice cracked with a half-formed sob.

A garbage truck rolled down the hill toward us, bumping Bobby Brown, "*I wanna rock with you, baby* . . ." Our interaction must've looked strange to the garbagemen. A fat one squeezed in the backseat called out, "Halloween to pussyclaat!"

The one in front had his arm hanging out. He smacked the passenger door and bellowed, "Careful, bwoy, ol' woman watah scratch prick!" They roared away laughing.

The dog never stopped yapping, snapping at my heels with its sharp little teeth. I kicked it away. Zetta took off one of her trinkets, a blue stone amulet, and rolled my fingers over it.

"Take it. You're not well, boy. Take care of yourself."

I grabbed at her bangled arm.

She pulled away, shaking her head. "Come to me for a proper reading. My spirit isn't settled this morning. It's like my head is gathering water." She clutched her jaw and seemed distracted. "See, I even forget to bring the squeeze bottle." She dragged the dog behind her.

I didn't dare raise my hand to wipe away the tears. I walked to the bus stop with my eyes clouded, seeing only blurred figures.

Someone disturbed my typing. I looked up from my laptop.

A man had come on at Stony Gut wearing a visitor's ID for the Gun Court. People were immediately anxious; it dampened the mood on the bus. "Take dat damn t'ing off! Who yuh be?" someone shouted.

"Make me," the man challenged. He was strapping, with bloodshot eyes and dark smoker's lips. He looked like a sad Black demon cast out of heaven or hell.

"Man, it better yuh did come on here wearin' a damn clown mask than dat fuckin' t'ing," said a heavily jowled man. "No one want to see dat early mawnin' when dem tryin' to build dem courage to face de workweek."

"Big bloodclaat Monday mawnin' an' yuh out here lookin' like de Grim Reaper in yuh hangman epaulette," snarled the wiry little conductor everybody called Bussy; he was staring the man down as if he wanted to throw him off the bus. The man was twice Bussy's size with big arms and shoulders, could've squeezed Bussy's head like a peanut.

A woman sucking a bag juice, jiggling a child sitting on her lap, said, "But Bussy, is you let him on."

Bussy began attracting uncomfortable and hostile looks. He defended himself: "Everybody rushin' dis bus in de mawnin', how I suppose to interrogate an' examine everybody? Is my *rass* fault dis bus so popular? Attract all type o' character?"

"Bussy, yuh need to be more vigilant," complained a bespectacled man wearing a bush jacket. "Yuh jus' bring crosses on dis bus. Anybody rub shoulders wid dis *hombre* bound to be salt de whole week an' even de whole month."

The man sat gimlet-eyed and miserable, his pockmarked jaws clean-shaven and taut with uncoiled aggression, gleaming with fresh perspiration. He was prepared to defend his honor, and was quietly proud of the stir he was causing. He was wearing the tag in public—not behind the barbed-wire brick walls of the Gun Court, where it was intended to be worn—as an outward sign of his grief. He had intended no malice; as a matter of fact, judging by his tight-lipped, red-eyed brooding, it was a call for sympathy and public communion. He probably didn't want to suffer by himself. The red line running through the plastic ID strung around his squat neck meant that whoever he'd been visiting was on death row. He shook his head and said to the empty seat beside him, "Yesterday an' de whole o' las' week dem rehearse de execution. Dressed up in suits to see a man die, as if dem respectable. Why would yuh wa'an sit dere an' watch a man die over an' over? Wid de same regularity yuh go to church service or funeral."

On the bus stereo, Deniece Williams twittered, "*But now that you've set me free, it's gonna take a miracle . . .*"

A woman raised her hand and swayed her head to the song, trying to drown out the man's elegy. "That's it, Niecey. Sing, gyal!"

He continued, "Ain't nutten damn respectable in watchin' a life being sucked dry from de flesh. Is evil."

"Ain't nutten respectable 'bout takin' an innocent person's life either," countered Bussy, trying to steer the man's anger like a matador toying with a wounded bull.

"I wa'an t'row me feelings to de bottom of de ocean an' bury dem," the man said. "Me cyaan sleep at night. Me keep seein' me twin bredda's face an' me know all who go attend him execution won't really see him. Dey rehearsin' away dem sympathy. Yes!" His red eyes blinked rapidly as if he'd had a eureka moment amid the deluge of grief. "De warden, de mayor, de custos . . . de whole fuckin' lot o' dem. Dem deadenin' dem nerves from now. All dem goin' see come dat day is de gruesomeness of death widout seein' de person sufferin' a few feet away. Widout sufferin' an equal penalty demselves for dem coldheartedness, for dem barbarous display. Dem wa'an see how close dem can get to Death's face an' escape. But we all go die someday!"

His words caused a sobering stillness, like a toxin; it sank into our bloodstreams and made us feel heavy. Deniece Williams was hitting the high notes, whirligigging her pretty cut-glass voice, "*It's gonna take a miracle, ooh, baby . . .*"

"Yuh brother was a murderer, plain an' simple," said Bussy, raising his screechy voice a notch, shaking off the gloomy stupor settling over the commuters.

The man jumped up. "See! See! Yuh doh get it! It never plain an' never simple."

"Go find dat river bottom fass an' drown yuh feelings an' doh come up," said the woman with the child on her lap.

Now the man got his release. He stepped out into the aisle and people pulled back and murmured. He paced the narrow space, blackening it with his frenzied shadow. "Why's there no love an' understandin' between man an' man? Why no honesty of feelings? Why two souls cyaan communicate widout all dis . . . posturin'?" He walked down to Bussy sitting on the patty-pan seat near the door, pointing his finger at the smaller man's tattooed face. For the merest moment, Bussy cringed and showed fear. "I tell yuh I miss me bredda an' yuh go tell me I ain't got no right to love a criminal—like I never born sensitive?"

"You is a faggot or wha'?" Bussy said stupidly, his droopy lips tremulous. "Bringin' feelings into dis." He had a long string-bean face and bulbous eyes that made him look funny, so people never took him seriously—it was a part of his charm that attracted passengers to Horace's bus. They liked Bussy's making fun of his own ugliness and chasing after girls, turning himself into comic relief.

Now he tried his best to look serious. Seeing the burly man bearing down on him, he started knocking the back of the front passenger seat, yelling over the music, "Pull over, Horace, pull over! Mek me beat de green shit outta dis mangrove crab!"

The man pounded his breast, his lips spreading into spit-shiny trembling flesh that looked like a wound in his face. "Me cyaan stop love, Clifton! Me cyaan stop love him—nuh matter what!" He continued raising his voice in bedlam, tears streaming down his face, beating his chest. "Cow nuh stop love calf even if him tear dung Busha fence!"

Bussy hit the back of the seat and shouted, "Pull over, Horace!" It was a cry of alarm, a terrible emergency we all suddenly felt.

Towering over the conductor, the man bawled, "Why yuh forcin' me to beat bloodclaat sense into yuh?"

Women started saying low and slowly, "Lawd Jesus, Lawd Jesus Christ . . ." Their voices knit so tightly with fear chilled me to the bones.

Bussy flicked out his knife in the cramped quarters and the man attacked him head-on. I jumped out of my seat and pushed my way toward the back row. With all his pent-up bitterness, the man was beating Bussy senseless. He didn't seem to mind the knife jammed halfway into his guts.

A girl beside me covered her head and ducked, rocking her body back and forth. "Bussy, yuh too fool! Why yuh tek people boostin' an' t'row way yuh life?"

"A godless David 'gainst Goliath," muttered an old woman. "Him cyaan win." She sank and closed her eyes, folding up in a sad, stiff stupor.

Bussy, meanwhile, was throwing wild stabs and kicks, but the man now had him cornered behind the front passenger seat. Horace pulled over into a stony patch of ground near Dragon Gym; before Bussy could manage to fling the door open, the man twisted his arm, pulled out the knife in his side, and stabbed Bussy in the nape. Women shrieked and covered their children's eyes.

Bussy staggered out, raising dust clouds, feeling at his neck till he fell heavily on his side, his arm twisted under his body. He attempted to get up, pushing himself off the ground with the arm that was free, but trying at the same time to stanch the flow of blood from his body.

The man ran toward a stone heap and then hit Bussy on his head with a rock. There was a thud and groan amid the screams, and Bussy pulled himself away like a shot dog, dragging his whole body weight on his elbows toward the man's shadow; he stopped only after he had firmly gripped the man's black boot. The lower half of the man's shirt was torn and blood-soaked, but he didn't seem to care; he took up another stone and raised it over Bussy's head.

"Trent! Trent, yuh wi' go ah prison!" screamed an Indian woman with a crayfish basket. She knew him—perhaps he was a customer or a vendor himself.

Trent bit his jerky lip, his big teardrops plopping on Bussy's dusty head like a perverse anointing. Bussy moaned and moved his limbs like a gross caterpillar, and Trent said, "Clifton, wait on me. We goin' home together, bredda. Jus' wait a bit. Dis worl' ain't no better or worse widout two neagahs in it. Tomorrow go still name Tuesday." He dropped the stone on Bussy's neck.

Several people scattered to the bushes and vomited. Some stood their ground in shock while others leaped and ululated like Maasai warriors.

Bussy raised his neck, the blood oozing over his green facial tattoos like a ruined canvas. "Remembah dat yuh kill me . . . pussy'ole."

Trent stooped and stabbed the conductor six times in the rib cage. Blood poured out of him. We heard sirens. It seemed like nothing after what we'd seen. When a blue-suited colonel disembarked from a police jeep, he yelled, "Nobody move! Everybody goin' big yawd!" He glared at Horace—who stood slack-jawed, bus keys hanging in his loose fist, looking half out of his mind. "What a wutless fucker like yuh, eh, Horace? Since Bussy was a bwoy, him workin' wid yuh like a son, an' it never occur to yuh to help him?"

* * *

It was my first time behind the Gun Court's famous brick walls that dominated the landscape of a downtown corner. They escorted us to separate rooms. The corporal stood there looking down on me sitting quietly. I didn't raise my eyes from his gleaming boots. He stood perfectly still, and from his shadow cast by the low-wattage bulb, I could tell he had his hands folded behind his back. He finally sat. I raised my head and looked directly in his face. He was young, maybe six or seven years my senior, but obviously full of himself. He had his red-banded black hat dangling on his crossed legs, sitting elegantly, but the smile on his small face was savage, toothy, subtly trying to rattle me.

"Name's Makepeace. Cigarette?"

"Yes, please."

He lit it for me, watching my face with his teeth slightly apart in a frozen grin, observing the steadiness of my hands. "Ol' habit of mine," he said of his staring, straightening his uniform jacket as he sat back. "Anytime I get someone in here, I feel they're guilty, even if it is only for routine questioning. I feel that anybody who end up here, even by association, have somethin' they want to admit. I can tell by the look in their face. No one comes in here by accident. And yuh have the look of a man who can't sleep. Am I right?"

I drew on the cigarette, exhaled. "Probably. But I didn't come here for sleepin' pills, did I?" Something caught on the tip of my tongue. I felt at it and checked my fingertips.

"Cheap cigarette, the only type in the dispenser here. Sorry." He stubbed his in the ashtray. "Yuh like this place? It seem cozy? Like somewhere yuh'd want to work or . . . We have a joke here." He leaned forward, loosening his body. "*Everybody* works here. Either plantin' evidence or plantin' vegetables. Ahaha! The prisoners have a nice garden out back. I should give you the tour later." He stopped short, checking his excitement. "Man, yuh smokin' that ciggy like yuh hungry." He looked at his ledger. "Nyjah Messado, teacher. Fresh outta college." He drew his chair closer. "I have one question. Yuh stood there the whole time and watch a man murdered in front of yuh. How yuh feel?"

"How *should* I feel?"

"Yuh know why I am in this chair and yuh sittin' there?"

"Because yuh not me," I said.

"Exactly. I have my feet firm on the ground. Where yuh stand in this world? What if that dead conductor was yuh friend or brother?"

"Are yuh callin' me a coward?"

"I guess I am, but answer the question. What if it were personal, what would yuh have done then?"

"I would—" I stopped, glared. "I don't have to answer that. Ask me somethin' relevant."

"That's the only thing relevant right now. You're not to be trusted with another man's life. That's what it all comes down to. Yuh know what's this department's motto? *No man left behind.* The weaker sex have a foot in the door now. So they'll probably change it soon. But it's still the same. You're a weakling, Messado, a pampered, underdone soft-boiled egg with a runny yolk. A man who has no taste for the fundamentals of decency. Selfish enough like all the other rat-belly bastards to stand back and watch a man bein' killed in front of their face and record it to put on Instagram as clickbait."

"Yuh finished?"

"No!" He slammed the desk and jabbed a finger at my face. "Any whorehouse or strip club I go and find yuh foolin' with any gyal, I fuckin' puttin' yuh under arrest. Howzat? I know yuh type—fuckin' *sketels* and uptown gyals alike, actin' like yuh own this damn place. But yuh hollow inside."

I leaned forward: "*We are the hollow men / We are the stuffed men / Leaning together / Headpiece filled with straw.*"

He looked befuddled, blinking a few times, clenching his fists and puffing his jaws.

I stood and looked down on him. "Did they teach yuh *that* in Police Academy?"

"Get out."

When I was at the door, I turned. "Who are you to put me in my place?"

He chuckled to himself, slipping his hat back on as he stood up, fixing his jacket again. "So, you is a big ol' puppy dog with a little bit of bark. We'll meet again, teacher bwoy."

"Don't count on it. Good day, Corporal Makepeace."

"Look at me!" His voice was so commanding that I did turn around again. "What yuh do? Stand by and watch. Might as well yuh stab him yuh bloodclaat self."

Mrs. Lombard let herself in with her keys (something I didn't like), and she came and knocked on the door to my bedroom. "Nyjah, darling, yuh hungry?"

I got up and opened the door. "The schools gave me special leave, so I came home."

She hugged me and smelled my clothes. "Yuh smell like a jail-bird. And yuh weren't even down at that awful place very long."

"I'm fine, ma'am, just a bit tired is all."

She started unbuttoning my shirt as if I were a child. "Take this off. Yuh smell like hell. The pants too. Give them here."

I passed her the shirt. "My girlfriend's comin'. She'll wash the rest."

She pushed out her lips and frowned a little. "Oh, well, I guess . . . yes, let her take care of yuh. I left some food covered on the table there. Cooked it yesterday."

"Thanks," I said, ushering her out the door. "I'll eat it later."

"Give me the pants, bwoy," she said, stepping back into the doorway. "Don't lie back down in it."

I took them off, handed them over.

"You saw him die, Nyjah?"

"Yes, Mrs. Lombard, I saw everything."

She shook her head. "What Montego Bay comin' to? Yuh can't even ride public transport in peace. Look at what that awful sight did to yuh, look at yuh face!"

"Good day, Mrs. Lombard."

"Goodbye, darlin'."

I lay with my hands on my chest, staring at the ceiling. Giggling and boisterous voices floated up to the window. I got up and looked down at the boulevard. It was a group of Chester College boys walking from the bus stop. One was saying to friends, ". . . that's how yuh kiss and feel on a gyal, that's how yuh enjoy them, that's how yuh take what them have to offer and not lose yuhself."

"Shut up, Jermaine," said a dumpy one, "talkin' like yuh go all the way when she only mek yuh feel her bottom."

The group snickered and walked on. I closed the window.

I called Dreenie. "What's takin' yuh so long?"

She got upset at my tone and hung up.

When she finally arrived, her hair was black and auburn, separated perfectly at the middle, with loose curls cascading over her shoulders. It was so beautiful it took my breath away as soon as I opened the door. She must have seen the wonder in my face—she leaned across the threshold and kissed me. Her breath was stale and chalky, and left a bad taste in my mouth.

"Yuh been smokin'."

She dropped her eyes. "I was worried about yuh, that's why."

"Don't use me as an excuse."

"I'll make cocoa." She huffed behind me as she went to the kitchen. "Two seconds an' we already arguin'. We make a fine couple."

I lay back down, playing the patient. She was waiting for me to comment on her hair, but I wanted her to feel sorry for me first. She wiggled out of her pants and sat spraddled on the bed's edge. My eyes made their way to her shaved crotch.

She reached across and stroked my head. "Feelin' any better?"

"I saw him die, Andrene. I watched the whole thing."

"Me see't too. On WhatsApp when me in de arcade. Nobody can believe Bussy jus' dead suh. T'row 'way him life jus' 'cause a man come on de bus in him feelings. I mean, how many people like dat him handle in de past an' get de better of de situation? Why him act de fool alluva sudden?"

I was surprised by her generosity of thought. I eased up on the pillow and looked at her. Her profile was sad and tired; she'd been selling all morning, God knows what, but had left when I called to go home and freshen up.

"Maybe he was just really wired and not thinkin' straight today," I offered.

She let out a nasty little laugh and scratched her inner thigh. "Him woman prolly nuh give him no pussy las' night." She batted her eyes, running her hand up my chest.

"Come here," I said. She leaned to me and I kissed her nose ring. "Yuh hair look so nice."

"Ugh! Nyjah, it take dem forever to set it. I think I'd die in dat chair. 'Zaas Christ."

I ran my fingers through it, then pulled her closer to enjoy her smell. "What am I fightin' for, Dreen? Why all this nonsense 'bout chasin' a job and family and writin' publishable poetry? Why am I puttin' all this undue pressure on myself? Is it worth it? Who decided it was?"

"It's what yuh want. Stop actin' weak 'cause yuh see a dead body. I don't like weakness. Yuh know how hard me life is." She pulled away, propped her foot on the bed, looking listlessly at her sparkly nail polish. "You can always jus' write for yuhself, if dat's what yuh want."

I gave her a cold stare. "Yuh not listenin'."

"I see an' hear an' understan' more dan yuh t'ink."

I rolled toward the wall and propped the pillow under my head. She got up and then sat before the dresser, toying with her hair like a child besotted with her reflection. She tried being upbeat and casual, cupping her bosom. "Yuh t'ink me breasts too small? Hey—worry puss! Doh turn your back on me, bwoy. What yuh wa'an do, t'row up your hands an' live free? How yuh goin' pay rent? How yuh goin' pay back all dem student fees?"

"What if I did just throw up my hands and say to hell with it?"

She swiveled around on the stool. "What's all dis? Where dis comin' from? Did sum'n happen on dat bus yuh not tellin' me 'bout?"

"Everythin' happened and nutten happened. I was in a space to be impacted upon by all I saw and did, and by all I didn't see and all I didn't do. It wasn't the first time. There were lessons to be learned about myself and other people in those few minutes, lessons it would take someone else a lifetime to understand. Lessons that forced me to see myself through other people's eyes . . ."

"Go on," she said nonchalantly, "get it off yuh chest. I may not understand all dat yuh sayin', but I get de feelin' yuh don't either."

I looked at her sharply. "What's that supposed to mean?"

"Take it any way yuh want, you're de great t'inker."

I humphed and thumped the pillow. "Fix me somethin' to eat."

She picked up a comb and worked on her ends. "But me see food on de table."

"Fix me somethin' else."

She narrowed her eyes and sulked. "Is me yuh want to t'ump?" She came and sat beside me and rubbed my back. "Yuh been t'rough trauma . . ."

"Hah! Yuh can't imagine."

"Take it easy on yuhself. But this t'ing about mopin' on black thoughts like is a field of study is a defeat in itself."

"Obviously you've never read *Hamlet*."

She got up. "No, Nyjah, I've not. An' I cyaan quote Shakespeare neither. Yuh'll be an original—a Shakespeare-quotin' bum beggin' bread on de street corner an' wipin' yuh ass wid literature."

The kettle squealed. "Aren't you goin' to get that?"

"Get it yuhself!"

I went to the kitchen. She had left the spout uncovered and water gushed out steaming and furious. It stung my skin so badly I yelped and cursed and braved the unexpected assault to switch off the knob and clean up the mess on the stovetop. "I should smack that bitch," I said under my breath. The enormity of the words frightened me and I balked at them. I wasn't sure about what I felt anymore—my emotions were blindsiding me. I went back to the room and huddled in the corner by myself, hoping she wouldn't do or say anything to piss me off. I felt I couldn't be responsible for my actions now.

"Yuh want me to leave?" she said, sitting on the stool with her hands between her legs.

"Suit yuhself."

At that moment, Rory arrived home. Dreenie dragged on her pants and skipped out to the hallway to greet him. I heard him smack a kiss on her cheek; I knew he had his hands on her waist. He was always handsy with other people's things, would while away his time in class doing technical sketches then "borrow" your notes. I heard her setting pans on the stove, happy to cook for someone who was grateful.

He put his head in the doorway. "How we feelin'?"

"I spent quite the time at the police station," I groaned.

"Did you?" he chuckled.

I looked at him seriously. He dropped his cheerful attitude.

"Bussy died," I said.

"It's all over the news. He was a character, wasn't he?" He was straining to hear Dreenie in the kitchen.

"A *character*, Rory? That's all you have to say?"

He sighed and looked at the floor. "Okay, you're a minefield right now—I'll come back later when yuh feel up to it. We can play some *Minecraft*."

"Yuh want her?"

"What?"

"Just say it—I won't mind. Yuh'd probably be better for her."

"Get some sleep, Nyjah." He turned back toward the kitchen. "I'm having dinner with you guys. I don't want leftovers today."

"She's cookin' for you, not me," I said.

As he closed the door, the cat padded into the room, her collar bell jangling like a jailer's keys.

CHAPTER 9

I met Briana for lunch at the food court in Baywest. She brought me a copy of the *Mirror*. She was fresh-faced with light perspiration on her top lip, her hair done in her usual bun on top of her head; her cool complexion made her look like an exquisite doll, especially when she smiled. The urge to kiss her was like a fever knotting my brain.

She saw the hunger in my expression and became fussy, fanning her face with her hand. "This mall too damn hot even in open space. What should we eat?"

"I don't know, anything yuh want."

She scanned the shops lined up small and neat: McDonald's, Subway, Dumbo's Chicken, the Fish Shop, ChuckleBerry's. "I can't decide. Suggest something."

"Yuh ever had a cake with a sausage in it?"

She slapped at my hand. "Nyjah, don't be rude. So juvenile . . ."

"I'm sorry, it just came out."

She gave me a hard look. "Stop right there, before your mouth gets you into further trouble." She shook her head. "Bwoys . . ." She opened the paper to my review. Her manner was editorial even outside of the office, the way she moved her hands and eyes over newsprint. "I cut a lot of what yuh wrote out of this one, it was too subjective. As if yuh had an axe to grind with the director. Even after cutting I wasn't pleased. Look here." She pointed. "'When Felix says pride about race and religion, he means unrepentant racism.' I don't like that either, but I left it in because we had a disagreement in the office."

"Saved by the soft-liners," I commented, glancing at a group of girls passing by. I really wasn't interested in discussing literature. She noted my roving eyes with a look of distaste and folded the paper. "Nyjah," she said in a wheedling tone, "do something, yuh go make me starve, enuh. *Cho*, I hungry too bad, man."

"I know what." I took out my phone. "I'll order lunch from my mother's caterin' service, best food in town. Trust me." Pearl picked up and I asked Bree what she wanted. "Not that far from here, won't take long."

Bree went quiet, as if bored with my company or just too hungry to talk. High school children were window-shopping and I had a flash of panic when I thought my students could be among them. Bree ordered a tapioca milkshake with coffee added to it.

I remembered she had mentioned a new manager from Kingston. "How's the new boss?"

Bree was talking but I was hardly listening, having just noticed Philip Moodie pulling a juvenile stunt. By a mall booth, he and two car-wash toughs were intimidating young nurses till the women abandoned their post. The sign above the booth said: *Vaccine Shots Today*. Philip tore away the *Vaccine* strip and pointed, shouting, "Shots today!" and started handing out tequila to shoppers like a kid at a lemonade stand. He saw me; we grinned mischievously at each other; he told the hooligans to "keep working" and walked over with two *caballitos* and a bottle.

Mugging, he poured us shots with exaggerated manners.

Briana looked appalled. "Philip, what are you doing?" she hissed. "You ass!"

"Long time no see, Bree," chuckled Philip. "Still babysittin' Perry?" He turned to me. "Yuh never tell me yuh two fuckin'."

"Philip . . ."

He ignored my embarrassment. "This is what people want. They're not worried 'bout flu. Come, Nyjah, come drink with us."

Surprising myself, I downed the glass he handed me.

"Nyjah!" Briana scolded.

Philip poured another eagerly. "Good, eh? Like old times at Smokey's den."

I raised the glass but then put it down. "I can't. A student could pass and see me."

Philip scowled. "Suit yuhself. Go on—run back to class, that's what yuh always did. Yuh know what we looked forward to in Smokey's, Nyjah?"

"No, Philip, what?"

"It wasn't fun or delinquency. It was death, as the great resolution. We never won or lost anythin' in that gamblin' den. But *she* escaped. She's still to die meaningfully." He strolled off after saying this and I watched his wake.

Rookie police in blue shorts and bicycle helmets came and broke up their devilry. The car-wash boys scrambled off with shoppers laughing.

"Who's *she?*" Briana asked, watching me. "Who's Smokey?"

"Nutten . . . nobody. What about that assessment you were so worried about?"

She stirred the tapioca pearls in the bottom of her drink and sighed theatrically. "My dear, they were to have got it tomorrow. Who knows? I don't care." She spoke very rapidly when she got worked up, almost without pause for breath. I remembered she was an uptown girl. Paradise Crescent. Uptown people speak as if they're flinging words at you, like a spear to your brain, showing off their facility with Standard English as if to remind others—downtown people who speak with deliberate cadence—that uptowners have breeding that no level of education or money can endow commoners—*hurry-come-ups*—with. I stared at her levelly, wondering if she was giving me a lesson now, consciously or unconsciously, being a *risto* bitch.

Her twin speaks the same way—that faggot bitch Perry, I thought, not understanding my sudden aversion to her. Maybe I was being reminded that we were still fundamentally different, after all these years. I wondered often if she was using me now to somehow save her brother—she was very clever—perhaps using her body as baleful poetry. Esther and Xerxes.

"How's it going at the job?" she asked. "Getting along? Making enemies?"

I snapped out of my revery. "What? Oh . . ." I could tell she was only half-interested in the response, if even that much. She probably thought my job beneath her, overachiever that she was with a master's degree from some fancy Canadian college, but I didn't care. I answered from my heart, about the thing that most worried me, that had only recently cropped up: "Some of them are Chester bwoys resittin' exams, and they're already lookin' to me for fraternity and friendship, maybe even guidance. It's funny."

She sucked the frothy green cream from the glass bottom and looked up from under her coppery eyelids. "What is?"

"What yuh tryin' to avoid, yuh land right back into. Anyway, I don't mind. They're aware and a little frightened of the hostility of other bwoys who don't like their cliquishness. But I have to be careful not to appear to show favoritism."

"You can't save them—some things need to happen as they always have."

"Who said I was tryin' to save anybody?"

"They're in the jungle—let them adapt. This is part of their education."

"You sure yuh not speaking 'bout Perry?"

She gave me a hurt look.

I changed the subject: "I'm glad yuh came."

She twirled her tongue around the straw. "You don't *look* glad. You're a proper teacher already, worrying about your babies."

"Yuh look really nice."

"Thanks. So do you."

"Yuh don't have to say that."

"Why not? But you do. Why do you look annoyed? You silly bwoy. Explain to me why I offended you just now."

"A man doesn't really care about his looks, not in the way a woman does. An ugly woman is infinitely fussier than a handsome man."

"Oh wow . . . wow, Nyjah. Where did that come from?"

My phone beeped: the food had arrived. When I saw who was heading toward our table, I froze midstep. It was Charmaine, tight-faced and so angry she was unconsciously crushing the food.

Briana whispered, "Why's she looking like I just killed her white fowl? Your ex?"

"I'll handle it."

"Please do," said Briana, staring frostily at Char and handing me her money.

I walked hastily toward Char to preempt disaster. I put my hand on her elbow, led her toward some potted plants by a corner elevator. "Look, I'm sorry—"

"Doh touch me! Yuh cyaan even look me in de eye."

"Here, gimme the food bag." I was being apologetic and practical at once and it infuriated her further.

She held up her hand. "Doh gimme dat bitch's money! Yuh mother say de food free."

"Char . . . I . . ."

"Yuh what? You of all people at a loss for words? Yuh wrong, Nyjah."

"I know . . ."

"Gwaan back to yuh *stoosh* gyal. Here. Yuh food gettin' cold. Yuh have sum'n comin' to yuh . . . look out."

"What can I do? What can I say?"

She laughed scornfully. "Not a damn t'ing."

I jogged after her to the steps, but she was jiggling her keys as if she would strike me if I touched her again. Slowly she calmed herself.

"I don't want us to be like this, Char. I don't want—"

She poked my chest. "Yuh don't want *what*? Yuh never get nutten from me. It ain't like nutten happen between us." She was fighting tears.

"I'm sorry for what I did."

"Yuh used me, Nyjah! How could yuh? I nearly lose me job! I have to go on me knees to beg yuh mother—me, a big ol' gyal." She let out a short burst of laughter and wiped her cheek. "*Char, gyal*—is like yuh bawn fe people tek step wid yuh. Look at all dese people watchin' us. Dem countin' on yuh decency, but dem doh know yuh like I do, dat yuh slime, yuh rotten! Does *she* know? Bye, enjoy de food. I should've spit in it. I know de curry goat is yours."

We attended Bussy's funeral that week. We squeezed our way into the piss-stained amphitheater behind the Civic Centre. It was around one o'clock and the funeral wouldn't start for another hour. "*Rahtid*," said Cress, "is like they declared today a national holiday. Look in front of Scotia!" The crowd by the brick-faced bank was so thick that only sections of the white pillars, flanked by baton-wielding policemen, were visible.

"We have to get inside," said Chadwell, "I ain't standin' here. The piss so rank I can't catch my breath."

"And people still shovin' in by the Handsworth end. Look."

"But what the fuck all of them comin' for?" asked Marco. "Some didn't even know Bussy."

"Yuh didn't know him either," said Rory.

Marco defended himself: "We ridin' with him from when we inna short pants. This is the last journey."

"This isn't natural," remarked Chad. "I mean, look at those people. Do they know somethin' we don't?"

"What *we* doin' here?" I said. "We are the same as them. Is a free circus."

"Is more than that," said Marco, looking over the heads. "Chad's right. Something's in the air here. A vibe."

A scrofulous bum named Louder Milk, accompanied by his dog Richard II, bumbled through the press of bodies and people were trying to avoid him, some of them shrieking and covering their noses. His whole body had sores, which he tried to cover under dirty long-sleeved shirts. One of his black shoes was a size too big and made a flapping noise like a scuba flipper. He scratched his face and chest and back and arms and head as if he were on fire, as if he wanted to tear off the grimy clothes. His dog barked. He started shouting hoarsely, as if his vocal cords were damaged, "Champagne poppin'! Celebrate, we ah celebrate de weak! De strong an' overbearin' can go suck a dick! Down wid de oppressors!" The mob came to a standstill at his words. They didn't make clear sense, but they did. He mounted the pink cut-stone wall encircling some potted palms, elevating himself a good four feet above us. "'All day long I been warnin' you,' Daddy voice in me head say, 'now get to the level dat belongs to *you*!'"

"De only level yuh belong is a sewer pit!" someone called out.

Louder, parroting the screech of Teddy Gilmore, a radio personality, said, "What we have in the Caribbean is Black pain. The artist representing the pain of his community. Not *pya-pya* materialism like Murica. The artist representing the neuroses of suburbia—well written yet sterile like reading the *New Yorker*."

Sunlight broke through a gap in the trees like a giant flame and dazzled our eyes. A man blurted out, "Damn mask get stuck in me beard an' itchin' me like cow itch!" It was as if a god had spoken—his words, though trifling, felt portentous.

Someone dragged Louder down; they spilled water over him. "Shower!" they screamed.

He shrieked when cold water touched his damaged skin.

A schoolboy said, "Yuh dare preachifyin' to us an' yuh doh even wa'an bathe."

A popular money-changer named Dalton, who scammed tourists with counterfeit currency, stepped forward with a filthy rope that he'd taken from a trash heap near a covered carousel. Richard II started barking in his master's defense; his loyalty to Louder touched us even then. "Yuh know yuh ABC, badman?" asked Dalton.

"How yuh mean, Dalton? Wha' yuh a sey, man?" quipped Louder jovially, beating the water out of his bushy hair.

"Den say it backway," the money-changer demanded.

The crowd waited with smiles on their faces. I was disgusted and looked around, hoping a patrol jeep would show up. Louder had done nothing to deserve this aside from being weak. He started reciting the reverse ABCs and then faltered, waiting for the blow—his face a collage of emotion.

Dalton, hollow-chested and dapperly dressed in a white merino, blue denim, and crisp white sneakers, showed Louder his platinum teeth and cracked the rope. His cronies started circling the bum, scratching their heads and making faces behind his back.

Louder sang as a prelude to his demise, trying his best to make fun of his own debasement: "My *donkey can walk, my donkey can talk, my donkey can eat wid knife an' fork.*"

People laughed, but barely.

"Pussy'ole country bwoy," I yelled at Dalton, "yuh don't even come from MoBay! Who give yuh the right to fuck with Louder!?"

"Who say dat?" Dalton swiveled his eyes till they rested on my face. Glaring at me, he told his friends, "Entertain him." So they started beating Louder with the rope, then Dalton said, "Now blow de trumpet, pussy'ole."

Louder Milk straightened himself and blew, "*Tara-tara-tara-ta-ta!*"

Now everyone got their release. They laughed and withdrew. They'd seen enough.

Chadwell grabbed my arm. "Come."

He had bribed an attendant and brought us in through the underground lot. We found a small space on the first floor. When the casket finally made its way down the aisle, people were oddly silent, respectful, not boisterous like they'd been outside. We were allowed an hour for viewing the body as it lay in the mahogany casket on the lower level of the marble podium. People took their time going up in groups, where they gathered in a huddle over the casket with heads bowed. I couldn't have moved if I'd wanted to. I couldn't go look, it was too personal. My friends did though.

"Him look good," Marco said, "him look really good."

A ditsy woman who'd taken a picture of the corpse showed her phone to the people around her. She looked at the screen and said, "This is the first time I feel like I'm actually seein' him." When she realized how it had come out, she had a look as if she wanted to clamp her own mouth.

"What?" someone said. "Him really come?"

"Yes," answered an old man. "He's here."

The big padded doors had just been thrown open so that those outside could come and see the body. Cress was humming Toto's "Africa" when Snow gate-crashed the funeral.

"The nerve of the opportunist!" Chadwell said.

Snow's knuckles were knitted together in frustration as he made his way down the aisle. People respectfully let him pass. He had a black velvet robe around his shoulders that trailed on the white marble floor, and his entourage was dressed the same—they looked like a murder of crows. "Rum Preacher," someone murmured worshipfully, stepping back with a stooped head. "Him look like a Black pope!" The man sounded immensely proud. "Dis feel like a coronation at Buckingham, to *rass*!"

A black-robed lackey held Snow's red oval Clairin bottle aloft like a chrism vessel. The old grief had hardened into something sinister inside me as I watched Snow. He walked to the head of the casket. Someone handed him a mic and the gathered went silent and fell back out of respect.

"Lissen to dem, Bussy," said Snow, biting down on a toothpick with his gums (a habit he'd had since school days) and sniffling into the mic, the sad sound reverberating through the high arches and dome. He continued looking down on Bussy and stroking the corpse's face with a feathery touch. "Yuh'll never be more popular to dem dan yuh are now." He looked as if he could weep for all the bitterness in the world and never stop, as if a black door had opened in his mind and he wanted it shut.

A roar of applause went up. "Eulogy!"

Snow half bowed and mounted the podium, then paused, peering over the expectant faces, sighing repeatedly. Slowly he raised the mic to his lips. "Sometimes yuh watchin' a game an' yuh doh realize how much yuh've invested in it till someone misses a goal an' yuh feel as if yuh could kill dem. Y'all know what I talkin' 'bout."

"Yes, Rummy—we know!"

Snow allowed himself a shallow laugh. "Now . . . we miss Bussy. We realize too late what him meant to us. Him was taken, taken in a bad an' cruel way him didn't deserve. But good men fall in battle . . . an' leave dem enemies in awe!"

"Yes! Send him home!"

"This city failed Bussy, just as it failed a lotta us as its daughters an' sons."

Watching Snow's infuriating showmanship, I was nevertheless thinking of myself and what was closest to my heart. I was finding that the best way to write was not to think about myself but other people: respecting their humanity no matter my personal opinion. But I couldn't seem to apply that concept in my personal life. I was too self-absorbed with nursing my perceived injury at the hands of others; I was thinking now of all the wrong I'd supposedly suffered at Snow's hands, which had damaged me in a way I feared I could never recover from, not least because he kept insinuating himself into my life. "He's an emotional opportunist!" I called to Rory over the din. "Let's leave!"

"Wait," said Rory grabbing my sleeve, "I want to hear him out."

"But I tell yuh, folks," Snow went on, hitting his stride, "we have wolves among us. Who I would jus' as soon knock de shit outta instead of cozyin' up to. 'Cause people wanted to see dis. Dem wanted to see Bussy's head smashed in 'cause dat's how some Montegonians are: we like perverse comedy and a little cruelty sometimes. I've seen women watchin' dem own—"

A loud melodic voice interrupted us, pulled all our attention away from Snow with its youthful sweetness and vibrato, like a yodeler in the Alps. It was a barker, a street boy of about twelve holding up a department-store poster on a tall stick, doing scrap work for merchants, marching around to gatherings promoting the latest sales. It was this poster that sent Snow into something that looked almost like anaphylactic shock. He stared on as the boy screamed, pushed through the crowd, stunning us with his vocal talent like a clarion, "We got the look! Ladies, get the look you will love at Hanna's Better Buy!" holding aloft the sky-blue poster of a woman under blissful duress, sitting on the floor in a miniskirt and bright-green stilettos with her legs splayed and laden with colorful shopping bags stacked all around her, as if she had suffered an avalanche of them, with more hanging on her shoulders and elbows and bent arms and one lifted up before her, rendering her faceless and mysterious. This lady shopper, practically buried by bags and looking wonderfully helpless—it was this image that sent Snow into a wave of panic. He grabbed his chest and his mouth fell open like a trapdoor. He hyperventilated, grasping wildly at the acolyte with the Clairin so that the bottle fell and smashed. Groans sounded at the front, and when Snow staggered backward and had to grab on to helping hands, people got confused and restless at his sudden breakdown.

The barker was still hoisting the placard and shouting amid the melee, "Get the look you will love at Hanna's! Ladies! Gents!"

CHAPTER 10

I had only a staff meeting at Willocks that morning so I went to the electrical store. Ska was outside with Greg, Scabby, and Ninja, his crew of electricians; the men were throwing their gear into the back of Ska's white Isuzu pickup to head out soon to another job. Ska, sitting on a big wooden cable reel resting against the shop's burglar grill, was having a morning drink from a white plastic cup.

"So early in the mornin', Ska?" I called out. "Where's yuh brother? What's this big surprise him have for me that can't wait?"

"He went out and got yuh a pony," said Ska, whistling at two girls walking down the lane. "So yuh can ride through those school gates like a real Prince Charming."

Two shops down at the car wash, the proprietor, Fruity Hastings, a muscle-bound gay man, bald with thin pink lips, a dangling crucifix earring, and a temper equal parts jovial and violent, sane and crazy, nodded to us in greeting.

"I thought he was dead by now," I whispered, though we stood at a far remove from him.

"He just got deported. He speaks like an American. Said he did a 'dime' in San Quentin. And Bussy got 'shanked.'"

"But nuh Mighty runnin' de car wash?" said Greg. "How dat sittin' wid Fruits?"

This was a name I hadn't heard in a while, Marvin Mighty, a name that had driven me out of Montego Bay, to try desperately to make myself over, to forget the hellish past we shared.

"Look at him finger," Ska said, his smile frozen in place at Fruits, who seemed to suspect we were talking about him. "Don't yuh see the big DeLaurence ring? Him *protected.* Last week he forced a jockey to drink a jug of horse piss after his horse lost at Caymanas. Not even Mighty cross him."

I watched Fruits. He was older than us, probably in his fifties, but hadn't changed since our school days—none of us had. All he did was sit at the gate and devour sweet tea and jerk barbecue, licking ketchup from his thick fingers. Passing children called him a "freak." As if on cue, Mighty came out of the car wash and my heart jumped, especially when I saw Perry Fischer step out after him, talking urgently into his phone. They were all dressed in pipe jeans and laced boots, like some kind of uniform or boy band.

"So everybody is a gangster now," I said.

Ska responded, "Yuh damaged goods, Nyjah. The best thing about yuh is yuh poetry. Don't think yuh better than them. Yuh back where yuh belong."

"Funny how they moved from the car-wash business at school to here."

Ska peered at me. "Funny how? It seem the most natural step to me."

But still I was surprised, even a bit disappointed, to see Fischer there. "I guess Perry done with medical school."

"Mighty operates the car wash now. He's second only to Fruits, and he's been grooming Perry all along, and now it's all in the open . . . as much as it could be open."

Mighty's voice was slow with drink—he was talking to Fruits but it was obvious they were communicating in code. After Perry ended his phone call and said something to both of them, Fruits snorted as he got up from a mortar-encrusted bucket he'd been sitting on. "Why dey keep barrin' de cellar doors as if dey feel de bodies go fly out de coffins? Tell dem we go double de price for dat."

I checked my watch. "Let Chadwell know I'll catch him another time. I go get some stuff done."

"Hold your horses, here he comes."

Chadwell slowed to the curb on a silver Suzuki Burgman 400—I knew because it was the same model I'd been eyeing in a magazine with him one day at lunch—throwing his foot down to lean the motorcycle forward and rev the engine one last time before releasing the kickstand. He got off the bike slowly with his hands on his hips, smiling broadly. "Yuh like it?"

"Yeah man, it kinda neat," I said, looking over the spanking-new brake levers, the leather seat, the gleaming engine casing, gears, and crankshaft. It was a beauty.

Chadwell gestured to the electricians and they quietly enjoyed my delight, then he threw me the keys. "It's yours."

"What? Yuh jokin', Chad."

"The paperwork's all done. Now let's hear a proper thank you."

I pulled him into an embrace and the men cheered. Ska opened the JB and started a proper round, humming to himself, then breaking into song, his screech alarming tourists entering the craft market across the road. "*That's what friends are for . . .*"

Ninja adjusted his dark spectacles and began playing air melodica.

"Ninja, we need to blind yuh other eye so yuh can be a proper Steve Wonder," said Scabby, lifting his gansey over his big hairy stomach to just below his fleshy breasts, trying to get relief from the heat.

Ninja wiped the fluids that occasionally trickled from his blind eye. He had lost it in a site accident but had never sued the family. Mr. Crichton had pledged to take care of him and school his children. But I often wondered about his loyalty to Ska, if a part of him didn't hate the guy. Ska was the one who'd caused the accident, from what Chadwell told me, because he'd been half cut on the job.

I still couldn't get over Chadwell's generosity, and he was pleased with this, like a father watching his child unwrapping gifts. I couldn't take my hands off the bike, I inspected every bit of it and was so keyed up I spilled my drink.

"See, round here, Nyjah, it has a luggage rack, a saddlebag, and book rest. And yuh can open this part and put yuh stuff in, very spacious."

"I swear, my little brother treat yuh better than him own flesh and blood, Nyjah," Ska remarked. "Here him dolin' out presents and can't even remember him own mother's birthday."

Chadwell took the cup from his brother's hand as if he were a child. "Ska, that's enough." He flashed the older men a warning glance and they lost some of their frivolity.

"I wish the guys were here," I said, running my hand down the smooth ash-blue subframe.

"Let's take it for a test ride."

"Nyjah, yuh need some killer bike gloves an' shoes now to really pull it off," said Greg.

I hopped on the seat, trying to get a feel of it before I put the helmet on. It had been so long since I'd ridden. Chadwell got on the pillion. "Okay," I said, "please keep all hands and legs inside the vehicle at all times." And we were off with raucous noise.

We rode all the way to Whitehouse and parked and walked the row of stalls fronting the seawall, looking at fish and lobsters swimming in plastic tubs, trying to decide which ones to buy. The fishermen's wives smiled at us as they flipped festivals on grills or splashed jerk meat with Red Stripe, giving vacationers a little show.

"I really wish the bwoys were here."

"Yuh keep sayin' that," said Chadwell. "Yuh sound like an itchin' cunt. Just enjoy the moment."

The stalls all looked and smelled so good. Seawater crashed into the bluff and sprayed our faces. The sun was high, warm. We walked to the back of a shabby restaurant and sat on some rocks where I could keep an eye on the bike. We hardly ate seafood whenever we stopped along the coast, something about the abundance put us off. Someone had spray-painted in yellow down the length of an old shithouse, *DON'T STAND ON CEREMONY IF YOU CAN*

HELP IT. STAND ON HER HEAD INSTEAD! I saw a trampled earring in the dirt and my heart fluttered.

Chadwell noticed my reaction and grabbed my arm. "It's okay," he said, "breathe."

"I'm a bag of nerves these days," I said after I calmed down.

"It's the new job and the new women."

"Yes, that's it."

"Yuh haven't told me how much yuh like the bike."

"Yuh jokin'? I love it! Now all I need is gas money."

He pushed my head playfully; we bought weed off a Rastaman with buds stuck up his tam, hiding them from bicycle police patrolling the coast. The weed had the damp frowsy smell of his sweating locks but got better with each draw.

"Is like we smokin' the Rasta's brain . . ." We sat there watching a grayish-blond woman feeding her child jackass corn.

Chadwell giggled. "She feedin' the little brat like a fowl. Come. Let's see what this bike can do."

"I thought we just did," I coughed, sucking the spliff tail. "I think Rory has the hots for Dreenie. She cooked for us that day Bussy died and he couldn't keep his eyes off her."

"Did she take it?"

I nodded.

"I shoulda tell yuh before. I saw her with Burberry Dalton, that *samfie* bwoy from the arcade."

I smiled at the information. "So he graduated from sellin' counterfeit dollars and added a title to his name." I remembered nearly tangling with Dalton that day of Bussy's funeral, when he'd had his cronies harass Louder Milk.

A skinny delivery boy pushed past the heavy red iron back door, causing us to jump. A fat man in a dirty white apron and chef hat trundled after him, swinging his big belly from side to side and wagging his finger. "Yuh gettin' foul-mouthed, Campbell," said the chef.

The stringy delivery boy turned and gave him the finger. "Fuck you!"

"That right there is a lesson," Chadwell said. "Always be a boss in your head, even when yuh work under people."

"*Fat* people. Let's go," I said, pulling him onto the bike.

We stopped farther down by a jelly cart.

"How much for the Graham mangoes?" asked Chad.

"Eighty dollars a dozen, I-yah," said the young Rasta, twirling his stringy beard and stepping toward us with a basket of fruit. "I tangle two roots togedda so de vines fuse, so dese Grahams mixed wid Julie mango too."

"A regular botanist," I whispered.

Chadwell wasn't so subtle: "I don't care for your lies, just gimme the damn fruit."

The Rasta, eager for the sale, handed a few over without taking payment and waited as we ate.

I inspected the yellow heart of the fruit with each taste; there did seem to be some Julie mango in it somewhere, the taste was curiously mild yet rich. "Give us two dozen."

"Yuh payin' for that," said Chad.

I dropped the bag of mangoes in the underseat storage. "No I'm not." When the Rasta passed us the second bag, I slapped his hand away and sped off.

The man hurled stones at the swerving motorcycle, jumping, spitting with rage. "Me go chop up yuh bumboclaat!"

I weaved patterns with the bike—this came back naturally from my days working as a delivery boy in Kingston. Chadwell clung to my ribs, laughing.

"Rich as you are, how can you cheat the poor?"

"*You* took it!" I charged, and we howled some more.

Daylight bloomed like sea light when tranquil under a yellow sun.

"Faster, Nyjah, go faster!"

I did. Soon we were breaking the speed limit. We beat the band all afternoon as if the town was ours.

"Let's go by Deelo and get some pumpkin soup!"

* * *

As I walked toward Bailey House, an Asian boy with a long plait down his back—a thing never allowed in our time—and a face as delicate as a flower opening to sunlight, a face filled with fragility and warmth, stood in the spot where I'd always stood as a student, next to the sundial.

"I used to do the same thing, wondering about the faces that passed through this place."

The boy rolled his eyes and snorted. When he spoke, his voice was countrified, coarse, something I hadn't assumed about him, erroneously thinking him refined due to his ethnicity and soft looks. "It ain't dat I t'inkin'. I wonderin' how come nobody doh have de balls to b'un dung dis *rass* ol' house. Like dem fraida duppy."

I was taken aback. His eyes burned with the sacrilegiousness of his words, as if he actually meant to do it one way or another. Of all the pranks we'd pulled, and we had pulled many, nobody had ever dared to harm the sanctity of old Bailey, but to this boy it was as worthless as an empty matchbox, an eyesore—in his head he probably carried no space for monuments, no ceremonial sense of history or permanence. I wondered if he was an imposter, someone trespassing on the compound in disguise.

"Yuh know Smokey?"

He flicked his thumb. "Here he come."

Smokey picked up a rock and feinted. "Peng! Yuh Chiney dawg, gwaan a class!"

The boy ran down the slope toward the old chemistry labs.

Smokey had the same small wizened face and rabbit teeth slightly jutting over his lip that made him look like a preserved corpse. He hadn't aged a day, still mincing in his manner and movements, going about his groundskeeping at a glacial pace as if he didn't want the work to catch up with him.

"Who that iconoclast just now?"

Smokey swatted the question away with a gruff gesture. "Nobody. Jus' a runny-nose runt. A scholarship bum."

"He said the strangest thing."

Smokey looked at me with shallow curiosity. "Did he?"

"He said . . . never mind. But there's something odd about him."

We stepped into the shed and sat on discarded school chairs; Smokey handed me a beer from a mini fridge. "Him a seventh-grader, tek a set pon me like me him daddy. But me never fuck a Chiney woman from me bawn." His right hand impatiently ordered God to bear witness.

I was waiting for the invite down to his den, like a first-time comedian on *The Tonight Show* waiting for Carson to call him to the couch. It never came. I stayed there a long time looking at him, feeling bad and not enjoying my drink; he opened another beer, drank, and peered right back at me with an empty face. "Yuh look good, Nyjah."

"So this is it?" I finally said. "I get only the shed?"

He took a cigarette from behind his ear. "What yuh expect? Homecomin'?" He pulled on the Matterhorn and regarded me. "Why yuh back here?"

"I can't remember," I bluffed. "Maybe it isn't that important."

He leaned against the reddish cement-splashed zinc and narrowed his eyes. "I t'ink it *is* important an' yuh remember perfectly well." He tapped ash in a cream-colored ashtray he used to keep in the den, the one that sat right next to his favorite couch. I looked around the shed with the slow horrific realization that everything that had been inside the den had been transferred here, thrown aside like junk, even the poster of an ice cream–eating gorilla screaming, *Uho!*—all that was left was the smashed frame and fragments of the print. The shed felt like a nightmarish funhouse.

"But why, Smokey?" I muttered, glancing around frantically, piecing back together an old life lying around me in sad disarray.

He kicked an empty blue water drum and it hurtled across the room. I jumped aside just in time to avoid it. "Because yuh ruin me fuckin' place, dat's why! You an' de rest o' dem ungrateful jancros! Turn me house into a fuckin' crime scene!" He had to breathe slowly to bring his temper under control.

So he *had* known all along, at least partially. He thought I was part of the gang rape because my friends had been there. I might well have been—that's the guilt of shared responsibility I'd been struggling with. Sometimes I convinced myself that in a way I *had* raped her too. And I wasn't about to deny culpability now. I felt dizzy, my throat dry.

"I'm sorry, Smokey."

He stood, advanced. I braced myself for a slap, a punch—anything would've been better than his smoldering anger. He grabbed my arm and pulled me outside. I allowed myself to be led. We walked behind Bailey House and up the long stretch of lonely road that fronted the teachers' cottages. The wind raged and the empty houses were silent witnesses. We were walking abreast in this suffocating silence, the wind in our ears and the distant murmur of boys filling the cafeteria slowly drifting toward us.

Finally he said, "Yuh goin' to do de right t'ing, Nyjah."

I whipped around but he dragged me forward. I had to keep moving to bear all he had to say. "How, Smokey?"

"Dis is what de Chester motto *Men of Might* means. De strength to stan' up an' be counted. Dis especially will make de institution stan' behind yuh. Dey will applaud yuh courage."

"Don't quote that motto to me!" I lashed out. "*Courage*! You're a fine one to talk. Sittin' up here still enablin' bwoys with slackness, feedin' them liquor and gamblin', and you dare be sanctimonious with me?"

He never lost his gentility, he was calmer for it, uncompromising. I was falling to pieces. "Nyjah, me wa'an what's best for yuh. Me wa'an yuh to be whole again. I wouldn't dare tell yuh to do anyt'ing else dan de right t'ing, 'cause I love yuh."

The wind spread the cold tears across my cheeks. But I didn't feel hopeless; in fact, I would've been miserable if he were to leave right then. "Yuh love me . . . ?"

"Yes."

"Yuh love me, Smokey."

"Yes."

"Then help me."

"Stop actin' so insipid! What yuh want from me? What yuh t'ink it mean to be a man? It mean one t'ing above all odders, not education or ignorance or poverty or riches—it mean takin' responsibility!"

"But what about you? Shouldn't *you* take some responsibility?"

He laughed and turned his face away, looking down the rolling green hill toward the J block and his den where everything had happened. A new clique of gay boys ran the car wash, their voices a howling tempest to mask their unhappiness. "Yuh know Castleigh is a teacher here. A teacher, imagine dat." He looked at me. "But you not like Castleigh. Never have been. I study every one o' yuh who I let in here. Dat was me greatest lesson over de years—studyin' all o' yuh. Is a blessin' I wouldn't trade for nutten else. *Dis*"—he put his hand over his heart—"an' yuh company gimme de greatest life lesson. Lissen to yuh heart, Nyjah. What it tellin' yuh?"

"Yuh corrupted us."

He shook his head and reached out, but I pulled away. "I wouldn't tell Castleigh all what I tellin' yuh, 'cause Castleigh ain't you."

"Yuh keep saying that."

"Castleigh cut from a different cloth. I could tell yuh right now what happen dat day widout seein' anyt'ing."

"Yuh don't know a thing 'bout what happened that day."

"I know de ringleaders an' those who were manipulated. But yuh haffe come clean, Nyjah. Else yuh'll never see yuh face in de mirror an' like it. A bwoy like Mighty look in de mirror an' see de devil smilin' back, but him doh mind. Him comfortable wid him breed. Sodomites an' reprobates."

"And what breed are you?" I asked.

"Me? It don't matter. Do what's good for yuh. An' Smokey will feel him done some good amidst him own devilment."

A cloudburst surprised us. A brown cluster of small sparrows darted from the clump of nearby lignum vitae branches. It was strange that their instincts were so dull that they hadn't fled before the rainfall. They seemed harried and desperate as they darted around in heavy wetness, as if foolishly trying to evade each raindrop. Smokey and I jogged back to the shed and waited out the cloudburst. There was nothing more to be said. We were like two strangers caught at a bus stop in the rain. When it stopped almost as abruptly as it had started—the sun hot and bright again—I walked down to the lower school, leaving Smokey to fuss with his bags of ruined seeds.

On a concrete platform in the quad of the eighth-grade block, a boy sat with his elbows pressing down on a desk and no chair under his bottom. He had to stay that way—in a sitting position, usually for half an hour, out in the sun—as a spectacle because he was a habitual sleeper. The punishment was called the Invisible Chair. The sadism made me mad now. I wished I could command him to walk away from the desk. Most of the unfortunates in my day were country lads who woke before dawn and traveled great distances since they couldn't afford boarding, so they nodded off in class. It had always seemed cruel to punish them.

Castleigh finished class and came out and stood quietly beside me, watching the boy. "I made him do it," he boasted.

He was muscular from gym training, looking as if he would burst out of his tight fashionable pants; he had grown sideburns and had a scar down his forehead I didn't care to ask him about, probably from some rafting accident or other. He was an extreme-sports fanatic—in a way he was like his brother Snow, a thrill seeker. I wished I could say I was happy to see him, but we'd largely avoided each other ever since graduation; he was never really one of us, was always too wild for our liking (or maybe we were too timid for his), and Chadwell had never appreciated his own status being challenged by Castleigh's strong-headedness.

"First-time offender?" I said without looking at him.

"Does it matter? Listen, all in all those who have suffered this punishment, before our time down till now, have deserved it, if only to make them better students and avoid sloth."

"I'm surprised at your own self-damnin' assessment."

He turned to me. "I don't follow."

"Never mind . . . What yuh teachin'?"

"Math and physics. What brings yuh here?"

"I need a transcript. Just thought I'd drop by and say hello."

"But wha' gwaan, Messado? Still tryin' to give the world meanin' with poetry?" He smiled broadly and slapped my back. "Ol' Nyjah the fixer! Always collectin' big on money football. Bwoy, I wish we had time to play a game like old times. Show these grubs how real Chesterites do it."

He shadowboxed with some of the bolder boys and pulled at a small one's head. I could tell he had good rapport with them; they probably respected his no-nonsense ways because he kidded with them too. The shyer ones took a speculative interest in our conversation, standing apart with their ears cocked.

Castleigh put his fingers to his lips and whistled to the boy in the quad. "You there! Take up your bed and walk!"

The boys closest to us laughed coldly as if it was expected of them; the shyer ones showed sympathy and remained quiet. The boy sulked and hauled the desk noisily toward class, still fuming; he could barely walk, his legs were jelly. Castleigh had a bamboo cane behind him, clearly itching to strike the kid if he made eyes with him as he passed. The boy, mindful of this, calibrated his behavior to show just the right degree of contrition and drifted past as if blind, greeting us quietly and lifting his desk over the threshold. Once inside, he immediately fell in a heap on his chair. Another boy volunteered to get him lunch, but he was too tired to speak; he put his head on the desk and opened his mouth like a dead fish.

Castleigh whispered, "Yuh know, I don't even remember the little bugger's name. Come, let's go have a drink."

We went to the convenience store by the teachers' lounge.

Castleigh eyed his favorite candy since school days, a chocolate-and-nuts wafer called Crunky. He fished for coins in his wallet, rolling them out in his palm. "Crunky, Nyjah! Do I have enough for a Crunky? I dare say I do." He threw the coins down and didn't even look at the cashier, and the girl muttered something as she worked the register. I got two coffees and we sat near the windows by the gardens.

"I bought a car, secondhand thing, with fish-shaped taillights, real trendy-looking."

"That's nice," I said.

"So yuh gettin' on at the schools?"

I sipped my drink. "*Timid, afraid of his own ambitions and self-honesty*. That's what someone wrote in the yearbook about yuh, as if it was a report card. I always wondered who wrote that."

He showed his teeth and ate his candy as if it had rocks in it. "And what did yours say?"

"They hit the nail on the head, didn't they? For all yuh bluster, yuh've always been a sad sack, punishing that bwoy just now probably 'cause yuh having a lousy day, on the pretext of being someone who believes in *values*."

He tried to laugh it off, jerking his head around to see if anyone was listening. "What's with yuh? Why yuh bitin' off me head? Did I fuck someone close to yuh?"

I took out a pack of Matterhorns.

Castleigh made a frenzied gesture. "This is a no-smokin' zone."

I couldn't stop laughing, tickled by his choice of words; his voice was so prim and forbidding, like a stage actor's. "Forgive me. What yuh goin' do if I light up? Cane me?"

He finished the candy, then sipped his own cup. Something changed in his demeanor. "Yuh not here for a transcript, yuh came to get yuh head shrunk. You're a bagga tricks."

"And why are *you* here? Because yuh love teachin' kids?"

He looked at me fiercely, with his old wild expression that always gave me a twinge of apprehension. "I'm here because I can stomach it. I'm like the guy who cleans up the bodies."

"A John Crow."

"Probably . . ." He drank as if the warmth was relaxing him, melting his tension. "I'll tell yuh one thing: nobody fuck with me. Smokey wouldn't dare try get round me with him fuckin' amateur-hour questionin'. I can make him lose him job like that! I'm his boss now—not a bwoy." He saw my surprise. "Yeah, yuh think I didn't see you two? I have eyes all over. This is *my* place, remember. I get to do the creepin' and tellin' of half-truths, not you. When were yuh plannin' to tell me 'bout that conversation?"

I stayed silent.

The cashier, young and trendy, with one side of her head a smooth perm of silver and purple tints, the other side arranged in rows of pink-jeweled snap clips that looked like a rack of ribs from a pig, had been edgy ever since we entered. I realized in retrospect that something had passed between them when he slighted her at the counter.

Castleigh watched my eyes flit back and forth. "Yes," he smiled, raising the cup to his mouth, "I live by the teachers' cottages. She get her daggerin' last week."

"Yuh one of them now, aren't yuh? One of the womanizin' masters."

"This was always home. I'm a simple man. In my case, *destiny* and *destination* are very much the same. I'm a Chesterite through and through." And just like that, he forgot her and got back to me. "What you two talk about anyway?" He was still smirking at having caught me off guard, mocking my overconfidence. I had played right into his hands and he was ready for checkmate. "Yuh know what? Don't tell me. I couldn't bear to have someone lie to me."

"Lie to yuh? Yuh lying to yuhself. Yuh whole life is a lie, if yuh want to know."

"Hey, take it easy. Keep yuh voice down." He leaned across the table. "Yuh don't get to come in here and tell me the state of things. Who the fuck yuh think yuh is? This ain't yuh place anymore. I'm a grown man. We aren't—"

I stood up.

He dragged me back down and I pushed his arm off. Staff were watching us, as was a security guard, who walked over casually, his hands on his big belt like a patrol cop. "Everyt'ing all right, Mr. Twentyman?"

Castleigh gave him an impatient glare. "Yes, Harry, just friends catchin' up."

"Yes, Harry, leave us alone for a bit nuh."

"Maybe yuh gentlemen would like to take it to de Oak Room?"

This was a lounge exclusively for Chesterites; staff who hadn't graduated from the school couldn't even go there.

"We're fine."

The guard returned to the double doors.

Castleigh kept flicking his empty cup with his finger, looking almost doleful. "I've something to tell yuh."

I waited.

"She's in Westmoreland, yuh know. We've been to see her. She's a museum curator in Seaford Town."

"*We?*"

"Me and Chad . . . I can take yuh there if yuh want."

"Somehow I wouldn't trust a ride with you two. I don't know what yuh could get up to."

"What yuh think we would do, bump yuh off? Even after permanently buying yuh silence with that motorcycle?"

"Yuh seem to know everything, Cass."

"Chad seems to think her having any reminder of that day could be disastrous."

"You don't get to decide that!"

"Oh, we don't? Yuh need to start showing some fuckin' humility and sense." Castleigh looked out the window at boys on cleaning duty, raking leaves and giving each other rides in the wheelbarrow. "Ask him where to find her, he'll tell yuh." As I stood, he squeezed my wrist. "Yuh owe us loyalty . . . don't yuh ever forget that."

CHAPTER 11

When he arrived in the Hummer, late as usual, he came out with two white delivery bags of food, like a peace offering, smiling as he advanced. "Bought yuh lunch," he said.

"I'm not hungry . . . I saw Castleigh on Wednesday."

"Eeh? How is ol' Shark Mouth?"

"You tell me—from what I heard, you two are chums."

Chadwell's mouth corners tightened. He had a very handsome profile like his older brother, it was part of his charm. "I see yuh have somethin' heavy to drop on me. Hold that thought. Le'we go look at somethin' first."

We walked two streets over to Waltham Crescent.

"What's this dump?"

It was a dilapidated day care, with a sign out front showing smiling happy children and parents; but the sign was sun-bleached and peeling, leaving the faces disfigured, missing eyeballs, hairlines, noses, mouths, and teeth, and looking instead like a gaggle of frenzied ghosts; rather than happy they seemed almost bitter against the world. The building looked as if it had been forgotten by the city even before the children and staff vacated it. Now there was no one to cut the thick weeds, and the smell of human shit was thick in the trash-strewn yard. Suddenly, light came filtering out from somewhere inside its dark concrete depths to flash across our faces; we covered our eyes.

A disheveled woman ran from inside, babbling deliriously, leaping like a spring hare down the steps and holding a piece of glass. It was Mad Lena, the bum who had complained of being raped near Fowler Bridge that day we saw Snow. At first she appeared so shy that she refused to even look at us, wandering about the yard, checking out her stained teeth in the mirror, and fixing her hair that was as twiggy as a bird nest, perhaps wishing us away by squeezing her eyes shut intermittently, lost in her own fantasy. When she opened them and saw us still standing there, she started screaming, "Get out! Get off me property! Police! The Dollar Boys come back to fuck me!"

Chadwell held his hands out. "Take it easy, we won't hurt you."

She backed away like a frightened animal.

"Take it easy . . ." He offered her the bag of food.

She took it with her dirt-caked hands, sat on the steps, pulled her raggedy skirt into her lap, and started eating greedily, licking chicken grease from her knuckles and black fingernails.

"Good gyal," said Chadwell, stepping forward slowly and patting her dirty hair as if she were a dog.

"We should leave," I said, already backing out of the lot.

He turned around. "Take it easy, Nyjah, don't be rude. We just got here."

Mad Lena smiled through a mouthful of food and ugly brown teeth.

Chad looked deep in thought. "Princess," he said softly, "who owns this place?"

Lena turned her wild eyes up to him and pulled strands of hair from her scarred cheeks. "The Matalons, but they abandon it."

"So yuh moved in."

"It's mine now. I take care of it." She gnawed the drumstick and picked her teeth, then spat out a chaw of bone like wet seeds.

"And yuh've done great, princess," said Chadwell, stroking her face.

She moved her cheek along his palm as if she'd lick it.

"What are yuh thinkin'?" I asked.

"Property, Nyjah. Real estate. I'm goin' buy it. *We're* goin' buy it."

Lena jumped and threw aside the food bag like a poisonous snake. "Yuh can't do that! And put me out on the street!" She grabbed at Chadwell's leg, but he kicked her off and cocked his fist.

"Get off me, yuh crazy bitch."

Falling to her knees, she grabbed her head. "Aah! Aah! Don't put me back on the street! They will kill me out there!" She crept on all fours across the stony yard and grabbed my knees. She must have seen my bewildered expression. She appealed to me through tears: "Please talk to yuh friend. Talk to him, please!" Her voice had a resonance like grating iron.

Chadwell had walked off with a spring in his step. "C'mon, Nyjah."

I shook my head at her and left, her sobs haunting my every step.

"Chad . . ." I began.

He turned with light aggression, as if I'd disturbed his thinking—his mind was running through all the permutations of future wealth, I could see it in his eyes. "This goin' to be *your* school. I go buy it and refurbish it. But I want it to be a group venture. I go talk to Cress and Rory tomorrow." I could see he had it all planned out; our involvement was an afterthought, though I would've been foolish to gainsay his judgment. "The Matalons movin' outta St. James. They're eager to sell. Don't worry 'bout yuh end, I'll cover yuh with a loan . . . Oh, what did yuh want to talk about?"

"Nutten. Some other time."

Briana kept pestering me to talk to Perry. So that Saturday, after returning to the electrical shop with Chad, I planned a coup. Dreenie had called, saying she wanted me to meet her mother.

I found Perry by himself for once, having grilled lobster and a stout outside the car wash. I hurried down the sidewalk. "Can we talk?"

He looked up peevishly, spritzing his lunch with lemon sauce. "Now, Messado?"

"Gimme a ride. I need to see me gyal."

"Liar. Briana put yuh up to this."

"Perry—"

He held up his hand. "Yuh know why Fulvia took Cicero's head, pulled out his tongue, and jabbed it repeatedly with her hairpin?"

I sighed. "No, why?"

"As final revenge against Cicero's power of speech. The man practically ruined Antony. Yuh goin' tell me the truth, Nyjah, or am I goin' have to rip yuh tongue from yuh head?"

"Okay . . . Bree put me up to it. But hear me out."

He called a boy over from the car wash, handed him his food. "See, was that so hard?"

We picked up Andrene at St. Claver's.

She lived in Concrete, a place that made both me and Perry nervous.

"So this your gyal, eh?" smiled Perry. "I like yuh dress, honey. Lemme have a look at it and make a muslin for you," he teased.

"T'anks," said Dreenie. "What's a muslin?"

"For your wedding, silly!" giggled Perry. "You goin' drag a lotta dirt up the aisle with that train, enuh. Nyjah is a ol' dawg."

"You should know," I quipped, flicking his ear. "Ah yuh tek me virginity."

We laughed, enjoying our homoerotic play like back in school.

"Yuh soun' like faggots," Dreenie said, smiling. "Hurry up an' marry aredi."

We talked some, then she called ahead to tell her mother we were coming. "Mummy, me finally bringin' Nyjah to meet yuh. An' a friend-a his, nice guy, trainin' to be a doctah."

When we got out of the car, we heard, "She too small for yuh, tall man." It was a young dread in an old orange tam, blowing *kutchie* smoke in my face as he brushed my shoulder in passing.

Dreenie clutched my arm and spat, "Fuck off, trash!" as the man gazed back menacingly at us.

Dusty-feet children outside a furniture shop, smelling sweetly of spray lacquer, fussed over their sales pitch, deciding how much to charge us. One ran up proffering guineps.

"Don't taste none," Dreenie warned. "If yuh taste, yuh haffe buy de bunch, even if it sour."

"Sorta like de gyal dem round here," said one of the gang of shirtless youths sitting on the bus stop wall. When his friends laughed, he added, "I talkin' 'bout yuh mooma!"

Dreenie tugged us along.

"Dreen, yuh man shoes bottom clean doe," one called out. "Ah foreign him come from? I go check yuh later fe some foreign currency."

"Why dat brown one walk like battyman suh?" squeaked another in a black and yellow hockey beanie.

Perry glanced back, but I yanked his sleeve. He chirped the BMW's alarm, still glaring at them.

As we walked off, one of the boys shrieked, "We nuh rob BMW—Batty Man Wagon!" They howled at their witticism.

Dreenie's mother and little sister met us in the dooryard.

"This is Nyjah an'—" Dreenie began.

"Her other boyfriend," Perry interjected.

The woman nearly had a fright.

"An' his friend Perry," Dreenie said, recovering herself.

"Perry, behave," I muttered.

"Hi, I'm Norma, Dr. Perry."

"He ain't a doctah yet, Mama," Dreenie snorted.

We shook the older woman's nervous hand.

"Hi, Norma, glad to finally meet yuh."

"An' me likkle sister Pearl," continued Dreenie.

"Hey, *jubie*," grinned Perry, pulling the child's cheek.

She had long pigtails and buckteeth. Her hair was as Indian as the mother's. I realized that Dreenie took more from her Black father.

"I savin' to get Pearl braces," Norma said apologetically.

"I'll pay for it," said Perry.

"Perry, that's not funny," I said sharply. "Be serious."

"I'm serious," he said with a perfect smile. He pulled out a checkbook and wrote a check right there and then.

Norma nearly fainted from surprise.

We helped her overcome the embarrassment. "Let's go in and see the house," I said.

"Of course," Norma stammered. She went on autopilot, overflowing with gratitude to the two angels visiting Sodom. "Dis is de living room, I know it ain't no Carol Gardens mansion . . . Over here is de dining room an' a piana."

"A piano?" said Perry.

"Yes, someone donated it for de church, we cyaan keep it dere 'cause dem t'ief de las' one."

"Dear God," said Perry.

Norma threw a dirty-looking frock at Dreenie that had been draped on a chair. She had one of those living-dining rooms ghetto people seem so proud of—the economy and ingenuity of space. "Dis is de kitchen over here. Me plan on gettin' all de new fixtures when me get dat pawdna draw."

"Please use the money to fix the child's teeth," said Perry.

"All dem rotten shelves go get taken out an' I go *lick* out dat wall dere. It go be much nicer an' bigger." Norma looked proudly for a moment at the imagined renovation. Then she shuffled past us with her wide frame. "An' up dere is de bedrooms an' bath. Plenty ah room." She peered down a dark passage. "An' this is ah—"

"Mama, dem never come fe a tour!" Dreenie snapped. "Lawd, man, yuh actin' like dem is building inspector."

"Yes," Norma said. "Gyals, come help me." She spun, said to me, "Dreen is a good chile. Some o' what yuh see here she buy. Buil' up her mooma wid de money she mek at de shoes market. I doh wa'an her to be a higgler all her life like me. Help her, Nyjah—she deserve better dan dis!"

After the females stepped away, Perry said, "Poor people have a disease. They're always desperate to impress people. Never comfortable in their own skin."

"How comfortable are *you*?" I lit his cigarette. "Dreen, babes, gimme a Ting," I called out.

"Yes, Dreen, Ting us," Perry echoed.

I chuckled quietly and whispered, "Who still uses a checkbook anyhow?"

"How can yuh stand her?" Perry said.

"What yuh care? Yuh don't even like gyals."

"I know yuh fuckin' Bree again. You're a big pussy man, ain't yuh?"

"Again?"

Dreenie came back, though Perry had caught the question and was desperate to pursue it.

But I changed tack when Dreenie left with the tray. "Bree worries about yuh."

"Yeah? Does this count as an intervention?"

"Don't get smart."

Sitting forward, he pointed his cigarette at me. "You, my friend, are in a curious bind: yuh have no moral authority here. Dreenie know yuh fuckin' my sister?"

"Keep yuh voice down! It ain't like that."

"No? I wonder how yuh'd feel if I fucked yuh aunties."

"That's enough!"

Perry leered, setting his drink down. "Oh, yuh goin' slap me now? Yuh think yuh more man than me, Messado?"

"Bwoys, play nice," said Dreenie, coming back into the room.

"Of course yuh do. After all, ol' Perry is just a *fish*. He walks like a gyal. Runs like one, talks like one, throws like one. Probably pisses like one too. Just squats right down. That's what yuh said when yuh first saw me in gym, remember? I overheard *everythin'*."

It pained me suddenly that he'd been carrying that around. I remembered my attempt to blackmail him—how he'd suffered. "You're a great athlete," I allowed. "I took all that back once we got on the cricket pitch. It's like . . . yuh became a different person. Someone I envied."

"Someone yuh could *almost* respect?" he said. "Yuh envied my talent, not *me*."

"What's the difference?"

"I'm more than my talent—look at me!"

"*I'm* certainly not."

"Then I feel sorry for yuh." He raised the green bottle. "Cheers, Nyjah, don't look so glum. Where would we be without true friends . . . you scum." He laughed maniacally, went to the piano, cracked his fingers, and started playing and singing, "*We were sailing along on Moonlight Bay* . . ."

Norma hugged Dreenie with Pearl between them, the three of them rocking slowly, enjoying Perry's voice, entranced by the melody, till Norma clambered over and squeaked, "No, Doctah, dem t'iefin' bwoys might hear an' come tek de piana!"

"Oh, I'm sorry," said Perry. Then his phone rang; he went off to a corner. I could hear Mighty shouting and watched Perry shrinking before me, drying up like a raisin, saying sheepishly, "Yes, Marvin . . . Yes . . . Yes . . . No . . . Sorry . . . Of course . . ." When he hung up, he lit another cigarette and paced with angry steps, knocking the side of his head and muttering, "Kill or cure, kill or cure . . ."

The words didn't make sense, but his pain was obvious. Even the child looked sad for him.

Norma muttered to Dreen, "Rich daddy, prep school, silk pajama, yet *Charlie* nuh happy."

Perry banged the piano keys and I had to run over and grab his arms.

He struggled in my grip, saying, "I'm going to shit and fall back in it! I don't care anymore, Nyjah. I don't!"

Norma approached. "Yuh know what fowl do when one chicken bawn wid *off*-color feather? Dem peck at dat discolored spot till de chicken dead. Dem cyaan stand dat it's different."

Perry fell on his knees before her. "Yes, Mother, I'm different—

we're different. This whole country would like to kill me and my crew!"

Zetta Rosegreen flashed in my head like lightning—as if Perry and I shared some sort of affliction.

Norma pulled Perry up, glaring in his wet face. "Doh let dem! Dem nuh deserve an inch ah space more than yuh! Run from coward dawg him chase yuh!"

It started raining in sheets, drumming the roof like a buzz saw. The light of glory shone through the window, holding our attention, then we heard a garbage truck honk, "Late pickup!" trailing a smell so sour we had to close the windows.

"What on earth!" fussed Norma. "Deliver me from dis place. Yuh have children—yuh leave dem in de hands o' Gawd! Who can touch dem? Who can JUDGE dem?"

A shiver pierced my heart at her power.

Perry huddled up and quickly fell asleep on the sofa, resting peacefully, sound. Till Norma woke him for a feast of a dinner.

CHAPTER 12

On the marquee, the smiling seahorse was flickering its green tail and winking at us above its white bow tie and tux. "Fuckin' freak-out factory tonight," said Ninja. We worked our way along the cold brick wall of the interior and stood near tall single-legged tables covered with empty plastic cups and cocktail glasses.

A middle-aged white man, his face smooth and his eyes like bulbs, sat in the roped-off lounge with a girl on his lap; she wore an electric-blue wig and blue contacts, which jarred with her shiny black skin. He was extremely taken with her; he looked at her as if she were an expensive painting. Whenever she ran her hand over the bulge in his pants, he purred, "*Goot . . . goot*."

"Must be German," said Cress, "they like the gyals with a lotta melanin. They come here to do a little coal mining."

We couldn't stop laughing.

Ska called a waiter over, relieved him of a tray of cocktails, and made a toast: "*Sláinte*! To the colliery!"

"To the colliery!"

A light-skinned dancer limbering up flashed her breasts in my face, but I didn't bite. She persisted, pushing them softly on me as I scowled. "If yuh not goin' look or buy ah dance, yuh can at least tip me or buy me a drink."

I waved her off, watching the young woman behind her.

Realizing she had competition, she half turned with her face screwed up.

The other one sucked her teeth in passing, "Dis Red Ibo gyal . . ."

"Talk again, bitch!"

Scabby stepped between them: "Hot patty! Hot patty, who go cool it?" The light-skinned one slapped his upturned palm to the other girl's face and they grabbed each other's hair and grunted and were soon rolling on the ground. Patrons swiveled around them like racing cars negotiating a chicane.

"He hid the money in the back of the painting," said a svelte greasy-haired foreigner to a bouncer, "so naturally the value went up." The bouncer didn't get the joke and the gray-suited man apologized and nervously ran his hand down the front of his suit, then walked off.

We baptized some strippers sleepwalking toward the dressing rooms—ostensibly for good luck, but really to piss them off—splashing them with liquor from our fingertips dipped in the cocktails. "Wake up, gyal," Scabby said merrily, crowding them with his paunch, "I doh get me eyeful yet. What yuh-all lookin' so *fenke-fenke* for? Hurry up an' come back out!"

They cursed us but were careful not to be too cross because they were gauging, courting customers. Pipes zigzagging the aluminum-covered ceiling sprayed disinfecting mist that billowed over strobe lights till the whole scene became hypnotic; a girl dressed in a skin-tight feline costume was playing a violin and wagging her tail, dancing through the fog and patrons.

"Probably some poor college student. She plays pretty, eh?" said Greg. When she stood before us, she played snippets of Mozart's slow-fast-slow "Turkish March" and curtsied.

I clapped and Rory complained to her, "My gyal left me today. Bad breakup at the beach."

To our surprise, she responded with sign language and pointed to her ear. Rory quickly wrote on his phone and showed it to her and she made a sad face, like a mime, performing for him. He pointed at her chest and mouthed, *Are they real?* She took his hand and put it on her right breast. I realized she was naked, that the costume was spray-painted on.

Scabby grabbed at her, but anticipating this, she skillfully sashayed away, taking Rory with her like the Pied Piper, leading him by the arm toward a balcony beyond the glass doors.

Marco said, "How the fuck they get the fish in the walls? Is like a hobby for Blofeld or Hugo Drax."

I glanced at rockfish swimming in green-lit mini aquariums set in bricks behind us, looking like thorny prehistoric gems.

Cress said, "Forget that." He was pointing with his jutted chin toward the stage.

The deaf girl arched her body and slowly suspended herself, her eyes loose in her head, her mouth slightly open. As she raised herself, her hair cascaded to the ground with a liquid motion as if she were slowly emerging from an invisible swimming pool. There was an inconspicuous barrier of light between her and us and she was performing for a directing figure we couldn't see, marshaling her movement to his instruction, listening to his joyous screams—he might have been an invisible cameraman working her through the angles, conducting her like music, turning her body into an instrument, and it was mesmerizing. What we saw was the interpretive dance between her and the spirit; we didn't see her nakedness.

"She's like a bird in a trapped space," said Cress, his mouth agape. "She's too good to be free . . ."

She seemed happy doing what she did well. *But can she really be happy in a strip club—in conditional captivity?* Throughout her routine, there was no sound. Maybe the only sound she needed, the only overmastering voice, was inside of her, protected. She finished her routine in sudden darkness.

Don Carlos mounted the stage to roaring applause when the strobe lights came back on. There were black circles around his red eyes, and his skin seemed to have shrunk on the frame of his oversized skull. It might've been makeup, or the stage might've really been hell. He donned a black velvet cloak with red lining and wore red trunks. When he dropped the trunks, everyone gasped. "Kiss me *rass*," said a teen beside us, "him cocky look like hose!" The little man twirled like a matador and stood akimbo, giving everyone an eyeful of just how well-endowed he was, smirking this second and scowling the next, changing expressions like a clown while moving clockwise on a rotating dais. The deaf girl in the leopard suit, Rory's violinist, reemerged from behind the curtains, jiggled her ass, and went down on her belly and moved like a snake, then the little man held her as if she were a wheelbarrow and tried initiating sex.

But the MC intervened: "Don Carlos!"

"Yes," said the little man meekly, talking so low into the mic that the MC had to signal him to speak up. It struck us that he was shy, was only doing his job, and looked rather eager to get it over with.

"Las' week him fuck a goat," said a man with sorrow thick in his throat. "De week before dat, dem mek him fuck a cripple off de street. An' de week before, anodda animal."

"Again?" I asked.

"No," the man said. "Dat week it was de Doberman dat fuck *him*—all Carlos had to do was lie down . . . mercifully." He made it sound as if that act had been a much-needed break. I saw his larger point—Don Carlos was indeed fortunate to have another human for a mate this weekend. The club owners' whims were varied and cruel. "Him on contract," the man enlarged. "Haffe work here till April. Him like a tiger inna cage, an exotic bein' rented out to one zoo after de next. Las' month he was contracted at Muck and Mire."

"So it's hell after all."

"Wha' dat?"

"Nutten."

I focused on the stage again. The red-jacketed MC tugged his golden bow tie and exhorted Carlos, "Yow, boss, 'lastic an' plastic up de t'ing, enuh."

So Don Carlos dramatically squeezed on a condom that was too small. It burst like a firecracker, amplified by the mic at his groin. There was a ripple of strained laughter. The MC dipped in his silver pants and handed Carlos another rubber, flashing it first at the crowd.

"Trojan XL for Don!" yelled a patron in an odd refrain, like a spectator at the Colosseum.

When Don Carlos straddled her backward, Rory looked away. The MC handed the girl a yellow ab roller, which she gripped by both handlebars, and Carlos started wheeling her around the stage with each thrust, a fluid yet brutal motion. The deaf girl made sounds like a strangled cat, then like an engine, then something more guttural, more unplaceable, that sent shivers down my back. The MC shrilled, "Uh-oh, dat pussy gettin' tackled by de holy ghost! Look at dat midget fuck! Dumb pussy speakin' in tongues!"

A woman to the left of the stage caught my eye. It was the surprise of seeing her here—in uniform, low-cut leather belly-skin vest and sequin batty riders—that made my blood surge. I couldn't believe my luck. I immediately forgot about the stage and grabbed Marco's arm. "Call that gyal for me. The one with the tray strapped to her chest."

Marco pulled away, his eyes glued on the sex. "Call her yuhself, Messado."

"I can't, she knows me, I want it to be a surprise."

He sighed. "All right, but yuh owe me." He went off.

She was walking around serving VIPs sitting on black couches in the roped-off section. She followed Marco over with an impatient look, almost as if she were in unfamiliar territory, as if she had never deigned to work in the regular area called the Pit, farthest from the glassy stage. She still hadn't made out my face. She didn't care to.

"What's yuh name?" I whispered, holding on to the US hundred-dollar bill while her fingers grasped it.

She leaned forward. "Melissa."

"What yuh want, Melissa, a drink?"

"*T'cha*! Yuh jus' a try buss yuh pipe." Her long oval face was pale and bewitching with the sparkly makeup. She had thick twisted braids and full red lips.

I took out another hundred-dollar bill. "Yuh very sure of yuhself, aren't yuh?"

"No tree nuh inna me face," she responded, "me can get any man me want." She stepped closer, resting her lips on my chin stubble, her tray touching my arm. "Me wa'an a man fe mek me skin crawl, inna de right type ah way."

My cock got hard and I moved my face into the light.

She gasped and pulled back. "*You!* De landlawd's bwoy!"

Greg caught the remark and made a sound like a gorilla, then elbowed Chadwell.

Now I have you . . . where's your priggish attitude? I thought.

She couldn't have moved for sheer befuddlement. It was like a cruel game of tag.

"Sumaddy out fe pay dem rent," giggled Greg.

The crowd was going wild as Don Carlos rode the girl's back like a conquistador, twirling his long fake mustache and waving his floppy hat. The girl panted like a flogged horse. "Giddyup!" said Don Carlos, while the speakers played "The William Tell Overture."

"So, yuh not a hairdresser," I said, pulling her roughly to me. "Yuh know, if I tell Papa who yuh really are, yuh goin' have to move out."

"Tell him!" she screamed, but lost her bottle when she saw I was serious. She struggled but didn't pull away. "Don't *grounds* me! Yuh don't need all dat—if yuh want me, jus' say it. Don't be a coward. Dis a place of business. Act like it—doh come in here wid yuh petty childish feelings. Me have regular customers an' employers watchin' me."

On the stage they had switched roles. The girl was fucking Don Carlos with a blackjack. The little man howled as if his throat had been cut.

"*Jesus mercy*," said the man beside me, turning away from the assault.

Studying Melissa more closely than I ever had, I realized she was older than I'd imagined, around thirty-five to look at. "I want yuh—there, I said it. Now what?"

She straightened her vest, all cool and composed, handed her tray to a shorter, full-faced girl in the same outfit, and led me away by a side passage with a plush rug trimmed with lights like shooting stars. It was intended to give one the feeling they were headed to heaven, even temporarily, the fragrance here redolent, heady, as if the AC had an intoxicant. I wondered what was really in the mist, the fog.

Ska called after us, "Mums, take time with him!"

When her hand was on the doorknob, I held it. "I promise you'll enjoy this," I said for some reason.

She lowered her eyes as if she pitied me. "Sex doh feel good. Gettin' *away* from it feel good."

The room was a bright offensive pink. For each piece of clothing she slowly took off, she said, "*Mmm-mm . . . mmm*," almost as if she were sorry. She looked sad and pretty, her skin clean and soft, yet she was so grave I couldn't enjoy her beauty. She had on white full-body lingerie hugging her curves.

She lay beside me and turned her back, raising her hand to put the light out. But I stopped her. She went limp like a rabbit in a dog's mouth. She kept staring at the wallpaper, and murmured, "De fish are swimmin'."

"What?" I said behind her, spreading her thighs.

"De fish are swimmin'."

I looked at the yellow and mauve fish covering the chintzy wallpaper. "Have yuh been in this room before?"

"Too many times." She turned around to face me, her hands resting under her head like a fleshy pillow, looking deep into my eyes. "Wipe de tears off me face for me."

"Do it yuhself." I took the last of her clothes off as she lay stiff as a mannequin.

Again she looked over my head to the wallpaper as if she were trapped in a dream. "De fish are swimmin'. Yuh cyaan see it?" She rose from the bed, naked and frantic, tore off a section of the wallpaper, then lay beside me and wrapped it over her face as if she wanted to suffocate herself.

"Jesus, what's wrong with yuh?" I jumped up as if the carpet had caught fire. I wondered if she'd had too much weed or alcohol, or harder drugs. She didn't look the type. But she was having an *episode*. Its true nature, though, I was clueless about. I wrestled her down and held her and she went stiff again, her arms bent at an angle, her fists clenched, staring blankly at the wall, her head and upper body twitching. I wiped the tears for her and found myself rocking her till she fell asleep. But the sleep wasn't because of any service I had rendered. I was incapable, in whatever capacity, of helping her. It was as if she had walked into a deep sleep in her head, like opening a rescue door and closing it off from the world to restore herself. Staring at the cheap wallpaper with all the fish, I wondered what she'd really seen.

When I found the card in her clothes, it said: *IN CASE SOMETHING HAPPENS TO ME, CALL FAT BOB, 952-6547*. I called Chadwell instead. He was in another room and I could hear at least two girls giggling.

"I don't know, she just passed out, as if she has narcolepsy, dead-dead sleep."

"Well, what yuh want me to do?" Chad asked.

"Shit, I can't leave her like this."

"She'll be fine."

"There's a number here, for a Fat Bob."

"Quiet," he said, shushing the girls. "Don't call it, Nyjah. Jesus, don't yuh know anything? That's her pimp! If yuh call, *then* yuh goin' be in trouble. You'll have to pay out yuh nose. He'll charge all kinds of fees."

"Oh, yuh right. But—"

"Get out now! Just leave her before someone comes. Meet me out front."

I left and made sure to remove any sign I had been there. On our way out, we passed the bug-eyed German with a new girl on his lap. ". . . Troubleshooting . . . access failure," he grinned as he worked his hand under her clothes. She had his wallet on the glass table, counting his money bill by bill and playfully twisting her thighs, making it hard for him.

Rory sat on the pavement outside, waiting for a driver to help him into a taxi. He smiled, a painful contortion of his lips, and waved insensibly at us. We saw him totter and fall as he tried to get up. The driver came around and opened the door and beckoned him into the car, but he belched his response and then vomited into the backseat. The driver hurried around to belt him but backed off when he saw us, then refused our money. He felt insulted. He drove away with the sour smell trailing his car like the garbage truck at Dreenie's the day before.

As we walked down the driveway, Rory grabbed my shirtfront. "I fucked up with yuh, didn't I?"

"What yuh mean? With Dreenie?"

He wiped his spit away. "I guess so . . . I'm sorry."

"Don't worry 'bout it."

He curled his lips bitterly. "That cat gyal though—she played Mozart so well, so pure."

"Yuh drunk, Rory."

He got up to a wild panting, grabbed my shirt again. "Snow kept poundin' her, pullin' her knees open, but she was beyond carin', like she was in some sorta trance. She said, 'Yes, break me open, let me leave behind all the sweat, tears, blood, and . . .' Then she started chokin' and just starin' at the wall. She said somethin' like, 'Look at the ghosts of the persecuted comin' out of the past.' Snow said, 'Christ,' then she started shriekin' with her mouth open as if somethin' was goin' fly outta her body and said somethin' crazy like, 'I took them all, and if I must be the messenger of blood, so be it!' Snow tried to muzzle her while he finished, but that's when she had the fit . . ."

CHAPTER 13

I rang the buzzer of his white-gated mansion. He came down shirtless, amid fierce barking from German shepherds chained in the yard, and looked dazed. "Yuh from de masseuse agency? There's a mix-up. Is a gyal me order. Me nuh tek massage from man!"

I removed my face mask. "No, Tom, it's me." He still looked confused. "Anthony's grandson . . . who own the cement and block factory in Tucker."

He scratched the coppery white hair along his temple. "I met yuh at de café?"

"Yeah man, that day you tangled with Zetta Rosegreen 'cause of the dog."

"Oh yes, I remember! You was carryin' a cat in a cage like a tiger."

"Yeah, somethin' like that."

"Yuh wa'an come inside . . . to me house?"

"Only if you'll have me, please."

He thought for a moment then waved me in. "Come, mind de dawgs." The gate hadn't been locked. The place had a rank vacated air.

He led me through a side door into a damp-smelling, poorly lit, nondescript room; I tried to keep in mind the man he once was; that there was weight attached to his name and maybe he had some native wisdom I could partake of. Inside, the passage had a faint reek of dog shit from the yard. He threw curtains open and light flooded the richly tapestried living room. He kept a neat house on days the helper came, I surmised, but when she was off for extended periods, like this long holiday, her work gradually deteriorated and he was comfortable living like a pig, in shambles, with empty lunch boxes and beer cans on the carpet. I focused on a painting on the wall, a rim of trees that made a paling around a river, a nature scene. "Me wife painted dat." He struggled along, dragging his oxygen tank, trundling toward the kitchen. "Lemme get us some drinks."

"Don't bother," I said quickly. "I just want to talk, no hospitality necessary."

He looked disappointed, sitting down and drawing the oxygen tubes free of his smooth brown legs. "So talk, me friend."

"I raped someone, a long time ago."

He leaned back with his hands going up to his chest, as if I'd thrown him a Frisbee he wasn't expecting. "How long we talkin'?"

"Four, five years, I don't know."

"Of course yuh do—quit the lyin' if yuh need me help."

"I do . . ."

"Well, first thing, there's no statute of limitations on de book, so yuh still culpable."

This is what I wanted—the no-nonsense police grit he'd been famous for. "I know, I looked it up in the court library and Internet."

"Good bwoy . . . Well, not so good. You're a rapist. Was it you alone?"

"No, five of us."

"An' you were a minor when it happen?"

"In the company of an older bwoy."

"But I don't get the sense yuh wa'an plea coercion. A good lawyer can get yuh off after confession, even a half-wit one. But yuh reputation would still be dragged t'rough de mud an' it will affect yuh job."

"I don't care 'bout all that."

"Of course yuh don't, yuh were raised right, I can see it. You're from Tucker, normally Tucker bwoys don't—"

"I'm a Chesterite," I said to stop his blathering.

He clutched his naked breast as if having a coronary. "De beacon on de hill? Say it ain't so!"

"It is. That's where it happened. We raped a trainee."

"Gyal or bwoy?"

"Gyal, of course!"

"Don't bite me head. Plenty faggots go to dat school. Yuh sure yuh doh wa'an dat drink?" He looked more worried than I was; he kneaded his forehead. "But how? Why? You bwoys are MoBay's pride. I follow yuh every victory, TV debates, schoolbwoy football, Schools Challenge Quiz! National Indoor hockey championships. You're a paragon not to be—"

"Are yuh goin' help me or not?"

He pushed his dentures in and out of his mouth like an animated corpse. "But what exactly can me do? Dis ain't Cub Scout business. Dis is big-bwoy trouble. But why hasn't de gyal pressed charges?"

I leaned back and thought about this. "I don't know. I think they threatened her that day, got to her somehow."

"An' is it dat yuh doh like de feeling of insecurity?"

"It's not that. I just can't live with myself anymore, knowin' what happened. I feel as if I'm drownin'."

"Are yuh religious?"

"Not particularly, but I tried to be religious once—just after it happened."

"What's yuh outlet for stress if yuh doh have prayer?"

"Poetry."

"How is dat workin' out? Is enough?"

"I'm here, aren't I?"

"Well, speakin' as a man of de law, I would tell yuh to do what's right, an' yuh already know what dat is. But I know dat's easier said than done, an' trus' me, I've done some terrible t'ings. Sometimes when I remember dem I cyaan sleep. I get de feelin' dat's where yuh at now . . . or gettin' there." I nodded. "It's dat Lady

Macbeth syndrome—yuh see blood everywhere. An' yuh see de duppy dem comin' back for yuh wid blood inna dem eye 'cause dem never ready fe dead." He was rambling his heart out, wiping his bristly cheeks like a bear. "De academy psych course never teach us how to deal wid trauma when yuh step outside de law. It wasn't dem time—de victims—but yuh took dem life an' siddung wid yuh family to say grace an' eat, but all yuh see is dem faces hauntin' yuh." It sounded as if it was the closest he'd ever come to a confession.

"Tom, what if it was *your* daughter?"

He wiped his mouth, sucked on his oxygen, then stretched out, moving the side lever so his seat reclined, still and pensive. "*Brother*, to get de taste of evil out yuh mout', yuh gonna have to spit it out, doh hol' anyt'ing back."

I nodded and got up. "Thanks, Tom."

"Doh worry, come back anytime yuh feel like—an' don't rush t'ings. I know yuh gonna make de right decision, just wait for courage. Patience is part of it."

"Thank you."

"It's too late for *me*, but I've made peace wid it."

I was almost out but turned and said, "Someone trod on my ankle on the bus today and it hurt. When I turned to see who it was, I saw it was a gyal and was no longer angry. Was that unconsciously sexist? Did I think she wasn't worthy of my true feelings because she was merely a woman?"

"We was all raised wrong—to hell wid it. I know egg-zackly what yuh mean. Emotional dishonesty is only a small part of it. Trus' me. We cyaan even begin to appreciate a woman. We're freaks." He turned on the TV; he'd had porn going when I'd disturbed him. A new scene started and the players introduced themselves. There was a porn star called Ugly Man—the shock of it was, he was *really* ugly. Tom laughed, already half forgetting me, his hand down his shorts. "Where de fuck is dat masseuse?"

* * *

The next day I met Andrene. When she realized we were going to the Georgian, she tapped her stomach in delight. "Bwoy, where me go find space to put all dat food? Why yuh never tell me we goin' eat? Hold on." She took selfies of us sitting on the bike.

As we passed by a fountain near the valet booth, she posed again before lions gushing water from brazen lips. "Okay, okay, me can take a hint," she said, looking at my face in the pictures. "No more pics for now, but remember—this is *my* day." She kissed me. "Smile for me nuh, babes."

As soon as she saw Chadwell, her bonhomie evaporated. "What's he doin' here?"

"He got us seats—they're very hard to get, especially on holidays—and asked to see yuh."

"See *me*? What for? *You* more likely. Yuh couldn't say no to him?" She made a clacking sound with her teeth.

Chadwell stood up and buttoned his blue blazer. "Guys, I've been sittin' here like a model without a painter. What took yuh so long?" He kissed Andrene, but she greeted him coldly and frowned at his cologne. He raised his eyebrow and mouthed, *What's her problem?*

I shrugged. But I figured it was her guilt at having seen Chadwell when she was with Burberry Dalton.

"Happy birthday, dearest," he said. "Yuh look nice. Love the feathery hair."

"T'anks."

I took out her present. She opened the box and gasped with a soft wet sound, removing the necklace that unfurled against her wrist. "Nyjah, me love it! Put it on, *please*!" She turned around. Chadwell narrowed his eyes. When it was around her neck, she examined the pendant. It was a fat little Buddha smiling inside a delicately wrought shrine. "It's unique." She batted her long gaudy eyelashes. "Where yuh get it?"

"Kingston."

"Yuh go Kingston? When? Widout me?"

I laughed. "I had a poetry reading. The jeweler said this was the only one she brought back from Japan."

She twirled it. "An' no one in de whole country have anodda one. T'ank you, sweetie." She kissed me again.

The couple beside us smiled.

I handed them my phone. "Can yuh take a picture of the three of us, please? It's her birthday."

"Sure," said the man. "Happy birthday!"

"Chad, take one of just me and Andrene."

"Oh, here he comes," Chad said with a smile.

The waiter walked over with a small white cake spitting sparks, accompanied by a violinist. "*Happy birthday to you . . .*"

Everyone turned to see who it was. When they set the cake down, Dreenie became shy.

The woman with the violin played staccato notes like a villain's score as Dreenie blew out the candles to courteous applause. The waiters bowed and left.

"Funny havin' dessert so early, before everythin' else," said Chadwell. Dreenie glanced up at him. "Enjoy—it's all on me."

"I intend to," she retorted.

Chadwell sat back, unbuttoning his blazer. "I've a sweet tooth today. How 'bout you guys? No? Mind if I get the ball rollin'?"

The waiter came back with wine and Chadwell made a show of sniffing and tasting it, even though I knew he'd never send it back. Clicking his full glass against hers and mine, he said, "To the birthday gyal, and friendship—with all its complexities." He sipped. "A lot has changed, yuh know, Dreenie. Otherwise, we—me and Nyjah—could have never invited yuh to this place. Yuh lucky I invited yuh here at all."

She put the glass down. "What yuh gettin' at?"

"I'm just sayin' . . . we have a lot to be grateful for." He avoided my eyes the whole time.

The food came and we looked down at it. Andrene started hurrying through hers, not enjoying it. When the waiter came around again, Chadwell ordered more food that he kept eating carelessly—empanadas, crispy baked wings. Andrene was too nervous to eat anything else, but he didn't seem to notice.

Chadwell reached for some popcorn shrimp, then pulled his hand away. "Where's my manners? Ladies first." Dreenie refused. "Oh, come now, don't be modest. Yuh don't know when you'll be able to feast like this again. Try the fritters. They cook them so well here." His face went big because he had a laugh sealed up in it as he watched her uncertainty. "There, there, dear. Lemme start yuh off with a little aperitif then. That course was only the warm-up."

She looked to me helplessly, but I turned away. Perhaps I should've rescued her, but my annoyance was cutting both ways so my charity was bankrupt. I grabbed one of the crab cakes and stuffed it in my mouth, miserable with myself.

Chadwell took his time chewing a fritter, then said, "Want me to suggest somethin'?"

To my surprise, Dreenie nodded, responding to his manipulation.

He gestured slightly and the waiter came over. "Waiter, brioche and more coffee for the lady, please."

The waiter said, "What flavor?"

Andrene could only blink. The waiter looked at her, then looked away in embarrassment and back to Chadwell.

"Maple," Chad said.

When the brioche came and Dreenie bit into it, she spat out the sugar crystals as if they were glass shards. People around us cringed.

Chadwell let out a harsh burst of laughter. "That's the French surprise!"

I went aquiver with anger. Why do this with Dreenie? *He's out to make a fool of me*, I thought, taking his oafish games personally.

From that point on, things only got worse. When Dreenie unconsciously leaned toward me for support, I pulled my chair away. She was furious, but shame stultified her rage.

"Would you care for a cordial, ma'am?" asked the hovering waiter, in on the game now.

"Ah wha'?" Dreenie said as she pushed away the milky coffee.

"A liqueur, my dear gyal, to warm yuh cockles," said Chadwell. "Reorient the buds."

"Orange juice," she said. "Cold."

"Freshly squeezed if yuh can," said Chadwell. He kept chewing until the plate in front of him was clean.

I got up. "I need a word with yuh."

Chad played the innocent.

"Now!"

We walked to the terrace. Before I could say anything, he began, "She's a zit. Pop her and get it over with."

"Fuck you, yuh actin' like a brat."

"Oh-hoh, the Good Samaritan!"

"Yuh just can't bear to see me happy—to see anyone happy. Why you always have to suck the fuckin' air outta the room?"

"This is *me* yuh talkin' to!"

I threw back my head. "Right. When were yuh goin' tell me?"

"Tell yuh what?"

"That you've been to see her—Maude."

He blinked, lost all his poise. "Castleigh . . . the sonuvabitch."

"Yuh goin' give me the address. If not now, then later. And yuh goin' back to that table and apologize. Yuh hear me?"

He stretched his lips. "Aye-aye."

We both heard a familiar voice saying, ". . . certain of the men at the car wash let it be known that . . ." When we looked around, we spotted Perry and Marvin Mighty sitting at a table, toasting over a bread basket. They saw us and waved.

"Perry?" I said. But he looked away.

When we returned, Chadwell sat, smiling at Dreenie as he dipped into his bag in the basket at his feet. "Here, I got yuh this. Nyjah told me yuh like stargazing."

It was a small golden telescope, beautiful, exquisite. She held it tenderly and was so overcome she couldn't open her mouth. He had surprised me again. I hated him for it.

He reached across the table to show her the inscription. "I could teach yuh the constellations."

"No," she responded, looking at him squarely. "T'ank yuh. I know all de major ones. Maybe it's *I* who should teach *you*."

I entered through the postern again, a gate I'd hardly used since I was a child. The taxi had brought me the long way around; I hadn't noticed because I'd been replaying the events from lunch and the driver had to shout. As I walked into the yard, I mentally checked if I'd put out enough food for PJ and glanced at Melissa's house. They weren't there. The curtains were closed and the chairs were upturned on the verandah. *A curator like Lois, hiding out in a country museum like an asylum*, I thought.

When I stepped through the back door, Mama exhaled softly in surprise. Cam gangled into the kitchen, smiling with her eyes and delicate mouth. "We'd given up on yuh."

Tony took my bag and mumbled his greeting.

"I went to Kingston yesterday and had lunch with Dreen today. It's her birthday."

Mama looked disappointed. "So how yuh goin' eat now? And when we meetin' this gyal?"

"He can't decide which one to bring," Cam smirked. "That's his problem."

After we said grace in the dining room, Mama told me, "Yuh grandfather leggo a ton o' money playing Kiwanis Club bingo."

"Ah," I sighed, "a man out of his depth on a freshly mopped floor."

Tony laughed. Papa scowled—he didn't like to be mocked, even slightly. "Den dey have de cheek to lie to everybody dat de money goin' to charity." He sounded genuinely aggrieved.

"But it is," Mama said. "Didn't Bradley turn over his winnings? Yuh see him wid yuh own eyes."

"I doh trus' it," Papa responded, breaking water crackers into his cock soup.

"What yuh doh trus'? Yuh eyes?" Mama teased.

"What happenin' at work?" Lois asked.

I was happy for this. Usually I was dinnertime entertainment till I crossed the invisible line of decency and Mama had to reel me in. "They treat the principal's office like a bomb shelter: only worthies are allowed in. I'm at my wit's end trying to elevate myself."

Lois cackled, "Nyjah, yuh too wicked."

"Is true."

"How the children?" Mama asked, trying to quiet us down.

I swallowed a spoonful of stewed plum. "I do not doubt that they will come. Come around to their senses, that is, if they have any. Most of them are so *dull*."

When my grandmother was vexed she was predictable; first she sighed, then fussed needlessly with things. She kept rearranging the crochet mats beneath the Pyrex dishes. "I'm worried 'bout yuh wid dat attitude . . . yes. A teacher is supposed to see de best in him students, not mouthin' off like a juvenile behind dem back." She herself was a retired schoolteacher.

"Mama, it's so hard with these kids though. Is like they go out of their way to make things difficult."

"Because dey wa'an see if yuh really care. Children are very sensitive. And dem hate condescension."

"I don't condescend."

"No? Then what yuh call tellin' dem, *There is an everydayness about crime now*? So dem shouldn't be unduly worried?"

"I call it givin' them practical advice. Why should they walk around with their hearts in their throats worried about being robbed? This country has more pickpockets than civil servants; we have to coexist."

"Too bad pickpockets don't pay taxes from their earnings," said Lois. "The informal economy is ruining us."

"Derails progress," echoed Cam.

"Yuh tellin' dem to let dem guard down, Nyjah."

"I beg to differ, Mama."

"Yuh givin' dem half-baked advice, which dem will unwittingly apply to dem studies. Yuh being myopic. Can't yuh see it will affect dem expectations and esteem?"

I sighed. "I wish I hadn't showed yuh that speech."

"So? What's the tale within de main story here?" Mama said.

"Excuse me?" She had an irritating way of using these turns of phrase that forced you to ask for clarification, like a game show host toying with contestants.

"What's behind dis half commitment to yuh job? What yuh jumpy 'bout so much yuh takin' it out on de kids? What's de true emergency?"

"The true *what*? Listen, if at least 50 percent of my final-year students don't pass with at least a grade three, I'm out of a job. That's it—it's down to performance."

"Results, yuh mean," said Lois. "I'll tell yuh what, Mama."

"What?"

"If not anything, he's outwardly committed. I saw him downtown with chalk on his backside and he didn't even care—the first sign he's immersed, finally and shamelessly a teacher."

"Child, doh be facetious."

Lois and Cam exchanged glances and muffled giggles.

"I can't pussyfoot around. I have bills."

"And yuh t'ink dem parents don't?" said Mama. "Yuh t'ink education is all about a grade on paper? A paper yuh can burn like trash?"

"I do. I don't care if they have to cheat to get it—I need to keep my job. It's like being sat there in the lunchroom with a stupid look on my face, thinking, *Hell, I'm goin' to hate this food but I need to be a chum, a team player*—punishin' myself. At the end of the day, none of that really matters, does it? 'Cause if the boss-woman, Hobart, comes April with the big stick and points at me, I can tell yuh, it's goin' to be my last supper."

"Yuh have to show boss-lady what yuh did with yuh talents," said Cam.

"The woman is practically Jesus."

"Don't blaspheme," Papa spoke up, chewing his hot yams with his mouth half-open and steaming like a demon's.

"Anthony, him not blasphemin'," said Mama. "Don't be ridiculous, him tryin' to make a point."

Papa dropped his fork and we all froze. He put his coarse-skinned elbows on the table and knitted his thick fingers, sucking his teeth clean with a nasty noise, then stuck his pinky in his mouth to finish the job, imposing himself with crude manners, slow and cold-blooded like a reptile. "So lemme get dis straight. Is yuh job to interpret for me now?"

"Why yuh actin' dis way?" Mama said without looking at him, her spoon stopping halfway to her mouth.

"How I actin'? I jus' wa'an know—not to stop all-yuh civilized conversation, but jus' to know if I so stupid I cyaan tell de difference between black an' white, an' need me wife to point it out—to shovel pap in me mout'."

I looked at Cam but she had her eyes on her plate, making swirling patterns with the curdling gravy. Mama wiped her mouth with her napkin and sipped her ginger beer.

Papa stared in her face, and we could feel her wilting, not daring to raise her head. "Answer me, woman!" he shouted, and bammed the table with his palm, knocking over the guava jelly. Tony started sniffling. "Dis bwoy insultin' de Lawd—wid him mout' runnin' like him nyam chicken batty. Dis truant—dis *runaway*—who nyam people money an' keep dodgin' duty at de cement factory! Who take responsibility for nutten! Yuh spoil him!"

For some strange reason, Mama turned her attention to the boy and scolded him feebly, "Tony, what yuh cryin' for? Yuh have tears to waste?"

Tony sobbed and dropped his arms. He could see what was coming like a wailing prophet. Mama continued smiling vacantly at the child, ignoring Papa's anger. He was seething now, blowing so hard his chest sent tremors into the table. I signaled Lois and she got up to take Mama into the kitchen, but Papa saw the play and preempted us. He struck her, full and hard. We all gasped as if it were the first time he'd done it. It always took us by gut-wrenching surprise, his calm, calculated violence. Mama's head sat back on her neck in awkward yet ugly defiance, her eyes aggressive yet scared. She looked him dead in the eye and got up and went from the dining room to the kitchen sink to wash the blood off.

Papa started eating again and made clinking noises with his knife and fork, and said into the dead silence like a gentleman, "Excuse me." The sink was still running.

Tears flooded my eyes; my hand went limp around my fork. I felt frightened of what I was about to do. Lois and Cam stayed quiet. Tony looked as if he wanted to run, though his tears had dried. Mama sat back down and started chewing her plantain slice, but couldn't manage it. Her top lip was still bleeding.

Cam covered her mouth in horror and screamed, "Mama!"

I pushed my chair back and stood, but he was ready for me. He flew up, reaching for his own chair. I didn't care anymore.

Lois blocked my path. "Nyjah, don't!"

Mama held her bust-up lip and bawled, "Anthony, him nuh know better!"

What does she mean by that? Making an excuse for my behavior as if I'm *the culpable one and he isn't a monster?*

Lois kept pushing me back. On *Willoughby's Evening People's Show*, they were playing "D.A.N.C.E." by Justice. "*Get ready to ignite . . .*"

Tony shouted, "No!" as I raced through the side door and picked up a stick and circled to the verandah. Papa met me coming down the steps, armed with his cutlass. My aunts were screaming.

"No more of this!" I shouted, pacing in the yard. "I told yuh I'd kill yuh and I ain't jokin'!"

"Come," he said, showing his big perfect teeth. "Come, Missa Nyjah, me ready fe dead!"

Mama stood at the living room window, gripping the curtains

with a blank terror on her face as if the house were on fire and she was trapped.

My rage had me in a vise. I wasn't even scared of the cutlass. "I warn yuh once," I said, dipping for a sizable rock as the yard fowls scattered and flapped and squawked. "I warn yuh twice. Stop puttin' yuh hand on them!"

Our neighbor Joyce rattled her fence. "Nyjah, you'll ketch trouble!"

I feinted and he moved in lumbering confusion. I gauged my aim like when we would fling at birds in *bud bush*. I fired the rock and it hit him squarely in the chest.

He staggered and bit his tongue and rasped, "To bum-willings!" He fetched up against the wall to gather his strength, but Cam threw herself before him. He used the back of his arm to shove her aside like a rag doll.

I took the opportunity to cover the space between us, then reached down and grabbed his ankle, sending him sprawling on his back. He hit his head on the landing and lay with his eyes shut, his fingers twitching. He looked like a big spider on its back.

"Papa!" Tony screamed, and it was the fervor of the boy's response that revealed everything, like Solomon's women and the contested baby. "Don't yuh hurt me fawda!" he shouted, wresting the cutlass from Papa's half-dead grip to come at me.

Lois grabbed his shirt. I felt weak-kneed and terrible looking down at Papa's face. Mama had rushed out and was bent over him, cradling his head.

Joyce had her hands on her head, screaming and jiggling her bosom. "Murdah!"

Mama called out, "Jocelyn, shut yuh mout' 'fore I t'row water on yuh! An' if yuh breathe a word 'bout Tony to anybody . . ."

Joyce went quiet and spiteful at Mama's belittling tone. She had ammunition to use against us, our family who people had always accused of being snobbish. She looked at us coldly, then hurried into her house.

"Come," said Mama, "gwaan back ah Porto Bello."

"Mama, who Tony be to us?" I demanded, glancing at the fuming child with his red eyes and runny nose.

"Shut up dis goddamn minute! Don't yuh see yuh grandfather lyin' on de floor?"

"He's breathin'," said Lois, wrapping a bandage around his head; it bloomed with spots of blood. "Cam, get a warm rag and pass the smellin' salts. Hurry, gyal!"

Cam dashed inside.

"Come gwaan, Nyjah, we'll take care of this," said Lois.

"What if he takes a turn for the worse?" I said, peering at his bearded face lolling in her arms, his lower lip hanging open to show his dark gums and food-stained teeth—he looked like a butchered ram. I wished he were dead. Yet my heart grieved for what I had done.

"Come gwaan!" barked Mama. "Tony, get Nyjah's t'ings."

Tony skulked off.

They stretched Papa out on the verandah and passed smelling salts under his nose and wrapped his head again. Cam phoned the ambulance.

I counted my steps all the way home and waited for my phone to ring, not knowing what would be good news or bad. My head was hot and heavy with all the deceits and debilitating secrets of my family. Now I saw the resemblance, the long, oval lower face like a capybara's. *So Tony is my uncle*, I thought with crippling shame and disgust.

CHAPTER 14

The principal, Mrs. Hobart, stuck her head in the staff room doorway and smiled at me. "A minute . . ."

We sat down and she came right out with it, looking on with her steely manner: her payday face. "I'm afraid this month's salary will be delayed for some time, Messado."

"What? I'm practically working for free now. You haven't paid me for the last two months."

She popped a Mento in her mouth and had the nerve to offer me one. "Listen—"

I jumped out of my chair. "No, *you* listen, I don't want a dragée and I don't want another excuse, I want what I worked for. You people jokin', man . . . Yuh serious? No, no . . ."

She screwed up her face, looking at me stolidly. "A *dragée*? What's that?"

"Look it up!" I stormed out of the poorly lit trailer office smelling of kerosene and wood chips. *The smell of stagnation, of failure.* "And I want my money by month's end!" I called back at her.

I returned to my desk but was too livid to carry on marking papers. I didn't have classes till three thirty, so I left.

Five minutes after I entered Juici Patties, Perry Fischer and Philip Moodie came in.

"There he is," beamed Philip, walking over and playfully slapping my chest, "the man with impeccable manners, who truly knows how to conduct himself. Nyjah, help me out, I'm tellin' Perry that Strand is the only movie house left with an old-fashioned marquee, with the white facade and red glowing letters." He looked at me like an importunate puppy, as if a rebuff would leave him heartbroken; it was almost sad to see what gangsterism had done to him.

"But how would *you* know, Philip?" I replied. "Yuh hardly leave town."

He was wearing an old Chester jacket, a yellow jersey with red details, and still had the small ageless look of a school brat. Someone had cut him, and they would've done it deliberately to spoil his pretty-boy looks. Just below his left eye was a thickly braided scar that trembled when he spoke. He pointed to it, half sneering, half smiling, in that crazy way of his. "Like it?"

"If I were you, I'd stay away from lineups."

He laughed hard, a big, bright, false-looking-teeth laugh; he smiled as if his face were going to fall off or break open, so ebullient yet horrific it made me apprehensive for him. They had also smashed his mouth in and he was wearing plates.

"Damn, Philip," I said, wincing, "they really worked yuh over."

"Nyjah, don't worry, the fuckers who did this won't see me comin'. I go use their evil 'gainst them. *May they not be my oracles as well. And set me up in hope?*" He put his finger to his lip. "*But hush, no more.*" After speaking these words, he left us.

"Bye, Banquo," I said, raising an eyebrow at Perry.

Perry said nothing and went to the counter to order. I noticed for the first time how thin he looked since he'd come back from medical school. Now all he did was loiter at the car wash. Kept dragging his feet about finishing his degree—this was what Briana was so worried about.

He sat before me, throwing pieces of beef patty in his mouth and rolling them around on his pierced tongue. "Workin' hard, Messado?"

"You know me . . ."

"I do—that's why I asked."

I chuckled. "Fuck you, faggot."

He lost some of his levity, eating slowly and watching my face. He could be unpredictable, even after he'd come out of the closet. He thumped my shoulder and blew cigarette smoke at me.

"Yuh can't smoke in here."

He ignored me; the guard didn't say anything because he knew Perry ran with Mighty. He looked at me through half-lidded eyes. "Work isn't beautiful but it's necessary. To keep the likes of you from going to rot."

"I don't need yuh half-baked platitudes."

"That's not what I'm givin' yuh," Perry said.

"No, yuh think yuh givin' me advice, but yuh only playin' God. That's all yuh like to do nowadays."

He dropped ash on the floor; the old lady next to us pulled away. "Well, not all. I like to fuck men too."

We stared at each other and laughed. "Has ever a man been more sorely tried than our dear Perry?" I tutted. "I hear yuh performin' like a backseat driver at the car wash, runnin' Fruity's crew like a cloak-and-dagger general."

"Don't believe everythin' yuh hear. Especially 'bout me or Fruits."

"No? Set me straight then."

"I've been trying to set my own self straight long enough—why do yuh tempt me with impracticalities?"

"Haha. Droll Fish . . . By the way, Norma said to thank yuh again for Pearl's braces."

"The whole city needs cosmetic dentistry." He flicked his cigarette butt through a window and scrolled through his phone, starting on a jelly roll and wagging his head; he showed me his screen. "Look at this nonsense: *Also charged with possession of a bladed article*. Why don't they just say *knife*? Who are they writin' for with this pompous language anyway? Reading the *Mirror* nowadays is like drinkin' cold porridge. Don't you work there?"

"Blame yuh sister—she edits it."

A wistful look twisted his face. "Briana . . . the optimist. How's school?"

"Perry, I've my worst batch later, every opportunity they wreck a class. Is like I'm smilin' while they cut my neck."

"Any hot gyals there?"

"What do you care?"

"Humor me, man."

"Okay, there's this one young teacher, I asked her if she was married and she answered quickly, 'No, but I have a rabbit.' It was so funny and strange."

"What did yuh say?"

"I said, 'It's good, it's good that yuh have a pet.'"

"Yuh fool, don't yuh realize *rabbit* means a dildo?" said Perry.

"No . . . really?"

He shook his head. "Yuh so naive, Messy. It's goin' to get yuh in trouble."

"Yuh jokin', right? Yuh runnin' with the mob and worried 'bout me? Seriously, Fish—how yuh copin'?"

He stopped eating and simply looked lost. "Yuh ever seen a leaf blowin' on the ground, Messado, and have the sensation that it's a butterfly? Like an illusion but at the same time . . ."

"But at the same time, what, *real*?"

He pulled at the scraggly beard on his long chin, his movements becoming slightly animated, along with the quality of his voice. "Sometimes I'd take up the leaf and hold it in my palm and wait, sure that when I open my hand things will be different somehow. That it will fly away."

"Yuh sound depressed."

"Do I?"

"Well, yuh not happy. That's plain. I used to follow yuh at school. Yuh never knew. Whenever yuh thought no one was watchin', you'd climb the staircase at eighth-grade block. And stand there at the top where Smokey kept his buckets and mops, facin' the wall. Why?"

"I wanted to get used to the idea of a dead end. I was preparin' myself for the future."

"Yuh still feel the same way?"

He didn't answer. He ran his hand down his long face; his red skin had turned almost auburn since he'd been out in the sun so much in the car-wash lot and by WOW, the disco nightclub across from it that the gay boys also ran, old-talking with half-wits he treated like his dearest friends, playing *Ludo*, drinking champagne from open bottles.

"Why yuh keep shirkin' med school? Yuh could be miles ahead right now."

"Miles ahead of what? Besides, Marvin's takin' care of me."

"That doesn't answer the question."

"It does, it's just not the answer yuh want to hear."

"Like the way he took care of yuh at school? Takin' yuh milk money? Extortin' yuh for 'protection'? Runnin' with the car-wash bwoys is the real dead end, Perry. I'm sure yuh see that."

He crushed the rest of his patty in the bag till it became greasy and soft. "My parents cut me off. Didn't Bree tell yuh?"

"With all that telephone-scam money Mighty's makin', he can pay yuh tuition three times over. Or is it that he doesn't want yuh to leave him? That's it, isn't it?"

He got up. "See yuh round."

"See yuh, Fish."

He saluted me and stalked off.

I put on my noise-reduction earphones and resumed writing a review of a new compilation album.

It's ironic that the greatest dancehall song, Sister Nancy's "Bam Bam," should be from a woman, when dancehall is such a male-dominated genre, very much a men's club, like the classical period of music in its European heyday. "Bam Bam," a song which almost didn't get made because she had to struggle for studio time,

I looked up and he was there the next second, like one of those cheap magic tricks. He sat before me where Perry had, drumming his fingers on the Formica surface, then scraping it with his chunky tarnished ring. "Enjoying yuh patties, Teach? I didn't know yuh eat at Juici Patties."

"Who are you?" I asked, taking off the headphones, trying to throw him.

"A close friend to a friend, man. Me lay dung wid yuh gyal too. She never tell yuh?"

A group of brown-skirted cosmetology students had bustled through the door and the noise had made me nearly miss his words. "Say again?"

"*Say again?*" he mocked, his smirk now a grimace. Keloid ran down his nose along the twisted bridge, surely inflicted by someone's knife. I went back to my writing, ignoring him.

has found rejuvenation through the sampling of Baby Wayne—our local DJ who is brilliant and overlooked, but who thankfully appears on this compilation.

He flipped my computer around and read what I'd written as if outraged, and snarled, "His brilliance is *not* overlooked! It's there to be discovered by those who care. Wha' de fuck yuh preppy bwoys know 'bout ghetto culture anyway? I first bring Baby Wayne go studio an' haffe bruk him hand when him doh pay me back me loan wid interest."

"That must've been painful," I said, biting into my callaloo loaf and pointing at his scar.

He leaned back and dropped his hands in the well of his baggy jeans. "I used to be a schoolbwoy goalkeeper, best in Cornwall County. But never win Dacosta Cup, never got me recognition. We school always lose to Chester. I hate every fuckin' one o' yuh. Even now when dem come to me shop, I doh sell dem a pin. I go outta me way fe mek life prickly fe dem, 'cause I carryin' a unhealable wound here." He thumped his bony chest beneath the white wifebeater.

"Must be tough. Carryin' around that grudge."

He looked scandalized, with the fidgety aggression and onion eyes of a cokehead. "Yuh t'ink I envy yuh—is that what yuh t'ink?" He showed me his silver-capped teeth.

It was Burberry Dalton—his hair in that odd bell-shaped high-top. But what did he want with me? I was afraid and I was not afraid—I was used to being intimidated from my days of getting robbed en route to school by Fuller Canterbury thugs.

"Hear me out," I said.

He raised his hand. "No, yuh doh get to talk—not to me, pussy'ole. Not today. Eat yuh food." He stood, stared me down, and walked out, making sure I saw the Cuban cutlass in his waist. The chubby guard looked away when Dalton froze him with a threatening glare.

I finished my lunch, watching him head down the street with his chest and midriff sunken, as if anticipating an attack, his arms not swinging when he walked—he might've been a dead man doing a bad impression of the living.

I went back to the parking lot behind Cheng's supermarket. My bike was gone. I threw my keys at a fence and shouted, "Bumboclaat!" I knew Dalton had something to do with it.

When I entered the Gun Court's Vehicle Theft Unit, it looked half-abandoned. Milk bottles with smiling cows on them were strewn out front. Two officers rounded the corner like ghosts, their voices startling me; they were both young and handsome, upbeat in their brisk demeanor and gait, and surprisingly courteous. When they offered a nod, I kept my mouth shut dumbly instead of asking for help. I walked through a passage with a gutted roof. The walls peeled and flaked with mildew, rats scurried about, busy and fierce, hardly minding my presence. I had to lift my feet to not obstruct their walkways. Someone had spray-painted the word *Magenta* above the cellblock and I heard inmates eating. The squishy sound of the food was even worse than the bland, warm smell. When I peered through the broken bars of another empty trash-strewn room, I realized I was on the wrong side of the building. I went back around.

"I made a bad turn just now," I said to the front desk officer.

"Did yuh? A walk on the wrong side of the law, eh?"

"No, the building."

"Same difference." He had a face like a pestered pigeon's, all jaws and mean little eyes. I reported what had happened and he frowned at something in his book. "Yuh been here before."

"Is that a question?" I realized I didn't like him.

He toyed with the mint ball in his mouth, then spat it in a corner of the cramped front quarters. No one else dared look up from their desks. "Makepeace!" he shouted. "Someone here to see yuh—an ol' friend."

The officer who came out was the same one who'd interrogated me that day of Bussy's death. He didn't betray any knowledge of our former meeting, though, and acted withdrawn as he led me to a room without a window. But instead of being hot, it was almost freezing in there, dank with a dungeon-like atmosphere; I was immediately uncomfortable.

"Listen, I made the report and need to get back to—"

He put his finger to his lips, pulled out two chairs—he sat me down and closed the door with an immensely pleased expression, as if he'd just sealed the Ark, as if we were the only two people left in the world. There was no table this time, no barrier. He leaned forward and pulled his chair close. His expression was empty of friendliness.

"What a coincidence. I had a strange case this mornin'—if yuh'd believe it, another bus killin'." He massaged his neck. "Buses ain't safe no more, bwoy. Imagine, a man seated and another standin' over him, and because him standin' he put his bag in the overhead, just to relieve his hands. But fish oil from his lunch dripped through the bag and fell on the sittin' man's head. And just like *that!*" He clapped his hands and startled me. "They fought—one end up dead, stabbed in the chest."

"Which one was it?"

"That's the question, isn't it? Was it the one anointed with fish oil?" He scratched his chin. "Who deserves to die here? Which bastard don't deserve to live? I hear the concern in yuh voice. Yuh rootin' for the man who'd been standin', no?"

I didn't answer his question. Instead I said, "Whoever was travelin' with a knife—him I have no pity for."

"Tell yuh what—last week an even worse case: a couple fight in their house. Man break in his wife's phone, find texts to Joe Grind. How she can't wait to feel his hood in her throat, so she comin' to fuck him at lunchtime. Yuh know what the husband did?"

My body stiffened with dread. *This room is like a fridge.*

"He delivered her bloody nose in a wedding-ring box to her parents. The mother fainted when she opened it. What kinda heart it take for a man to cut off his own wife's nose and ride halfway 'cross town, cool as yuh like, and deliver it to her mooma?"

"Mummy used to cheat . . . with that fat bastard, Senior. That's why they divorced. It's her fault. They're probably still fuckin'." I didn't know why I was being so generous with my thoughts, but when I said this I felt relief, like a cold shower down my back. And there was more I longed to say.

He could see it. He screwed his face tight as if trying to decide whether or not to bestow pity on me. He said flatly, "Both men sharin' a bunk 'cross the yard. Now tell me, what happened?"

I could hardly open my mouth now. My complaint seemed so petty. But it was just one of his intimidation tactics. I realized something: I was learning not to be shocked by any of this, I was learning to see the bigger picture of his small-mindedness, this pathetic little world where he wielded negligible power. "I'm sure they told you—my bike was stolen. I filled out the form."

He threw his legs open, sighed, looking into my eyes. "We grew up rough, Nyjah—can I call you Nyjah? When I was younger I was afraid all the time. I kept askin', *Is this the day? Is it goin' to be me?* I grew up in Fuller Canterbury during *the regime*. Toughest times in MoBay. Friends tried to survive the turf wars. Yet we kept dyin' one by one and no one really survived—not even me—'cause with each funeral, a piece of yuh was buried, a piece of yuh was lost. Yuh became less human. Easier to be controlled by the 'spirits,' the gunmen who were like gods. I developed an oversensitivity, a sixth sense that makes me good at my job, that makes me sniff out criminals like they wearin' Cuss Cuss."

The phrase alarmed me, brought Maude back to mind because that was the cologne she wore during gym, that musky manly scent—as if trying to become one of us.

"Yuh mentioned yuh mother. My mother survived a heart attack at the age of thirty-six, when I was young. The fear of losin' her was constantly with me as I grew up. I could tell she'd die soon. She died of a second heart attack at forty-seven, though we're not quite there yet."

"But it'll have to do," I said, standing. "I've made my report and I need to get out of here. I can't hear yuh out—sorry."

He stood too, straightening his jacket and putting a hand on my shoulder. "Yuh med-student friend, Perry Fischer, tell him to get out."

My knees wobbled and I sat back down. "Wha'—wha' yuh mean?"

"*Wha' yuh mean*, haha! Yuh sound like a yardie. Real patois!" He crossed his legs and played with his pants hem. "We watchin' those car-wash bwoys, story soon come to bump. The scammin' is baby steps, what they're spreadin' 'bout to make people feel their *pettifoggin'*. Movin' big numbers. They mix coke like baby formula—they fill the spoon with powder, level it off with a knife. Get the picture?"

I nodded.

He patted my cheek. "Warn him, tell him to get out. It too late for Mighty and Colin and Bolo. And we all know Philip Moodie is a psycho. Him beyond the pale."

Now the room did feel like the Ark. And he was either God or Noah. How deep was his knowledge? *Is he omniscient?* A heat rose through my stomach that told me I couldn't take much more of his bald-faced baiting talk. "You're a narcissist, Makepeace, yuh like playin' God. Yuh expect me to run to Fischer and make a fool of myself? Yuh sowin' seeds to help yuh own operation. Don't try to use me. I've been manipulated enough for one week."

"Somethin' tells me that's the pot calling the kettle black."

"Yuh sizin' me up now?"

"Careful there, I've some years on yuh. Yuh still have some ways to go. When bird fly too fast, him pass him nest."

"Don't quote me yuh insipid proverbs . . . Now I'm itchin' for a cigarette."

He took out a Craven A.

"No, I only smoke Matterhorn."

He lit it for himself and shook out the match. "'Course yuh do, yuh one of Smokey's bastard children."

To this day, I don't remember exiting the room.

As I walked home that afternoon, I saw Zetta Rosegreen waddling over Tucker Bridge without her dog. She swayed so badly it looked as if the wind would pick her up like a sheet of zinc. The last time I'd seen her she was snatching up cigarette butts on the beach with a tong and dropping them in a scandal bag, a very far way from home. I'd worried for her that morning, hoping she'd find her way back.

As soon as she saw me, she sobered up a spell and thrust her neck out, but was still moving with the same sluggish motion, probably trying to shake off the cobwebs of drink. I was sure she had a message in her mouth.

"Where's yuh dog?" I began, meeting her halfway.

She batted the question away with a truculent wave. Then she grabbed my palm and half opened her mouth, her breath burning my face. "You know where you get your lines from? Your mother's womb."

"Huh?"

"Human hands develop palmar creases in the womb; I can see your lines were developed at around the eleventh week of gestation. And you're in the eleventh hour. You're in trouble, son."

"Tell me."

"What have you been doing?" she demanded.

"I've . . . been writin'," I said weakly.

"No! You've been sitting! A writer does his best writing away from the computer screen, when he's thinking on his feet. Have you been pondering your sins?"

"What must I do?"

She did it with a brass neck, mumbling, half-cut: she tossed the quarter bottle of JB into the grass. She was obviously coming from the river shop, the rum bar almost exclusively catering to men near the bridge where Tucker's tributary plunged toward Great River. That was where she "walked" on her waters—where people often saw her communing with river spirits, shrieking at reeds as if they were witnesses—after running up her tab at the bar, promising to pay in gold coins. Was I that desperate, so overwrought to be duped by a madwoman? Yet I couldn't release her. I felt I could tolerate anyone who took even a scant interest in my anguish and offered a way out, or the semblance of one. Her movements were heavy, stolid, filled with slow blood, filled with concern from the bottom of her dusty feet up.

"I come from the river with a message!"

"What is it? Am I to . . . ?"

The silvery lids of her eyes fluttered, the corners of her painted mouth danced with the shock of all she'd seen in my future—or past. She was reading me thoroughly. She had her spirit on today like a cap. She hadn't been in her element, I remembered, that morning near the beach—there had been no drink in her. Now she rocked back and forth. "You knew you'd meet me today, didn't you?"

"I did?" I said like a dummy.

"The dream you had."

"Oh yes," I lied. Or maybe I *had* augured this meeting—I was all mixed up. I wanted so badly to believe.

"Don't worry," she said, then threw her chiffon scarf around my neck and pulled me into her caustic breath. "Come, take me upstairs."

"You mean . . ."

I did it without question, like an automaton.

Mrs. Lombard was on the verandah peeling carrots and Irish potatoes into a bowl, and gave us a strange look, as if watching a funeral procession, or a circus act, something sad and absurd rolled into one. Maybe the burial of a clown. It didn't help that Zetta Rosegreen was high-stepping like a ballerina and being peremptory with me, fussy like an old hen in clownish makeup and her pale chiffon dress rustling as she tottered.

"Where's my bottle?" she asked suddenly. "Did you take it?"

Mrs. Lombard stifled a laugh and sucked her teeth, watching with disbelief as we plodded up the steps.

Zetta Rosegreen led me to the bedroom as if she knew where it was. It was meant to be as sacred and ridiculous as it all was now—we straddled two worlds when she straddled me, the sacred and profane, the faith-filled and absurd. She was tiny-boned and light, like a jockey on top of a horse. The blood turned to water in my veins. *Am I really doing this?* She dipped into her shirt and took what looked like smelling salts from somewhere between her withered breasts and stuck them up her nostrils as if to give herself a boost, then ran her green claws down my chest, popping open my buttons. She moved her hips back and forth over my body, her bony pelvis digging into me like a spur. "I'm sucking the poison out of you," she moaned, "I'm reversing the curse!" It was hard getting inside her because she was dry at first, almost like sandpaper, but the raking of her fingernails warmed my blood and I was soon throbbing hard, as if she'd raised the dead. "You don't have to worry about the rape again."

"What?" *She knows? How? Did Tom tell her?*

"I only want to feel you pressed against me," she said, her face contorted, her body jerking. "A woman has needs, you know." She tore through my underwear with her fast-paced grinding. She wrapped her panties around my neck and squeezed. "I only want to give you comfort against your constant pain."

The harder she strangled, the more I struggled. The air in my lungs sounded as if it were being run through a rickety purifier, filtering out pollutants maybe—spiritual impurities—half catching in my throat only to run back inside me and up again with each pelvic thrust. I felt like I was on the verge of passing out—she took me to the brink and back again, fully in control.

"I owe you the truth—it will end bad *and* good for you. But be brave . . . you're halfway there. It's all right now, dearest. It's . . ." Her face looked as if it would slide off her skull; her eyes shifted to one side of her face, and she climaxed, rocking, rubbing on top of me. "It's done," she panted, toppling sideways like a shot cowboy off a horse. "All you have to do now is . . . *mmm.*" She turned her ugly face away.

My mind seemed to come back to me from somewhere else. I sprang up like a ghost from its coffin. She took a Matterhorn from the nightstand, watching me warmly, scratching her hair. Inhaling a deep lungful of smoke, she leaned over and blew in my face, looking sleepily into my eyes.

"Yuh tricked me," I said. "That's what yuh wanted to do all along, ever since yuh set eyes on me."

"Stripling," she said huskily, running her fingers up my arm. "Hush . . ."

"Y-you *exploited* me."

"Oh, get over yourself! Don't you see it *had* to be this way?" She reached for her panties, yanking them lopsided over thin speckled legs the color of eggshells. I shuddered at the sight of her muddy feet. She said calmly, like a weary teacher, "When a forty-leg stings you, what does your mother put on it? The same venom—am I right?"

"Get out!" I pulled the sheet from under her so that she slid off the other side and thudded to the floor. "I must be losin' my goddamn mind. What have I done?"

She struggled to her feet, the alcohol seemingly still warming her, a barrier to pain, and searched for her slippers, keeping her eyes on the ground with a crooked grin around her cigarette, her yellow hands scaly like a chicken hawk's. She pulled her dress back down below her knees and stepped past with her head held high, satisfied with her work, her hair looking like a ravaged nest, turning to peck me on the cheek. "I'll be seeing you, lover boy."

I shoved her out of the bedroom. In the living room, walking backward, she blew a kiss, leering and patting her pussy with jeweled fingers, stumbling over the sofa to avoid the cat. "I hate cats!" she rasped, kicking at PJ.

I was mortified. I felt dirty. Snow snapped at her heels as she left. All the way down the patio steps, she twittered like a bird, "*You'll never get to heaven if you break my heart . . .*"

PART III

ST. MAUDE

CHAPTER 15

The moon paled in the dawn sky, which was beautiful in its first suggestions of daylight. After Chadwell gave me the address, I had double-checked with Lois to see if she knew Maude. Curators were a small community in Cornwall County. She did. They'd met on multiple occasions at socials and some annual conference or other. Lois said she hadn't made an impression, had seemed shy and withdrawn. My heart had fluttered again and I was only too happy Lois hadn't questioned me closely, but she'd looked wary, as if she knew better than to pry, perhaps informed by some collected wisdom, or from the look of complete collapse on my face. Now I was finally going to see Maude, taking the early bus to Seaford Town.

As I sat there, I mused on the conversation I'd had with Papa after he'd recovered and I'd apologized for hitting him. We had gone to Irwin Hills for the Heroes' Day boar hunt, a tradition among Messado men, and taken Tony along.

"I dreamed I was gettin' married to the devil," I had said, "and God was doin' the marriage. She raped me, Papa. And the whole time it was like a wakin' nightmare I knew I had no right escapin'."

"So? What yuh wa'an me do 'bout it? After yuh nearly kill me," he said in grim humor.

"You're the only one I can tell."

"Yet yuh doh seem angry." His eyes searched my face like a sweeping beacon. "What's really goin' on wid yuh?"

"Maybe I wanted it."

"Is only *you* can answer dat. Till yuh come clean wid yuhself an' everybody else, yuh cyaan put t'ings in proper perspective. Is like yuh wearin' foggy lens."

"Like how yuh came clean 'bout Tony?" I replied with a measure of hurt.

But he wasn't interested in wounding me, he was genuinely concerned. "Yes, egg-zackly. I took a vow, Nyjah. I'll never hurt dem again. I mean it. Maybe dat rock yuh fling to me chest knocked somethin' into it. An' you be careful too. Yuh t'ink I doh know yuh tongue goin' *lucku-lucku* for dat Red Ibo gyal Melissa who live in de apartment?"

The driver sighed loudly up front, breaking my revery. "People, de highway traffic too much dis mawnin'. If we drive pon it, we not reachin' Seaford Town till after eleven."

"I cyaan reach so late, Ziggy," complained a wiry higgler beside me in Jheri curl. "De likkle touris' business go done by ten t'irty when de tour bus dem lef'. Tu'n yuh han' mek fashion."

Ziggy mumbled something, then turned off the highway. "De road bad, sistah," he said to a woman beside him. "Almos' every week accident happen ah Fel'man Kawna 'cause how it narrow. It never use to be dat small, but every time heavy rain fall it wash 'way piece ah de road."

"Guv'ment doh care 'bout Fel'man Kawna people," said the Jheri curl craftswoman. "Ongle roads dat de white people drive on get de attention. Is as if is de touris' dem country an' we doh live here."

"Driver, is it really safe to drive on this road?" I called out.

Several people turned around and looked back at me with bright-eyed mockery.

"Yuh soun' like yuh from Montego Bay, sonny," said a bearded man peeling an ortanique. "Yuh feel yuh too good fe dead wid country folk? Yuh know dat AIDS start in MoBay? Yet why yuh Montegonians always gwaan like yuh shit can mek patty?"

"Prento, leave de bwoy alone," said Ziggy, who made eyes with me through his mirror. "Son, de road drivable, I jus' haffe mek sure once I comin' from dis side, I blow me horn when goin' roun' de kawna. Dere's no road sign to sey dat; but everybody who familiar wid de area know dat rule: just remembah de kawna."

Somehow this brought me back to the purpose of my trip. Why was I going anyway? Why was I so adamant? What could I give Maude more than a fresh reminder of her trauma? My throat lumped; the passengers' giggles rang dully in my ears like an accusative chorus, a gallery of reproving faces scrutinizing my motives. Ready to cast lots and toss me overboard.

Ziggy continued lecturing, as is a minibus driver's wont, and chatting up the young woman beside him, showing off, marking territory. "Wha' dis guv'ment wa'an anyhow? I ask yuh—to deliver modernity?"

"Den brag 'bout it come election," said Prento, the epidemiologist who'd pinpointed the origin of local AIDS.

"You wa'an talk 'bout de vanishin' beauty of Westmorelan'?" rhapsodized Ziggy. "'Cause dem buildin' a dam 'cross Negril River—dem give de contract to Chiney, who only hire neagah as laborer. Dem nuh wa'an employ locals wid college degree an' pay dem proper money fe proper work."

"Dem goin' flood King's Valley too," wheezed an obese man seated in front of me. "Is a massive project. Transformin' de whole parish."

"Benji, doh talk 'bout *massive*," sniped Prento, "you is massive yuhself."

"Who give dem fuckin' Asians de right?" Ziggy bellowed, shaking his scarred jowls. He had the ferment of people who called into local radio talk shows.

"Dem drownin' de river, man," piped someone behind me.

All this bus *labrish* was for some reason making me hot under the collar.

We talkin' to YOU! said their faces, pouring hostile glances into me because I refrained from joining in.

"Negril River jus' about de las' virginal, untamed beauty spot, like Joseph's Cave. De unpolluted, un-Chineyed river in Westmorelan'," said the craftswoman.

"Dere ain't goin' be no more river when de Chiney dam done. De fuckers doh even care."

"Jus' a big dead lake," mourned another woman. "All in de name ah *progress*."

Maude used to be a roaring river, I thought, *now she's one big dead lake*.

"Wha' yuh t'ink, MoBay?" said Prento, finishing off the ortanique.

"I think . . . a dam is a nice clean way to generate electric power."

The ensuing silence condemned me.

The fresh-faced young woman beside Ziggy finally came to my rescue: "That lake will provide people with new recreation." She had a cultured voice like my aunty.

"No!" Ziggy exploded, glaring at her, looking betrayed. "Yuh push a likkle more power into Negril. *So what!* What nex'? Likkle nuclear power plants for yuh fancy fuckin' gated communities? Yuh see de protests happenin' in Japan? An' yuh know wha' goin' happen eventually? Dem goin' rape dis whole landscape. Dem goin' rape it!"

"Oh come now," said the fresh-faced woman, "that's an extreme view."

"Stop the bus—stop the bus!" I bawled.

I jumped out and retched by a dusty eucalyptus, then wiped my scummy hand on a leathery leaf.

It was the same woman in the front who came out and said, "Motion sickness? You all right?"

"I can't do this—this is a mistake. It's all selfishness, I shouldn't have come."

She smiled. Her hair was done up in two small bleached Afro puffs; a silver snake nested in her navel. "Sure you can—you've already come this far, haven't you?"

After we reboarded the bus, the road twisted around a quarried hillside; I couldn't see what was beyond the curve. The edge of Feldman Corner had a sheer drop and I had to look away to check my nausea.

I stepped from the bus with bravery I didn't feel, sucking in the salty wind like a tonic. As I wended down the street, women offered me whole melons just so I would stop at their stalls, piled high with deep green fruit, a particular shade I hadn't seen in years, which I felt a craving for, not just from my gastric glands. The place was replete with shops selling cutlasses, hoes, shiny knickknacks, and fishing wares, and a few tawdry tourist shops plastered with sun-bleached Tourist Board posters. Vendors were doing a brisk business near the station. They sent children with fruit samples among queues along the yellow buses. "Pick up yuh strength!" chirped the children weaving through, "Pick up yuh strength!" as if they were coaches handing out glucose to athletes.

"Hey, yuh likkle white cockroach," roared a man at one of the boys, "sell me half a melon!" On either side of the road were freshly dug melon patches, and on one side a stretch of beach.

"Where's the museum?" I asked one of the vendors.

Putting a hand above her pale eyelashes to block the sun's glare, she pointed. "Right down there—yuh can walk or tek a hack."

"A *hack*?" I smiled at the strange word.

She noted my tone with scorn. She was proud—the people here in Seaford Town didn't like outsiders judging them as bumpkins. "Yesh," she responded with her mashed mouth, "or if it suit yuh, aksh someone elsh."

"I didn't mean to offend. But I'll need somethin' specific."

"Right round de bend, Talbot, yuh cyaan mish it." This was another vernacular quirk of theirs: they called men *Talbot*.

"Talbot is an extinct dog breed. My name is Nyjah. What's yours?"

She pushed her dirty-blond hair from her liver-spotted face. She looked like Mother Teresa dug up from the dead. "Look here, *pawdi*, for all de time yuh jus' cosh me, yuh haffe buy a melon."

"I thought I was about to get one free."

"Yuh talk me outta it!" she snapped, clicking her tongue against her scattered teeth. "Or yuh talk *yuhshelf* outta it. Which one?"

The other women nearby fiddled with money bags below their sagging breasts and smiled. The tan lines along their necks shone with a healthy golden tone.

I saw the laugh starting at the corners of her lips. I smiled back. This whole town of displaced Germans, dropped in the middle of nowhere by Lord Seaford to make up for labor shortages after slavery, deserved a case study. Their skin, especially at the backs of their necks, was sunburned to an almost syrupy brown like the potatoes they sold, their hands and faces leathery, their rotten teeth stumps the color of brown sugar. They had been abandoned but had kept a strong and impressive sense of community.

Mother Teresa must have noticed my discomfort. She foisted the melon on me like a ticking bomb.

"What's yuh name?" I repeated.

"Heidi," she said, then called over to her children playing with bleached shells.

"I could've guessed that."

A dirty little white girl holding one of the shells ran up to me and said, "Me sell yuh dis fe twenty dollar or a Malta an' banana chips." She was very serious about the barter. Her sea-green eyes, floating in her coppery face, finally settled on my trousers. "Where yuh billy?"

Heidi glanced at the girl with a mixture of awe and amusement, then yelled, "Tek weh yuhshelf! Yuh dutty likkle whore, yuh soon start sellin' yuh likkle coco bread!"

The child stood her ground, ignored her mother; the other women laughed at her determination.

Heidi took my hand and felt my palm. "Yuh hand sawf—yuh from MoBay," she concluded like an empiricist.

"But see dis though," said another woman, "what a way she eager!" The two of them seemed both proud and ashamed at the child's effrontery.

"Lemme see that shell," I said, taking it from the little girl. It turned out to be a hairbrush that only looked like a shell, with a pink glassy texture that shone with many colors when it caught the sun. For some reason it made me think of Briana. "Twenty dollars?"

The girl shook her head. "Me said twenty-five."

The women laughed again, but heartily. "Her blood common but she know how fe *grawf*," said one of them.

I smiled. "I won't ask again, yuh might raise it to thirty." She had dirty-blond hair like her mother, but hers was scraped into a ponytail. "Here, brush yuh hair with it one last time, for good luck."

She brushed her hair perfunctorily. "Yuh go give it to yuh girlfriend?" she blurted out, grabbing my hand. "Tek me wid yuh."

"Mona!" Heidi snapped. "Dat's enough, yuh likkle *tegareg*, don't embarrash me. We not starvin'. We not hard up."

Mona pumped my hand and looked fiercely at me. "Dem found Jakey dead from epilepsy," she said with a rush of breath, "stinkin' and rotten in de seaside hut, and dem scraped him up wid a shovel."

"Mona, come here, yuh dutty bitch," said Heidi.

This unrelated tale embarrassed and startled me; the child looked stricken with a dreadful panic. "Who's Jakey?" I asked her.

"Him was a ol' sea dawg. *Fischer*. F-i-s-c-h-e-r. Him did promise to tek we back to Germany. Every night when him on de beach an' warm wid drink, de back of him eyeballs begin to sweat till him see de *Cutty Sark* out pon de sea. De tea clipper dat bring we here. He was buildin' an ark!" Mona tugged my arm around her neck and gave me an earnest look as if I were Jakey's replacement, as if I should continue his work of repatriation. "Tek me back to MoBay wid yuh!" I might've been Jakey's reincarnated self.

Heidi ran over and pulled her away. "Sorry, Talbot, she *tallawah* dis one—but a likkle gone in de head."

The child hollered and kicked as her mother dragged her behind the shops and peppered her with licks from her slipper. I left fifty dollars and pocketed the brush, hoping the women were honest enough to give Mona her just reward. I couldn't help being slightly unsettled that the German word she'd used for fisherman—*Fischer*—was Perry's surname.

When I got to the museum, I hesitated. A voice said, "Tek a breath, man. I know yuh drive a long way." I turned to see a small, lively faced man with thick, wavy black hair, though his whiskers were turning gray; he looked old and young at the same time. "De melon any good?"

"I bought it from Heidi."

"Mus' be sweet then," he declared, leaning on his rake. "She have de best field."

"Can I tell yuh a secret?" I broke the melon and bit into its juicy deep-red flesh.

"I doh wa'an dat responsibility, Talbot."

"I was kinda hopin' it was closed. I'm dreadin' what I'll find here." The melon had a fibrous taste, chewy and firm.

"Nutten but bowls an' spears an' bones, Talbot. All dead an' rottin', nutten livin' in dere, nobody can hurt yuh."

"One last question . . ."

He sighed and bit his lip. He seemed to regret having been friendly to me. "Talk quick-fass now!"

"The curator—the gyal that works there."

His hazel eyes rolled back in his head and he flicked his tongue like a lizard. He was a mulatto, a product of the Germans and Blacks, a man whose face held a deep-set angst, as if he were at a crossroads, as if he had a lot of history inside him he didn't like carrying around. He leaned back on a granite gate pillar and scratched his chin. "Miss Dallmeyer? Strange creature . . . quiet. Keep to herself mostly; she belong in dat museum. Somet'ing inside her dead . . . an' somet'ing inside there holdin' her *arden*."

"*Arden?*"

"Firm, stubborn—like tree roots. People say she connected wid de pieces she collect in a way a shaman connected to him commune. She set down roots in dere dat tek up invisible space, dat bind her, for better or worse. She's an attraction herself."

"Yuh not makin' much sense."

He smiled and whistled through the gap in his teeth. "Yuh Mo-Bay people—everyt'ing mus' mek *sense*, like de two ugly holes in a dawg's face. Maybe dat's why she run 'way an' leave yuh. You is de boyfriend? Yuh used to cut her tail?"

"No . . . not—"

"Doh lie to me, else I ain't sayin' anodda word to yuh."

I threw the melon bark on the rice bag spread on the driveway. The man looked disgusted, as if I'd wiped my muddy shoes inside his house. I remembered he had been cleaning when I approached. "I'm not lyin'. We're connected, but not intimately . . . Well, put it this way: I belong to her *former* life."

"Den why yuh come see her?"

"We have unfinished business. Somethin' I have to confront."

"Confront *who*? Her? A delicate soul like dat? Come gwaan, Talbot. I won't let yuh disturb her." He was now a centurion; she was his empress.

"I'm goin' to have to insist—"

He waved me off and seemed ready to tackle me down the driveway, with his rake held like a spear.

"Please. I promise I won't upset her."

He watched my face, considered, then led me away by the arm. "Come, yuh goin' haffe wait awhile, dis de time-a day she like to be alone."

"Really? Why?"

"Enough questions, Talbot."

We had to navigate past four very big buildings—government centers holding artifacts and records about Seaford Town's German settlement—as well as a grand marble statue of Lord Seaford on a horse, then a church and a cemetery, to get to a gazebo where we sat down and watched fishermen mending nets.

"Wait awhile, *pawdi*, me soon come back an' tek yuh inside."

When the groundskeeper deemed it right to return, my heart started hammering and my knees went weak. I noticed a bevy of children and a swarthy hipshot woman practicing welcome routines in the shell of a hurricane-damaged building. He brought me to an open window and showed her to me. She was wearing a brown dress, rose-framed glasses, and had her brown arms folded over her chest. *What is she doing?* She stood still as if she were nailed to an invisible cross. She might have been studying something on a shelf.

He whispered, "Today she has de museum to herself—Huntley, her boss, will drop in only if a delegation comin'. Very boasty fella, likes to see himself on local TV every Wednesday mawnin' talkin' 'bout dis an' dat an' *tarra* knows what. She nevah does interviews wid de community channel, no matter how many times dem request. Dis her sanctuary."

The museum was mostly empty. She started walking across the room like she had eggs between her thighs, almost as if she were moving within invisible lines she daren't breach. She glanced around and kissed the wind with her spongy lips, that mouth that had almost driven me to tears.

The groundskeeper looked on, appearing enthralled. Then he whispered, "Her favorite phrase is *for no natural reason*. Dis gyal always shake her head like de world on her shoulders an' say, 'for no natural reason.' Come, time to head in."

I grabbed his thin shoulder. "Wait . . . I can't. I just want to watch her."

He seemed frustrated, as if his time had been wasted. "Yuh sure?"

"Yes, I'll be fine. I'll rent a room at the inn and stay a couple days. I've got time, I don't want to rush anything."

"Bird-watchin'." Now he seemed appreciative. "I like yuh style, Talbot. A man should always know what him gettin' into, t'ink t'ings t'rough."

"Isn't that the truth. If I'd stayed longer at the gym that mornin', none of this would've happened."

"*What* would've not happen?" he burst out.

She whipped around at his raised voice. When she saw us through the open window, she froze—something in her hand which

I hadn't noticed dropped to the ground and swirled and swirled, ringing with a tinny sound.

The groundskeeper waved to her and sniggered, but I ducked down below the ledge. After several moments, I stood back up. Maude had resumed her egg-walking, moving through the building as if in a different world.

"I t'ought she'd piss herself jus' now, de fright I give her," muttered the groundskeeper.

"She used to be quite tough, yuh know, a disciplinarian. I once saw her throw a shot put so far she dislocated her shoulder—but she just popped it back in herself."

"Yuh tellin' stories now. Le'we go," he said. We turned to leave, crab-walking down a knoll like men with crooked knees. "I go leave yuh. I'll be over here cuttin' de lawn if yuh need anyt'ing. I call dis section de Deep 'cause it a sunken garden, it still part marshland. Salt water from an estuary use to run all de way here."

The first tour bus soon arrived and the welcoming committee fanned out while passengers disembarked. "Damn!" said a cigar-chomping red-faced man in a sun bonnet, wiping his broad neck with a yellow cloth and smiling at the little dancing girls in bandanna skirts, holding braided zinnias. "It's a hootenanny here. Howdy, gals!"

I moved with the stream of bodies, keeping just outside Maude's range of sight and walking alongside the cigar chomper. He smelled like brake fluid.

"I watch the museum," I heard her say to a spectacled tourist.

"You mean you *run* it?" the woman replied, trying to soften her condescension with a smile, passing her fingers through her bobbed cherry-colored hair streaked with a skunk-like strip of gray.

"No, I mean just what I say," Maude responded curtly. "I watch it."

The tourist walked away to another exhibit of honey-colored glassware and a school of brightly painted wooden fish. I stepped some paces back. A Toyota Coaster arrived with eager visitors, making introductions or talking to each other, mostly in German, people who'd probably heard of the town and come to trace ancestry with a vulgar gaiety about them, like ugly Americans.

"Hacker," said a rangy man to the idle bus driver. "Is the name Hacker common around these parts?"

The driver retired with a shy nod.

They pushed past me at the door as if I wasn't there. I might've been a ghost. A teenage girl, stripping a John-bellyful with buck teeth, brushed her elbow against my chest and looked at me, wiping the yellow pulp off her chin. Internally I had a hostile reaction: *Stupid foreigner doesn't know how to eat a mango*. I was suddenly protective of the place and said rather sternly, "No eating in the museum, please."

Her parents, thinking me a guard, quickly apologized.

The child glanced back as if suspicious of my intentions, and I backed down.

Maude was busy, but took her time moving through visitors at her own pace. I walked almost parallel to her on the other side of a sea of bodies crowded around a low table of carved conch shells. I observed her change in features since I'd last seen her, but somehow my attention was being pulled from the physical toward the stirring of something deep down.

Her age had begun to show, but the more significant shift was in her temperament. In demeanor, she seemed to be an entirely different person—a fragile introvert: the way she moved among everyone but held herself apart as if she'd been disturbed, like a caterpillar displaced from a leaf. She was professional but almost aloof, and wouldn't be beholden to their constant stream of questions and demands.

The space between us started to shrink, yet I was wary of growing careless. I moved with the giddy tourists like a shark outside a school of fish. A man came at me with a question bursting through his pink face, and Maude started to turn toward us, so I slipped behind a door. From where I stood, I saw the hawk-featured man looking over at me. I kneeled down, pretending to tie my shoe.

"Son, you don't have laces," he said.

I hissed at him, "Go away, Alan Arkin. Buy yourself a clue, you mutt."

He looked flabbergasted and shook his head, then turned back. I decided to step outside.

In the driveway, I remembered Lois's advice when she would take the family on museum tours on Employees' Day: *You have to respect people's space, Nyjah. Remember, yuh not just here to look around.* I had to be aware of boundaries. Hadn't the groundskeeper referred to it as her sanctuary? I needed to be thoughtful, sensitive, like a chemist; I needed more time for observation.

I took awhile absorbing the surroundings. The museum stood between two gigantic almond trees with sand at their roots. When I stooped and scooped up sand, it occurred to me that the sea had once come this far and the building was a recent construction, erected on the lip of a shallow bay famous for its shape like a chin. The damaged building in the yard, bathed in poincianas, with a wide wooden verandah where children had gathered, had been the original museum. Now it was the most important relic. Its roof, dark and torn, still had bits of handcrafted shingles along its spine that looked like the backbone of a gutted grouper. It had not survived the hurricane.

The groundskeeper startled me again. "Like many of us, it lost t'ings," he said, pointing at the wreck. "Sixty-three artifacts were sunk, scattered, or swallowed by wind. But I like to believe dey found a spiritual home."

"They didn't like to be cooped up in a museum. How did *you* manage in the storm?"

"Me try not to dwell too much on de hurricane. Dey say de more yuh t'ink 'bout somet'ing, de more yuh experience it—an' once was more dan enough. Believe it or not, a Taino village used to stan' somewhere here—dis a *real* burial ground. Sometimes when we feel that unusual chill in de air, we know duppy walkin' t'rough us."

I returned inside. The red-faced man with the sun bonnet was jabbering at a taller tourist: "I came to see the mummy couple they found in the cave. Especially that Arawak gal the media's calling Yo-Yo Ma or Yamaye." Several other visitors regarded him with gentle scorn, but he didn't seem to mind.

Another man was pestering Maude, invading her personal space with his unctuous, almost smarmy way. Her unease was plain (though maybe only to me) as she explained, "I organize tours, talks, and updates to the archives."

"Yes, but tell me . . ." the man pressed, reaching out and taking hold of her arm. She gasped audibly. Then something strange happened: for a moment she stood stock-still, with one arm half hanging away from her like a crooked wing; time might've stopped. All the other tourists in the room seemed to have noticed too, and the air went dead. Then they sort of reoriented themselves with a calm urgency around her motionless figure, like ants adjusting their marching lines around an injured straggler or some object in their path they knew better than to mount. Their whispers crowded her like tides without a seafloor, then crashed, and everything started moving again like clockwork.

The pesky man released her arm and said shallowly, "I'm sorry, I didn't mean to be . . . touchy. I have disported myself so much in your country the last few days that I got carried away."

She was hardly listening; she was looking in my direction. Sometimes the misreading of something could lead to a whole poem for me, as if the poem had lain there in the fissure of a lapsed thought, in a synapse, but needed the unintentional miracle of that split second of error. I had fallen into her eyes while she was stupefied, yet pulled back because I feared she was about to have an epileptic fit like the one she'd had that day in Smokey's den, but I had misinterpreted the situation, had gone against instinct and perhaps had missed an opportunity to connect with her while her spirit soared, the thread of memory snapped between us. Now I was looking back at her, though I withdrew as quickly as I could. I felt almost like I was being swept away. My heart rose, then subsided with gentle poisonous swells. Everything was going wrong. In distress, I hunted for the groundskeeper for advice, but he was gone. I took refuge in the original wreck of a museum like an almshouse.

I waited there in the ruins until the tours moved away. The noon sun, hanging in a cradle of watery mist above the sea, was red at the top and pink at the bottom; the sky looked like a smudged painting. Maude shuttered the general entrance and exited through the back door, a lunch pail in her hand, then locked up with her keys and hurried through the backyard toward a backstreet instead of the main one. I watched her heading toward the red cemetery gates where some tombs were visible, a hill dotted with crosses. I took a shortcut, ran along a marigold hedge to the cemetery—but to the other end of the property that I'd observed from the gazebo. I sat with my back against the cold surface of a mausoleum and waited. The earth was sandy on this elevation too (had this once been beach land?), mixing with the loamy darker soil edging the tombs.

I waited several minutes until I heard her. She squeezed between a column and a half-torn fence instead of walking through the gates. In the coppery afternoon light, she bore a haunting resemblance to her younger self that had dominated our lives for the space of a few tragic months. She moved very close to where I was hiding and sat on a grave, under a tangle of shedding cedars, and brushed some falling twigs off her brown dress. She crossed her legs and took what looked like a diary out of a pocket in her dress and started reading. Her face was replete with the contentment of aloneness. I felt almost disgusted with myself for violating her privacy. She pushed her bleached-bronze hair from her face and removed her rose-framed glasses. For perhaps the first time, I truly took in her eyes. They had a ring of gray that caught fire with the sun. It occurred to me that she, too, might have mixed blood, German and Black, and had come home, returned to her hometown. Why hadn't I figured this out before? It made perfect sense. She finished her sandwich and wiped her mouth with a napkin; her phone rang. "Yes, Mr. Huntley," she answered with stiff courtesy. "I see . . . Okay, I'll be right there." In her haste, she forgot the little book.

After she left, I couldn't resist. I hurried to the grave and read her bookmarked pages:

The Burial

"Who is the favored one?" That was the question on everybody's lips when Tamu emerged from behind the screen. He looked around the caney like a man lost, like someone contemplating boundaries nobody else could see. The women glanced at the bohique's puzzling mien, trying to mask their trepidation. Tamu drew a dignified breath, lines of consternation crisscrossing his leathery face as if he'd slept facedown in his hamaca. Bamboo creaked somewhere in the tense stillness with the rattling sound of a coney's teeth grinding nuts. Tamu raised his hand vaguely. "The cacique has made his decision. He's at death's door. The poison from the arrow entered his bloodstream, there's nothing more we can do . . ." Quiet keening started. The head wife's body crashed to the floor and sank but the others ignored her. Tamu spoke on as if he couldn't hear them, "The zemís have sealed his journey to Coaybey. It was their favor that saved us from the Kalinago raid. And every man in Batabanó fought bravely and saved the cacicazgo. Now it falls to the royal household to do one last duty—chiefly the wives of Cacique Baba Ata." A hush reimposed itself; the wives dried their eyes and considered their position. The priest-healer continued, "I will shortly announce who is so favored as to join the chief in . . ." But Tamu couldn't bring himself to finish; waves of murmuring and unrest ran through the ranks of beautiful women and their jittery hands clutched at things, some their golden beads trailing down their stomachs, some over swelling bellies.

"Surely a pregnant wife would not be chosen?" some thought with a glimmer of hope. They drew nearer and each could hear the other's lifeblood pulsing against them in thickening horror. They

waited desperately for the bohique's next words like an executioner's pardon. Tamu's expression slowly softened—they were like his daughters. He'd known all of them since they were little girls running around, playing batú with other children, bouncy as the rubber balls they bound on their naked bodies in the batey. Now they were grown, some with children of their own.

They continued shuffling their jeweled feet, eyeing each other in suspense. Generally they cohabited peacefully but many didn't like their co-wives and stepchildren, and had often engaged in petty squabbles and sought to curry favor with the cacique for the sake of their children and lineage. But this—this they would've never wished on their worst enemy, much less their family. Tension suffocated them inside the caney. From behind the screen, the dying man's groans filled their ears like a muffled scream. The earthen floor was cool under their feet and the sound of cicadas falling from trees filled the air with heart-stopping thuds that normally would've gone unnoticed, just the sound of seasonal change, the coming of the hurakán season, on the heels of a victory over their perpetual enemies, the Kalinago Caribs, that hadn't been without displeasure. Because their leader now lay dying. "Come," said Tamu, "we'll make the announcement in the courtyard."

Afia blew his guamo, but the batey already teemed with people. Sunshine glittered iridescently on the herald's shell trumpet as he stepped back deftly, making way as nitaínos gathered in a semicircle, sitting on their dujos to form the village council. The naborias hung back a few yards, watchful, murmurous, keeping a respectful distance. The wives lined up with their backs to the sub-caciques, facing the crowd, making eye contact with family members who'd had their hearts in their mouths all morning too, and whose limbs stiffened with dread anticipation.

Tamu fingered the dark polished stone, looking down the row of women; shadows crossed the ground, his head flitted upward as chinchilin fluttered and sang telltale notes of mourning. Ev-

erybody held their breath when he made his first step. He took his time walking down the line, avoiding eye contact, slowly rotating the ceremonial axe blade over his wrinkled fingers. The atmosphere became unbearable, dreadful. He had stepped past the eighth, twelfth, fifteenth wife and still hadn't made his decision. People sighed in relief when their daughter, sister, or cousin was passed. Just as Yamaye sucked in her breath, closed her eyes, and opened them to look directly at her mother Coati's gaze, Tamu dropped the celt at the girl's feet. A gasp of horrific disbelief sounded as Coati fainted and was quickly taken to her hut. There was an outburst of joyous shrieks. "Yamaye has been chosen to accompany the cacique! What a great honor!"

People queued to congratulate the girl. Yamaye stood there as in a dream, receiving bows and hugs she could barely feel. She felt so paralyzed with shock and a bottomless sense of loss that she had to physically will herself to breathe, to open her mouth and say, "Thank you," to the endless stream of blessings. "Why me?" kept running through her head, countered by: "Supreme Yúcahu, if it is your will . . ." But this voice was joyless, stripped of life and sincerity, an additional poison to her wilting spirit. She feared she would fall. She very nearly did. She could see smug malice underneath some smiles offered by royal wives and their families. "Why me?" she almost cried out loud.

She heard someone say in the background: "It's the best choice, she's yet to have a child. Perhaps her womb wasn't blessed."

"As if this is a way to make up for my unblessedness!" screamed Yamaye in her head.

Coati recovered and emerged from her bohío and threw herself at Tamu's feet. "Yamaye, my only child, why must she die so young?" Tamu, too, felt like weeping when he looked at the girl's youthful beauty, her radiant coppery complexion, her dark bewitching eyes and prominent cheekbones, her lustrous hair cut short over her smooth forehead and flowing down to her shapely figure. Her father, Guacuba, had been a warrior—the cacique and sub-caciques had declared him the bravest of men, and he had died in battle defending the cacicazgo from raiding Caribs. It was his strategy that had saved the village. He had died with honor. It wasn't a stretch to say that many of them owed him their lives. And now to repay his only daughter with death? Coati kept weeping bitterly, "Bury me—bury me instead!" She wallowed in the courtyard till well-wishers, embarrassed, balked at their own hypocrisy. "If the cacique truly loves his people, how can he treat them like this? What am I without my daughter? I am nothing, Tamu—I'm already dead!"

"Get up!" said Hutiey. The sub-cacique rose from his dujo and advanced with menace in his eyes. "You dishonor us all. How can you put your interest above the gods? The cacique loves his people. Your daughter will spend happiness eternally in Coaybey. How can you not rejoice?"

But all this time Tamu pondered: "How will the spirit of the village survive the death of their beautiful daughter?" To him, Yamaye represented all that was good and pure about their people.

"Why choose my child? She's all I have!" Coati grabbed Hutiey's ankle. "Mercy, great Hutiey. Intercede for us. Yamaye won't say anything because she's proud. But I . . . I'll lay down my life if necessary to save her."

Tamu pulled her up. "It is not your life that's required, Coati. The cacique has spoken. If he doesn't recover, which seems certain, then Yamaye, his favorite wife, will be buried with him alive tomorrow."

Coati wheezed a long breath and fell back in the dust, like a hutia tranquilized by a blowgun. "Leave her. All she needs is a good draw of tabako," said another shaman with disdain.

At that moment, a servant ran out of the royal caney and cried, "The cacique is dead!"

The cacicazgo erupted in screams that chased birds from trees. Yamaye's fate was sealed.

Before I could read on, I heard rustling through the overgrown path—it was Maude doubling back for the journal, or whatever this was. I plopped it down and scrambled over to the mausoleum unseen. From where I hid, I could see her reading it for a long while, almost studying it, as if she could tell someone had tampered with it. Ghosts maybe.

CHAPTER 16

As we drove down MoBay Proper, Rory said, "I wonder if Harding ever fleeces the school when he budgets for these events every year."

Harding's name brought back the memory of that day when I burst into his office. I looked over at Rory. "Yuh know, that day yuh raped Dallmeyer, I told Harding everything."

His hand got jumpy on the steering wheel. "You're lyin' . . . I don't believe yuh."

"Why would I lie about that?"

"I don't know. Why would yuh?"

"Yuh don't believe me or yuh don't *want* to?"

He hit the steering wheel. "It was an accident—the whole sequence! Chadwell didn't trip her on purpose, he was trying to move his foot outta the way."

This ludicrous reasoning brought back Ms. Dallmeyer's scolding about a domino effect of actions that she'd given me in the gym before the incident. "Like hell he was! And that's beside the point. Yuh went into the den anyway and finished the job, didn't yuh?"

Rory started fidgeting in his seat. "Yuh don't know what happened in there."

"Yuh didn't go in there to get yuh tonsils taken out, yuh went in there to do one thing."

He hit the steering wheel again. "And what did *you* do? Yuh ran. Coward!"

A quiet settled between us the rest of the way.

Rory was so lost in thought that he startled when I said, "Yuh just drove past the gate."

When we pulled into the parking lot, Carey Halls rushed over, rapping the passenger window as if he would break it and baring his big teeth, then pantomiming a bum spraying dirty water over the windshield, squeegeeing the glass with manic energy and wiggling his bottom. Chesterites standing below a blue awning laughed and slapped their knees.

"I should run him over," said Rory, flipping Carey the bird. "I never liked his Black ass, always seekin' attention. So fuckin' needy."

We parked and some of the young men greeted us heartily. The dinner was exclusively for our graduating class. We mingled a bit on the cobblestone patio while they set up inside.

"Here come Cress and Marco."

"They're ready for us," I said, eyeing the waitresses standing on either side of the white glass doors.

Rory held my arm. "Let them go ahead, I hate queues. I feel like I'm back in the cafeteria."

Two Chesterites passing by were engaged in a lively conversation. One looked over his shoulder and said, "What's her ambition?"

"To work in a public bath," answered the other.

They laughed, but the humor went over my head.

Nearby, Carey was talking with some old classmates, including Randall Hughes. "The gyal we chose tonight, the actress, you know what she said? That she wants to meet a famous person—that is her goal in life."

"You make a mistake thinking she's shallow," said Randall. "They're the cleverest sets. They put so much pressure on themselves, these attractive types."

"But we'll ease her burden tonight, won't we?"

"We shall certainly try. What should she care? She's getting paid for our service; it's not the other way around."

"It's an absolute privilege—she *should* be thanking us."

They became aware of my presence. "Nyjah, you ol' Anansi, still eavesdropping? Where's your master?"

"Who might that be?"

"Where's Chadwell?"

I didn't respond, I simply stepped back so they could move ahead.

"Messado, we have a bone to pick with you," said Randall. "You've been avoiding your alma mater ever since you left. We hardly see you. This is the first dinner you've attended in years."

"Get off it, Hughes," I responded. "What do yuh do here anyway? It's like a stompin' ground for cripples."

They regarded me with slightly wounded looks. The queue was moving like mud because of a bottleneck near the marble fountain; someone had been pushed into the water, a superstitious sacrifice to ensure the night went well. The young man was cursing and flapping around in his wet suit.

"We're going to show you the power of the *enfant terrible*," said Randall. "We're going to raise ourselves in your opinion by the time we get round to the salad course."

"Don't strain yuhself. I came for the entertainment, not for tears."

"Oh, but that's the fun of it, Messado," said Randall, bobbing his big head. "You never get what you expect."

It was a large open room that faced a wall of glass overlooking the illuminated golf course. The room was carpeted in thick paisley the color of bourbon and the walls had an equally rich oak paneling up to waist height; hanging all around the room were photos of club members and wealthy patrons—mostly Chester brass. The property was owned by a certain Vivian Debruin, himself an old boy.

We sat down in the back row just as cocktails arrived. The ice cream bowls were lined with lettuce and fruit in school colors. Cress sat beside me, and the waitress who served him a lobster cocktail lingered at his chair with a smile on her face. Cress nervously fingered the lemon wedges around the rim of the glass. Chadwell nudged his knee under the table to get him to say something, but Cress nearly ate his tongue. The waitress pushed a strand of her curly brown hair behind her ear and waited, standing bowlegged with her silver platter pressed to her chest; her initial pleasure at seeing him flustered then turned to polite embarrassment and she walked off with quick light steps. There was something about Cress—he was quiet and even mannered and well bred, but not usually flustered. He got shy around women because of his appearance: his bottom teeth weren't straight and his mouth had a dilapidated look as if there was something wrong with his jaw. He depended on us to set him up with women, and even when they found him attractive, he'd screw things up because he couldn't believe they'd ever really accept him. He was always suspicious, always looking for a way out, always testing the girls, and they would grow tired of his insecurities.

"Get up, jackass," said Marco, "go after her!"

"She's workin'," Cress countered, looking to the rest of us for support.

"Go after her now and don't come back without her scalp," ordered Chadwell.

So he got up and moved forward like a one-eyed dog searching for a thrown ball, treading on people's toes as he weaved through the white tables.

Right then, Fischer and Marvin Mighty came in. "Perry brought a date," someone snickered, but no one dared look in Mighty's direction for too long. Instead of the traditional school blazer, Marvin was wearing blue jeans, a long blue jacket that reached almost to his knees, and a cashmere and silk paisley shawl with fringed edges tied fashionably about his neck.

"He's not even dressed like a gentleman," Claudius Paulwell remarked at the table next to ours. "And graduated ahead of us!"

"But he's the only one that can get away with it," said someone else. "He's showing us who's boss—he's not here to blend in."

Before anyone at their table could get another word out,

Castleigh Twentyman walked over to them and whispered something to Claudius with a firm squeeze to the shoulder. Claudius went completely stiff as if stung by an adder and started apologizing. Castleigh said nothing and returned to his own table, smiling coldly over at us before he sat down.

"What the fuck is Cass's deal?" said Rory. "He's a henchman? Is he on the car wash's payroll?"

"Dunno," I said, "don't care." It occurred to me that with Cress temporarily away, we were now a party of four, a guilty party, the table seating only rapists. Through some undesirable telepathy, we all eyed each other and glanced around, twitching our necks like chickens, desperate for Cress to come back and relieve us from the latent discomfort of each other's company. I realized that it would always be like this.

Marco fiddled with the menu, clearly searching for something to say, and we watched him with disfavor. He pressed ahead anyway: "Big Eye's the MC—a controversial choice, don't yuh think?"

"Why controversial?" I said. "He's a theater director and actor at Fairfield."

"Really?" said Rory, feigning ignorance.

"Yeah, doin' lewd roots plays, and he's as flamboyant as ever."

A new waitress, her hands wrapped in a towel, gently slid the hot plates before us. Marco cooed at his oxtail and boiled potatoes.

Cress sat back down with us and said, "You're such a misogynist, Bow Dog. Why do you always say *cunt*-troversial?"

"Cre-e-ss!" Marco cheered, patting his back. "There he is!"

"How did it go?" said Chadwell, leaning forward with a smile.

"*Racing pools*," Cress said, mimicking Charles Magnus, the horse race announcer, "*get in it and win it!*"

We gave him high fives. "Nutten to it, eh?"

"We're going out tomorrow." Cress grinned from ear to ear, then his phone beeped and he read her message with delight.

"Don't answer yet, don't be too eager."

"But she's watching. Her name is Dianne . . . Sheriff. But it's spelled Scherif, almost pronounced *Shereef*."

"Nothing is *almost* pronounced, stupid, it's either pronounced or it isn't."

I started on the Mannish water soup and felt like being wicked. "Chad, yuh remember that mute gyal who Don Carlos rode like a donkey?"

"Uh-huh," said Chadwell, swallowing his spinners dumpling whole.

"Rory playin' kissy face with her, having sleepovers."

"Rory . . . no . . . they don't come cheap, yuh know," said Marco. "Expect a handshake in the mail from her pimp. Yuh goin' pay even the cab fare."

"It's not like that," Rory responded.

"Oh?" said Marco, wiping his mouth. "Have yuh ever heard the phrase *on the clock*? Look it up."

"And Marco should know," Cress said, "he only sleeps with whores."

Marco acknowledged the compliment and beckoned to a waiter, who came over and asked if we had everything we wanted.

"Bring us a bottle of the house wine," said Chad.

"Red or white, Mr. Crichton?"

Rory didn't really mind our harsh humor; he savored his soup, his top lip perspiring from the Scotch bonnet. "Tell yuh what: I like when she wears my boxers and shorts."

"Yuh gay, nigga," said Marco. "Go join the car wash."

"Yuh like when she straps on too?" said Chad.

"Yuh jealous," Rory barked. "You approached her first and she didn't like yuh, Chad. They never do. Something about yuh puts women off."

Chadwell, showing a surprising flash of hurt, said pointedly, "I'm no different from you."

"Oh yes yuh are," Rory said. "Must be lonely being you."

The tense exchange made us miserable, except for Cress, who didn't grasp what was driving all of this.

Perry walked over right then and tried being wry, but then thought better of it when he saw our strained expressions.

"What yuh want, Fischer?" groaned Marco.

Perry spread his arms and said with bluff charm, as if we were his houseguests, "Hmm . . . so far so different, eh? Same ol' crew, but different venue." When he was in his element, he never lacked confidence. He could be almost proprietorial when he was enjoying himself and had a flair for orchestration, whether it was people or events.

"And what have you been up to?" said Marco, breaking a prawn as if he wanted to break Perry's neck. "What holes have you been pluggin' to keep the ship afloat, Captain?"

The tables right around us went quiet; everyone cocked their ears because Marco had always been a class clown.

Perry was easy: "Don't criticize *me*, check out Greenlaw, he has man-boobs!"

Chadwell seemed to notice for the first time that Cress was putting on some pounds. "By God, yuh right, Perry. Titties, Cress, Jesus Christ."

We laughed. Perry could always find wiggle room in a conversation, could always disarm us, it was a part of his gift, an MC's glibness. But it ran deeper—he had a hopeful optimism that worked as well as Marco's comical cynicism. Even Marco chuckled begrudgingly.

"I see what it is," Perry said, looking overhead at the frosted-cake ceiling and chandeliers. "The streetlights this side of town don't work, eh, Messado, leaving you with rats for company." We laughed again, but while Perry was entertaining us, it was clear he wasn't enjoying himself, perhaps giving us humor to draw attention away from himself, like a comedian doing community service. His life was a tolerable hell that required all his skill, this neurosis of his to keep heat-seeking missiles off his tail. "I saw yuh just now, Cress," he continued, gesturing like a waiter, his manner all theatrical humility. "I have an even hotter gyal for you by the car wash."

"Sure," Cress replied casually, "bring her round when Mighty gives you a water break."

Perry looked at him as if he'd expected a different reaction, but then seemed to once again recognize the strange mood at our table, so he left without another word, glancing neither left or right, heading straight toward Mighty like a buoy.

"Fuckin' shit dick," grumbled Marco, spooning a mouthful of tamarind chutney. "And who would've thought Mighty was really a faggot. He used to fuck St. Helena gyals by the cemetery all the time."

"He used to have a funeral every week. Sometimes he buried three bodies a day."

"But how many times can a man bury himself?"

"Funny, whenever he cleared his throat, there was always a sound like an axed tree fallin'."

"That's true!"

"He was dyin' inside."

Chad made a low catcall and Marco said, "Who are you, Fischer, the bitch or the pants?" But I didn't think Perry could hear them. Watching his treacherous walk through those close tables, I had a strange sensation that he was carrying all of us on his shoulders, through choppy waters and rocks that could've dashed our brains out because we were lesser men, that he was a giant, like Talos of the bronze race, and no one could find the vein that ran from the sinew of his ankle to his neck, so he was safe in the fortress of his own flesh; nobody could break his thick skin and let the blood pour from him like molten lead. In a hall that barely had elbow room, he had all the space in the world because he'd made the decision to be himself.

"Perry never wanted to be a doctor," Marco confided to Cress, as if suddenly feeling the need to be gracious. "He always said he wanted to be the next David Selznick, but in a sorry close-minded country with no artistic rigor and even less resources, he has to settle for being a party organizer, producing dancehalls at WOW and five-hundred-dollar Mondays at the car wash."

It was funny to hear Marco say *close-minded*, like a Pharisee uttering, *Praise Jesus*. But it was true: we all led compromised existences in some way, navigating limitations, regrets. This was what I'd meant by a stomping ground for cripples.

Then something happened that took our breath away, something completely unexpected. From where we sat, we couldn't see the delicate details; we viewed it as through a lens, in almost delayed time. Sitting side by side, Fischer put his fingers on Mighty's face, just below his left eye, and pulled something free with a feathery touch, then showed him his fingertip and said something in his ear. They gazed at each other as if they were the only ones in the room.

Mighty closed his eyes, then opened them. For a moment, we thought they might kiss.

Perry blew what appeared to be an eyelash away like a dandelion tuft. Young men seated nearby pulled back as if ash had spewed from a volcano.

"Mighty Marvin!" Perry shouted, clapping childishly.

"This goin' be a long fuckin' night," lamented Marco.

"Take heart, Bow Dog," said Chad.

But Marco was inconsolable. He said quietly, "Yuh know, I used to think I was a good singer. I was such a star in the shower. But that day when Master Throckmorton made me sing in front-a class, I sounded so terrible I realized I'd been foolin' myself. I felt the same way in Smokey's den that day. All the time I'd been thinkin' I was tolerably good, but when I dropped my pants in that room, I realized I was a monster."

"Huh?" said Cress.

The white wine was an almost golden peach in the changing lights. At the same moment the entree was being served, Big Eye took the stage, wearing the traditional yellow cummerbund of the MC that matched the golden nuggets in his ears. He said, "Y'all see Snow preachin' fire and brimstone downtown?" Many people laughed and clapped. "He wanted to be here tonight but had to attend the Last Supper. He's Judas." More laughter. Big Eye raised a hand to cut the noise and grew more serious. "Gentlemen, tonight we're inductin' an honorary Chesterite into our ranks. A man who needs no introduction. The man who got most of us started on fags. Matterhorns, to be exact . . ."

My heart thumped. The room suddenly got smaller. *It can't be*, I mouthed.

There was a general hubbub. Big Eye continued, "Patience . . . patience, everyone. The man who gave us our greatest education, who told all of us fortunate to have had an audience at his footstool that the only things a man needs are ears to hear and a brain to think and a—"

"Dick to fuck with!" someone shouted.

"Who are we, gentlemen?" asked Big Eye, cupping his ear for a response.

"We are the bwoys who knew where to find the key for his whatnot!"

"The what?"

"De waknat!"

"De what?"

"De what's-it-not wid de blue movie tapes!"

The general din grew louder; the hankering for the guest of honor was palpable. People were getting up, looking all around, standing on chairs, not sure what door he would emerge from, not sure what to do next. I caught a glimpse of Master Harding standing inside a far doorway, as if he was neither in nor out of the room, masking his presence, his pipe spewing smoke like a dragon's nostrils, his hands tucked firmly in his waistcoat pockets.

"Who can forget the gorilla and his ice cream cone, the classic kung fu tapes with fuzzy lines that yuh can't find on the Internet?"

"*Uho! Uho!*" we roared, getting up and pounding our chests and making sounds that appalled the waiters—they looked as if they'd suddenly found themselves in a cage with dangerous animals. When the noise reached fever pitch and utensils began shaking, when we started banging tables and drowning out Big Eye's talking, Smokey stepped out from behind one of the doors of the white-ceilinged room, smiling. Our breathing stopped, as if a dog whistle had gone off that only we could hear. Everybody stood still, oriented toward that door, for a full three or four seconds, completely quiet. Smokey raised a shaky fist, then dropped it. He opened the door behind him, stepped back through it, and slammed it on himself.

We went crazy. "Smokey! Smokey!"

Finally, he reemerged with a playful grin and walked to the middle of the room with his peculiar gait, the one he used when pushing a wheelbarrow, his chest slightly sunken, his fists half-clenched. He stopped before Big Eye and stood there respectfully. He was dressed identically to us, sans blazer.

A youth behind Big Eye who I didn't recognize moved forward with a red box resting on his forearms. Big Eye opened the package and carefully lifted a jacket from the crinkly white paper, unfolded it, and pronounced, "What do yuh give to a man who has given us life?"

Hearts were too full to answer; some of us were near tears. The standing ovation seemed insufficient; we yearned to give him our hearts. Smokey shook his small head and ground his dentures, his face blank of emotion against the loud applause, and we could see the gravity of the moment sinking into him, shrinking his presence. He was overwhelmed and his eyes welled with tears. He lifted his arms as if he were about to fly. And when Big Eye put the blazer on him and smoothed it down, Smokey didn't dare look about the room, he just stared at the frosted ceiling. When he opened his mouth to say thank you, his voice trembled and we understood, but we weren't about to let him off the hook.

Big Eye foisted the mic on him and signaled to us, so we shouted, "Speech!"

Smokey tried again, stopped, mumbled, then wiped his tears. A big extravagant chair, upholstered in tufted white velvet with hand-finished gold leafing along its edges, stood at the center of the space in front and he was gently ushered into it.

"Relax, Uncle," said Big Eye, "now is time for the refreshments."

He gestured to an usher, who put a spotlight on the high-back chair that gradually crept forward to settle between Smokey and the first row of tables. The murmuring gathered momentum. I remembered Carey saying something about an "actress." Big Eye was starting to warm up: "Gentlemen, they say dancin' with a gyal is a shortcut to intimacy, yuh dig?"

"We dig!"

"Awrite then," said Big Eye, his frog eyes going almost as big as his wide-mouthed grin. "Comin' out to the stage—Melissa Marvelous!"

I fell back in my chair holding my chest.

Chadwell glanced at me. "The fuck wrong with yuh now?"

Melissa came out in a long, tight burgundy dress, her hair done up in a high, jeweled pompadour, and a glittery color-changing butterfly mask pressed to her face. She was so enchanting that nearly everybody drew breath as one, wondering what had happened and who she was and where exactly had she come from. It was as if Big Eye had pulled off a sleight of hand. It was then we realized that he was about to put on a play. The excitement ran through our ranks like a current. Everyone leaned forward and those at the back moved their chairs up.

Smokey's face went stony. We had known him long enough to grasp that he wasn't pleased, but Big Eye was hell-bent on his spectacle, giving the best way he knew how: through his talent.

Smokey looked disgruntled, disgraced, as if his throne were a toilet or a dunce's chair. "Travis," he began, speaking for the first time that night, calling Big Eye by his real name and putting that scratchy heft in his voice, "Travis, what—"

But Big Eye took his mic. "Enjoy, Uncle."

The old boys from the debate club, the Gadfly, in their rosy magenta jackets, stood up from a long table, stagehands, and quickly set up the props for Act One. Big Eye bowed and stepped back to a table near the low podium.

An actor came out from behind the curtains near a piano, an old boy dressed as Master Harding, puffing on his pipe and pulling on the lapel of his tweed jacket. He sat at his desk and said in his rotund inflection, "Bring in the sex slave!" Then things happened rapidly in something like a mise-en-scène. Don Carlos, the little man from Punkie's, came out in bronze makeup and wearing nothing but a bronze spray-painted thong, dragging a life-sized inflatable blond doll with a leash around her neck. The boys fell over in their chairs with laughter like wailing hyenas.

I had noticed that at the words *sex slave*, Melissa had first looked terrified, and now she looked blank—she didn't get the humor, and as it escalated she got a dull sickened look, clearly wondering what her role would be. But she seemed determined to play along, perhaps more out of fear than interest.

Most of the waiters and waitresses slowly withdrew from the room—they were used to hijinks like this from drunken old boys, so for them it was nothing new—but some of them stuck around, watching with bemused grins.

"Master Harding" puffed his pipe and smacked his desk. "Dare I say she looks cold, don't you think, Don Carlos?" The little man nodded, and Harding pointed at Melissa. "Would you mind giving her the shirt off your back, dearest?"

Melissa slowly wiggled out of her dress; there were hoots and howls. She stood there in her black two-piece lingerie and threw the dress to Don Carlos, who put it on the inflatable doll with sartorial care, humming to himself and rubbing his hands over her big pink plastic breasts. He pressed his lips to hers.

We laughed because their expressions were almost identical. The doll had a look of suspended shock, with big painted eyes and a gaping red mouth. I glanced over at Smokey. He stiffened, then simply covered his eyes and groaned. Big Eye watched him too, with a vicious grin.

"Master Harding" walked over to Melissa and grabbed her crotch. "How much for this?"

"Plenty thousand dollar, yuh cyaan afford it," she replied.

The young men giggled in fits. They were growing impatient.

I ran forward and tried to pull her away, but she protested. "'Low me to earn me money! Yuh know how much dem payin' me for dis?"

More laughter. "Messado is her messiah!"

"Master Harding" went back to his desk and took out a paddle, then curled his finger, calling her over. Her eyes went big and she vehemently shook her head.

"She never read the fine print!" The laughter sounded like fiends in hell.

She shrilled, her voice shaky and terror-stricken, "Pay me for me services or let me walk away!" She realized her mistake too late—she was in no position to bargain. Everyone watched her closely. Bow ties dangling, sleeves rolled up, jackets thrown aside. Don Carlos was playing horsey with the doll and through puffed cheeks made trumpet sounds. Perry was sitting on Mighty's lap with a bottle to his mouth, leering at Melissa like a fallen prince.

"Do what yuh've been told, gyal," said Big Eye.

I reached for my wallet. "How much they promised yuh?"

"Messado, step aside!"

She looked half-dead refusing the bailout, as if she'd already been eaten. "Keep yuh money," she said, weakly pushing me away.

"Yuh don't understand what's happening here," I whispered to her.

"Oh, and *you* do?" she responded.

"They'll eat yuh alive. They'll fix yuh."

"Me a whore!" she snapped. "What's new?"

The Gadfly members grabbed her; the boys hooted, "To the threshing room!"

"Master Harding" smiled. "How's your Latin, dear? Just two words from the school's motto and we'll spare you."

I crumpled next to a table. "Smokey, do somethin'!"

"For the love of God, man, somebody throw Messado outside!"

"Don't be so sensitive, Kierkegaard!"

Something intruded upon my gloom, a kind of reckless death wish. I was willing to lose my life in that room without any thought of nobility or redemption. "Don't call me that!" I said, whipping around, braving the sea of faces.

Smokey finally stood and quieted the proceedings, as if everyone had been waiting for the guest of honor to show a pulse. He was back to his old self—we could see it in the way he took off the jacket and threw it aside like a pair of his dirty overalls. The playacting was over. He picked his words like a man picking grapes in a vineyard. "Pity it is such a difficult world," he began, tracing his fingers along the lines of his rough hand, "which refuses to give satisfaction. I dream las' night I fell an' knocked out me front teeth. Now I see I have painfully lost me children."

That's all it took from him—we blushed to our ears, deeply ashamed, silent.

Big Eye fumed though. He felt the weight of rejection, and like Cain he was confused by his own self-sabotage. He walked up to Smokey with fight in his manner, pointing at the older man's face. "Don't flatter yuhself. Yuh don't own us. Never did. Never will. Yuh sense of loss and responsibility is misplaced, a delusion that belongs to another time and place. Who yuh think yuh is to look down yuh nose at us? Yuh came here so yuh would learn yuh place once and for all. Yuh don't get to feel sorry for us. *We* have moved on."

We couldn't even raise our eyes to Smokey's. Big Eye had presumed to speak for all of us and had embarrassed us thoroughly.

Smokey stared at Big Eye till the latter dropped his eyes and fierceness, then he beckoned to Melissa. "Come, chile, yuh need a ride?"

In an absurd display, something Big Eye couldn't have scripted, Melissa struggled to wrench her dress off the blow-up doll but was so flustered she abandoned it and clip-clopped to a side door in her heels and lingerie, rubbing her hands along her upper arms when chillsome wind entered the doorway, her glittery face mask catching moonlight like liquid drops. Smokey threw the blazer around her shoulders and left without a word. We couldn't have enjoyed ourselves after that even if we'd wanted to. We had spoiled our own fun like brats trying to show an adult who was boss. It was as if there'd been a blackout in the room. A tear slipped down Big Eye's face and he was too ashamed to wipe it.

Carey Halls, seeking to seize the moment, said with forced casualness, "There, proud-a yuhself, Big Eye?"

Big Eye fell upon him and beat him with the paddle.

CHAPTER 17

That Saturday after the Old Boys' Dinner, I headed to my grandparents' because Cam had taken ill. I sat at a window writing and caught Melissa watching me through her curtains. I went outside and up to her house. She pulled the curtains closed and came to her door. The ordeal of the night before was visible in her bleary eyes, and fresh sleep lines crisscrossed her face like thin bleeding cuts. She had on Hammer Mouth's gray undershirt that he worked in at my family's cement factory; it stretched almost to her knees.

"Where's yuh man?"

"Gone ah work." She spat the words at me like venom.

I stood there staring her down.

She slowly lifted the shirt with spite in her eyes, backpedaling into the blue living room. "Come, John Crow, come tek what yuh t'ink yuh earn!"

It was frightening how much this hold I had over her aroused me. I stepped inside and gently closed the door. "Yuh tell Hammer yuh turnin' tricks?"

"None of yuh business!"

"Who wicked, gyal? Me or you?"

She watched me cock-eyed as she sat down at a table, pegging an orange and crossing her legs. "Yuh sleep wid me dat night when me knock out?"

"No! I didn't—I swear. Did someone—"

"Doh ask me no question!" She uncrossed her legs to show she had only panties on. "Tek de likkle pussy an' gwaan. Hammer nuh haffe know nutten 'bout today or tomorrow or any odder time. As far as him concerned, I'm a massage therapist an' hairdresser—see me certificates dere on de wall."

"I'm not here to blackmail yuh."

"No? Jus' here to colleck some pussy like how yuh colleck rent?" She looked tired, there was strain in her eyes, yet she tried to force the issue, moving to the small bed below the window and taking off her shirt, throwing it languidly on a chair. Her phone beeped and she stretched across the bed to get it, half lying, her limbs in an awkward pose, like a coney incapacitated by a hunter's bullet. She had long legs and a birthmark on the back of one knee in the shape of a gallows, like the cat's birthmark in that Poe story. Reading the message, she smiled bitterly at the phone. "*Thank you for your business*. That's what him say to me. So courteous, such a gentleman."

"Who's *he*?"

"An' de whole time him huffin' on toppa me, him smell like under John Crow wing. I had to hol' me breath, fightin' not to vomit when I see ringworm leakin' pus on him fat disgustin' neck. Me felt like a toilet for him to piss him cum in."

I sat on a chair and watched as she stared blankly at the wall. We were in the room at Punkie's again, that same aloof attitude of hers, the pink chintzy wallpaper and endless circles of fish swimming around us. "I know why yuh keep this bed here—yuh can't bear to sleep with him in the bedroom 'cause it holds no more intimacy for yuh than a telephone booth. It feels like betrayal—"

"Doh flatter yuhself, smartypants. I keep dis bed here for when de cataplexy start an' I too weak to walk." She wrapped an arm across her abdomen. "*T'cha*! Wha' do dis bwoy though? Look here, me nuh have time fe waste."

"What does it feel like when the narcolepsy comes on?"

She softened, and her arm slowly went limp, falling to her lap; she sucked her bottom lip like a lonely child left behind in a schoolyard. Her gaze went inward and she tilted her head back slightly, making slow circles with her finger around one of her breasts. "Yuh wa'an talk to me now?" she scoffed. "Yuh wa'an play counselor?"

"I'm sure yuh gettin' medical help, but is there somethin' yuh'd like to get off yuh chest . . . personally?"

"Me confidant," she sniggered, peering coldly at me, her eyes like bright little beads in her unslept swollen face.

I wondered if they'd had a fight that morning. Lois had told me that sometimes when the shouting started, or a dish smashed, it would be too late—by the time Lois or Cam would go look, Melissa would have already dashed out of the house, at times half-naked. Hammer would stand on the verandah, screaming something like, "Me nuh wa'an yuh back inside here, dutty germsy gyal! Whore!" According to Lois, sometimes he'd throw her clothes out, even her most personal items—contraceptives, sanitary napkins, pills. Melissa would only reward the women in my family with mumbles or terrified silence, and a few times they allowed her to spend the night at their place.

Now she cut into my thoughts: "I'd like to get yuh off me fuckin' back—first t'ing!"

"I mean it, Melissa, I want to know what it's like for yuh. Yuh probably don't remember, but just before yuh blacked out that night, it was almost as if you were becomin' another person. Yuh started talkin', bein' very forthright. Till you tore the wallpaper off—"

"Okay, you first: tell me somet'ing unpleasant—somet'ing dat annoy yuh recently."

I thought. "Okay . . . I ran into an old classmate at the tax office, a bwoy I'd never liked, who made neat notes but was stupid. Now he had a desk with his name on it and I had to see him."

She laughed a little, plucking at the flesh of her upper arm. "Wha' him name?"

"Strachan. Paul. Pronounced *Strawn* but spelled S-t-r-a-c-h-a-n. We used to pronounce it in ugly syllables and drag phlegm up our throats, especially when we did roll call or picked teams. Some bwoys would spit at his feet after hawkin' his name up their tonsils. I could see him rememberin' all that. I used to be one of the spitters."

"So yuh felt guilty den?"

"Yes, but annoyed too, begrudgin' the fact he had the upper hand for even a few lousy minutes as I sat there toleratin' his condescension."

"Yuh felt powerless."

"Yes, yes, that's the word."

"Well, dat's how I feel whenever de sleep paralysis comin' on. I'm talkin' to friends, at de bus stop, in a bar servin' drinks, dancin' onstage, at de racetrack or Jarret Park wid Hammer, in bed wid a client. On de toilet. I'm you an' de narcolepsy is Paul Strachan. But de difference is you *deserve* punishment an' still unrepentant. See dis here?" She opened her thighs and showed me a long crinkly scar that ran close to her panty line. "See here too?" Her elbow was also blemished. "An' here." When she pushed her hair behind her ear, I saw she was missing a lobe—it had been burned off. "More dan once I get an attack while curling me hair; dat's de worst. Hammer keep sayin' I should stop use it, but a gyal in my line ah work cyaan go widout it, no more dan a carpenter can go widout a plane."

"That's why yuh need him—he keeps yuh from accidentally harmin' yuhself?"

She nodded and started ponytailing her hair with a scrunchie. She was looking at my crotch with resigned misery. "Him more dan dat, him me guardrail, safety belt . . . me angel. Widout him I'd be dead arredi. One time him catch me on de bathroom floor jus' as I was about to roll over on de damn curling wand an' lose ah whole side ah me face. I would-a ended up wid one eye fe sure, an' me face is me business."

"So yuh scared of losin' him—if he finds out you're a prostitute."

She dropped her hands and exhaled angrily. "It was *burlesque*! Dat's what I did at Punkie's, till I get inna jam an' Fat Bob bail me out."

"And yuh repayin' an everlastin' debt. I've heard it all before. How pimps send agents to bus stations to scout gyals fresh off de country bus."

"Yuh doh know shit! An' lemme tell yuh sum'n. You're a whore too. Yes—you! Why yuh lookin' at me like dat? We all t'ink we free, but we not, we follow de same path again an' again."

"What's that supposed to mean?"

"If I change me past, I'll change who I am right now. Doh t'ink yuh can interfere wid me life. It doh work like dat. If I was you, I'd tek de likkle *kratches* yuh mout' been runnin' water for an' leave dis room an' doh come back. Dis might be yuh house, but it's my *life*. Doh confuse de two." She stared at me when I refused to move, then went down on her knees and waddled over and started at my zipper.

I got up and put the money on the table, along with Chadwell's card. "Come to that address if yuh ever want to talk away from here. It's all there, the amount Big Eye promised yuh. How weak is the heart of a woman?" I said to her coldly, genuinely mad at her for misreading me. "That's why Fat Bob will never let yuh go. You're a chicken who think it can outsmart a hawk. Don't gimme yuh self-pityin' speech. We have nutten in common."

She stood, pushed me to the wall. "Who de fuck yuh t'ink yuh be?" She looked around for something to attack with, then grabbed the money and shoved me to the door. "Here—tek it!" She forced the money back into my hand.

I wedged my foot against the doorjamb.

She reached for an umbrella. "Tek de fuckin' money! Stop actin' prideful an' indignant!" Then she stepped back. Perhaps something had flitted over my face that betrayed my deepest feelings. She stood at a remove and grinned, pulling her lips back to show her teeth, her eyes shining with some secret knowledge. "Yuh did *somet'ing*," she said. "I can see't in yuh face. Doh use *me* to buy back yuh conscience." She slapped my hand and the bills went flying.

I left them on the floor and finally walked out, but turned and snapped a pic with my phone of her raving. "Yuh tell Hammer stories, I can tell a few too," I said.

She spat at me as I moved away, then hurried out and threw the money over the verandah railing. She spat on the last bill, crumpled it, and hurled it at my head. "Hypocrite! Blackmailer! Me freer than *you*. Stop watch me pussy. Me a big woman fe yuh. Me nuh bawn a Bay—but no pimp nuh tek me offa country bloodclaat bus. Nobody cyaan frighten me wid dem mout'!" She stormed back inside.

Mama came out to the clothesline looking horrified. I walked to the other end of the house, but she followed and confronted me: "Nyjah, what yuh doin' wid Hammer Mouth's woman!"

"Mama, please, it was a misunderstandin', that's all."

"I go ask yuh only one time . . ."

"Is not what yuh think. Trust me."

"*Trus'* yuh? After I see yuh leavin' hotfoot wid a half-dressed woman screamin' an' spittin' at yuh? T'rowin' money in de yawd? Jeezam peas . . . Lois, get in here!"

"Yuh can't put her out," I said. "She needs to stay, she's narcoleptic. They'll break her like an egg. Yuh just can't do it."

Mama stood before me. "How yuh know all dis?"

"That's my business, and no, I didn't sleep with her."

"Hmph," said Lois, approaching us like a judge back from recess. "Seems to me yuh still haven't told us half of what we need to decide whether she stays or not."

"Stop being so fuckin' superior. I'm sick of yuh primmin'. Yuh no better than she is, no matter what she does."

"Language!"

Lois arched her eyebrows. "What she *does*? What does she *do*, Nyjah? Fess up."

"Aie!" said Mama, pressing her wet hands on her head tie. "Enough!"

"And *who* will break her?" said Lois.

Perhaps what happened next was divine intervention. Cam cried out. When we raced inside to her room, she was clutching a sheet to her chest. "It hurts . . ." she wheezed. Her rash trailed drops of blood like when she'd pick at her face in her sleep. She'd been bedridden, suffering from fever and muscle pain almost a whole week. "It hurts!"

"Tony, call an ambulance!"

"No, let the doctor come. I hate those frowsy hospital beds!" She began stuffing the sheet in her mouth, writhing with tears brimming her sore eyelids. It was all Mama could do to pull the sheet from her grip.

I stared out the glary window. The hotel overlooked the fire station and I could see firemen, some of them former classmates, shirtless around a *Ludo* table. Their daredevilish voices reached us on the eighth floor.

"I just need some time to think, Bree. This thing with Cam out to kill me."

Briana avoided my eyes as if not willing to be drawn into my depressive thoughts. "Why yuh bring me here? Yuh want me to stay all day cooped up in this shabby hotel nursing yuh and drinking cheap tea bags?"

"Is not like is the first time we comin' here. I hardly see yuh."

"Yuh don't *want* to see me. This is an emergency on your terms. I can't spend my life waiting on yuh, Nyjah. And I'm afraid yuh've made the right choice. She loves yuh more than I do. Let's just enjoy what we have as long as we can."

"Will yuh come to the hospital?" I asked.

"No, that's too complicated. That's family space."

"I want yuh there."

"It's not your decision alone to make. Don't be such a worrywart, yuh aunt will make it. She's young. Worry about yuh job and all these accruing absences."

"My problems feel unimportant. But Cam . . ." I sat down beside her.

Briana wiped the tear from my cheek. "I know . . . it's hard."

"*Hard*," I laughed bitterly. "I know she doesn't have long. We all do. We discuss it when she's not around. My grandmother has even prepared her funeral gown. Imagine what it's like for a mother without hope for her own child."

I broke down. She let me cry and put the *Do Not Disturb* sign outside. She pulled the curtains together and turned up the TV. I couldn't believe how easily it had happened.

"Yuh finally in my arms—freely." She released a girlish giggle and gently kissed my cheek.

"Bree . . ." I held her waist and tugged her in, pulling strands of her hair in place along the sides of her face like a child playing with a doll.

"Bwoy, what yuh doing? Don't pet me like a dog," she said with a small smile.

I put my finger to her lips and laid her down. She relaxed and threw her arms above her head, her mouth pulled back in a slightly frozen, nervous grin. I put my hand up her skirt and she pushed it off and pulled her skirt back down, and we struggled as she giggled till she was out of breath. I slowly pulled the blouse over her head; her armpits were shaved and darker than the rest of her skin and had lines of deodorant stuck between the creases. I traced my hand down the swell of her firm breasts and let it rest on the stubbly warmth between her legs. She arched her back and stared up at the ceiling. Her fingernails played over my back and lifted my shirt off.

"I'm dancing in my head, Nyjah," she said. "It hasn't reached my body yet."

"Follow my lead," I said, turning her over. Cinnamon-colored plaits cascaded down her bare back, her skin a deep, smooth brown.

When it was over, she drew the sheet up to her chest, quiet, contemplative. "Yuh spoke to Perry for me?"

"Bree, *lawks*, man, let's not spoil this," I said, sucking my teeth.

"Okay."

I rolled over, went to sleep. I don't know how long I was out before something knocked me awake. She picked up the phone and hurled it harder. "Ow!"

Her face had gone almost purple with hot-blooded rage. She

pointed at the screen, at the picture I'd snapped of Melissa. "What's that, Nyjah!? Yuh mean yuh tell me yuh have a gyal, Dreenie or Dreen or whatever the fuck her name is, and I say, 'Okay, I'll work with it. I'll be the second wheel 'cause I like yuh,' and yuh go and take up another one?"

"What gives you the right to search my phone, gyal?" But my protest was ludicrous in the face of her wrath.

"I must be the stupidest gyal in St. James in the first place to *deh* with people, man, and expect them to be satisfied with two women. Not you Montegonian men! Yes! I must be some kinda stupid, 'cause they say man scarce and woman nuff like salt, so take whichever man yuh can get, even if yuh have to share him. But no, this is the heights of disrespect! How the fuck yuh hang this on me?" She launched at me, wringing my neck. "This is why some of us turn *rass* lesbian without regret! Man too fuckin' wicked!"

I went to Pier One that weekend. The old kindergarten was fully refurbished and we'd be opening the school within a month. But Chadwell could see the traces of misgiving in my face. "How many checks do they owe yuh now—three, four months? Yuh think the kids aren't payin'? She's divertin' the wealth to her Kingston branches to prop them up."

My head jerked up. "Yuh mean Hobart?"

"All the patty shops yuh work for. The so-called MoBay Branch and staff is just an experiment, a cipher. Don't yuh know anything 'bout Kingstonians? They're crooks. They don't respect us. Yuh school is a pawn brokerage, a trout pool. They pay excuses and expect servility 'cause yuh desperate for a job. They know they have yuh by the balls."

"I need a steady check though, Chad. I got student loans."

"Are yuh gettin' a steady check now? Don't be daft. This is a chance at wealth. It might be rough at first, but the kids will come. Think about expansion. Two schools . . . six schools."

"Chad, this is not like buyin' me a bike, enuh."

"Nyjah, is time yuh start carryin' yuhself. Fix yuh fuckin' face. We here to celebrate."

We took bottles of Moët down to the dunes, the area along the beach where partygoers were thickest. We saw the car-wash crew. Chadwell went over to Mighty for a word. Perry nodded to us but he wasn't in the mood to be friendly. He was red-eyed and coughing with one tightly trousered leg propped on Mighty's baby-blue Mercedes. Some of the car-wash crew sat on sand buggies they'd arranged like a circle of wagons. Mixed emotions melted inside me, broke like water shaken from a tree. I was about to step out of the shadow of servitude, become my own man, but I wasn't free—I was shackled to Chadwell. When I saw Philip Moodie with an older man hanging on to him, greedily eating spoons of ice cream Philip fed him over his shoulder, when I saw the man kissing Philip's neck, till Philip had to push him off just to reclaim his personal space, I knew I was in trouble, that my life would never truly know happiness until I purged my conscience. Then Philip walked over.

"New boyfriend?" I indicated the man who'd stepped into shadows and was now watching us.

"Jérémie . . . it's French," Philip said. "He's from Martinique. How's the writin'?"

"You tell me, you were always the real talent, sans discipline."

He smiled sourly. "My life's my work. Somethin' you'll never understand. We could never be artistic rivals. I'm tryin' to engage in a special type of promiscuity. Abandon my body the way my country has abandoned me."

"It's called suicide, Philip, and it's hardy poetic."

He flicked his ice cream spoon up and down, squinting. "See, that's where yuh wrong. Snow is—" But Jérémie came over right then and pulled him away.

"Bumboclaat Babylon, bwoy, dem cyaan mek we hol' a vibes in peace," someone lamented, and the camouflage jeeps had already rolled down. People quickly threw spliffs and other contraband into crags in the long stretch of limestone.

A fierce soldier named Karate Georgie, who had lost an eye in the drug wars and now proudly wore a patch, walked over to the wagon circle with his gun hoisted like a golf club, smiling viciously. "Would yuh look at dis, Townsend," he said to his partner, stepping up to Fruity Hastings, "a hothouse of ambition dis car-wash crew is, eh? Fruity, look at yuh ugly fuckin' face, smilin' over here like de sun shinin' out yuh ass even at night."

People laughed timidly.

Fruits grinned broadly and blew weed smoke in Karate Georgie's face. A searchlight came on as soldiers combed the property, frisking people and using the opportunity to fondle women who cursed them like pigs. Fruits wouldn't back down from the one-eyed officer.

"No, sonny, keep yuh hands down," another soldier said to Colin. "Me never put me hand up a *chi-chi* man's pants, me doh wa'an feel a maxi pad."

Raucous laughs poured out. People felt emboldened when there were soldiers around.

The gay boys were momentarily stripped of their power.

Another soldier spoke up: "I hear yuh faggots' battyhole so loose dat when shit come, yuh cyaan hol' it if a toilet ain't close, so yuh haffe wear dat Donald Duck nappy." He grabbed Fenton, roughly spun him, and shined a flashlight on his jeans. "Look—puffy pants. Advertisin' yuh indifference to good opinion like a whore wearin' her pimp's flea collar."

"Lemme go, pussy'ole! *Kirrout!*" Fenton shot back.

"Dis one a bitch," said the soldier, as if inspecting a kennel. He clucked in disgust, "Such a fuckin' shame, I know y'all mothers wa'an grandchildren."

"Come check if I wearin' a nappy nuh!" yelled Moodie.

"Philip, buil'," Mighty warned.

Philip clacked his tongue against the roof of his mouth; the sound was so loud in the tense stillness, it was if a gun had been cocked.

The soldier walked over easily. "A who dis Copper Kid? De hothead SilverHawk me hear 'bout?"

"Suck out yuh mooma pussy!" Philip spat.

The soldier smashed Philip's nose; it squirted like a ketchup squeezer.

"Bumboclaat!" Philip erupted, reaching for his gun, but they pinned him and stomped his face into the sand.

"Dis how we party, pussy'ole!" yelled a soldier at the shocked crowd.

The instigator could hardly catch his breath he was so excited; he looked down at the unconscious body and marveled at his handiwork. "Awrite, back to work," he said as they hauled Philip into a jeep.

A halo of light suddenly crowned Mighty's nappy head as he ran an Afro pick through it; with headlights trained on him, he stood still like a catatonic. He looked like a mosaic of the Byzantine Christ with all the deep lines running through his face; there was profound sadness in his bloodshot eyes and tight mouth, holding back a scream against the world that had been building for years. His countenance was so unflinching that we had to look away from it. He seemed both alive and dead—a sinner and a persecuted saint. The soldiers had all circled their jeeps now, and their combined headlights might have been pinning Mighty to the Cross.

"Yes," said Karate Georgie, biting the top off a cigar, "yuh Missa Marvin, yuh t'ink we doh know yuh runnin' t'ings? Yuh t'ink is dunce Fruits we wa'an?"

With that, they drove off.

Venting frustration, the car-wash posse retrieved their weapons and fired several rounds when the music came back on. "Come, yah bitch!" cursed Mighty, a champagne bottle held aloft. He yanked on Perry's long braids and almost tossed him to the ground.

Perry yelped in pain and surprise, and Mighty gripped his shoulders, bent him over, and lifted his shirt to grind on him as Perry wined, his hips in slow rhythmic rotation as Mighty slapped his rump in time to the bassline.

Some big fat gyal cyaan handle buddy
yet still wa'an ride pon Kabasaki,
mawga slim gyal cyaan tek winery . . .
Hood top, hood top, if yuh love bike back . . .

Mighty pulled Perry in for a tongue bath and the other gay boys fired more shots in the air. People scattered and shrieked. "Fuckin' battyman dem!" someone called out. But that's all they could do—sneer. Mighty had become too powerful to care. He ruled downtown as he had ruled school.

DJ Bobby Cornflakes roared, "*Showaaaa*! Hailin' up de big bad Mighty Mouse an' de car-wash crew! MoBay finery! Big-money winery! *Pu-ull up!*"

The car-wash crew threw cash in the air and everyone scrambled for it. Someone ran off with a loud yelp; there was blood on some of the five-hundred-dollar bills. It came to our attention that someone was hobbling around and moaning like a wounded dog.

"Dem shot him in de leg!" a woman shrieked. "Stray bullet!"

They circled the unfortunate man as he lay stiff on the shore. "Fuckin' shit-smellin', cock-suckin' Sodomite dem! Oonuh shot me! Fuck all-ah yuh cunt-hatin' faggots!"

Perry examined him as he screamed and wriggled. "The bullet went clean through."

"You a doctor?" the man asked Perry.

Perry stared at him steadily and must've seen the hate he radiated like a carburetor. "Bite down on *this*. We're goin' move yuh and get yuh some help."

Mighty came over and placed a hand on Perry's neck; the man's eyes went wide with disbelief. "Yuh—doc . . . yuh one ah dem too?"

Mighty gave an ugly smile.

"Yes," said Perry, "yuh still want me to help yuh?"

"Leave me!" the man yelled. "Me nuh wa'an nuh *chi-chi* man touch me. Suckin' one anodda balls! Eatin' man hood like termite!"

Mighty covered his hand and lit his spliff, then said, "We bring our destinies into dis world wid us like de finest ah spiderwebs an' weave it gradually, blind to its pattern an' numb to its fragile hold pon us. Why yuh hate us, really? Were yuh born to hate us as how we born to be what we is?"

The man laughed scornfully. "Somebody shoulda cut yuh t'roat while yuh still in de crib."

"Bring him, Perry," said Colin. "Put him in de car."

The man realized his mistake. "No! Me tek back every word!"

Bolo, the cast-eye one with the broad chest, who'd lost some weight since school days, scooped the man up by himself and brought him to the Escalade. The man never stopped screaming, asking forgiveness and praying aloud. He took out his ID and threw it at some bystanders. "Desmond Haynes me name! Me live ah 33 Hopeview Road!"

"*Hope*," Bolo giggled. "C'mon, Dessie, le'we tek yuh home."

"No, me wa'an go hospital," the man whimpered, grabbing Mighty's arm.

"Yes," said Mighty, bending two of the man's fingers backward. "We should sew the cell phone under yuh skin—dat way yuh never miss yuh calls."

Desmond seemed to have lost his capacity for speech.

Bolo reported jovially, "Him shit himself."

Mighty chuckled and tossed the spliff. "Who the shit-smellin' bastard now?"

They rolled out in a cortege with the man still screaming.

"Mercy," said a girl in hot pink. "Battyman turn undertaker now."

"A boneyard him gone."

On came the voice of Frisco Kid over the speakers: "*A bai juvenile run downtown, run downtown, run downtown . . .*"

CHAPTER 18

I returned to the museum three weeks later. I was reading *Genji* on the bus to calm my nerves.

> *The strangest thing was that her robes were permeated with the scent of the poppy seeds burned at exorcisms. She changed clothes repeatedly and even washed her hair, but the odor persisted. She was overcome with self-loathing.*

I wondered how Maude would be when I found her. *Yamaye, the ghost who Maude's spiritual gaze is pinned upon / A vision in the flesh.* But I couldn't go on with this poem—the words dried up in my brain. I'd felt so horrible after reading her journal without permission that it kept me up some nights. I had to apologize—to make it right. *Make* what *right?* I castigated myself. Yet I had to try. The thing I wanted to be never seemed to gel with the thing I was. I wanted to be brave with her, to confront my fears and not think of an end result, to abandon totally the notion of self-regard or my own absolution. I wanted to come out of the shadows and show my face. What was the purpose of all these near meetings if not to intersect meaningfully, once and for all? But I had faith in her story—her writing had confronted me in a way that confounded my own.

When I entered the property, the groundskeeper had to look hard before he recognized me, twisting the filthy ascot on his head.

I wondered if all groundskeepers had a proclivity for this fashion. Smokey wore one of those ascots as well.

"Yuh here to see yuh princess?"

I nodded.

He smiled at my being tongue-tied. "Gwaan, yuh timin' immaculate as always. She in dere by herself."

I stepped into the building and watched her moving around at the far end of the room; her presence filled the place. It became even clearer to me that this was more than a museum to her. It seemed to be a willing vessel, a kind of body she utilized. It was impossible to tell where she began and where it ended. She went into a small room marked *Staff*, and I took my time looking around. The museum, though well-appointed, was marked by certain absences. Strict time lines had been avoided in favor of a less temporal grouping of artifacts. Ceramics and wicker craft overflowed from one shelf to another while ceremonial costumes and sea-rotted clothing swam between rooms. Great canoes, carved some six hundred years earlier by Taino hands, sat alongside estate records and a bottle with a churner. There was an entire room dedicated to the ritual use of the hallucinogenic *cohoba.* I soon realized that coherence wasn't the point, that to spend time trying to appreciate her curatorial decisions was to understand that rooms led nowhere and labels served no purpose, that time itself was unwelcome and boundaries were real yet not, that exhibitions weren't dead displays but gateways—pulsing with life like the ritual Dujo throne with its zemi head and inlays of eyes, ears, mouth, and humanized feet—gateways that, when passed through at just the right pace and in just the right order, could send you somewhere outside of yourself. Had she unconsciously arranged it like this to escape *herself?*

I saw two silhouettes behind the staff room's glass door. She soon came out and walked over to an exhibit, then pulled something heavy that looked like a horseshoe crab from a tilting overhead shelf. I cleared my throat and approached. "Yuh need any help?"

"What?" she said.

"That looks heavy, could I lend a hand?"

Her eyes flickered for a brief moment. "Current exhibit closed till further notice, check the press."

She didn't face me as she said this—I might've been talking to the automated service for a cinema.

I decided to leave her alone. Fortunately, her boss came out. This was probably Huntley, the man who the groundskeeper had said was fond of seeing himself on local TV every Wednesday. He was an old white guy with a wide gait and a complexion like cinnamon oatmeal. He gave me a cheeky grin as if he thought I was her boyfriend. He walked over briskly, alarming me with his radiant assuredness, and had the temerity to take my arm and lead me aside.

"Please," he said gently, "you look like a boy of good breeding, am I right? Take her out sometime. Buy her something nice. She walks around here sometimes as if she's lost."

I did my best to formulate a response that would dispel his assumptions. But what was the hurry? It was good of him to talk so openly—I could learn more about what I was up against.

"I'm thinking I need to change the AC unit," he mused, scratching his chin and looking around. "What do you think?" The atmosphere of this wing was cloistered and the air dank and still. It had the feel of a monastery.

"Huh?" I replied, watching her sit down at a small table by an open door. She sat with her back to us, catching fresh air. She had old-fashioned earphones on and was eating a sandwich, swinging her legs like a child, enjoying her music, in her own world.

The white man gave me a quizzical look and excused himself. I waited a few moments and then approached Maude. I could hear the buzz of Lionel Richie's tenor coming from her earphones: "*Oh no, I'm going crazy for love . . . over you . . .*"

"Really?" I said. "Lionel Richie?"

"What did yuh expect?" she responded with equanimity. It was now plain that she recognized me, though she was calm, as if she were on holy ground, safe and protected.

"I don't know. Not that, though."

"So for once I surprise yuh," she said easily, crossing her legs and biting into her sandwich. Her smile was crowding me into a corner, as if our roles were reversed. She noticed my apprehension, my surprise at her lack of surprise and annoyance, and she stood and put her food away. "Walk with me."

I felt such a relief that she wasn't angry, but it was surreal, like a murderer walking with his victim's ghost. "Yuh know," I said, "we had a nickname for yuh."

She smirked, then ran her tongue over her teeth. "I do know. *Ms. Daydream.*"

"There was another one."

"I know it too. *St. Maude the Epileptic.* I saw yuh that day, yuh know, when yuh ran away."

"Do yuh hate me?"

She looked me full in the face.

I balked. We were now walking side by side, past the garden and off the property, yet there was something missing, a vital gap, a lacuna in our interaction, something that had to be filled immediately before it all crumbled into disaster. I was seized with a strangling shortness of breath and knew what it was—the truth was fighting its way up.

"What saved yuh that day . . . how did yuh recover?"

"Who says I've recovered? God comforts. He can save you too. Are yuh faith-filled?"

"I was, for a while, after what I saw them do to yuh, but . . . I'm afraid I was shammin'. Plus, it was a primitive religion, not anything as effective as yuh own. It was my mother's Pocomania church."

We stopped at a polished gray stone monument that bordered pastel-colored bungalows and motels near the seaside. She sat down on a bench with a modicum of movement, folding her black skirt neatly under her thigh.

"I've got somethin' I must say to yuh," I began. "I must apologize for—"

But Maude's head swiveled toward a ruckus: a quarrel was breaking out between tenants of the villas. A burly Black man stood beside a sagging chain-link fence with his camera trained on a white man sitting on his verandah, smoking and enjoying his Sangster's rum cream. The white man's young lover had just put a plate of food before him.

"Why are you videoing me?" the white man was saying in an American accent. He got up from his white plastic chair and slammed his phone down. "Am I in a fucking zoo?"

"Ain't got money for shit," the Black man responded.

"Why—what's . . . ? You don't do that. You *can't* do that," said the American, gangling toward his white burglar bars. We couldn't really see what was happening.

"Come out yah," beckoned the Black local, smiling savagely.

The American limped toward his steps, his green Jamaican soccer jersey billowing in the sea breeze's brackish reek. "You still videoing me?" He was either injured or disabled.

His Black girlfriend tackled him on the faux-marble steps. "Jerry, doh t'row nutten." She clawed at strands of her own curly bronze wig, her pretty gamine face set off by big ears, looking almost like a black Tinker Bell. "Jerry!"

Then I saw her resemblance to Maude.

But Jerry palmed an ashtray and launched it at the fence. "Take a video of *this*!"

The ashtray smashed on the Black man's wall. His white girlfriend on the balcony above, wearing only black panties and an Arsenal jersey, covered her mouth and jumped back.

"Irma, control him!" Maude called out, scrambling toward the fracas.

I was confused, excited, and apprehensive. I never knew country people to behave like this, and with foreigners to boot. "Who's that white guy?" I said behind Maude.

"He's a sex tourist," she said dismissively. "The gyal's my cousin . . . Irma!" she repeated.

"Yeah, bad bwoy?" mocked the bald Black man, whom I figured for a returning resident come to show off his white woman. The whole interaction was quite bizarre. "Yeah, bad bwoy, yeah!"

Irma and Maude grabbed the guy's arms as he moved menacingly toward the limping white man.

"Nuh bother lick him, Dwayne. Nuh bother with him," Maude begged, then screamed at her cousin: "Gyal, gwaan go talk sense into him!"

Irma jogged toward Jerry as he propped a crutch on the railing and dragged his hurt leg behind him, his thin lips trembling in anger and his black-rimmed glasses steamy.

"Oh my god," said Dwayne's white girlfriend on the upstairs balcony. "Oh my god."

"Yuh t'ink dis a bloodclaat joke?" muttered the Black man, pushing Maude away. "Come."

"Dwayne, no!" pleaded Maude. It was the most spirited I'd seen her since school days.

"That's invading my privacy," said Jerry. "Who gives you the right?"

"Yeah? An' wha' de fuck yuh go do, white bwoy?" Dwayne bellowed.

"Just get that fucking phone off of me," said Jerry.

"Nyjah, don't just stand there!" Maude yelled, pushing Dwayne back with all her strength. "Help Irma!"

But I froze. Like I froze that day at the J block. Like I froze when Bussy died.

Maude and Irma struggled to keep the men apart.

"Relax yuhself—relax!" Irma scolded Jerry, who looked twice her age.

"Don't get in the way," said the white man as Irma pushed him back into his doorway.

"Let him go, man—mek him come," taunted Dwayne.

"Stop fighting me," whined Jerry. His weak left leg meant he could offer little resistance to the young woman's strength. When she snapped both dog tags off his stringy neck, his Adam's apple bobbed violently below his gray stubble and he grabbed at her wig.

"Leggo offa me!" Irma exploded. "Behave yuhself!" She started slapping him until he fell down on his bony backside.

"To bloodclaat!" laughed a nearby fisherman. "I doh understan', how yuh come to a Black country an' doh like Blacks? Beat him *rass*, Irma."

As Irma administered more slaps to the man on the ground, her blue jeans rode down her hips to expose a tattoo just above her ass. "Behave . . . pussy'ole," she finished, swinging her small pink Chanel bag around her neck, getting it tangled in her long weave.

"You don't support me, you slut!" yelled Jerry as she moved away, rising to his knees and feeling around for his glasses.

Maude glared at Irma. "Pick him back up, yuh likkle *sketel*. That's all yuh good for."

Strangely cowed, Irma turned around and walked back over to Jerry, still on his knees, looking pitiful. "Behave." She raised her palm again and Jerry flinched.

A growing group of fishermen and bystanders held their bellies and laughed.

"Thanks a *lot*," said Jerry, then pointed at Dwayne, who was still recording. "You want that on TikTok?"

Maude snatched Dwayne's phone out of his hand and threw it to the ground. "I'm sick of all-ah yuh! Sick! Laughing at this poor man!"

The fishermen quieted.

"So she have a white man and Dwayne have a white gyal?" said a local white teenager standing with the fishermen.

"Cyaan even walk right but him wa'an ack hawd," said another bystander. "Him mus' t'ink him still deh ah 'Merica."

"*Yuh doh support me!*" someone mocked Jerry, who I now realized was fairly drunk.

"Him should respeck de people an' de lan'—him is a visitor here," said a woman. "Dose rights yuh have in 'Merica doh work here. How de fuck him go be racist inna Black country?"

"Who give any of yuh the right?" Maude yelled. "And *you*!" She turned to Irma. "Tellin' a grown man to behave and smackin' him like pickney. Why don't *you* behave and straighten out yuh dutty life?"

"But Maude, Irma jus' save him from an assin'," a vendor offered tentatively, twisting the sunburned dreads on his chin. "If Dwayne hol' him, it done."

"*Save* him? She saw her green card slippin'," said the local white kid.

"She save both him an' Dwayne 'cause Dwayne would-a go to prison for killin' tourist."

"What she doin' for that green card, Peter?" Maude said, facing the white teen. "Didn't yuh just hear him call her a slut?"

Irma dropped her head and pushed Jerry back inside the guesthouse.

"Dwayne, yuh wrong too," Maude continued. "Why yuh provoke the man when him sittin' on his verandah? And you, with yuh self-respect under yuh foot bottom. When yuh goin' change?"

Irma, meanwhile, had had enough. "At least me have a life! 'Low me mek me fuck who me want! Yuh actin' like yuh savin' yuh pussy fe Jesus, Maude. I ain't runnin' from life or hidin' inna museum. Yuh fuckin' cripple more dan Jerry! Come back here, come siddung pon yuh hands like *mumu*. After Auntie Mila waste so much money pon yuh edukayshon. Boastin' to everybody 'bout yuh."

Maude's face darkened as she pushed through the gawkers and hurried back to the museum compound.

"I come to de garden alone, while de dew is still on de roses," crooned the groundskeeper the next day, in a sweet rumbling baritone, picking his way through yellowing breadfruit leaves piled high like a young yam hill. He was in a good mood; he winked at me. "Yuh

goin' marry her someday, bwoy. I see't in me cuppa cerassie." He had fingers like grated carrots—they looked as if they belonged in the museum, or he might've borrowed them from some prehistoric collection.

She wore her hair in a bewitching style; she had dyed it blond today, almost fawn-colored, parted down the middle with the midsection a deep black like wet mud, with cream pearls beading each side of her scalp like a jeweled runway.

I stole over to the wooden bench and stood behind her. She was watching a soap opera and eating a sandwich. The short girl on the phone screen said to the tall bookish man in glasses, "*I love you! I can't help it!*" The man, whom I realized was a lecturer (and she a student), backed out of the empty classroom as if being mobbed by phantoms. "*Love me? You don't even know me.*" The girl threw herself at him: "*Love is its own knowledge!*"

Maude paused her chewing, tilting her head at the girl's rejection.

"You're a sentimental sap, aren't yuh? First Lionel Richie, now this."

"Nyjah? What are yuh doin' here? Didn't yuh go home?"

"I rented a room at Sea Blue."

She went back to her soap.

"May I sit down?"

"No."

"Well, can I at least—"

She breathed noisily. "No, no, no, to anything yuh goin' ask. This has to stop, Nyjah. What yuh want, *bwoy*?"

My stomach grumbled loudly.

She rolled her eyes at the sky and slapped her knee. "Ugh! Here!" She passed half her sandwich to me.

I sat down quickly. "Much obliged. Hotel breakfast didn't agree with me."

"Be quiet—don't talk till I'm through watchin' this."

"Okay . . . Can I—"

"Nyjah!"

"Right . . . quiet, eating . . . quietly . . . not a sound."

She flashed her eyes. "I'm going to wave my pinky and hopefully you'll be gone by then."

So I left her to the soap. I started eating, surprised that someone could make a saltfish sandwich better than my mother's, and observed the garden. The waxy green leaves had long tendrils with buds like green sparks, like a freeze-frame of some chemical explosion. I looked around to ask the groundskeeper what they were called, but he was busy. I took a picture and googled it.

When she finished, she sighed for all the injustice in the soap-operatic world, then remembered I was still there and didn't bother hiding her disappointment. "So I guess I've got to entertain yuh now, is that it?"

"Do I look that bored?"

"Come," she said, flicking her fingers, "want to see somethin' interestin'?"

I followed her inside. The museum had only a few patrons, a smattering of out-of-towners in sandals, sandy shorts, and poorly printed T-shirts advertising some Negril run-a-thon.

"I heard Perry Fischer's in med school," she said.

"He took time off—family matters," I lied, not wanting to get into the details.

She brought me through a turnstile, the floor inside patterned with black and white tiles. Upon a pyre-like table, the mummy lay behind a screen, and a hay-colored rug covered the floor. It was musty in there, and we moved toward the centerpiece with soft steps as if not to disturb it. The shrunken body was lying stiff on a board bed with a rough sheet partially thrown over it and one of its withered hands hanging over the side.

"The cover has an antibacterial property. It must be terrible for her," said Maude.

I saw that Yamaye was young. Her face was unchanged, in a sense, and quite pretty.

Maude was there physically, but had left me behind again,

talking to the corpse: "Won't yuh let me hear yuh voice again?" She took one of its fingers. "What was it that made me give yuh all my love, for so short a time, and then made yuh leave me to this misery?"

Did she really think the corpse could hear her? Did she think their lives were entwined somehow or that they had lived in the same period? I had never figured her for a mystic. Yet I wondered—had I unwittingly stepped through one of her gateways?

I didn't know how to step in and comfort her, not wanting to break her spiritual connection because it seemed so emotionally real.

"Taino?" I asked quietly, feigning ignorance.

She nodded almost imperceptibly. I might've been at a funeral disturbing the bereaved. "The priests did not know who she was," she told me. "Chauvinists!" She sounded like a near lunatic.

I wondered if she was having a quiet episode, something internal. But then something remarkable happened: I felt my eyes mist over.

She put her ear to the corpse's straw-like mouth that still had a few stony teeth. "What? Come with yuh to the zemi festival?" Her face colored with hesitant grief. "We've been together since I was very young. I've never left yuh side, not for a single moment. Where am I to go now? I'll have to tell the others what has happened to yuh. And I'll have to put up with their accusations." She began crying and swaying. "I want to go with yuh, sister! It's only natural. But it's the way of the world. Partin' is always sad. Our lives must end, early or late. Try to put yuh trust in me." She drew herself to her full height and released the charcoal-looking finger. "Put yuh trust in me—I fear I have not long to live myself."

"What's her story?" I asked, after the séance ended.

"She was discovered on the outskirts of Lime Gut, in the burial chamber of a cacique. The university people believe she's around six hundred years old . . ."

I wondered how much her rapture had affected me; I could no

longer discern the corpse's gender—perhaps it had been the power of suggestion.

". . . preserved by the cave's dry atmosphere and limestone. They also found evidence that she was buried alive."

"Why?"

"She was probably his favorite wife . . . She's set to start a traveling exhibit, still shackled to him."

"Where's the cacique?"

"He's at the university," she muttered scornfully, "being feted."

"Where's her resting place?"

"Here." She pointed to a grand gleaming coffin I hadn't noticed, ensconced on a low-lit dais in the corner. "It's silly, of course, but the funeral home donated it so they could attach themselves to the buzz."

"How vulgar . . . but what a fine coffin," I said with a smile.

"Sometimes when those Grantsview bwoys have a turf war and nightfall catches me here, I sleep in her coffin. It's very peaceful in there."

I swallowed my alarm and said, "Yes, one is like the other, isn't it? But it's not a matter of safety for yuh, I imagine it's somethin' more profound."

Maude's face flushed crimson. "For a long while after it happened, I slept under the bed. I didn't even want sunlight to disturb me, or cold. I slept so well there, in the dark. I never knew restful sleep was so important. So is closure."

"I get it: sleepin' under a bed is like sleepin' in a tomb."

"Not quite, but . . ."

"It's yuh cloister."

"I saw magic today and it gave me hope. This mornin', one of the women dustin' a piece of Taino pottery dropped it, and it immediately became a heap of dust, not fragments or recognizable pieces. Dust."

I didn't say anything. The blank misery on her face was too much.

"Ever heard the joke about the man who went to Canada?" she asked.

"No."

"Guess what he found there?"

"What?"

"Canadians."

"Right."

"That's my stage-exit joke, by the way," she said.

"I realized."

"Come, enough of the babysittin'."

We went back outside to sit under the trees. "My grandfather said that by the time yuh get to forty, yuh'd have seen all the types of people in the world. I wonder what type I am."

"I'm afraid I'm too young to tell," she said. "I know one thing though: I never liked most masters at yuh school. They lived and died by the respect people showed, and if they felt they were ever slighted, they cried foul and pouted. Master Lindon once signed a time sheet for me, and when he handed it over I thanked him, but I was distracted by a Skype call. He fumed quietly for weeks that I hadn't made eye contact during the transaction. I had no idea why he was acting strange to me, till the bursar told me what I'd done. She said, 'Maude, yuh made a man feel small, yuh can't do that on this campus. They goin' tie you to a tree and put yuh feet in a ants' nest, gyal.' But my suffering had already started—the ants' nest wasn't limited to Chester College. When I volunteered to leave Westmoreland, my true education began."

"To volunteer for anything is to die in a way, to kill a part of yuh, fear maybe."

"That's true."

"The others have been to see yuh, yuh know."

"They have?" she feigned ignorance.

"Yuh already know they have. Yuh tryin' to catch me out."

She laughed softly. "I know, man, I saw them. I can't stop them now, can I?" She tapped my leg playfully. "What's been happenin' with them?"

"Well, yuh already know about Perry, but in a way yuh don't."

"I know," she responded judiciously. "The car-wash crew—I've heard."

"Big Eye is a playwright, Marco's playing semiprofessional football—"

"Mark Snow?" she cut me off.

"He's a performance artist, distributing his pain like holy water."

"He's incapable of change," she said.

"Have you and Irma made up?"

She avoided the question, said, "I dropped a baby *nanka* down her shirt once; she ran and fell, her knee skinned to white meat. I used to be a tomboy. Headstrong as anything."

I pictured Mona. "Jesus, I hate snakes."

"Yuh should've seen it—golden-green around its head with black zigzag crossbars down its length, its small forked tongue playing from its mouth like an electric spark."

"Ugh," I said, shivering. "Poor Irma."

"Yeah, poor *Irmela*. My mother whipped me. I could've apologized to Irma in a million different ways—I was spoiled for choices, but I never did. I blamed her for that assin'."

"Yuh feel responsible for her?"

"I just wanted her to grow up for once, stop bein' such a little pest. I hated her adulation and clinginess. But for a stroke of luck, she too might have become a victim."

This last statement made me lurch, and Maude noticed. "There, there. These people are goin' to start thinkin' I'm yuh girlfriend. Chin up."

I was ashamed that she had to comfort me. It didn't seem at all fair. "Will yuh ever go to the police?"

She didn't answer.

"Have yuh told anyone?"

"God. The less yuh know, the better, Messado."

The thin tapestry of empathy between us was unraveling.

"Because yuh still sufferin', I know."

"That's not a stupendous deduction."

"Yuh don't owe me anything . . ."

"But? Yuh don't give up, do yuh? What yuh want, absolution?"

"I want to know how yuh did it—how yuh keep yuh faith."

Her face darkened and she gazed off into space. "Somethin' happened to me once. *You . . . the spider following me . . . are yuh listenin'?*"

She might've been talking to the shrub. I wasn't convinced she was addressing me. But her words were captivating.

"My key broke off in my lock once and I jumped. It gave me such a fright. Somewhere in the process of the metal losing its constitution, I lost my own molecular composure. I screamed, and when I took out my phone to dial the emergency number, I got so nervous, it fell and the screen smashed. I was unprepared for this, like I'd been that day when I dropped my guard and put my faith not in a key but in bwoys' hormones. I scrambled up the window, breakin' into my own house. I felt like disaster was chasin' me again. I smashed the window with my elbow and threw myself over broken glass. When I got inside, I realized I'd shit myself, but I wasn't embarrassed; I was alone, safe. Why should I be embarrassed? I was only relieved, I could even say happy, that my mind and body were still functionin'. I'd survived."

"Are yuh seizures all like that—did it start with us?"

"It all started with *him*, he was masturbatin' with a book hidin' his penis, watchin' us across the aisle. Irma and I were high schoolers at the time, but I had my first divine call then—somethin' rescued me from calamity. He followed us off the bus and walked five paces back. I called my mother. She said, 'Find a police station and wait there. I'm on my way.' I couldn't find any. It was like a trick the devil was playin' to make all the buildings look the same. I whispered to Irmela that we should split up, but she thought we should stick together, so I pushed her away. He kept pursuin' me, yet somethin' stopped me from screamin'. *Why me?* I wanted to shout. *Why me and not Irma? Why not go after Irma? Did I draw the short straw?* He must've somehow heard my thoughts. He was closer than

I thought and grabbed my neck. 'Yes, bitch, yuh grasp de shawt straw an' when me done wid yuh, yuh go dead!' I wriggled free and jumped on another bus just before the door closed, but he boarded too, hangin' off the door like they rode them before the Road Safety Act. Why not a *Child* Safety Act? He sat a few rows down, Satan, his eyes burnin' into my back. I called Mommy again, she told me she was on a parallel street but stuck in traffic and I should go tell the bus driver a strange man had been followin' me from Chatham. At the next stop, I glanced back and he showed me his knife. When I got to the driver's chair, my mouth couldn't open. I ran down the steps and the driver yelled, 'Yuh likkle bitch, where's me fare?'

"He was hot on my trail again, and tears blinded me so I was only waitin' for him to grab me again and be done with it. We must've been the only two people in the world, lion and gazelle, cat and mouse. I took out the phone but it fell and I kept on walkin' and somethin' took over my head. Autopilot. I kicked off my shoes, tore off my crimson tie, and ripped my uniform dress open all the way to my knees. I heard gasps around me but couldn't see—I was blind to the world. I made a leap of faith and turned into the next open yard, not knowing what it was. I lay there half-dressed on the grass and saw him with his knife outside the gate; he didn't dare enter. I looked up at the weather vane on the green spire and said, 'Father, forgive my selfish thoughts. Thank yuh for sparin' my cousin. I'm ready—fill me with yuh arrows!' Then my head and tongue went heavy, my eyes rolled back, and the fit started. But I was saved."

"A churchyard," I said.

She stayed quiet.

"Yuh still drawn to religious spaces—the cemetery."

Her eyes went wide. "Were yuh there? I knew it! Did yuh read my journal? Leave, Messado—now!"

I was so shocked by this rebuff, I almost fell off the bench. She moved at me with her fists raised in a pugilistic stance, like those boxing toys with two fighters perpetually facing each other on a plastic mount. She looked lost inside her head. I knew she was struggling with the emergence of her battered alter ego: it had something to feed on, it had a grip on her again. Something fundamental had been ruined, maybe her accord with God to watch over her and seal her protection. He had not revealed to her that day that she was not alone with her infinite struggle, that there was a devil in her private space, corrupting her solitude.

It had all come to naught because of my intrusion. I was her undesired witness and she wanted me gone once and for all.

"Leave!"

CHAPTER 19

"How's it going with the deaf violinist?" asked Cress.

Rory smiled through a mouthful of food. "Nice. We climbed the mountains on my grandfather's property to pick mushrooms. Nyjah brought Dreenie—all bells and whistles, Cress."

I whispered to Chadwell, "I followed her."

"Again?"

"I wanted to apologize—and still haven't. I fucked it up. I should have just left her alone."

"You're James Stewart."

"What?"

"*Vertigo*. And she's that blonde."

"Don't yuh want to know how she's doin'?"

Chad shrugged. "Why do yuh want to punish me with status reports?"

"Punish *you?* Okay, fine." I was suddenly embittered, annoyed. He avoided looking at me and ate his stuffed green peppers with mincing bites. He said offhandedly, looking up at the clouds, "I like when downpour catches us on the terrace. It feels like we're in a movie."

Rory was still gushing about Petra-Gaye to Cress: "I told her I wanted to become a photographer and she said I should go for it. She's seen my pictures."

"Is that what this is about? Someone to feed yuh dreamin'?" I said.

He held his chopstick like an ice pick. "Why's it a fantasy? You're a writer."

"That's different."

"How?" he asked.

"There's craft involved—by craft, I mean sacrifice. It takes more than talent."

"Yuh sound like a blustering showoff, that's why I don't—"

"Yuh don't *what*? Show me yuh pictures? 'Cause yuh don't want an honest opinion."

"Who's the blonde anyhow?"

"Blonde?"

"I heard Chad mention—"

"Gentlemen," interjected the waiter, "the drink bar has the oolong tea you asked for."

We were sitting near the duty free shops and the sidewalk was buzzing. "*Ya ya yah yah*," rapped a stray dog running by the car-park barrier as if its tail were on fire. We stood up to watch the rumbling procession the mutt had forerun. People jogged alongside the crawling pickup where Snow sat, signing autographs in their Bibles and on T-shirts, dandling and kissing babies hoisted toward him, sometimes even thrown like flesh-bound footballs. He looked like an Ashanti king, in a silver and purple dashiki with beads and chicken feathers around his neck and wrists. The pickup had to stop where the crowd was too thick to continue.

People waded into traffic, just so they could get a glimpse of him or touch his robes. "Rum Preacher! Healin'!"

Snow sat on a red-velvet throne erected in the truck—like a popemobile seat—and looked plain exhausted, too exhausted in fact to speak, and he started playing a recording of a previous sermon he had given about the recent vaccine campaign.

Rather than complain about the noise from the loudspeaker, the restaurant owner, Mr. Chung, simply said, "He's the only poet in the Bay people care about. You're outta luck, Nyjah. You have no crisis of circumstance and heart."

People soon tired of the recording. They started demanding a message, even just a sentence, a word. His rest prematurely ended, Snow stood up. He stirred them with only his gestures and meaningful looks—squints and frowns and neck-bobbing. He turned off the loudspeaker; the place went still. He had them thinking before he even opened his mouth. And he was a long time employing this body language—grunting, grinding his teeth, hemming and hawing and turning over papers on the little desk he had set up in the pickup, turning himself into a holy roadblock. The clouds darkened above. More strays were barking, like shepherds rustling a human herd.

Finally he spoke: "Accountability!"

"Yes!" they erupted. Traffic had to squeeze around his vehicle, motorists honking angrily and cursing but quickly winding up windows, wary of hostile bystanders.

"Slaves spent dem whole lives fightin' for recognition of dem humanity," Snow began. "Dem souls was exhausted, dem was too downtrodden inside to be truly free. Blacks abroad are livin' de same lives now, tired people on a battlefield dem cyaan retire from, a war dem can never win, fightin' as soon as dem born, fightin' as soon as dem step out de front door. Fightin' for others to see dem as corporeal beings who feel, and not as shadows. Soul-tired beings, like de women in dis country."

There was a stir—no one had seen this coming.

"We're Black an' free here, comfortable but not homologous. Women struggle like dem ancestors."

"Careful now, Rummy, faggots an' trannies will hop on yuh argument like a Jolly bus!"

But Snow was dead serious. He looked sad, angry, disgusted, as if he suddenly hated the very sight of them, like a mother sneering at mud-covered brats and thinking of the laundry and scrubbing—wishing she could scrub out their nature, too, with a brush.

"Yuh can never bargain wid a man more powerful than yuh," he continued. "Sin—dis casual, internalized, institutional misogyny—

made a deceitful bargain wid us, den cut our t'roats like sorry children. We were victims—all of us at dat school. Left to die in de dust . . ."

A man barreled his way through in something like a yukata, his arms hidden beneath shabby robes. He broke past the line of self-appointed guards, and when they accosted him, they realized he was one-armed. He wielded a stick and fell to the ground screaming himself hoarse.

"Who de fuck him t'ink him be? Yojimbo?" someone said.

"Big Monday, an' yuh nuh have nuh manners," said a woman. "Ah show yuh dutty colors."

"Leave him!" ordered Snow.

They pulled him to his feet, but he dropped back down to his knees. "Preachah, me come fe healin'!"

"I cyaan heal yuh." Snow looked miserable, like all the old hurt was coming back up and drowning him.

"Why?" asked the one-armed man.

"I'm not pure."

The man considered this. "Well, at least help me clear me name. Dey sayin' I t'ief hubcaps at Skateland an' sell to de car-wash bwoys, an' dey settin' up to lynch me at a public trial—I need a lawyer too bad!"

People laughed. Some tutted in sympathy. "Finally de trut' come out!" someone shouted. "Ol' dutty *rass* like yuhself, yuh doh need healin'—yuh need licks!"

Snow considered the thief. "Lissen, friend, a trial is not about justice, it's about manipulation. If dem manipulate de facts better dan you do, dem win—it doh matter if yuh steal an' resell dem hubcaps or not, yuh goose still cook."

"So wha' me should do?" croaked Yojimbo.

Snow threw up his hands. "Ah, me friend, where are de law an' prophets dis side?"

"Where were the laws and prophets when yuh raped that woman?" I don't know why or how the words escaped me, but they did, and I couldn't take them back.

Snow's face dropped open like a cargo plane's hatch. "Who said dat?"

But it was so feeble coming out of his mouth that to answer would have been to kill him right then and there, to knock him over with a truthful wind. Chadwell glanced at me and seemed quietly alarmed, as if expecting me to say something even more damning, as if he was warning me with his eyes not to draw attention to ourselves—but my brain told my mouth it had said enough and could rest easy.

Snow, meanwhile, could not. He kept looking around as if searching for an exit door in a crowd, in that big open space, in that position of power—he was trapped and scared and it was hard to watch.

The people saw his fear and trembling and they waited for its resolution.

Snow parted his lips in a derisive smile. "Yes, come get me, whoever yuh are. Show yuhself!" But he was obviously miserable with his own shadow. We saw the suicidal urge plain then, like stripes on a whipped tiger. "Come!" he roared. "Yuh sonuvabitch! Doh hide behind odder neagahs! Step forward an' claim yuh statement!" His mouth trembled. "Please show yuhself. Please. Jus' raise a hand, yuh doh have to come up. I wa'an satisfy meself I hear exactly what yuh said. Dat I ain't paranoid . . . *Please*."

Everyone was befuddled by the turn of events; he was like a man being slowly crucified, but we couldn't see the nails or cross or blood. The derision in his original smile had been a door to madness and pain that was eating him inside. Some people looked away.

"Come . . . somebody tek off dem belt and pass it to me . . . Now!"

There was an outpouring, a raucous jabbering of uncontrollable tongues. Snow tottered with the tide of emotion swelling inside him. Two of his acolytes tried to hold him steady, but he tore away.

"A belt! Anybody!" His head bobbed as if it would drop off his shoulders as he scanned the crowd. "Somebody go part wid dem life today!" The words were now venomous and filled with all the violence and aggression of the Canterbury Snow we'd known as boys, his face as devilish as his thuggish days, as wicked as that time he'd browbeaten boys and spread a woman's half-dead legs. "Somebody go lose dem life!" The words might've been meaningless, but people looked worried. "I was a man widout a spirit then," he moaned, "but I know an' feel de violence of meaningful change. Why can't yuh leave me alone? Why? Please leave me alone!"

"Duppy ah ride him," someone surmised. "Him possessed. It hard fe a man when him so spirit-filled—when him so blessed. Devils always tryin' to tek a portion of him rich reward!"

A cloudburst surprised us and we left the Rum Preacher to his torment.

CHAPTER 20

At low tide, sunbeams interlocked in the clear shallow water like the wavering scales of a giant fish. We let the green-brown strands of sea moss drag through our water-wrinkled toes, drank Red Stripes. Briana and Birdie, the waitress Cress had met at the Old Boys' Dinner, were fishing with other women and small children for crabs and snails stranded in the low tide; they waved buckets at us.

"I'll commit to teachin' the business subjects for a reduced salary till you guys get goin'."

"*You guys?*" said Chadwell.

"Okay," said Cress, "us. And what are *you* doing?"

"I told yuh," Chad replied casually, his hands tucked in his Dockers rolled up at the knees. "I'll get the school everything it needs."

"I wonder how soon we can see a profit."

"Don't think that way, Nyjah. Yuh can't eat stew beef just yet, yuh haffe settle for patty and coco bread. But soon. And it's the best time, right at the start of the year. Exams not quite round the corner, but everybody sharpenin' up for May and June."

"Can yuh cover math too?"

Cress wrinkled his forehead. "That's going to stretch me."

"Stretch yuh? You're an actuary."

"I thought yuh said Rory would—"

"Yuh might have to convince him in sign language."

"Oh that's low, Chad, even for you."

"He'll drop soon."

"Yeah, like a constipated turd."

"Did yuh just call Rory a turd?"

"I'm sayin' he's a pain in the butt."

I felt the rich labor of my life was gone. I was back at my mother's after I'd worked so hard on my independence. I hesitated to mention to my friends that I was no longer staying at Rory's place, that I'd gone back to my mother's house with my tail between my legs. I remembered getting off the bus in Porto Bello and seeing Zetta Rosegreen gossiping with a bunch of people. Some had snickered at me when she flicked her tongue and I'd known immediately that I had to pack and leave.

"Marco teachin' physics and chem, and we can rent lab space at the community college. Perry knows someone . . . Nyjah, yuh still with us?"

"What? Yeah . . . I was just thinkin' 'bout somethin'."

Cress pointed along the reef. "That's where they found Haynes's body—dead with his eyes open and bullet holes in his boots."

"Why his boots?"

"A mark—to show that the car-wash crew did it."

"Yuh sure it was Haynes's body? I heard it was someone else."

Briana and Birdie were coaxing barnacles from sun-dried calcite shells streaked with purple. The reefs were covered with these cream shells, like so many tiny volcanic colonies. The air was tangy with the brackish smell of sea eggs. The three of us were quiet for a spell, watching the women.

". . . her version made the original sound like a bad cover," Bree was saying to Birdie. They talked at once, their words flowing over each other. It reminded me of prep school, of girls jumping rope or playing Chinese skip and laughing at our begrudging admiration.

Cress must've been thinking along the same wavelength. "Let's take the old oath," he said, "like when we used to *scul* classes to come here."

So we took the fisherman's oath—dragging the backs of our hands on barnacles; the surf washed away the blood.

The women gave us horrified looks. "What y'all doing?" said Birdie. She was handsome, in a dark brooding way, with bewitching eyes and a slight mustache over her sensuous mouth.

"They're being men," said Briana, standing loose-limbed with her plastic bucket. "Cruel and oafish." Her eye shadow looked like a hummingbird's underbelly with its glittery UV colors flickering in the sunlight. She had cut and curled the sides of her hair and dyed the flattop bronze like her lip gloss. *I wonder if I can do without her when the time comes*, I thought. She looked beyond us to a familiar patter of feet.

Cam strolled down the beach in a blue-striped blouse and white shorts, hands in her pockets, grinning at everyone. I was speechless. I hadn't seen her since she'd been discharged from the hospital. She came right up to me and planted a kiss on my jaw. "I wanted to surprise yuh."

"How did yuh know I'd be here?"

"Yuh mother told me." She waved at the others. "Hi, guys, I'm his de facto lifeguard. Don't ask—terrible hours. He's always gettin' in above his head."

Everyone laughed except for Bree, who had a detached look.

Cam noticed and took the initiative: "Briana, right?"

Bree took the proffered hand. "Nice to meet yuh . . . Camille?"

Cam gave her a broad grin. "Yuh face is in the papers all the time. Quite weird, that. An editor with a face—I'm used to faceless editorials."

"I have a feeling yuh prefer them that way," responded Bree icily.

"Perhaps," Cam said, still with a smile, "but then I never liked picture books either. Faces can be distractin'. I feel they're *sellin'* somethin', like Colonel Sanders."

Bree regarded her as she might a talking rattlesnake. "Sorry to have offended—"

Birdie stepped in: "Yuh not dressed for swimmin', Cam."

Cam saw my consternation and tugged my arm. "Look at him—

in the doldrums amidst company. Yuh've got to be *elected* to life, Nyjah. Else no one wants yuh. Look at me, back from the dead."

"Elected to life," smiled Chadwell. "I couldn't agree more."

"Without self-election, one doesn't find one's métier," said Cam.

Bree rolled her eyes and snorted, then started down the shore, swinging her clam bucket.

"What's her problem?" said Cam. "I guess I'm not everyone's cuppa tea. The editor don't like me, Nyjah." She made a crybaby face.

"Your aunt's charming, Messado," said Cress, nervously eyeing Birdie's reaction.

Chad was transfixed, staring at Cam as sea breeze tangled her short hair. "Hey, Cam, long time no see."

"Hello, you. Chad without a date." Cam looked sweetly plucked from a stem like a delicate rose, her pale cheeks still slightly blistered.

Inside me a poison bloomed, and quite suddenly, so easily, I hated Chadwell afresh. Yet I remembered it was on this same stretch of shore that I'd found him weeping for Obadiah, his baby brother who had died on his watch. That ambiguity—that inability to confront and condemn him—hit me again like the nauseous smell of green sea-foam.

CHAPTER 21

The first thing I didn't like was the way they'd stack my desk with miscellany, as if the desk were only partially mine, and grab up this junk the minute I approached as if playing some kind of mind game. Initially I had tolerated it, but it's hardly possible to ignore a box placed before you that takes up half your desk. I felt as if I'd been working in a stockroom. And the encroachment games had continued, though I refused to complain, so they got worse. But what decided it was the paycheck situation. Mentally, I'd walked away, yet I tried to remain committed to the kids. I started giving them lessons away from school, at shopping malls, at Mummy's catering business, dropping hints that I was soon to start my own school—*dropping the crumbs*, as Chad called it.

Now the building was open and the school was up and running. Chadwell had fast-tracked most of the document processing and the only significant hurdle had been obtaining something called a Scheme of Management. But Cress's father was a lawyer working as an adjunct to the ministry and finally we secured it.

We started with an enrollment of about eighty students, but had soon maneuvered to split the day into halves, which doubled our intake. Word of mouth, more than advertising, brought in signees by the day. We hired only three teachers. I even persuaded Eddie, the guard from Willocks Academy, to join me for a slight salary bump at reduced hours. We hired Louder Milk as a barker. He went into a clothes shop upstairs at Blue Diamond Plaza with some school flyers and ended up stealing tie pins. And Mad Lena never went away—she would wander around the premises wringing her hands and wailing, harassing Eddie to be let in, screaming bloody murder.

I was coming from Chad's late one evening when I had the inspiration for a poem, so I popped into Ice Cream Station, ordered a caipirinha, and set to work on my laptop.

Someone in the booth behind mine said, "I know what yuh doin', yuh datin' him for de stimulatin' conversation."

It was Burberry Dalton—I instantly recognized his voice. I peered at their shimmery forms reflecting off the Stippolyte glass. He had his arm around her.

Dreenie laughed and pushed him off. "Shut yuh mout'—yuh doh know him."

"Dem all alike," he said, smacking his straw. "Dem expect people to wipe dem ass for dem."

"Jealous?" she teased.

"Far from it. Jealousy is a weak emotion. I am a man, not a manframe like dem."

"Him selfish doe," she snarled, stirring her drink (I knew she was having a chocolate malt). "Mean, very self-absorbed. When him havin' a bad day, him tell me him tek it out on de students. An' him tell me all dis as if expectin' sympathy, Dalton."

"Dat's de type ah man all-ah dem be: *jubies* playin' dress-up, t'inkin' dem can tek out dem frustration pon odder people 'cause odders less deservin' of respeck. Yuh 'membah Beres? Him used to drive Chester school bus. Beres say when him drop dem off at school, him doubt dem even see him, dem operate like dem on some fuckin' cloud up at Orange Street hill."

"*Leadership* school," Dreenie put in.

"Dem doh *see* people, Dreen. Dem train dem to be some kinda Black buckra, like St. James is dem plantation, feelin' entitled to everyt'ing—point to yuh an' say, 'You there, could you pass me that pair, please? No, lower, my good man, on the penultimate shelf. Thank you kindly.'"

Dreenie laughed at his stiff accent.

The waitress came with my caipirinha and saw me eavesdropping.

I raised a finger to my lips and jerked a thumb over my shoulder. My *girlfriend*, I mouthed.

Nasty! she mouthed back. "The drink is free, poor t'ing." She padded off, shaking her head.

Dalton said, "I hear dem car-wash bwoys ah use de Wicked Man Syndrome on Snow, somet'ing dem adopt from Trelawny mob. Notice how Snow's pickup plaster all over wid car-wash ads? What yuh t'ink him really peddlin', religion or drugs?"

"Not my business," said Dreenie.

"Why de fuck me eat banana muffins wid de plantains? It ridin' me from mawnin'."

She had her head down checking her phone, almost mumbling, "Dat's somet'ing we doh do in MoBay. If yuh goin' have plantains for breakfast, yuh never eat bananas, not even banana muffin or fritters."

"Who de fuck yuh is to lecture me 'bout manners?"

His anger jerked her to attention; she put the phone away as if in a gesture of apology.

He stared at the side of her turned-away face, loudly grinding his teeth. "What yuh doin'? Condemnin' me 'cause I doh bawn a Bay? Dat's why yuh tek all dat shit from him? 'Cause him bawn up a Regional wid all de odder shit-smellin' faggots?"

"Maybe . . ."

"Lemme tell yuh sum'n! It nuh matter where yuh bawn! See't deh, I come from Trelawny, countryman who everybody scorn, now everybody know Dalton name! Me run de fuckin' arcade!"

"Doh underestimate dem," she said quietly, "not because dem go to a good school an' talk posh. Doh t'ink dem sawf. Dem know dis place like how David know psalm."

"Stop bloodclaat kowtow to dem. Dem a nuh nobody! Nuh fall before dem graven image 'cause yuh nuh come from nutten."

She bore the insult with sly mockery and he began fidgeting. "I'm ready," she said, standing.

My heart thudded against my ribs, but they didn't notice me. I dropped some cash on the table and furtively followed them out.

They stopped under a pool of light near Dumbo's, their backs to me. I slipped into shadows against a wall, close enough that I could still see and hear them.

"Yuh t'ink him better dan me? Is dat it, Dreen?" Dalton pressed.

She chawed gum and said simply, "No."

"Den why—why I haffe prove to yuh dat I jus' as ambitious an' have more potential?"

She peered into his eyes. "Dat right dere—yuh need to *prove*. Dat's all yuh talk 'bout. Bwoys like dat bawn to win, Dalton. It write in dem blood like code."

He wiped his finger under his nose like a cokehead and jigged about, chuckling at the passing faces, pulling at his cornrows and flicking his fingers as if he wanted to hit something. He kicked the wall and she jumped aside.

A Dumbo's waitress, emptying garbage in the side lot, said something I couldn't hear.

Dalton was clearly unhinged, but Dreenie watched him coolly, one arm folded across herself, the other swinging her handbag. When he stepped toward her, she backed off as if she smelled something bad.

"You an' me, Dreenie. You an' me go tek over city center an' all downtown. Like de Syrian dem. Me have it up here!" He pointed at his temple.

"Up *where?*" she scoffed. "What yuh have up dere, de map fe success? Yuh can barely read."

"*Cho*, bumbo rassclaat, man!" he barked. "Ah wha' do dis fuckin' dry-foot stink-pussy gyal doe?" He moved in and repeatedly poked her forehead with his finger; she rocked back and forth like an inflatable punching bag. "Hey, gyal, sey bet me kill yuh rassclaat right, yah so! Sey bet me ground yuh inna manners!"

She lowered her eyes and gently swung the bag by her leg, waiting out his anger.

"Answer me, pussy'ole! Yuh t'ink yuh or yuh batty-bloodclaat man betta dan me? Me nuh haffe bawn a Bay fe run dis bloodclaat! Me go show everybody dat a Burberry Dalton come fe lock dung dis bloodclaat! Who run de arcade?" Glad for the audience, he was aiming his vitriol at everyone who'd gathered, including several people motioning to Dreenie to come away. "Yuh t'ink Napoleon did bawn a France?"

I was about to confront them when I heard: "Oi! Bonaparty, wha'ppen, yuh lookin' conscription for de last big push?" It was a blue-seam.

Dalton became shifty-eyed and quiet but still tightly wound. "Officer, me nuh wa'an nuh trouble, me jus' have a likkle disagreement wid me sistren."

"Come, Josephine," said the blue-seam to Andrene. "Lef' Bonaparty to work out him geopolitical intrigues."

People gutted themselves with laughter. Dreenie peeled away from the spot where she'd been cornered and walked off with the policeman. Dalton watched them with his mouth open. He looked heartbroken. He pulled out a Mudslide from his bosom, sucked on it, then smashed the bottle.

I cut around to Gravel Lane to intercept them.

When Dreenie saw me, she jumped. "Jeezam peas! How yuh . . . ? What yuh . . . ?"

The officer cocked his head with a tired expression on his face. "You two know each odder?" He dropped his hand from her waist.

"Is me boyfriend," she said.

The officer swallowed his laugh. "Who, *him?* So who de odder one be to yuh, dearie?"

"Me uncle . . ." She couldn't bear to look at either of us.

"Of course," said the blue-seam. "Uncle *Tobias* . . . Yuh tek care now." He pushed her toward me with his baton to the small of her back.

She stiffened and sucked in her breath and flashed him an angry glance.

"Careful wid dis one," he said to me, "she a barn burner." With that, he tipped his cap and strolled down Union Street.

"Relax," I said, taking her elbow and whistling for a taxi. "The cameras are gone, relax."

I pushed her into a cab; she scooted to the other side. The driver was someone I knew, a man from my neighborhood named Winston, but Dreenie and I stayed silent, sitting apart like strangers. I mused on the fact that it felt like half our time together was spent fighting. I remembered asking Papa how I'd know when my heart was taken. I shook my head, laughing bitterly to myself. *So this is what it means to be in love*.

She gave me an odd look, half loathing, half endearment, then turned away. She misted the glass with her breath. She had full pert lips that were almost too big for her petite face, but it was her charm point, the feature that stood out most, particularly with the right shade of lipstick.

I said to the cabbie, "Winston, yuh know what I caught her doin'? Playing dolly house with Burberry Dalton."

"Him change woman like how him change foreign currency," Winston replied, and gave an almost embarrassed laugh. "T'ings nuh sure in dis world, Nyjah. Tek science, for instance: yuh cyaan even trus' science! I put on two egg fe boil inna me likkle green pot an' put on me teapot same time an' yuh know de egg dem bubble before de teapot, like dem nuh have de same boilin' point? Now, if yuh cyaan trus' science, how yuh go trus' a woman? An'—"

"What yuh think I should do with her?" I cut in.

"Stop talk 'bout me like me nuh inna de fuckin' cyar!" Dreenie snapped.

I jerked my hand and she pulled back and hit her head on the glass.

"Nyjah, ah swear! Jus' put yuh hand pon me! Yuh such ah animal! Who yuh get dat from?" She had her hand on something inside her purse.

Winston whistled. "We haffe find weself inna dem likkle cracks of uncertainty, ah deh so livity deh, ah deh so yuh work out yuh soul-case. Me workin' on a philosophy, it's called de Not Philosophy. It mek t'ings very simple. Yuh either sick or yuh not."

"Yuh either faithful or yuh not," I said.

"*You* faithful?" she spat. "Yuh t'ink I doh know why yuh back at yuh mooma house? 'Cause yuh fuck dat ol' bat an' she walkin' round tellin' everybody in Porto Bello! Yuh nuh shame?"

How did she hear about Zetta?

Winston pointed a finger at me after I gave him the fare. "De weatherman have a forecast for yuh—yuh betta listen."

I entered the house quietly so as not to wake Mummy, but she called out, "Nyjah, dat you? Turn off de outside light."

I mumbled a response as I stepped inside; she went back to sleep.

"Me wa'an wee-wee," Dreenie said, kicking off her heels, her hostility dialed down.

I knew she was taking her time in the bathroom, hoping I would calm down, but this infuriated me. I almost started beating on the bathroom door but remembered Mummy had to get up at four. I felt outmaneuvered and powerless in my own home.

Dreenie soon came back stirring a fizzing cup of Andrews Salts from the kitchen cupboard, and there was a perverse spell of comedy, like the condemned having a laugh with the hangman.

I rattled off the opening line of the Andrews Salts commercial, playing the part of the concerned mother: "*Too much pawty las' night . . .*"

She replied in the griping voice of the debauched son, her back to me at the dresser, sipping the antacid, "*What ah mus' tek?*"

"*Andrews, of course,*" I finished.

After she downed the glass, she looked glassy-eyed, collapsing to the stool with one hand drawn up to her bony elbow like a marionette, ready for her punishment.

"Take off that dress. I know he bought it for yuh and I can't stand the sight of it."

She slowly slid out of it, then sat haplessly in her satin slip with her knees open, her neck and shoulders tilting forward like her strings had been cut.

"What yuh have to say for yuhself?"

"Why I should even bother? Wha' yuh wa'an hear? Tell me, I'll say it—I jus' wa'an go to bed." She yawned and scratched her armpit.

"So is that it—I should just turn yuh over to him?"

She half sneered, wiping her eyes. "No, me wa'an yuh fight him. May de bes' man win."

"Yuh havin' a laugh?"

"Who tell yuh?" she replied tartly, lifting her head and dropping it.

"Yuh think I can't bloodclaat do somethin' 'cause my mother's down the hall?"

"Stop huff an' puff, Nyjah, yuh nuh scare me."

"Oh, 'cause yuh roll with badman Dalton?"

She looked at me through half-lidded eyes, toying with the strap of her slip, her mouth downturned as her belly made an ugly noise. She burped. "Ah never realize how damn ugly yuh be when yuh vex—yuh mout' look like fe hog." She covered her face, giggling through her fingers, watching me stew in anger.

"I'm sorry I ever said a word to yuh on the bus that day."

"Ahaha!" she cackled. "*You* sorry? I pas' sorry . . . I doh even know wha' fe call it."

I now saw that she'd gotten a tattoo below her armpit, along the swell of her left breast. "Did he tell yuh to get that? Yuh sleepin' with him?"

She braced herself and jerked her head up. "Yes! An' me suck him cock too when him wa'an! Wha' else yuh wa'an know!" Her hand dropped loosely with a hairpin—the marionette movement again. Something inside her had snapped too and she teared up. "Look pon me . . . Look how me likkle an' fine, yuh t'ink it easy to hol' space over de arcade where everybody tryin' to get even an inch ah space? Wha' kinda world yuh livin' in? How yuh t'ink

I manage shop rent? How de fuck yuh t'ink I manage to do dat so long? By Gawd's sweet grace? Yuh so naive, Nyjah."

"So yuh go keep fuckin' him for more acreage then."

"If me have to! I cyaan ask yuh for money, can I? Yuh never have none! A man suppose to take care-a him woman."

"Yuh know I have things doin', Dreen. I just can't afford it right now."

"Look how yuh run 'way from Porto Bello! Stop actin' like a fuckin' knight in shinin' armor."

"Don't throw this back on me. I didn't tell yuh to—"

"But yuh cyaan provide for me neither, an' yuh cyaan stop me. Do what yuh want." She shook her head.

"So this is it?"

"Yes. Why yuh swell up like bullfrog? Yuh did expect better news?" She swayed on the stool, bone-tired. "*Dat whosoever thirsts for life may have it more abundantly*. Me tired ah yuh neediness, Nyjah. Stop sweat out me wig. Me t'irsty, an' tired ah yuh rules . . . yuh fuckin' rules."

She flopped down on the bed more dead than alive; her soles were ugly and cracked and showed the rough side of her upbringing, as if she'd never worn shoes in her entire life. I saw the hardship and cruel irony of her enterprise, the shoe seller with battered feet, the girl hawking in the crowded arcade with her beggar's twang pitched high above the competition, chasing after people with straps of leather slippers gripped over her knuckles like leather thongs binding an ancient Greek boxer's hands, some of them turning to repay her with casual insults. I saw Dalton with his paws all over her, perhaps even in the shop. It didn't match her beauty or her resilient spirit; but it did match too somehow, viewed as a whole, like stepping back from a collage.

I took her place on the stool, trying to understand life the way she inhabited it, trying to hear the seller's bittersweet song in the market, trying to see her hands counting crumpled bills, trying to see her swallowing her pride to go down on her knees. My gorge rose; her vantage eluded me. I couldn't live in her shoes, I was too squeamish, I had led a protected life. When I stepped outside of myself, I was cold and miserable—and she was out like a light. My feelings didn't matter. I let her sleep.

"Careful," Mummy said, suddenly appearing in the doorway. "I ketch her spittin' like she pregnant."

"Yes," I said, and stepped out of the room, gently closing the door behind me.

"If is yours, make sure yuh do right by her."

"The way yuh did right by Daddy?"

"Yuh have to let dat go, Nyjah . . ."

"Whatever happened between you and Missa Senior, or still happenin', I understand better now. Dreenie think she fuckin' that man Dalton for the right reasons—to become a businesswoman like you. But yuh never stop payin', do yuh?"

"What yuh wa'an me to do, deny it to yuh face? Yuh t'ink dat go bring yuh daddy back? Grown-ups doh operate dat way."

"No, they certainly don't. Yuh ever see those women sellin' their teenage daughters to white men out by the craft market? Like is a slave port?"

"Yuh need to mind yuh own business." She pulled her nightgown about her, heading back to bed. "Doh let dat gyal give yuh *jacket*—make sure yuh demand a paternity test."

CHAPTER 22

We had just finished playing Saturday-morning football at Old Hospital Park and were cooling our sweaty backs against the cut-stone wall below road level, looking at waves battering the bluff at the end of the savanna. We changed clothes and headed down Leaders Avenue. At the old amphitheater we saw a gathering laughing at something on the sidewalk. It was Louder Milk, standing next to his dead companion.

"Richard II," he screamed at the corpse, "yuh abandon me!" He fell to his knees and sobbed, "*For God's sake, let us sit pon de groun'. And tell sad stories o' de death o' kings.*"

Chad shook his head. "Shakespeare wasted on a dead dog. What's new in this place?"

"I think he brought it to the amphitheater for a service," said Castleigh.

Even now they refused him sympathy, turning his pain into spectacle.

Louder had begun singing to the tawny carcass, "*Press along, saints, press along . . .*" but grew angry at my friends' irreverent comments and sprang up, waving a knife at passersby; everyone jumped back.

"Louder, wha' de fuck, man!" Fruity Hastings shouted. "Suppose yuh stab somebody!"

Louder spat at Fruits.

Fruits, squat, well-muscled, and bouncy like a rubber ball,

knocked him so hard that Louder bit his lip. But he screamed with filthy delight, as if relieved that they'd finally acknowledged him. He jumped forward and Fruits kicked him back. When he sat up, there was blood in his mouth.

"They took his thunder," I said to Cress.

"He ain't done yet," said Castleigh, like a ringside coach praying for a miracle. "What we always do when bettin' on crab races? Spit on the crab shell for good luck. They spit on Louder enough—he 'bout to win now."

Louder Milk spat again and picked at his toes pushing through his old shoe—he always wore only one shoe, and had toes like charred barbecue. He staggered to his feet and turned his back to everyone and, as if praying for the corpse, went still for a spell, then suddenly heaved it up and foisted it on the car-wash boss. "Hol' him, Parson!" he yelled. "Christen him for de ride home!"

Fruits was so shocked he dropped the filthy carcass, then started brushing off his blue silk shirt in disgust. We laughed. Seared right through with embarrassment, like the laughingstock on a playground, Fruits tackled Louder, wrenched the knife free, and opened his face right up.

"No, yuh cyaan do dat!" someone shouted. "Yuh tek it too far, Fruits! Louder nuh mean nutten!"

Louder screamed and wiped blood from his cheek, then fell to the curb. Fruits dropped the knife and gave us a look of begrudging apology, as if to say, *He asked for it.* Louder eventually calmed down; the cut hadn't been that deep. Someone in the amphitheater pit behind him stepped up and put a bandage on his cheek.

Louder smiled. "Thank you, Lady Montego." He fixed his grubby vest—we hadn't realized that we'd played into his hands and were giving Richard II, his companion of so many years, exactly the service he desired, that we were actors on his street stage, that he'd bled for this honor, probably would've died for it too. He said, "Ol' age kill Richie. Many dawgs doh get dat privilege. Him better performance was him own life. De role he played for de worl'. But wha' him lef' me to do widout him? I watch a man talkin' to him chick in de front-a him car dis afternoon, and I muse to meself, *Dat's all a man need, a pretty woman to lick him asshole, an' when him put two fingers in she pussy, it shoot water in him face . . . maybe couple children.*"

People were so appalled they clucked their tongues in shame and shook their heads, even the men.

"Well, not even pretty," he continued. "I would sekkle fe a gyal who look like donkey bite she face." His honesty clearly perturbed the onlookers, took them to an uncomfortable time and space.

"Man, go to a whorehouse!" a sky juice vendor called out.

"Dem won't have me," Louder responded, shaking his head. "My money ain't no good at Punkie's. Nobody wa'an lick a bum's balls. Dat whore's stock would drop. She would lose business from de fallout an' gossip."

"Pick up a streetwalker, a gyal from Sunshine Plaza."

They were actually trying to be helpful now; this tickled Louder. He grinned and scratched his dusty beard; people stepped back when he flicked something wriggling from his fingernails. "Yuh sorry fe me? How 'bout takin' me to de Chiney man instead, de one wid de new shop? I hear him have Haitian gyals as young as twelve who run 'way from the deportation center at Hopewell."

"No, he buys dem from de guards," Fruits said. "Dey keep an auction."

Louder seemed to weigh this update. Checking his wallet stuffed to bursting with junk, he licked his thumb and took out a greasy hundred-dollar bill that looked like dried callaloo, then some coins, and counted. "I've a bills an' forty. Who willin' to gimme a mek-up? How much Haitian pussy cos' now?"

We laughed easily—this was what we liked about Louder, the chameleon quality, the humor.

He said, "I hear dem gyals fuck to live and live to fuck. Dat dey fuck anyt'ing dat walk, even croakin' lizard."

"No, Louder, a prison wuk dat," someone said. "Leave de Chiney out, him days numbered."

"All-ah we days numbered," Louder Milk warned. "Look at Richard II. Doh fool yuhself, MoBay is ah cesspool and de plumber come. I jus' need to sort out me tools."

"Yuh need some pussy—dat's what yuh need."

"Vermeer is de painter I like," said Louder, heading somewhere else in his rambling thoughts, as was his wont. He could be very encyclopedic sometimes; he spent hours in the parish library reading indiscriminately, silent and solemn and bad-smelling, and they'd have to throw all the windows open and turn off the AC. "Him de firs' one to realize de potential o' gloomy cartoons. Yuh ever look good on *Girl wid a Pearl Earring*?"

Right then we heard a voice amplified through a megaphone.

Louder jumped to his feet as if Snow's attendance at Richard II's send-off was a crowning achievement, a pièce de résistance not even he had thought possible.

Standing in the popemobile contraption, Snow was shaking his fist. "Dese modern-day Babylonians! Dese King Ahabs who work iniquity 'gainst de house ah Israel an' de lifeblood ah Jesus!" When he noticed the dead dog lying in the gutter, he went speechless, his eyes blinking like traffic signals, as if he'd seen something prophetic. He beat the glass for the driver to stop and hopped down, approaching like a cowboy about to draw his pistol, his arms cocked and his feet wide. In his papal cassock billowing in the wind and his silk skullcap, he cut a handsome figure. People were rapt. What would he do to the corpse? He moved with purpose, his eyes glued to the dog already buzzing with greenbottles.

Louder scrambled forward and Snow couldn't help showing his disgust. He screwed up his clean-shaven face and pulled his white-flowing dress tight to his body and visibly stopped his breathing. Louder wasn't discouraged, but two bodyguards stepped between him and Snow at just the right moment. Beating his fists against them, Louder screamed, "Rummy, is *me!* De one yuh ordain at Bussy funeral! When yuh t'row water on me dat day, yuh doh realize yuh baptize me?"

Snow looked intrigued now, and motioned for them to let Louder go. "What's yuh name, fella?"

Louder swayed with the wind, reciting soundless words as if he didn't need an audience anymore, his lips, face working, as if getting a signal from some frequency we couldn't hear, and when that frequency stopped, his lips and body stopped too, like a device running out of juice. Then he started swaying again.

Snow waited with his hands crossed before him.

Louder snapped fully alive, his eyes popping like beans from a pod.

"What's yuh name?" Snow asked again.

"Maesaiah," Louder hissed, and started in on a sort of jittery rain dance.

"Spell it," said Snow, reaching for the Clairin from his assistant.

"M-a-e-s-a-i-a-h," said Louder Milk, undergoing a transformation, walking on the corpse-sniffing wind.

"Yuh pullin' me leg or what? Yuh cyaan spell?" mocked Fruits, but he was quickly hushed by aggressive stares.

It wasn't a funeral anymore. It was an awakening.

"No!" Snow exploded. "Addlepated . . . sick to de stomach! Yuh ambition too small. Dig deeper!"

"It's African!" Louder responded, waving his arms and lifting his knees to show the insides of his chaps-like pants, torn down the inside seams so his hairy balls and penis swung like a donkey's, spreading a peculiar smell. "I'm the king of Lesotho!"

Mad Lena muttered in rapture, "Hail the chief," and ripped her dress open—her long, loose, flat breast moving like a cobra when she danced. "Hail the chief!"

The refrain was picked up, and louder: "HAIL DE CHIEF!"

Louder Milk, the king of Lesotho, danced his peculiar jig beside the corpse, and we wouldn't have been surprised if Richard II had risen.

Snow grew self-contained and solemn almost immediately. He shook his head and tutted, "Yuh mus' pay fe everyt'ing in dis world, one way or anodda. Dere's nutten free except God's grace." Yet he allowed himself a smile, evidently pleased with his public service. He said to the awestruck crowd, "See, bredrin, transformation is possible. But yuh need a bruisin' sometimes, ah crisis of circumstance. We need a jerkin' outta soul-damnin' slumber!"

The crowd murmured agreement.

Removing his rope tassel belt, Snow grew full of righteous fury, looking for someone to hit. Mad Lena presented herself and he started whipping her. "Out! You iniquitous demon, get out!"

One of Snow's assistants prostrated himself on the sidewalk. Men and women began slowly coming forward, lying down in a long row by the blue ledge curving around the sunken old amphitheater.

Snow struck their legs and buttocks with the belt till his hands shook and his breath grew ragged and his voice hoarse. "Drive out de devil from among us—drive him out! Now, who goin' whip de biggest sinner?" He knotted the cassock above his hairy legs. "Who goin' whip the biggest sinner among yuh?" He held out the belt, but no one dared take it. "Come on!" he exhorted. "Answer de call!"

I stepped forward and he offered the belt gladly, as if I had relieved him of a poisonous serpent.

"Yes," he beamed, kneeling. "Yes, Nyjah, do it. It was meant to be like dis." He lay facedown on the ground with his pants around his knees, full of swelling grief.

I flung the belt across the street. "Yuh don't deserve a floggin'—that's too good for yuh. Yuh deserve a stonin'!"

Snow began weeping and beat his head against the concrete till his forehead was cut open and bleeding like Louder's cheek. They had to pin him so he would stop, but still he shrieked, "Come back here! Messado, yuh owe dis to me!" When people tried to lift him, he struggled and kicked. "Lemme go! All-ah yuh leave me before me kill sumaddy! Messado! Crichton! Cass, me bredda! No!"

A gun went off and people scattered as police cleared the way for the sanitation truck.

* * *

It was my first time setting foot in the car wash. When I crossed that particular threshold, it felt like being back in the J block at school, though I swallowed my reservations. The sign on the yellow board above the gate said:

Basic Wash $300
Tire & Wheel $600
Protect $1000
Perfect Shine $1500
Polish Tunnel $2000

Men in the yard sat around small square tables playing *Ludo* or *Othello* for cash. An oldish woman named Bev, a former drug addict, sunken-cheeked with big eyes and hair that stood on her small dried-up head like a borrowed wig, waddled over like a hostess. "Sit over dere," she screeched. "Lemme get Marvin."

"What does she do here, wash cars?"

"Product tester," Chadwell replied cheekily.

"Yuh seem to know a lot."

We walked past a semi trailer converted into an office-cum–rec room. From inside came the high-pitched sounds of video-game fights; smoke poured through the small windows. "Is that *Tekken?*" said Chadwell.

We sat at an empty table.

A gambler at another table tugged at Bev's miniskirt as she passed. "Bev, me jus' decide me New Year's resolution," he said, squinting at the black and white *Othello* pieces like a mystic reading tea leaves. "A fresh start!"

"Yuh doh need gawd to give yuh a clean pair ah drawers," she quipped.

Someone let out a belly laugh that sounded familiar. It was Big Eye, sitting at a table off to the side, banging away on his laptop with sunglasses perched on top of his head, wearing his customary crewneck sweater, his ankles crossed neatly and his face pinched like a church boy. He wiped the spit from his mouth that always appeared when he smoked. I hadn't spoken to him since the Old Boys' Dinner; even then, he'd only been giving out hollow exhortations like a colonel sending faceless troops into battle. There'd always been something cold and unfeeling about him. Yet the odd thing was, Mighty and Big Eye were inseparable, true friends. It was almost admirable, if it wasn't so strange. And they were still partners. His eyes went big like golf balls as he pulled his lips back from impressive teeth. "Wow, evil has found a groove or two—what yuh grubs doin' here?"

"Business," said Chad curtly.

Big Eye raised his cup to us and pulled on his Matterhorn, then went back to his writing.

A few minutes later, Perry came out from the small white bungalow in the center of the property. He had straightened his hair and wore it in bangs and had on loop earrings.

"The fuck yuh do to yuh hair?" I said.

He beamed, flapping his arm in that way that made me uncomfortable, and it occurred to me that I'd never been truly accepting of him, that I was very much a bigot. "Yuh likes? An angel came down from heaven and combed it and made it straight. I hear yuh have some trouble."

"It's Dalton."

"Who sell all those Burberry knockoffs at the arcade?"

"He's extortin' Dreenie. I think he stole my bike too."

Perry was only half listening. I suddenly remembered how I had once seen him in a yellow raincoat when it was pouring out. He'd stood on the eighth-grade landing, out of breath after climbing the stairs. I had opened an invisible door for him. But he hadn't jumped. He'd wanted to live. Still full of a survival instinct.

Right then, Mighty came out of the white house with someone we knew. He'd always been with this girl, Tammy, slim and brown with a perfect face and a Toni Braxton haircut, a beauty queen from St. Helena's. He'd always treated her coarsely in public during school days, and she would play it off though it obviously hurt her. I wondered why he still kept her around, seeing as he no longer needed a beard. She had a boy's body, and her jeans sat on her frame like a mannequin's; she was all business, with a smile like poison, her lipstick and eye shadow a shade like a rotting star apple. As they came over, she sniggered about something, then he kissed her. She tried to resist at first, raising her arms before her chest, but he grabbed her elbows and pulled her in.

"Still pretendin' yuh love panty puddin', Marvin?" said Big Eye.

"No," Mighty answered, "she jus' lose a bet an' haffe pay for it."

Tammy was smiling at first, then got serious and thumped his chest. "Leggo me . . . fuckin' cock breath. Me nuh wa'an taste anodda man's dick on yuh fuckin' lips!"

The place went quiet, as if all the air had been sucked out of the car wash. The only sounds were workers spraying cleaner on tires and squeaky Asian female voices—loafers inside the semi playing *Tekken*. For a moment, Mighty's face wore a weak grin, like that night at Pier One when soldiers had shot him with light beams. He reached toward Tammy and she didn't back away; she wasn't intimidated even when it looked like he was about to grab her throat. His mouth stiffened and he drew in through his teeth. "Fuck you . . ." He backpedaled—I could see the hurt twitch around his mouth. Now I thought I knew why he kept her around—she was more than a business partner, she was his emotional foil, a sort of abused therapist. I wondered if I kept Briana around for a similar reason; I'd realized I didn't feel as strongly about her as I did Andrene.

"Gentlemen," Mighty said, trying to mask his embarrassment, "glad yuh could mek it. Welcome to de car wash."

"Le'we talk by the gate."

"Of course," he said, still looking back at Tammy; he didn't glance at Perry once. Then he and Chadwell went off together.

I stood near the gate feeling a vague dread about bringing Mighty back into my life. Perhaps what happened next was a wake-up call. I heard a man say to someone else, "Hol' yuh bloodclaat kawna. Yuh cyaan gimme spliff when me nevah see yuh a smoke." I looked up as the voice drew closer. It was *him!* He'd come to Harbour Street to lime with the Dollar Boys, his old cronies who roamed back roads waylaying tour buses. When he saw me, he got cross and started forward, dipping in his waist for his Cuban. Just then, Mighty and Chadwell returned. He halted and released the cutlass, then laughed bitterly. "All yuh scumbags stick together, eh? All yuh slimy Chesterites—gay, straight, an' in between, fuckin' setta nawsiness!"

Mighty signaled to the car-wash boys; some stalked forward. "Dalton, yuh life ah scratch yuh dis mawnin'?"

Dalton backed off, ranting, "Leave Andrene alone! She doh belong wid yuh. She belong to her own kind. Ah warnin' yuh!"

Chadwell made at him. "Yuh warnin' who, pussy'ole?"

Dalton skulked off with his sunken-chest walk, his hands swinging, muttering and watching us with eyes in the back of his head.

Mighty sucked his spliff. "Yuh cut out for dis, Nyjah?"

"I asked him the same thing, Marvin," Chadwell said.

"That's *my* business," I said, and left them.

CHAPTER 23

"Fine way to spend Labour Day," said Cress, "cooped up in Punkie's trying to look cute. We getting too old for this."

"We here to celebrate," said Chadwell. "Is three months since the school's been open."

I hadn't even realized it. It was three months to the day. Chad was always a stickler for dates, another feature of his single-mindedness.

"So we do need some gyals after all," laughed Rory.

Marco touched my elbow and I saw Master Bremmer walking in.

"Ol' Curry Beard!" Rory gasped.

"I haven't seen him since school days . . ."

The odd thing was, he was wearing the same old green G.C. Foster College jersey he'd been wearing that day Ms. Dallmeyer was raped. We looked at each other, suddenly fearful he'd notice us, approach.

"The same damn shirt," said Rory. "He's probably been wearin' it the whole time."

When Bremmer turned, we saw the words *BIG BODY BRUISER* on the back of his shirt.

"It's not the same one," Chadwell said.

"Not exactly," I said, feeling bewildered.

"Bremmer goin' crush some pussy upstairs," said Marco, as if trying to lighten our conscience.

"Shut up," hissed Rory.

"We're more than ourselves," said Cress, "to remind us of all that's worth saving. I don't know what's going on, but—"

"Nyjah . . . about Cam," Chadwell cut in.

Marco and Cress both scowled and turned away.

"What about her?"

"Well . . . I've designs upon her."

They burst out laughing.

I lost my appetite. The luncheon felt like an ambush, as if it had all been leading up to this. "You can have any gyal yuh want, Chadwell."

He smiled and put his hands on the table, trying to soften me with his earnestness. "I'm drawn to her frailty—she's like a delicate flower."

"Isn't she a cripple?" said Marco.

"She has lupus, dummy," Cress said.

Marco chewed the purple flower from his mule cocktail. "Tomatoes tomahtoes."

Chadwell steepled his fingers and gave me his businessman mien, but calibrated it a bit, his head leaning slightly, the way he did when closing deals. "I want to marry her and become family. Give her a baby."

"Booyaka!" chirped Marco.

"Stop talkin'," I said, "I don't want to hear it."

"I know yuh don't, so I'm puttin' it out there."

"Well put it back, it's absurd!"

"Why's it absurd? Yuh know what? I don't need yuh—"

"Oh yes yuh do! Don't even try it. That's a line I'd never thought yuh'd cross. You're a bum, always have been, a poison to all of us and yuhself, so this shouldn't surprise me, but it does."

He smiled bitterly to himself; his eyes seemed teary. The rest of us went quiet. No one had ever managed to hurt his feelings. We looked at each other and waited for him to do something, perhaps erupt. We braced for it. But he simply stood up and walked out.

"*Designs upon her*. My word, he sounds like Edmund Blackadder."

"Was he really cryin'? Where yuh think him gone?"

"I don't know. I don't care."

"Let's leave."

We bought cheap umbrellas at a convenience store. People were laying wreaths at the egg-shaped Civic Centre monument for a stuntwoman who'd died on set, saying prayers for the actor charged with her death. A woman was holding up her phone, playing Tramaine Hawkins's "Goin' Up Yonder" and screaming through tears, "Dis is for you, Terrence!"

Rory sneered at her. "For a TV star—for a fuckin' actor yuh don't even know!"

The woman looked outraged and cocked her fist. We pulled Rory away.

"What's wrong with you?" said Cress, jerking his lapel. "Lay off the fuckin' bottle! Fuckin' lightweight."

Rory pushed Cress aside and made his way back to the mourners as if he wanted to fight them. "*Prop gun*," he sneered. "And he'll be back doin' his schtick in no time, for *her* sake, with the credits ending, *In Memoriam*. Because the show must go on. And her death was meaningless, except as airtime for a *heartfelt* promotion sponsored by SureBrite. That's what made her famous. Her greatest moment was a tragedy that maybe only her family cares about!"

"Fuck, he's havin' a meltdown." Marco ran over and grabbed him. "You okay, Rory?"

"No, are you? We raped her, Marco, we *raped* her!"

"Keep yuh voice down! The fuck yuh tryin' to do right now?"

Rory grabbed my arm, his breath sour in my face. "He's takin' from you again, Nyjah. Even that fuckin' school—who really has controlling interest? He uses people! Take a look at the books; it doesn't add up. Ask Cress."

"*What* doesn't add up?"

Rory laughed, then emptied his bottle and threw it on a sodden trash heap. "When I mounted her, she wanted to cry but somethin' wouldn't let her. She kept starin' at Smokey's DVD shelf and she said, 'God, when I wake up on the mountain, kill me, throw me to the bottom.' It turned me on and I tried to muzzle her, but I couldn't for some reason."

"Yuh drunk."

"Yeah? And Chad's sleepin' with her. Cam's his regular score."

"Shut up." I struck off down the street toward the Strand.

Rory hurried to catch up with me. "I swear. We even double-dated. And they told me not to tell yuh 'cause yuh not ready to see them together yet."

"Keep talkin' and see what yuh get!"

He followed me like a shadow past the marquee and up the Strand's steps. "All right, I go prove it to you."

I joined the short queue at the box office. "How?"

"Next time he let anythin' slip, I go call yuh. He so giddy he can't keep his mouth shut about it. I never seen him this happy since he cut Brown B a deal to sell his fudges at school."

"Go home, Rory, call an Uber . . . You're a disgrace."

I bought my ticket, and as I entered the dark carpeted passage, he called out, "I'm a disgrace? Yuh think name-calling can hurt me after I've *raped* someone? But you raped her too, Nyjah . . . Yes, yuh did! Yuh not innocent. And you'll never have a healthy relationship with anyone!"

A theater attendant smiled at me. "Enjoy your movie."

My thoughts kept drifting back to Maude. But I kept stalling. I felt I'd earned the right to enjoy my newly found success with the school and I didn't want to find myself struggling in deep waters all over again. It might sabotage my progress. So I struck a compromise with fate instead and took Briana to a museum. But I think she could see I'd rather be someplace else, that she wasn't the object of my preoccupation.

"Reminds me of Seurat," she said, drinking in the painting.

"Huh?"

"Okay, dark-skin Aunt Viv or light-skin Aunt Viv?"

"Hmm, that's tough," I said, fondling her wrist.

"Just testing if you're still with us . . . What's wrong?"

I looked at her and sighed. "I'll tell yuh soon . . . but I may be goin' away for a while."

"For how long?"

"I don't know. I've got to see someone. Why do people in museums walk so slow?"

"Why do you walk so fast?" She gently pulled her hand away. "I want to sit down."

There was a detailed charcoal drawing of a body louse on the wall, on a piece of transplanted concrete, with a message:

LISTEN YOU FUCKIN' TOURISTS
DIS IS CALLED A LICE
NOT NUH RASSCLAAT COOTIES

"How is this art? It's not even witty graffiti."

"Maybe that's the point," she said. "Why do they call that tramp Louder Milk? No one knows, but the name fits, like that piece fits the space there. Anyplace else it'd be worthless, anyplace else he'd just be a bum."

"Maybe it was all right where it was."

She took my hand in hers and rubbed my palm like Zetta Rosegreen. "I saw you having breakfast at the restaurant below MoBay High."

"At Overton Plaza? I eat there free."

"I figured. Chadwell's family owns the building, right?"

"Yuh shoulda stopped and said hi. I like listenin' to that chatty waitress."

She smirked as if she wanted a confession that I was actually chasing skirt.

"I do my best revisions there."

"Exactly. I didn't want to disturb you."

"With black coffee, listenin' to them complain 'bout the building supe named Fudgy, who's handsy with women but stingy."

We walked to a grainy blowup of train tracks buried in a road. I could see it taking her somewhere in her head. She smiled wistfully. "We used to hang off old railway lines whenever we went to Westgreen Clinic for dental checkups . . . me and Perry. Daring each other to jump."

I sighed. "I'd signed up for aid—meal vouchers, everythin'. The cement factory went into receivership and my family was in a bind. Perry was in the bursar's that day. I hated him for it."

"My brother did *nothing* to you!" She stepped at me but I grabbed her wrists.

"But he knew, Bree—can't yuh see? He *knew*. That was enough."

She shook her head. "So you tried to *destroy* him?"

"He destroyed himself."

"Meaning what, exactly? By being himself?"

"Sometimes that's all it takes. Look at me, look at Chadwell . . . we are what we are."

"Ugh! How pathetic," she said.

"And that day in bed after I promised not to touch yuh . . . I did."

"You mean . . . ? Forget it, we were children." She suddenly deescalated her ire.

I hated this. I wanted to be condemned. "And there's somethin' else that happened."

"Save that for your conscience. You think you have a dick 'cause you felt yourself puttin' it inside me? Grow a real one and be a man. Do what's right! Don't whine to me."

I shouted like Al Pacino, "*Leave him out! He's chasing that calico ginch from the track houses again!*"

But she didn't even smile. "Be quiet," she muttered, "people are watching." The next moment she grabbed my arm and whispered, "I know my brother. I *know* my twin. He has separation anxiety. He's had it since we were children. He's afraid of leaving Mighty. He needs a shock to the system to break free. I pushed him off the Westgreen railway bridge once. When he realized he'd landed in grass and not the river, he lost his fear of heights. That's what he needs: a push. And you *owe* me."

"Fuck you an' yuh hurt feelings. Yuh actin' like yuh have me on a leash and I just shit on the sidewalk." I started toward the exit.

"Nyjah, what's wrong with you? Bwoy, slow down!" She grabbed at my arm again.

Outside, I whistled for a taxi. She started to get in the cab with me, but I pushed her back, closed the door, and told the driver to pull away, leaving her there on the curb, looking miserable.

"Yeah, Bree, fuck you and yuh faggot brother," I groaned as we pulled away.

The driver glared at me through the glass. "What she do, me dads? Why yuh treat yuh gyal like dat?"

"I don't even know. She just piss me off."

"Yuh wa'an me go back an' get her?"

"Could yuh?"

"Awrite, me dads, nuh say nutten." He turned the car around and went back. She was still standing there at the curb, limp and hollow as a scarecrow, her eyes trained on her phone.

"Tek time wid dem, dads," counseled the driver. "Dem mout' ah dem strength. It tek a man to appreciate a woman's weakness."

I wasn't sure what he meant, but I didn't want to hear any more. I saw crabs emerging from the marshlands behind the museum in a steady martial line, heading for the back gate as if to either ambush or attend the next exhibition.

The car stopped at Briana's feet, and she just stood there glaring at me.

"Get in the car."

"Apologize first."

"I'm sorry."

She got in, then said, "Now *you* get out."

"Excuse me . . . ?"

She wouldn't look at me. The driver, however, was smiling in the mirror, enjoying himself.

"You heard me," she said. "I ain't riding back downtown with you."

I took a breath to say something but the driver checked me with his eyes, winking. "I'll take care of her, dads."

"How much?" I asked, taking out my wallet.

"Get out!" screamed Bree.

I finally stepped out and traded places with her on the curb, watching the car head down the street.

As I walked toward the stoplight, Rory rang me. "They're here," was all he said when I picked up.

"What? Who's where?"

"I followed them . . . I want yuh to see for yuhself just how rotten we all are—and Chad is the stinkiest cabbage!"

I knew then what he meant and wished I didn't. I knew where "here" was and flew down the street to catch a Bottom Road cab, praying that Rory was wrong and she wouldn't be there.

When I announced myself at Jack Tar Village, the guard gave a smile that didn't mask a thin veneer of irritation. "Hol' on," he said, reaching for his radio in the sentry box. He sat there listening and I knew Chadwell was asking him to get rid of me.

"Tell him it's an emergency," I said, "he'll understand."

The man seemed genuinely tickled as he buzzed me through the pink gate. "I doh haffe worry 'bout yuh, do I?"

"Worry 'bout yuh damn self."

Chadwell was standing in the entryway of the beach cottage tucked away in a corner of the property. His smile cracked as soon as he saw me.

"What's this, the honeymoon suite?"

He held his hands up and backed away.

"Waterfront villa," I said. "Cabin-stabbin'. Remember how we used to throw them down back in sixth form?"

"Nyjah—"

"Move outta my way!"

The house girl twirled the flounce of her flower-patterned uniform and tutted in sympathy, probably thinking I was the boyfriend. Chad signaled to her; as she reached for the white telephone on the wall, I flew by him right up the short flight of steps.

"Where is she?"

Cam started after me, then thought better of it. She scurried into the room at the top of the stairs, catching her sheer negligee on the door handle. She jumped on the four-poster bed, backing up to the headboard with a crab shuffle. The AC did little to mask the peculiar odor of a latex condom. I'd brought Briana to this same room back in high school. It felt like poetic justice.

"Put on yuh clothes."

"No," she said, wrapping her arms around her legs pulled up to her chest, looking at me like some poor little orphan.

I couldn't find the concentration I needed to think what to do next.

She saw this and seized the opportunity: "Why did yuh come here? To rescue me? Yuh fuckin' outta order. What I do is none of yuh business."

She kept yanking at the negligee to cover her crotch; it sickened me. I was torn between having a go at her or going after Chadwell, who was now standing in the doorway. I closed the door in his face. Sweat thickened on the tip of Cam's small nose. I focused on it to calm myself. It was no use acting so angry; I had to show her reason. But I still couldn't collect my thoughts. "How can yuh be with him—sleep with him knowing what yuh know?"

"Get off it! I'm older than you, stop treatin' me like an invalid! It happened long ago, he's a man now! And who I fuck is *my* business. Is not a decision by committee. I don't need yuh protection."

I paced the semicircular room; I felt like screaming, tearing at the white curtains. "Cam, yuh don't know him—Chadwell's an animal. He'll chew yuh up and spit yuh out."

She twisted her mouth into a spiritless grin. "Stop actin' silly.

I don't need yuh to fight my battles. Yuh bein' unreasonable. Managin' expectations—that's what I'm doin' with my life."

"What's that supposed to mean?"

She stared out the glass doors at the white-tiled sundeck, which was half in shadow. "I know I don't have long to live."

I turned away and collapsed on the edge of the bed. I felt faint and had to grab the ornamental cloth hanging from the canopy.

"Stop *grounds* me, Nyjah. Don't fuck things up for me."

Chadwell opened the door and came in. "Nyjah, lemme talk to yuh."

I followed him out, closing the door after me.

"Listen," he began, "I love her. I didn't mean to . . . it just happened."

"Yuh give a funny joke once—don't tell it again."

"I'm serious. Why yuh never care 'bout my feelings?"

This caught me off guard. *Is he playing sly mongoose?* "Why yuh tellin' me this? It's not like you to want sympathy from anyone, not even yuh best friend."

"Yuh don't care, do yuh? Yuh wouldn't care if I dropped dead right here before yuh."

"What's with yuh? What yuh anglin' for?"

"Yuh think I'm some cold animal, so yuh treat me like one," Chad said. "I *get* it—yuh think she goin' die and yuh powerless to stop it. I feel the same way 'bout Obadiah . . . to this day."

"Don't yuh dare!"

"We're more alike than yuh think," he said.

"I'm sorry, have I done something wrong here? Yuh used her, just say yuh sorry. But only if yuh mean it."

He chuckled and leaned against the wall beside me. I shuddered with disgust when his leg brushed up against mine. "And yuh think I could never mean it—that's why yuh added that last bit."

I stood up to face him. "Oh, yuh playin' this really well."

"I never meant for any of it to happen, Nyjah."

"But it did! It did, Chad, and yuh drew me into it."

"I'll understand if yuh don't want to be friends anymore. But leave Camille outta this."

"Oh no, yuh don't get off that easily. And yuh comin' to see Ms. Dallmeyer when I go back to Seaford Town."

"I can't."

"So yuh can use a gyal and rape another, yet yuh too scared to accept responsibility?"

"Do the right thing like you, eh? Where do yuh get off bein' so high and mighty?"

"Stop actin' like yuh lost, yuh know exactly what yuh need to do. Yuh weak, Chadwell, and yuh *afraid*. The day yuh admit it, yuh can move on."

"Yuh took a part of me that day. Whether yuh like it or not. Is like how I suffer over Obadiah . . . whenever Mummy gimme that look of doubt."

"Yeah, well, I ain't the one to pour yuh heart out to. Try apologizin' to Ms. Dallmeyer. *That* tragedy yuh definitely had a hand in."

"Do it for me next time yuh see her."

I shook my head. "Yuh can't even say her name, can yuh? Yet here yuh are, professin' love for a sick woman."

He started heading back out of the room. I threw him down and started pummeling his upraised arms guarding his face. At first he laughed, like when we used to play fight by the hockey field. "Quit! Mind yuh break my teeth . . . Nyjah!"

But I was dead serious and started hitting him harder.

"Stop!" Cam screamed. "Nyjah, yuh goin' kill him!"

In my rage, I couldn't even remember where I was. Chadwell now gave in fully to the assault.

"You sonuvabitch," I muttered, "she's weak." I didn't know whether I was talking about Cam or Maude. "Sonuvabitch!"

Cam shoved me off and pushed me into a chair. I sucked at the torn flesh on my knuckles. Chad got to his feet and left the room.

"Yuh makin' a mistake," I said to her.

"It's *my* life. I don't need you or Lois or Mama treatin' me like a patient."

I couldn't pull the hand away from my mouth. I bit down to check my emotions.

She sat in a white cane-bottom chair, tense, almost wincing. "I'm tryin' to live *my* dream, I'm not afraid of the enormousness of it. I'm tryin' to be happy and satisfied with enjoyin' what painless life I have left."

I bit my hand harder, wishing to God I were deaf.

She started chewing her fingernail. "I've always believed in yuh dream, Nyjah, I've even been jealous of yuh. Don't fear, my bwoy, you'll succeed. Yuh talent was always yuh X factor—when yuh come into a room, yuh so different from the twenty other people there. Yuh have this X factor and yuh can take this gift and yuh can be proud of it. What do I have? Faulty fuckin' genes."

"Cam—"

"No, don't, it's fine. I've embraced it. Because it's a part of me, whether I want it or not. I just need y'all to understand that I'm not afraid, that I don't blame anyone. I never have. I'm thankful for what I have, I'm not bitter . . . I just need some fuckin' breathing room. Chadwell didn't kidnap me and bring me here." She looked squarely in my face. "I came because I *want* to. Now get out. Stop stiflin' me with yuh expectations."

When I got up, she looked out the screen doors at the serene blue pool and dwarf palms swishing gently beside it.

Chadwell stood outside with a towel to his swollen jaw. "Did yuh tell her?"

"What if I did? Doesn't she deserve to know the *real* you?"

But the next second he was staring at a Latina guest in a bikini heading out to the poolside. "Her ass move like a waterbed," he smiled.

Something occurred to me watching his face. "That day when yuh raped Ms. Dallmeyer, were yuh projectin' yuh own pain about Obadiah onto her? Like that time you bullied Omar Binns?"

He bit his lip and looked down at his feet. "I was watchin' Obadiah . . ."

"No! Yuh mother stepped away to finish cookin' dinner and left yuh in charge of his bath time. Yuh filled the tub with water, placed the baby inside, then left the bathroom."

He covered his ears. "Nyjah, don't!"

"To do what? Play fuckin' computer games?"

He sank against the wall, dazed. "When she found the bathtub overflowing, it felt like only a second had passed . . ."

I left them and walked the beach. Sundown bled into dusk. At a thatched *barzebo*, a blind woman ordered a Dead Bodies Don't Float. A blue cap was walking down a big-bellied tourist who had three duffel bags jammed under his arms. When the tourist glanced back at the security guard, he scuttled like a crab, kicking up sand; the blue cap laughed and called out, "Leavin' us so soon, Joe?"

"Just going for a swim," the American replied.

"At dis time o' night?" the blue cap said, slyly quickening his pace downshore.

"I like to swim when it's dark," huffed the American. "Plus, the pools are always crowded in the evening. You know what I mean? Heh heh."

"Yuh like to swim wid yuh suitcases too or yuh jus' bein' extra cautious? Yuh know what I mean." The blue cap turned toward me: "Like dem tek people fe damn idiot."

"Fleein' responsibility?" I chuckled at him.

"Some o' de cheap, no-good tourist dem run up dem hotel bill high-high an' den try sneak outta de premises by walkin' pon de beach an' climbin' over de reef an' into Cariblue. Credit-card scammers."

"Shame on him," said the blind brunette, sipping her drink.

"Hold my passport?" the American was saying. "My passport is not my property, it's *government* property." He heaved his luggage over the big pink rocks and dove, swimming around the reef toward the stony beach that fronted Cariblue Beach Hotel.

The blue cap blew his whistle and gave chase. "Yuh goin' answer wid yuh neck!"

CHAPTER 24

My phone rang and the voice down the line was formal. "Mr. Nyjah Messado?"

"Yes?"

"This is Sergeant Pusey from the Summit police station. Could you come in to see us as soon as you can?"

"What's this about?"

He relaxed his tone fractionally, "Don't worry, young man. I think we have some good news that we hope you can validate at the station. I don't want to get into details over the phone."

"Okay, Sarge, I'm on my way."

I walked up to Lapeyrouse, as they called it, a smaller station across the road from the Gun Court that was like a clubhouse to the main building. Corporal Makepeace met me out front with a smile.

"Welcome back, Teach. I told yuh I'd be seein' yuh again."

"I'm here to—"

"I know why yuh here, hold yuh horses. What, yuh ain't glad to see me? Come, man, don't look so cross. How life treatin' yuh these days?"

"I'm well."

"That's good to hear. Yuh don't look well though. Does he look well, Shirley Temple?" he said to the German shepherd at his side. "No, he don't look well at all. But come, le'we go find this bike of yours and cheer yuh up. We picked up the youth yesterday on a separate robbery charge and yuh bike was the getaway vehicle." He took me down the corridor to the Vehicle Theft Unit.

Sergeant Pusey, a tall man with a pudgy clean-shaven face and an open but sly manner, tapped at his computer, informing me that he was looking at my file, then brought me to the backyard where scores of scooters were parked or lying on the ground.

"Where did yuh catch him?" I asked.

He didn't answer right away, taking his time weaving through the junkyard of bikes. "Paradise Meadows," he eventually said. "You're lucky, usually they scrap it or sell it across parish lines within the first week of theft."

"Yuh said yuh arrested him this mornin'."

"Two culprits, actually, but they out on bail."

"Why didn't yuh wait till I could ID them? Tell yuh if I'd seen them before?"

"You can't trust everybody in this station. I was thinking about your own protection."

I didn't believe a word of it. We stopped at a pale-blue and gray bike, not even close to mine, which was blue and white.

"This is not my bike, mine had XE plates. It's right there on the report, and the colors are different. Look at the paper you're holdin', see? XE 83640."

"Sometimes they respray them and change plates—this city have plenty bikes so nobody goin' notice."

"Even so, this is not mine, I can't accept it."

"You can't or you *won't*? You know something I don't? Or perhaps you want to tell me how to do my job, or how to subscribe to some new moral code?"

"This isn't mine," I repeated uneasily.

He laughed. "It is now."

I realized what was happening. If I refused this one, they would close my case and forget about me.

He glanced at his watch and humphed, as if he had someplace to be. "Look, man, you want it or not?"

I thought about my initial love affair with the one that was stolen, how besotted I'd been. When I had signed the ND release form and brought it home, I'd parked it in the backyard under the breadfruit tree and stared at it a long time—I couldn't even bring myself to put it in the shed. I hadn't fallen asleep till after four that morning. But I hadn't mourned it properly after I lost it. I'd been too caught up in myself, and now I was paying for it. I was having an absurd reaction, as if I could feel the bike taking revenge with these sadistic little games.

Before I could respond to the sergeant, my phone rang with a call from Chadwell. I picked up and said hello but there was a long silence before he spoke. "They're doin' an audit," he finally said.

My hand holding the phone started shaking and Pusey narrowed his eyes at me. "What? Who?" I said feebly.

"I don't know for now, but there might be trouble. I'll keep yuh posted."

"Wait! Chad, don't hang up."

"Something wrong, Teach?" Pusey asked.

"I'm goin' to prison," I responded. "His voice . . . it said more than his words . . ."

Pusey looked genuinely worried about me. "You involved in a mix-up?" he said in a hushed tone, stepping closer to me. "I could help you out, just say the word."

My mind was spinning. *What did he mean?* I forgot where I was, forgot I was talking to an officer of the law. "I'll have to flee . . ."

"Take it easy," Pusey said, setting a weighty hand on my shoulder. "Come, sit down. Tell me what happen, maybe I can help before it gets more complicated. You're a good man. I see it in your face. You're a victim. I have experience with these things."

We walked around to the open front yard facing the dusty street. Police dogs had tangled with a mongrel that strayed into the yard and were biting him bloody on the ground. The policemen didn't bother to intervene. The dogs, suddenly tired of their vanquished victim, growled at me. I looked to some nearby officers for protection, but they merely laughed and kept sipping their soup.

Pusey grabbed my arm. "Wait, man. Wait till they got them on the leash. You sure you all right, Teach? You might be in shock."

I pulled away and took a step forward. The nearest dog backed off, watching me, gauging if I was brave or just plain stupid. Another snapped at my pant leg and I heard it rip, but I didn't dare look down. I remembered Perry at the Old Boys' Dinner, swiveling through tables amid hisses, hostile stares, and remarks. Then I took a breath and stepped past quietly, tensely, my breath tremulous, out of the lions' den, into the sun beating the band. The day had cleared up.

Makepeace looked at my ripped pants when I entered his office. "Wha'ppen? Makin' new friends?"

"The bike isn't mine," I said, though my thoughts were elsewhere. I glanced at his face and knew he'd been right that we'd be seeing each other again. His instincts frightened me. My eyes stayed glued too long on posters of Desmond Haynes plastered all over the precinct wall. They had the same effect as the chintzy wallpaper that night at Punkie's with Melissa.

Makepeace watched me, smirked. "Look who's ridin' on the coattails of evil."

I felt my food coming up.

He reached over and held my shoulders. "Betsy, get a mop!"

My lunch was all over the floor.

"Come, man, sit down." I sat and he leaned my body forward, rubbing my back. "Let it all out . . . confession's good for the soul."

I stood and shrugged his hands off me.

Shirley Temple barked and grew excited.

"Easy now," Makepeace said. "Easy, Messado. How can yuh live like this? When yuh goin' come clean? I heard yuh buss up yuh grandfather real bad in the chest, nearly kill him." He saw the surprise in my face and smiled. "That night they disappeared Desmond Haynes at Pier One—who did it?"

I laughed in his face. "I did."

"Look at yuh—yuh sick."

"Pity yuh not a doctor."

He snatched a gray metal chair and slammed it on the floor three times, startling me. "Who gave the orders? Talk, yuh fuckin' mutt!"

"I don't know!"

"Come clean and we'll work somethin' out. It not too late."

"I have *nutten* to say to yuh."

"When we crack this case, we pinnin' it on all-a yuh! Not just the car-wash crew! I'm makin' it my goal to bring down all yuh rotten Chesterites who think yuh run this town with impunity!"

I walked out, but he kept yelling.

"We have eyes and ears everywhere! Yuh life is like that *Twilight Zone* episode 'Special Service.' I'm a submarine, Messado, you'll never see me comin'!"

CHAPTER 25

"This thing's gettin' itchier than a bum's balls."

"How deep we in?"

Chadwell looked pained as he sent someone out after writing their receipt, could barely force a smile to go along with the customer service. "There could be trouble," he said, sitting heavily in the chair. "It might not even be a matter of doin' the right thing, we might just have to roll with the punches."

He wasn't making sense to me. "How bad is it?"

"Yuh have to ask? Bad enough? The school income's tied up with Mighty's investments."

"Wash?"

"I had no choice—remember that favor we asked of him?"

"Yuh mean *I* asked of him? Don't play generous. At least the auditor general didn't stop our students from sittin' finals."

"Okay, *you* asked of him," said Chad. "Listen, I'm not blamin' yuh, but . . . he played us, right into his own hands."

"How much we in for?"

"Yuh have to ask? Over a million. Too much."

I stopped picking at my food. "From when? This can't be 'bout me and Burberry Dalton, then . . . From when, Chad?"

"Since . . . well . . ."

"You're a liar. Yuh planned it from the start. All those times I see yuh two together, so chummy, you were business partners. The school was just another fuckin' pipeline."

"Nyjah, it ain't like that."

"Look me in the eye and tell me yuh never plan this." He couldn't. "They hold a gun to yuh head so yuh could take their drug money?"

"Scam money alone . . ." He had said more than he'd intended to, or had answered too quickly—it told me all I needed to know.

"So yuh in on the telephone-scam racket? What's yuh cut?"

"That's *my* business!" He stood up and grimaced, as if the chair had coals beneath it.

"Why? Why get me involved? I never wanted this."

"Well, it's too late for that now, isn't it."

"So I should buck up? Is that it? Share the responsibility?"

"Listen to me, shithead. We in more trouble than yuh think—Fruity Hastings is runnin' drugs from Colombia, usin' MoBay for transshipment to Puerto Rico. There are Colombian agents all over the island, not just MoBay. Remember the ones we see by the car wash? That's just the tip of the iceberg. They even buy out funeral parlors to ship cocaine in coffins. They own dozens of businesses. Ownership structures across this city like a maze. They create shell companies and hide funds everywhere. You think I got involved painlessly? Who yuh think we lease school property from? Matalon? Colombians. They refuse to sell. They own the car-wash lease too. We all work for them. And now yuh want to sweat out my wig for some fuckin' shitbag school? That's the least of my problems!"

As I closed my food box, something else occurred to me. "See what I mean? It's always about *you*. And yuh don't care who go down with yuh."

"Get real, Nyjah! This fuckin' Mary Poppins bullshit—enough of the speeches!"

"This is why I don't want yuh involved with Cam."

"I don't even want to *see* pussy now—much less fuck it. Yuh talkin' to the wrong man."

"No, it's the truth—admit it. You've never wanted to help me to be my own boss. Yuh had an angle all along. I don't even know how much to believe of what comin' out yuh mouth, but I tell yuh what. I'm not runnin' no more. This is where the buck stop—time to pay the piper. We always had this comin'. Sooner or later."

"Stop being melodramatic," Chad said.

"I can be whatever I fuckin' want—I'm a dead man anyway. I could be in my bed and Colombian come take me out and shoot me. Kill my whole family. Like they did to those people in Hopewell. Is that melodramatic enough for yuh?"

"I never meant for this to happen. I was makin' a one-time investment, then get them off the books and protect yuh end, keep the school clean, but—"

"But yuh made a deal with the devil. Books, equipment, furniture—everythin' tainted, eh?"

He spoke to himself more than me: "I can't afford for Daddy to go to prison. I'd rather dead first . . ."

I hadn't thought about that—his father would've had to sign off on everything, and would be hardest hit. Chadwell could probably wiggle out of real responsibility if push came to shove. It hadn't occurred to me that this might sink his father, ruin the Crichton name, destroy his whole life's work because of Chadwell's lunacy in thinking he could overreach the devil.

"He works too hard . . . He was countin' on me." Chad sounded whipped, like a frightened bully. There wasn't any of the bounce-backability at the bottom of his voice. He was a drained well.

"Yuh father know exactly who yuh are—give the people closest to yuh some credit."

"Come with me tonight—we can talk things over with Mighty and Fruits."

"I ain't goin' nowhere with yuh. I don't want to get shot."

Ska's pickup rattled outside and three men hopped out of the back with electrical cables and toolboxes. Ska walked in and we immediately became self-conscious. He said nothing, didn't jest as usual or grumble about his slow lunch, he only put his tools aside then stepped back out. Cigarette smoke swirled into the shop along with muffled talk, someone, maybe Ninja, muttering, ". . . him in over him head."

"Yuh see't," answered Ska, sucking smoke into his lungs. "Sometime calf nuh fe run before cow . . ."

"T'ank gawd I'm jus' de electrician," laughed Greg.

Ska came back inside to put down his tool belt; he lowered it slowly like a holster, a hateful look passing between the two brothers, an ugly family resemblance.

At the sound system below the neon-green inflatable arch advertising *Wet T-shirt Weekend* at the car wash, DJ Bobby Cornflakes warmed up the early crowd with classics from the nineties soundclash era. When the horns of the "Real Rock" riddim blared and Tony Curtis crooned, "*My sound a murdah, a jump-pon in yah,*" people whistled and flicked lighters, mimicking Jigsy King's grating interjection, "*Wicked every time!*" We walked down to the dunes where the car-wash crew parked their sand buggies, where Karate Georgie and his goons had beaten Moodie. Mighty came over with his arm around Perry's waist. Perry smiled and batted his eyelash extensions at us.

"Look at him," Chadwell muttered. "Yuh think *we* have it bad? Perry's so hollow he don't even know who him is anymore. When you see him in Mighty's car front, he always looks spaced out. It's like Mighty's drivin' round with someone's ashes, lookin' for the right place to bury them."

Perry wore skinny jeans and oversized UGGs in the warm weather, and a roomy coat with long pockets that swallowed his arms to the elbows, his hair in a lank bun on top of his square-jawed face. He had a measured stride like a model's. If you could picture the actor Robert Pattinson, you could picture Perry, that's how handsome he was, but he'd tried to scrub all manliness from his features, and he didn't look healthy. Mighty was dressed with masculine abandon, in dirty blue jeans and red All Stars and a gray knapsack so grimy it looked as if it had been dipped in grease. He dapped us and pushed Perry off his shoulder. Perry stared, waiting for a remark. But Mighty saw from our closed expressions that we'd come to talk, so he snapped his fingers and Perry left. He watched Perry swiveling his hips to the bar, putting on his best strut, his arms slightly raised like crooked wings.

Mighty shook his head and chuckled. "Dat bwoy, him tek me breath."

Chadwell snorted. "Just wait till Tammy catches him goin' through her makeup kit."

Chad and I laughed, but Mighty didn't find it funny. Something of his schoolboy savagery, the gamester swindling boys out of their lunch money, crept into his face. But then a chubby, bleached-haired gay man named Craven passed us and Mighty stretched a finger out and pulled his belt loop. Craven sidled over and wedged himself between Mighty's legs and pushed him against a lamppost. They kissed deeply; when they pulled apart, Craven ran a bright-pink nail down Mighty's long jawline and walked on ahead.

Reflexively, we glanced over to the bar. Perry was apoplectic with rage, stomping the footrest of a barstool, probably imagining Craven's yellow hair beneath his furry boot.

Mighty glared at him, then turned back to us. "I hear yuh runnin' round like headless chickens 'cause some guv'ment sow call and t'row figures at yuh."

Chadwell tried to sound calm. "How we goin' get out in front-a this? Who goin' take the reins?"

Mighty screwed up his shaven eyebrows, half-annoyed, half-amused. "De fuck yuh lookin' at me for? Wha' yuh wa'an do, play rock, paper, scissors? Every tub haffe sit pon dem own bottom." He fished in his knapsack for a loose cigarette.

Bobby Cornflakes started playing Beres Hammond's lover's rock songs and men began harassing women for slow dances, scooting away with their victims to fences and poorly lit corners; someone dimmed the lights.

Mighty motioned us over to some sandy palms strung with pepper lights, as if uncomfortable in the sudden darkness. He tugged my shoulder and smiled. "How Melissa? She poppin' de pussy like popcorn?" It took me awhile to respond and he saw I was flummoxed. "If she nah perform, jus' tell me, mek me light fire under her bloodclaat tail." He took out his phone and called mine. "Dere's me numbah. Consider dat de customer-care hotline. Call if yuh have any problems wid her." He sucked his Matterhorn down to the butt, watching me with dark humor, tickled at my confusion.

I didn't want to ask anything and hear something I'd rather not, so I stayed quiet.

Mighty became withdrawn, contemplative, sitting on a tree trunk and peering out beyond the shore, listening to night swimmers laughing and fooling around in the dark waters. "Yuh know what I readin'? JFK biography. Yuh know he was de youngest man to serve as president, elected at forty-t'ree, and was also de youngest to die in office, at de age ah forty-six?"

Chadwell and I looked at each other.

Mighty continued, his voice mellowed with tobacco smoke: "Him know he was goin' dead. Dem try kill him four times before dem finally succeed. Was even given last rites by a priest 'cause him adrenal glands all fucked up while still in him twenties—nobody t'ought him would make it off dat sickbed. But him did. Him knew him had a mark on him back, a short time to live; that's why him help write him biography at just t'irty-nine . . ." Mighty looked up from under the hoods of his eyes. "Philip's brain-damaged, a vegetable, cyaan even wipe him own ass."

"No," I gasped.

Mighty nodded grimly. "An' de bloodclaat soldier bwoy dem who put him in hospital bring him disposable period panties, like dem havin' a laugh."

"That's a terrible brain to waste," said Chadwell stupidly.

Mighty looked like he wanted to hit him. But the three of us laughed; we had a Chester moment, boys enjoying gallows humor.

Then it vanished. The world was real again. We didn't feel privileged or sheltered.

"What we need is shadow diplomacy, I learn dat from de book," said Mighty, "where de leaders o' two warring countries visit each other. I'm volunteerin' Nyjah, we'll send yuh as a diplomat to Bogotá."

"Marvin, stop fuckin' around!" Chadwell snapped. "This is serious!"

Mighty sprang up. "Doh fuckin' presume to tell *me* what's serious! 'Fore me use me knife an' open yuh bloodclaat t'roat! De fuck yuh know 'bout—"

Right then, a woman's face swam out of the darkness on that stretch of sand and she grabbed my shirtfront and shrieked, "Missa Mighty—*duh*! Jus' tell me where me bredda bury! Me nuh wa'an nuh trouble! We jus' wa'an give Desmond a decent burial!"

I struggled out of her grip and barked, "I'm not Mighty! I'm afraid yuh have the wrong man."

But she kept coming at me as I stumbled to the sand. "Have a heart! T'ink 'bout yuh own family! Wouldn't yuh want to see dem restin' peacefully underground?"

Fenton and Colin moved in. "Awrite, sistren, dat's enough . . . We come here fe drink an' party. Nuh bada come fuck up we vibes wid yuh dead talk."

Bottles smashed and a cry went up. "Fuck him up!" cackled someone with lighthearted evil. "Drink him doctorfish soup!"

We saw patrons scrambling toward the fountain, which was strobed with the neon-pink letters *PIER ONE* that dissolved and reappeared with swirling water patterns. When we ran over, all the car-wash guys had their phone cameras trained on two men on the ground pulling each other's shirts. It took awhile for me to realize it was Perry and Craven. They looked exhausted, locked in a stalemate like mating crabs with tangled claws.

"Do it properly!" an effeminate voice called out to Perry, who had the slight ascendancy.

"Craven, open up her bloodclaat!" screamed someone else in a hot-pink onesie, the hood thrown over his head.

Perry peppered Craven with weak licks with the side of his fist. "Yuh fuckah, yuh! Yeah . . . yeah!"

Several people screamed as Perry stood up and started kicking him. Perry gripped Craven's thin shirt and spun him on the sand like a breakdance tag team.

"You're a bad gyal?" Perry harangued the pudgy shorter man. "Yah bad, gyal!"

Craven gave a muffled yelp, shielding his face.

"Nuh gyal nuh beat me!" Perry slapped his chest and shouted at the stunned crowd, "Me nuh play wid gyal!"

The mood was such that people could barely appreciate the excitement. It was something altogether different to see a gay man in pain, not caring what anyone did or said, not caring about their judgments yet unwittingly providing entertainment.

Perry beat his chest again and lowered his head toward Craven. "Me! Ah bad bloodclaat gyal!" He started thumping Craven again, the blows poorly aimed and feckless. "Wha' me say? See me an' wish me bloodclaat well!"

"Yes, Perry!" the gay boys now cheered, jumping and swinging their legs. "Tek it to him!"

"Hey gyal, run in!" yelled Perry. "Ah pussy me sell, gyal! Ah pussy me sell fe Mighty! Yuh cyaan hurt me! Why yuh nuh leave me alone when yuh see me?"

"Yuh fuckah, yuh!" cheered Perry's corner, working their cameras, swerving around the fighters like referees.

It all made sense, but it was still gut-wrenching. Perry wasn't Mighty's steady—he was a prostitute on Mighty's payroll. Everyone had to earn their keep.

"Wop her! Oonuh call de police now!"

"Nuh, gyal—nuh, gyal!" Perry shouted as he wound up another punch.

"Ah dis yuh come for!" someone jeered Craven, who was

wallowing on the sand. "Yuh lef' yuh bloodclaat yawd an' come fe dis!"

Mighty, meanwhile, looked as if he was at the cinema, a thin smile spreading across his lips, his hands jammed in his pockets.

Craven struggled up but bumbled over someone's wheelchair, the gay accountant everyone called Stick-'em-up because that was the last thing he'd purportedly heard before police rounds crippled him.

"Clumsy!" rasped Stick-'em-up, shoving Craven back down.

Craven tried to run, but Perry rode his shoulders like a country boy at a goat race.

"De battyman dem serious tonight!" a woman shrieked.

"Doh let her go!" one of the gay boys exhorted. "Wop her! Bumboclaat, ah dat yuh come out yah for, 'cause yuh a bad gyal!"

Craven's shirt was drawn all the way up to the top of his fat belly, and Perry was behind him, his arms tucked under Craven's armpits, both of them stumbling down the beach, raising laughs and screams.

"Outta order! Wop him, Perry!"

Perry pushed Craven up against a car for more slaps. At this point, Craven wasn't even trying to hit back. He seemed ashamed, waiting out the punishment.

"Me will kill yuh!" screamed Perry. "Yuh cyaan shame me wid me own business, gyal! All yuh have is mout', nutten else!"

"Perry, lemme go . . . Lemme go, Perry . . ."

Perry shoved his neck, pushing him toward the sea. "Bloodclaat gyal . . ."

"See't yah now!" Mighty called out, dapping his crew, who were laughing and throwing wagers on the ground.

Craven struggled at the water's edge, appealing to the bleached-face pretty boy who had replaced Philip as the car-wash beauty. "Noel, ah so yuh do me? Ah so yuh sell me out after me swear yuh to secrecy?"

"Yes!" screamed Noel, flashing his braids. "Ah beatin' yuh fe get. Tek lick inna yuh bloodclaat. Yuh bad company dem, nuh deh yah fe back yuh!"

"Not even de battyman dem have loyalty," someone lamented.

"Perry, stop . . . stop," croaked Craven when he was let up for air.

Perry pushed his head back under the surf. "Me nuh trouble gyal ah bloodclaat! Ah pussy me sell! Why yuh come inna me inbox? Me nuh respeck yuh so me nuh wa'an yuh fe fuck me! Me nuh care how much money yuh have!"

Chadwell ran over and grabbed him. "Perry, control yourself, you're goin' drown him! Yuh want to go to prison?"

"Doh *you* tell me to control meself!" countered Perry. "Doh yuh dare! Control *what*? Who go bloodclaat mek me? Control how?"

"Yuh actin' like a bitch!"

"Fuck off if yuh nuh like it—me cyaan control it! Dis is who I am, Chadwell!"

Chad shook his head and backpedaled up the shore bubbling with pepper lights hanging from palms. "Yuh despicable."

Craven used the distraction to sucker punch Perry.

Perry simply laughed and wiped away the blood trickling from his mouth. "Yes, me know . . . I'm scum." For a while he seemed to lose himself, his voice alternating between the charming cultured boy from Paradise Crescent and the streetwise prostitute. He wasn't fighting over Mighty or gossip anymore, he was just fighting to let out his anger. He dipped for a smooth white rock and knocked Craven out cold, then released the front of his shirt as if he'd vanquished the world.

Craven fell backward and his arm went up over his head at an awkward angle and he started shaking.

"He's seizin'!" someone screamed. "He's concussed!"

Perry noticed the bills scattered on the sand and sneered over at Mighty.

Mighty responded, "Yuh jus' a dollar sign to me, bitch—yuh cyaan even suck good dick."

"Fuck you, Marvin!" Perry yelled.

The car-wash men started grabbing up their money. It wasn't clear who'd lost or won their bets.

"Call an ambulance," Chadwell said to me.

But my phone was jammed with some kind of virus. When I opened the browser, a pop-up of a fiftysomething white woman appeared, her face as dark as beef jerky and looking just as tough, like a sailor who'd seen better days, her silicone breasts bursting over the top of her black one-piece, tugging on a bra strap and lecherously saying with a robotic cartoon mouth that kept opening and closing like something out of a nightmare, "*Show horny women near you. Click below.*"

I was so dazed with misery I nearly hurled the phone into the sea.

CHAPTER 26

On Emancipation Day, Snow was slated to appear at Sam Sharpe Square for a National Heroes' tribute. His public appearances had dwindled, as if he was preparing something big.

We made sure to get there early and camped outside the Civic Centre.

The sun labored through a strange midmorning mist. "This way," I said, and pulled at Cress, for I'd heard a commotion and felt the propinquity of evil.

"Townward!" Louder Milk shouted. "There he is! The chief compositor, rewritin' history!"

He was in an open-top car this time, had ditched the popemobile for a bee-yellow Subaru. The crowd ran forward as one. Snow sat in the passenger seat like a guru on a mountaintop, and he looked spaced out, the line of his mouth bitterly drawn. He watched a policeman fling aside a scarf which had been thrown in his direction, then got out of the vehicle, retrieved the scarf, and wrapped it around his neck.

A woman ran forward and nearly pulled him onto the brick steps of the Sam Sharpe monument. "Rummy, one young bwoy got killed at de quarry," she cried, "crushed by machinery he too young to operate, and a busload-a us come so yuh can scatter him ashes at de monument."

One of her company pumped his fist. "We go sue de fuckin' Chiney dem who hire him 'cause dem nuh wa'an pay full wages! How guv'ment let foreigner abuse we so?"

Snow took the urn from her shaking hands and read her blue T-shirt, stenciled with an epitaph, along with a picture of the boy's beaming face. Snow wept and fell down by the woman's feet. We all stood glumly and watched. When his acolyte Shepherd helped him up, Snow gathered himself and asked, "How old was he?"

The woman looked caught out.

"Your T-shirt, dummy!" snapped a girl standing nearby.

The woman looked down at her shirt, calculating the boy's age, but got the math wrong; some people groaned, others snickered. She stiffened in the face of her embarrassment, but kept her eyes on Snow.

Snow walked up the monument's steps and scattered ashes at Deacon Sharpe's broad foot, glancing momentarily at his bronze body with the immenseness of a charging bull, holding a Bible, preaching to four other statues. "So people not only support dis city when dem alive, dem support it when dem dead. This bwoy is a sacrifice. Just like you, just like how dem hang yuh—so all-ah us could live." Then he moved into the shadow of the most upsetting figure, the statue that was most lifelike, which babies cried at—that of the muscular slave, his sinewy, ugly face full of anguish as he runs forward to warn Sharpe of the coming Redcoats, a tragedy so aptly captured that people didn't even like their pictures taken with it, it was too haunting and ghostlike a figure. Snow stood on the monument's lip as if he had come full circle, as if he had started at the edge of the city in a spiritual path that had finally brought him to his center and the journey was over.

The hush continued.

A young woman traipsed down her apartment building's driveway in shorts, T-shirt, and slippers, scratching her rumply hair. She didn't seem to care about the idlers and nonsense of street preaching.

"Watch dat batty," said one of the constables, eyeing the woman as she headed toward the convenience store. "Yuh know what dat swingin' ass sayin'? *Work yuh money, bring it come—work yuh money . . .*" Men laughed dutifully. The constable's eyes glinted with malice; he looked over the woman's head up into Bogue's distant hills, churning his humor into something more thoughtful. "Dem like pets—dese women, dese *housewives*—not a care in de *rass* world but wa'an break man back wid naggin' an' greed fe money dem doh earn. Jus' a little above pets: piss, shit, an' eat an' breed an' dead an' yuh pay to bury dem, while me out here me whole life dodgin' bullets an' chasing in de shadows o' self-appointed gurus or sayin' to de supe, 'Yes, boss. No, boss. Have a nice day, boss.' An' when yuh go home dead tired an' say, 'Evenin', honey,' dem doh even answer. 'Cause yuh come home too early an' spoil dem fun. Not even a *rass choops* yuh can get."

"Dey worse dan pets—at least yuh doh have to put pets pon yuh health-care plan," offered a joker.

The constable didn't laugh. He looked almost exhausted from his disquisition. "Yes," he summed up, "dat's why man drop lick ah dem backside—dem too damn ungrateful. Dere's always a reason to beat dem. Dem whole lifestyle is a violation o' some kinda natural law. I jus' cyaan name it."

"Would yuh wa'an someone beatin' yuh sister?" Snow spoke up.

The constable mashed his lips. "If she deserve it."

"Would yuh wa'an someone rapin' her?"

"If she deserve it."

The gasps were subdued.

The policeman pressed his point: "What yuh care? Yuh doh even like woman. Yuh t'ink I doh know yuh is a self-hatin' faggot?"

Snow regarded the policeman, passing the urn slowly back to the woman in the blue T-shirt. "Squaddie, yuh believe everyt'ing yuh say?"

The young constable rolled his eyes but deescalated his frustration. "Women are only sweet in de beginnin', Preacher . . . when dem want yuh. As soon as dem have yuh dem sour, an' when dem get a baby by yuh, yuh affection and needs become an annoyance, den a imposition, an' den a burden."

A senior officer cocked her eyebrow. "Who tol' yuh dat?"

"Me father. Him wouldn't lie to me. Is not in him nature. So me can t'ank him for savin' me."

"So yuh never gettin' married?" said the full-faced policewoman.

"I would be a fool to even t'ink it."

The policewoman laughed. "You're a fool now—doh let yuh fadder spoil yuh life becah him doh enjoy his."

Snow added, "You're a broken young man in need of healin'. Yuh own self-reliance an' cynicism are a poison."

The two officers looked at each other as if they'd only just met, though they probably worked together in the same unit.

"You're a sin vial," Snow said. "I'm goin' break yuh open so yuh can praise de Lawd."

"Don't bodda," said the lanky policeman, "you is de biggest scam of all, even bigger dan dem car-wash bwoys. You the type-a disease people enjoy, like a child pickin' a scab, a disease rottin' dis town. Yuh like eye boogers. Nobody can see clearly in dis town anymore, dey all blinded wid delusion. T'rowin' dem hands up an' livin' empty lives like hungry-belly shamans."

Snow looked genuinely insulted. He worked his dark face, pushing his lips in and out, clenching and unclenching his fists. "Dem didn't believe dem could see freedom either . . . de slaves . . . even as Sharpe preached. Matter o' fact, dem was de ones who sent for de Redcoats to arrest him."

"Ahaha," laughed the constable. "What yuh wa'an—to be buried at Heroes Circle wid Bogle an' Nanny? Is dat yuh aimin' for? Is dat what dis twelve-year itch o' yours about? Dis citywide circus? You is a damn fuckin' joke! Sam Sharpe had more integrity inna him bloodclaat eyeteet' dan yuh have in yuh whole blasted body!"

Snow motioned for Shepherd to move back and the acolyte fingered something under his green silken shirt.

The constable sneered. "Come, Barabbas—if yuh t'ink yuh bad. Come mek me send yuh to heaven."

Grinning, Snow peered above everyone's heads. "Yuh know, as egotistic as men are, dem often gracious to each odder when dem sense one-a dem company is wounded. Aren't we breddas, Constable? Strivin' for de same goals? Equal opportunity an' respect for every citizen, no matter gender or sexuality?"

"Fuck you," said the constable. "Dat clear enough?"

"No one is de Rum Preacher!" someone cried out. "Him a special player dat never been seen in dis league!"

"Him an exploitateer," said someone else. "Peanut drops, no coconut custard! Shepherd is de real deal!"

Louder Milk, his eyes glazed like whenever the Dollars Boys give him bad drugs, skulked behind a tall, shapely woman in a Motown Supremes hairdo and began stroking his half-dead cock near her pert buttocks. When the woman wrinkled her nose at his stench and turned away, Louder quickly tucked his cock back into his pants and stepped level with her, gesturing as if smoking a cigarette.

"No, Louder baby," said the woman, smiling gently, "me nuh have nuh loose ciggy."

A man who'd been watching Louder stepped forward as if to clobber him, but several people intervened.

"I see dat yuh wounded, Constable" said Snow, calling for calm, "but too stubborn to ask fe help."

"Yuh wa'an heal me, Papa Snow—is dat it? Yuh wa'an *save* me? Yuh know what I t'ink? Yuh write a big bogus check dat nobody can cash. Why yuh doh tell dem, Preacher? Why yuh doh tell dem yuh have no truck wid de banks?"

Snow looked pained all of a sudden, his eyes going inward. He opened his long satin coat and ran a hand over his hairy chest, took a deep breath, then removed the robe and threw it into the mob, where it was immediately ripped to shreds. Fights broke out with foul curses as Snow stepped past them.

When their savagery was spent, they offered him blank looks of apology.

Snow said somberly, removing his glasses, "Sometimes yuh haffe take off yuh glasses to see better. Dat's de point when yuh not lookin' wid yuh eyes but yuh soul. Like when people give yuh bad news, yuh haffe remove de glasses from yuh face to truly grasp what dem sayin'. Pure understandin' needs no aid. It go beyond mere words. I done talkin'."

The words didn't make sense immediately, but people slowly absorbed them like subtitles in a foreign movie. Snow got behind the wheel of the car and sped down Harbour Street toward the old Palladium theater, which served as a half roundabout for taxis, and which locals called the Wailing Wall because it stank of human feces and crack pipes. The car smashed into the wall of the theater and a stray mutt limped away from its nest of puppies with its stomach busted open, its entrails hanging down to the gravelly road. It kept up its mewling, then started running in circles as its life leaked out. It faltered, stumbling onto its hind legs, then tried to stand up, then crawled, dragging its guts through pebbles and broken glass.

People shook off their panic and pulled their eyes away from the dog, and a bunch of us ran over to Snow's side of the car. He was slumped over the steering wheel, his head split open and a shard of glass sticking out of his eye.

"Don't move, Rummy!" Shepherd screamed.

Snow eased up onto his elbow, turned toward Shepherd, blinked his good eye, tried to speak, then went quiet.

Bawling broke out. "Bumboclaat! Rum Preacher dead!"

"Move away, Nyjah!" Cress yelled. "They're going to riot!"

"Bumbo bloodclaat! Me spirit grieve! Rummy dead—Rum Preacher dead to pussyclaat! Jus' dead so like aunty fowl dem! No, dis nuh real!"

People started kicking the car, moving around erratically, venting feelings against the Wailing Wall.

Cress pulled me back from the Subaru as they stampeded. They pulled Snow out, tearing off his clothes, even taking out his bootlaces—everybody wanted a piece of clothing before the police shut things down.

"First stripe! Second stripe!" Louder Milk shouted, tearing away pieces of clothing as if offering some sort of bargain.

Shepherd and several other acolytes moved in, trying to give the corpse some dignity.

Someone ran past us with a kerosene torch, screaming, "We nah lef' nutten fe Babylon meddle wid! Le'we sen' de preacher home!"

A group of men hurriedly built a pyre with trash and sticks, then doused and lit it. Black smoke billowed up the piss-stained wall. Someone scraped up the remains of the disemboweled mutt with a shovel and hurled it at the windshield of an arriving police jeep. My mind flashed back to Mona, the dirty little white girl in Seaford Town, and her tale of Jakey's abandoned devotees shoveling his rotting body.

The smoke was incredibly foul and people started choking, falling down. Some of them appeared to be deliberately inhaling the carbon monoxide, as if intent on getting the last of Snow's essence, willing to die with him like the slaves had died with Sharpe.

Shepherd walked around in a half daze, clutching his head then grabbing people's shirts and saying like a shell-shocked soldier, "Snow broke him leg and have some face cuts, but him fine. Except fe a piece-a metal lodged in him flesh dat de doctors say dem cyaan get out. De police say it look like attempted suicide."

People pushed him aside and clambered to get a look at Snow before fire burned away his features. Cress pulled me toward One Man Beach. Camera flashes lit up the cul-de-sac like artillery flares.

"Trumpetin' cherubs!" Shepherd shouted. "Is true? Him dead?" As if to enshrine his own legend, or scupper his madness, he wrenched a fuel jug from a rioter, doused himself, pushed his way back through, and jumped onto the pyre, which blazed with a *whoosh*.

People backed away from the flames and tortured screams of the writhing man. Two other acolytes, not to be outdone, doused themselves and jumped on the pyre too, like boys competing at Coral Cliff, diving into blue summer waters.

Others gathered burned rags, bone fragments, even flesh, and brought them to lay at the feet of Sam Sharpe.

* * *

They lamented Snow and the acolytes for a whole week. The acolytes who hadn't died with their master and brethren were condemned as frauds; they had to go into hiding to avoid verbal abuse and beatings.

CHAPTER 27

Chadwell listened but gave me only half his attention—he was increasingly worried about the investigation. He kept reviewing his sales book, kneading his forehead. Without looking at me, he said, "Yuh go really have to get out. There might be violence. Fruity Hastings ran off with more than his cut of some money, and the South Americans are lookin' to cut everybody down if they don't recoup their funds. And they plannin' to use lawmen on their payroll to do it. Yuh won't even see it comin'. Is like this: Fruits was plannin' this the whole time, ever since Mighty took over at the car wash. He's bitter 'cause he lost his face and power."

"Does any of it matter—who did what and why?"

"Nyjah, don't go all Hamlet on me. We need to think our way outta this."

"I ain't choosin' sides. Yuh shoulda been there, Chad. Snow went mad . . ."

A shadow darkened the doorway and a familiar perfume wafted in. I looked up to see Melissa peering into the shop, flicking her bangled wrist. Chadwell glanced from her to me; he could see that something had passed between us.

I stood and stepped around the counter, buzzed my way through the security door.

Melissa snarled, "Me come," as if she'd been sure I would be there all along, waiting for her. I hadn't even remembered I'd given her the shop's card.

"Who's this gyal to yuh?" said Chad, getting up.

I ignored him. Even now she was breathtaking, her hair twisted in red and white braids, interspersed with black beads, forming a swirling candy pattern in a big bun at the back of her head. She wore silver loop earrings, a long white frock, and sandals. She looked how I imagined an Ethiopian woman might look, or a nomad, and she had luggage by her feet. Her mouth was clamped shut and she refused to enter the shop.

Finally she answered the hostility in Chadwell's face: "*Who dis gyal?* Yuh wa'an know who I be, Shoppy? Somebody who come to colleck on a favah."

"Look, girlfriend," Chadwell began, "right now we sorta busy. Unless yuh lookin' for work as a bodyguard, keep movin'."

I brought her bags inside and offered her a chair, but she remained standing at the door.

"I know yuh," said Chadwell, stepping through the security door. "Yuh work somewhere . . ."

"Punkie's," she replied shortly. "So yuh been dere." She turned to me. "Ah go need dat money . . . Hammer Mouth put me out."

"Come sit down. Yuh want somethin' to drink?"

"No, me all right. I kinda in a rush, Nyjah. I need to leave de city tonight."

"Yuh in trouble?" Chadwell asked.

"Hey," she said with a scowl, "Missa Sunshine alluva sudden."

"So it done for you and Hammer?"

She folded her arms. "Yes . . . we cyaan work it out dis time. I goin' back to country."

"She's my family's tenant," I said to Chad.

But he'd already figured that out. "*Melissa Marvelous* . . . you were the stripper at the Old Boys' Dinner too. Yuh busy, eh, gyal? How much money yuh want?"

She bit her lip, thinking this over, twirling one of her silver earrings, when suddenly she looked down the road and shrieked, "Fat Bob! Him go bruk me up!"

We hurried to the doorway and saw Mighty down the sidewalk talking to customers leaving the car wash.

"Ah sh-should be at de clinic now gettin' vaccinated!" she stammered, so thunderstruck her jewels rattled. "Him go kill me if him know I plannin' to leave town!" She tilted her neck in an odd direction and her fingers stiffened, then her mouth dropped open and she simply tumbled to the ground—we barely had time to catch her.

"She's having an episode," I said to Chad, "let's get her in the shop."

When Melissa woke up more than twenty minutes later, she looked refreshed but pestered, trying to figure out where she was. Chadwell's sister Marsha gave her some orange juice.

"Who Mighty to yuh?" Chadwell asked.

Melissa looked puzzled, so I said, "Yuh called him Fat Bob."

"Me pimp," she replied quietly.

"Mighty?" said Ska. "Yuh sure, sister?"

She nodded, rising from the cot in the stockroom where Mr. Crichton and the electricians took naps. "De battyman dem mek de best pimps. Dem nuh wa'an no pussy from yuh."

Marsha flinched.

"Excuse me language. Most pimps, when yuh sign up wid dem, dem practically rape yuh before yuh can join de *gayelle*. Battyman nuh do dat, dem respeck us as people 'cause dem know we struggle. Dem understan' discrimination. But Fat Bob different—him *mean*. Is like yuh have shit pon yuh top lip dat yuh always smellin' but cyaan get rid of. An' when he sen' dat uppity bitch Tammy to punish yuh, dere ain't no tellin' wha' go happen. She more evil dan him."

"Yuh suppose to be workin' now?" asked Ska.

"No, him make appointment fe me to get vaccinated. But I doh wa'an it."

"You're a vaccine skeptic," said Marsha.

Melissa appeared defensive, started looking for her things. “Some customers doh wa’an sleep wid unvaccinated gyals. Some even want to fuck yuh in a mask. Fat Bob scared o’ losing business wid unvaxxed gyals. But is *my* body, me have a right to choose what go inside it.”

Chad and Ska looked at each other and sniggered. Marsha shot her brothers a scalding look.

“Well, sister, that’s the least of yuh problems,” said Ska.

“We’ll talk to Mighty,” said Chadwell. “Don’t worry.”

“No!” She grabbed his arm, looking terrified.

“All right,” said Marsha, “we’ll get yuh out tonight, or tomorrow. And write yuh a check.”

“T’ank yuh . . .” Melissa glanced around the cluttered, dusty stockroom as if in a cathedral, and her face held something like reverence. “So dis is where it all start . . . Yuh Missa Crichton children?”

The siblings nodded.

“How him do it?” she asked them. “How him turn de tables an’ mek sum’n of himself? How him beat de whole worl’?”

My phone rang with a call from Dreenie and I had to hurry away.

I spotted her on the other side of the fountain and waved. She puckered her lips in playful reproach. I choked as the fiery stuff of fear scorched my throat, stopping my breath for a moment: the sight of her smiling beautifully, leaning against the bank’s pillar like a stone angel, holding her belly.

“Come,” she chided gently, “I doh wa’an late fe clinic. Nurse sey is like de whole MoBay pregnant dis month.”

“Did she?” I thought how ironic it would be if the baby was Burberry Dalton’s.

We headed off, and when we turned down Baker Road, Mad Lena was sprawled in the middle of the street, naked as the day she was born, drinking a bottle of cream soda. She poured libation.

"Cris-muss, that's for Rum Preacher! He need a statue like Daddy Sharpe!" To the horror of a group of onlookers, she furnished a charred finger from her witching bag. Nobody knew whose corpse it was from—Snow or one of his dead acolytes—but she stuck the fetid finger up her vagina and began masturbating, yelling with religious fervor, "This ol' pussy is a reliquary! Rummy is the only saint that can violate me! Rape me, Snow . . . lustrate me! Make me *wo-o-rthy*!"

But nobody disturbed her—not even the police.

"Holy roadblock," muttered Dreenie.

It felt like everyone there was thinking with one heart, bent on studious forgiveness. But we couldn't stop watching. I remembered Louder's disgusting sexual exhibition.

She worked the finger till she shook with a violent orgasm and her eyes rolled back in her head—then she stopped moving completely.

PART IV

THE MUMMY

CHAPTER 28

"Funny," I said, "this is the same minibus I took the last time. And we had to turn off the highway too 'cause of traffic."

"Where we goin'?" Cress asked, chewing gum. "Why all the secrecy?"

"I wish I could restrain myself and let her be."

"Who? You're an egotist, Nyjah." He half smiled at me.

"I feel like my heart's wrapped in a blood-pressure cuff. Squeezin' the truth outta it."

"Yuh sure that ain't the bumpy road? Where the hell *is* this place? Even the potholes have potholes."

People poured glances at us just like on my first trip, and again I regretted my decision, doubly this time for taking Cress along.

"Maybe it's not too late to turn back."

"What? Why? Messado, yuh have me in a fog here."

The rain intensified, lulled us.

"I never understood why the Black guy in *Putney Swope* has a white voice."

I chuckled. "*How many syllables, Mario?*"

"Slow down likkle deh, Ziggy," called out a passenger, "an' remember to blow yuh horn."

But Ziggy wasn't listening. His neck had a big bulging scar as if his throat had once been cut open. The weather seemed to be making him cranky.

"Ziggy!"

"Ziggy!"

Several passengers began beating the seats in front of them. A child sucking a purple Kisko broke into tears.

The conductor shook Ziggy's shoulders from the patty-pan seat.

I closed my eyes, then felt a big jerk and the tires skidded.

"Hey, you all right?" Cress said, shaking my shoulder.

"Did we have an accident?" I asked, touching my forehead, realizing I'd slammed into the seat in front of me.

"Everybody out de bus!" ordered the hipshot conductor.

We were at Feldman Corner and had to squeeze right up against the rocky hill on our side of the road.

"Sorry I got yuh into this," I said to Cress.

He looked at me as if not understanding my words. I wasn't sure I understood them either.

Ziggy was now berating an old man: "Why yuh never blow yuh horn, pops?"

"I doh have horn to blow, is a cart!"

"Doh matter," Ziggy pressed, swinging his fat belly aggressively. "Yuh is a motoris' an' everybody mus' follow road regulations. Lawlessness killin' dis country!"

"Go easy pon him, Ziggy," chimed a skinny woman covering her head with her leather handbag. "Everybody deserve mercy. Even reckless ol' fools."

I looked down the road and spotted the cart with its shattered wheel fetched up against one of the few metal railings still intact on the corner. The beast was skidding around in reddish mud that was washing off the hill, braying miserably.

"De poor donkey," someone said. "Le'we help it."

A few more meters and the cart would drop right off the cliff. The bridle was strangling the donkey; it worked its ash-gray mouth in panicky anguish.

"Is a mule, not a donkey, dammit! Him name Nationwide," said the owner, as if it mattered.

"Holy Fawda," cried out the slim woman with the bag over her hair, "de road givin'!"

People started hollering as the animal began slipping.

The old man shrieked, "Nationwide, me comin'!"

But three men grabbed him before he reached the mule. "Dere's nutten yuh can do for him, daddy!" one of them said.

Then passengers started tossing their "vices" on the animal in local superstition as if it were a Levitical scapegoat: the skinny woman removed her ruined wig and flung it at the cart with a curse; a man tossed his bag of ganja and Rizla smoking papers; a fat man his box of jelly donuts; a young tough his ice pick; yet another his bottle of JB and an X-rated comic; a schoolgirl dug in her knapsack and launched a black vibrator at the animal. The rain pelted heavily and I felt I should've tossed *myself*.

We heard a cracking sound and the metal railing lifted a huge piece of asphalt—cracks started spreading like a spiderweb. The mule kicked its forepaws and brayed a heartrending appeal.

"Nationwide!" The old man fell to his knees.

We watched the cart slide away and disappear, pulling a big chunk of the road with it.

"Me nevah even have a chance fe save him," whimpered the old man; his fingers had rigor-mortised around the whipping stick.

Passengers, coming back to their senses, were too ashamed to look at him.

The sun peeped out with a white crown like a judge, then withdrew.

"Joshua of Nun," breathed Cress, "it can't be true. Nyjah, the donkey's gone!" He peered over at the precipice as if expecting the mule to rise with wings.

"Yuh in shock, daddy," said the jelly-donut man as he embraced the old man. "Shock is a sorta exile . . . Exile frees yuh from uncertainties an' responsibilities."

We were *all* in shock. But I was far from free. And what was *my* responsibility? Could I be comfortable in my own skin knowing I had walked away without doing what I could to bring *her* peace? Or was I thoughtlessly adding to her burden? Weighing her down with my own selfish expectations? Certainty was impossible. But I had to try.

We stood on the second floor and peered down through the glass. It was the first time I'd seen her from this angle; she looked like a bird in a cage, collating items on a long white board.

"You remember her?"

It took Cress some time to respond. "It's her: Daydream. She's put on weight, finally looks half-decent in that dress. Are yuh involved?"

"More than yuh can imagine. Remember that day at gym when she tossed the ball around with Chad?"

"Yeah . . . ?"

"They raped her."

He looked as if I'd just handed him a strange package. He blinked. "Say that again?"

"They took a shortcut by J, returning from the sick bay. She came upon Snow gettin' a blow job from Perry. Snow panicked an' dragged her into Smokey's and fucked her brains out. Him, Rory, Chad, Marco, and Castleigh."

"Yuh jokin', Messado . . . Wait, yuh not. Yuh serious! I remember that day walkin' home, you were all so . . . But who?"

"I just told yuh—yuh deaf?"

"So wait, what's this visit about?"

"I've decided to come clean, not to keep yuh in the dark any longer, 'cause the secret's been strainin' our relationship even before we left school."

"Hmph. So what was the fallout? Obviously they weren't caught and she didn't . . . You mean she's been dead inside all along, keeping it a secret?"

"That's a way to put it."

"And how yuh know this?"

"I was there, on the hill above the car wash. I witnessed the whole thing. They saw me."

"And you've come here for *what?*"

"To be real, Cress, not a hypocrite, like yuh said. I'm tired of carryin' this around."

"What do yuh plan to do? Ask her forgiveness?"

"I've been driven ever since comin' to Seaford Town to write her this poem—it's finally finished. I need to give it to her."

"As what, a peace offerin'?"

I shrugged. "I just have to."

As we walked back to the parking lot, I said to him, "Yuh know how sometimes yuh walkin' and yuh suddenly feel a cobweb about yuh face or head? And it bothers yuh that yuh weren't more alert, even though yuh couldn't have seen it?"

"Are yuh saying yuh walked into a trap that afternoon and it wasn't yuh fault? Because it *is* yuh fault—no one held a gun to yuh head and made yuh remain silent. A silent witness is the worst kind. An accomplice."

"You weren't there," I said almost bitterly, "so don't pass judgment!"

"You want my advice? You will always feel that cobweb about yuh face, in yuh eyes, in yuh nostrils, as long as yuh don't come clean."

I had a jarring experience when I went to visit her the next day, after Cress had returned home. I saw her walking toward me with her mouth closed, but her voice was coming from the other side of the Deep, where the gardener was working in isolation. I turned my head to look over the hedge at him, trying to clear my brain fog. He was holding a fat ladybug with his thumb and one knuckly finger, saying loudly to it, ". . . when yuh smell de lawn mower, metal death could be very close by, milady, it could even be *inside* yuh." Then he released it and admonished, "Fly 'way from here!" But the insect plopped back down into the cut grass he was about to burn. He looked disheartened because he couldn't find her.

I turned my attention back to Maude as she came closer. Her hair was black with auburn streaks. She had wrapped her long ponytail in a golden clasp emblazoned with a Gorgon that caught the sun and looked like Athena's shield. She had her journal under her arm. I had her poem in my fist.

We sat under the same poui, which was gently shedding yellow blossoms on the grass that the gardener began making a fuss over with his rake, trying to eavesdrop. We didn't look at each other for a while, till I said, "I saw yuh last night . . . at the beach fire. Yuh didn't seem to enjoy the storytellin'."

"I heard what happened to Snow."

"I was there, I saw everythin'. It happened so fast it didn't seem real."

"That's the way tragedy looks to outsiders and perpetrators, but trust me—he felt every bit of it."

"I'm sorry."

"Stop apologizin'. Yuh can't take back yuh words, nor what yuh did."

"Here, I wrote this for you."

She took the poem without even looking at it or saying anything.

"I want my poems to transcend into the psyche."

She stared pointedly at me.

"No, I mean—fuck it, I ain't goin' say nutten else."

"Why did yuh bring Greenlaw here yesterday—to watch me like some animal in a cage?"

I threw my hands up.

To my surprise, she grabbed my shirt. "Answer me! Do I amuse yuh? Am I fodder for yuh wet dreams?" She was back to the steely, scary side of her personality—the intimidating gym teacher who could overpower us, who easily caught heavy medicine balls and balanced soccer balls on her head.

I broke her grip. "Let go of me! Yes, I told him the truth—but only because . . ."

She seemed almost excited by this piece of violence, by the reaction she'd got. "Because *what*? He deserves to know? What happened, yuh lost some bet? Why don't yuh bring the whole posse here next time to have a reunion, show them where the victim is hidin'? Their spunk mattress. Their high school lay."

I stood up. "Stop."

She walked me down as I backpedaled. "Why? Make me. Go ahead—take me with yuh strength, Messado. Bend me to yuh will—do it! Be a man and take what yuh want! Who am I to stop yuh—I never stopped *them* before. I couldn't have. I'm just a weak woman. A joke—a piece of ass in gym clothes for yuh to jerk off to in the showers."

"Stop . . ."

She crushed the poem into a ball and flung the paper at my face, then shoved me backward. "Make me! Put the mouth-a-massy bitch in her place!"

I grabbed her and jerked her upper arms. "Stop! What yuh tryin' to do? What yuh tryin' to prove?"

She laughed and widened her eyes at me, her mouth half-open with a toothy grin. "I want more—I want to feel the *real* you. Show me all yuh have bottled up. Let it out!" She pushed me again and again, but I slackened my body, absorbing the blows.

"Feel better now?" I said.

She leaned against a tree and something went dead in her face. "I'm goin' to kill myself."

"*What?*" I watched Maude's eyes with terror. Then I closed mine, and I could hear her lips opening and closing.

"I'm going to kill myself one day," she said. "I'm going to bury this body yuh friends destroyed so I can break free. You should do the same, yuh sufferin' too."

"Suicide?"

She turned around and marched off. What exactly did she mean? Some perverse version of *Romeo and Juliet*?

I followed her, breaking into a jog.

"Come with me," she said, her gaze fixed, ferocious. She took my hand and led me through a shortcut by the sunken garden, to the side door of the museum. "We must save her."

"What?"

"Yamaye," she said. "The university people are comin' for her today. They'll shackle her to that horrid cacique again before the travelin' exhibit."

I dragged my hand away. "Yuh can't save her. She already lived her life. Live yours."

I could see her reliving her own misery as she contemplated my rejection, and fought to avoid her own meltdown. Moving to the mummy's room, she swayed as if ready to drop, struggling in a chaos of confused fury. But I couldn't help following her, vaguely chasing my own deliverance too—allied to her rabid fantasy.

She entered the room and gently lifted Yamaye from the table like a baby.

"Where will yuh take her?"

Maude seemed to be thinking quickly. "We'll hide her in the ruins of the old museum. Nobody'll think to look for her there."

"And after that?"

She bit her lip. "I'll take her back to Lime Gut, so she can at least have a proper burial this time without the cacique."

"You do realize we're stealing state property . . ."

"She's *nobody's* property! Not the cacique's nor the museum's nor the government's—you men and yuh sickenin' sense of entitlement to a woman's body. She was buried *alive*. Can yuh fathom how cruel that is?"

"Is that why yuh wrote her story? To humanize her? To give her power she never had?"

"What do you care? I wrote her so she could be real."

"She's dead, Maude . . . she's dead."

Without another word, like a madwoman, like Mad Lena entranced, Maude stalked through the side door and across the yard to the brown shell of the hurricane-riven museum.

I walked behind her like an acolyte, not sure of my role in her obsession with this unburied dead woman.

A blackbird—like the *chinchilin* in Maude's story—flew so low it startled us. The way it flapped its wings in the sky made it look like it was moving to the rhythms of someone's dream.

"That's her spirit fightin' to soar," Maude said fiercely.

"If yuh say so . . ."

"Take yuh shoes off," she ordered as we entered the condemned building. We walked down its cracked leaf-covered floor and stopped on the right arm of the cross-shaped structure as if it were a transept. Toting the shrunken brown corpse, she crossed a barrier of life into a dim shadowland. We listened wearily and indifferently to all the clamor of trees, sea, and voices, Maude began silently crying, as if she felt all the pain and cold and hunger that Yamaye must've felt as she was locked away in the cave, left to die and rot. As if she was having a seance again. "Sister, I won't let them take yuh—no! Not again!" A slow, bitter horror twisted the corpse's face in dancing sunlight streaming through the museum's wind-torn roof, a constellation of light filling Yamaye's dry skin.

Laying the body down, Maude seemed to float through this sidereal space, jerkily, as if she were Yamaye's reanimated ushabti. Then she started reading her journal, almost as an obituary. It was that story, "The Burial," which I'd partially read that day in the cemetery. "I used to be twenty-eight . . ." she interjected, breaking her narrative. "I would've been twenty-eight if I'd read this a month ago."

"Happy belated birthday," I said like a fool.

She railed in an angry crescendo, "Don't yuh get it? I'm *dead*! Not alive."

I remembered Cam's words. "You have to be elected to life, Maude . . . it's not over."

To pay worship to the spirit that now filled her, she paused her ministrations and went back to the preservation room for the celt—the stone axe, the terrible arbitrary weapon of the shaman, that had condemned Yamaye to death.

How long am I willing to wait on this woman? I looked at the sky through the broken roof, vaguely hoping for some sort of miracle, like the connection we shared over the corpse. Then I heard a spine-chilling scream. When I ran back to the main building, she was banging on the other side of the bathroom door. I tried the lock. "It's jammed, hold on!"

"Hurry, please!" she yelled.

I could hear the claustrophobia withering her, mummifying her. She was back in *her* burial chamber—Smokey's den—without the agency of mystical words. Dying before my eyes with a panic attack. The letters said: *In Case of Emergency, Use This*. After I hefted the fire extinguisher and smashed the lock, I found her lying on the floor, hyperventilating, her eyes widening as if prepared for some awful vision. There was a large water stain on the ceiling, right over her head.

A feeble cry escaped her lips. "Yamaye, you're free now . . ."

I saw from her wild stare that the stain had the illusion of movement, that perhaps she'd found her gateway where she least expected it, lying with her head next to a toilet, her spirit improvising to rescue her from complete shock. I lifted her head. "You're safe."

"The celt," she said, rising with a new clarity of vision.

We had no qualms about our crime this time. We brought the stone axe out to the backyard and each took turns bludgeoning it with the fire extinguisher. It gave way with the precious magic of powder—of a relinquished past. Then we scattered it like ashes.

For Philip Moodie

When the sandstorm was high,
it looked as if the fishermen were walking
on clouds like ancient priests. I knew what I had to do
as I watched her lay Yamaye down,
I had to bury myself to become the new me.
I had to break the bond of empathy to make it real.

Makepeace came out of his office and I closed the notepad; he took out his pen and docket. I was still in my head, playing over our last conversation.

"It . . . it goes against the culture," I had stammered.

"What's culture?" Maude had responded. "Culture is what we make it. We're the vanguards and the vandals. I'm going to say somethin' to yuh, Messado, but don't laugh."

"I won't."

"I think humans are given power by dreams."

"What do yuh mean *power*?"

"Like somethin' extraordinary."

"Somethin' spiritual? Supernatural?"

"Somethin' we cannot define with words, only feelings."

"Hmm . . ."

"I think I know what I have to do now . . . I saw it. I'm finished with the museum."

Makepeace's voice broke through my reverie: "Messado, why yuh here? Don't bullshit me today."

"Makepeace, I'm ready to talk now."

He laughed. "Somebody beat yuh to it. He gave everybody up—brought us hard drives from the car wash . . . and then some."

"Who?"

"He did it on one condition: that we never arraign him or open a police record. Came with his lawyer." He sized me up, smiling. "I guess he was right 'bout you too. He said yuh'd be at the crease to see out your innin'."

He brought me to the back room and I sat beside him.

"You were always a step ahead of me," I said.

"Was I?" Perry laughed dryly.

"Yeah, even in school—the way yuh allied with the car-wash bwoys at J block for protection."

"That's how it all started . . ."

"That's how it ends . . ."

"I was never really a part of them, was I?"

"No. Yuh did what yuh had to do—like yuh doin' now. You're a pragmatist, Perry."

He reflected almost proudly; I saw the glint in his eye. "*Hunh*, come now, Messado, yuh can do much better than flattery. I was never any good at bein' a moral guidepost."

"What does this mean for you?" I asked.

"Freedom . . . Funny, I never had a vengeful bone in my body. Even after how Marvin treated me. I guess this is the definition of pity—the way I feel about him now. Now that it's all washed from me."

"Secret witness?"

"No, Messado—catharsis. My chains are gone. I feel like I've operated on my own body. Like that American doctor who biopsied the lump in her own breast in Antarctica."

I dropped my head in my hands. "Briana . . . Everybody gave up on yuh, except her."

Chuckling, Perry patted my back. "Thatcher said, 'If my critics saw me walking over the Thames, they would say it's because I couldn't swim.' I shut out that noise a long time ago. But my sister won't get credit for my Prodigal Son act. Come, let's have a smoke."

We moved to the smoking room, lit Matterhorns.

"Remember that cricket talk yuh gave me?" I said. "When I idolized yuh and coveted yuh spot on the Sunlight Cup team?"

He sobered, ready to school me. "*I'm on a mission to figure out how I can fulfill my potential as a player and a person. While not drivin' myself mad with the standard I'm seekin'. It can be a terrible place to live, 'cause yuh never goin' be perfect, 'cause when yuh set that as yuh standard, yuh set yuhself up to fail.*"

"What the fuck? That was perfect recall!"

"*Total* recall," he quipped, ashing his cigarette and rubbing his neck. "I'll need it when I head back to med school."

We laughed, but tears glistened in his eyes. Now he spoke just for the fun of it, still schooling me in cricket: "Yuh must be self-critical. *What can I do better in this situation or scenario?* So when it does arise again, you'll be prepared and go out there and make the right play."

"How do yuh rebuild a life?" I said seriously, checking his verbiage.

He thumped my shoulder. "Come to Cuba, I'll show yuh the blueprint."

"Yuh remember when we visited Dreenie's mother in Concrete?"

Perry laughed. "Yeah—queer, wasn't it?"

"*Queer*, haha."

The way he kept rubbing his neck made me realize how nervous he was looking back; I'd hit upon something between us. "That day, I felt like we were angels visiting Sodom."

"We made it out, didn't we?" Perry said.

"You were so worried those kids would scratch your BMW."

"If yuh have children, yuh leave them in the hands of God—that's what Dreenie's mother said. I thought about that and my worry was gone. Fuck the car."

"Norma."

"Precious Norma. By the way, how's yuh girl?"

I looked at him and was strangely transported back to the hospital with Dreenie, checking out the ultrasound scan. In MoBay, to "turn the bill down" means to set the bill facedown on a customer's table—but to "turn down the bill" means to flee a restaurant without paying for the meal. It's a joke among Montegonian men that to "turn down the bill" also means to flee responsibility when you think a woman is giving you a *jacket*. I felt I'd truly graduated to the ranks of these men with this most bitter of circumstances: a baby whose paternity was dubious. Yet it somehow rang like justice.

"Everything's up in the air," I said. "We'll see what happens after I tell Makepeace what I know."

"Yuh haven't answered my question."

"I have, it's just not the answer you want to hear."

He smiled. "Touché."

Acknowledgments

I would like to express immeasurable thanks to my family, who love me perfectly in my imperfection: Mummy, Sabrina, my wife Ayako, my son Julian, my aunts, uncles, cousins, nephew, niece, grandparents, and in-laws—my cup runneth over.

Thanks as well to friends who have supported me constantly and acted as family: Nikane, Bertie, Stephanie, Andrew, Oshayne, and Husayn. And to all the people who read early drafts and offered encouragement, including Jeremy Logue.

I would also like to thank my creative family, for reading, listening, inspiring, encouraging, including Dr. Andrea Shaw, for her invaluable advice and patience in the beginning; Opal Palmer Adisa, for her faith in me; Kei Miller, who shopped around my first manuscript; Tanya Batson-Savage, for her great advice and help with this book; the library clerks who introduced me to the form and steered my passion; and the *Caribbean Writer*, which opened the gate.